Veil of the Goddess

Rob Preece

BooksForABuck.com

2006

Veil of the Goddess is a work of fiction. Any resemblance to actual events, people (whether living or dead) or geographic locations is coincidental.

Veil of the Goddess is published by www.BooksForABuck.com. Check with us often to see the latest and best in affordable electronic fiction.

BooksForABuck.com

ISBN: 978-1-60215-007-2

Chapter 1

"Sergeant Newland. Take your squad and give us room to operate. We'll take it from here."

The civilians were arrogant enough to be CIA, but Ivy Newland didn't think they were. She also couldn't follow their orders. She couldn't see any enemy combatants, but in Iraq, that didn't mean a thing—the only time you saw them was after they started shooting.

"Sorry, sir. This is not a secured area."

Not secured was putting it mildly. The ruins of the mosque still smoldered from last night's bombing raid. The Air Force had done a great job transforming it from a city block of downtown Mosul from a beautiful medieval building to a haven for snipers. A haze of dust and smoke from where wood continued to smolder hours after the mosque had burned out reduced visibility and made the always hot, dry air stick in her throat.

Infrared was useless in Mosul's hundred-and-twenty-degree heat, so Ivy used her telescopic sights, continually sweeping the area for any movement.

They'd already rooted one sniper out of the remains of the bombed mosque and Ivy would be real surprised if he was the only insurgent handy. They tended to run in packs.

The civilian gave her an impatient snarl, his pale face flushing an angry red. "Sergeant, we're undertaking a sensitive mission. You and your men are not need-to-know, and you have been ordered to support us, not baby-sit us."

She ducked reflexively as a clatter of automatic rifle fire sounded off to her right. The sound no longer panicked her, but she still felt as if a fist tightened in her gut every time she heard it—what if they got another of the kids in her National Guard unit?

Mosul was supposed to have been pacified months before, firmly in government hands. Like so much else in this war, if anyone had bothered telling the locals, the message had gotten lost in translation. Of course, no matter how pacified the place might be, a bunch of Americans digging in the newly bombed ruins of one of the city's biggest and oldest mosques were pure chum.

Ivy squeezed off a quick burst in response to the insurgent's AK-47, made sure her boys were safe, then she joined the rest of the team in taking cover. The civilians weren't as quick, though. Maybe they thought their black business suits provided more protection than infantry armor.

Bad thinking.

Her burst didn't have the desired effect of making the insurgents keep their heads down. A rifle shot banged from behind her. Its bullet spun one of the civilians around, dropping him to the ground. Hellfire. She hadn't liked the guy but he was an American.

She swiped sweat from her face. "Williams," her voice sounded hoarse, even to her. "Take five men and root out that sniper. Anderson, take James, Lennox, and Slocum and secure the area. Move."

She tossed her radio to 'Mr. Smith,' the civilian in charge of their operation, and dragged the injured 'Mr. Jones' out of the fire zone.

"Is he badly injured?" Smith didn't look like he cared much. His voice was about as cold as a snake and his gray eyes showed nothing but contempt for his partner.

She gestured for him to take cover behind the low mound that was all that remained of one of the mosque's once fabled mosaic-works. "It's bad. Call in a Medevac."

"It's imperative that we continue this search, regardless of the risk. Jones can take care of himself."

Ivy didn't know whom she'd pissed off to be given this assignment, but she swore she'd find out. And when she did, payback was going to be sweet.

"Mr. Jones isn't going to be doing any more searching today." She kept pressure on his wound but Jones bled in gushes. That couldn't be good news.

Keeping one hand on his wound, she sliced through Jones's impractical black suit and the starched white shirt underneath it and discovered about what she'd suspected. The bullet had ripped a hole out of his arm big enough to swallow her entire fist. Jones might live, but she doubted even the best surgeon would save that arm.

Every American soldier in Iraq carries emergency first aid equipment. Like many others, Ivy had been given practical experience. Luckily for Jones, blood no longer bothered her—much. Ivy yanked her largest sterile bandage out of its wrapping and pressed it hard against Jones's upper arm, then gave him a shot of morphine.

The civilian moaned and thrashed but he wasn't strong enough to get away.

"Take it easy, Jones. Helicopter should be on its way."

"I'll pray for him," Smith offered.

"Oh, yeah. That'll help."

"Of course." Smith missed her sarcasm.

"While you're praying, how about pouring some water on a bandage and swabbing off his forehead," she suggested. "We've got to keep his temperature regulated. If he doesn't bleed out and shock doesn't kill him, he might make it."

In Iraq, keeping body temperatures from skyrocketing was a constant challenge. She couldn't remember the last time the outside temperature had dropped below a hundred degrees.

She had found Jones a bit of shade: better yet, shade that was protected from the sniper who had shot him. That meant he was lying on a mix of stone, mortar, and huge shards of timber.

It wasn't much for comfort, but it was better than getting shot at, which was what was happening to her squad. Sending them into danger without going herself increased the nagging sense of unease that pushed her toward panic. But she didn't trust Smith to keep Jones under control without her staying. Smith didn't look much interested in what happened to his partner. Despite the repeated chatter of automatic weaponry, he was champing at the bit to search the bombed-out mosque complex.

She sighed. Once again, the civilians had found a way to stick their noses into a beehive and expected the military to bail them out.

Ivy crouched low, made sure Smith kept his head down, and hoped her guys would survive this latest civilian cluster.

It only took minutes, but it felt like an hour before she heard the whomp-whomp of the Medevac helicopter. Jones had lapsed into a semi-conscious state, intermixing shallow breathing with occasional heartfelt murmurs requesting that Jesus take a personal interest in his welfare.

A pair of fighter-bombers jetted over as the Medevac landed, blasting randomly at the neighborhood around the mosque complex. Under that dubious cover, the Medevac stretcher team dashed through the dust and rubble to collect their casualty.

Smith watched in complete disgust as his partner was flown away.

"So much for the armor of his faith. I had thought better of him."

"Civilians aren't trained to go for cover as fast as soldiers," Ivy said.

Smith looked at her, then used a handkerchief to wipe Jones's blood from his hands. "I'm going to need your help after all, Sergeant."

"Yes sir?" Of course it was too much to expect him to be rational and shit-can the mission.

"We have reliable intelligence that an important, ah, let's say weapon, was hidden inside, or beneath, this mosque. We're going to have to make a complete search."

Ivy risked lifting her head above the shattered wall and looked around the ruined mosque complex.

Once, the complex had been centered by a huge building rising hundreds of feet above the city. The building and grounds sprawled over a couple of acres near downtown Mosul. It had been built in the fourteenth century, on the grounds of an earlier mosque destroyed by the Mongols.

Now, only a single minaret remained intact. Around that spike toward the sky, the bones of the mosque baked under Iraq's summer sun.

It was likely as anything that weapons had been hidden inside the Sunni mosque. Hell, there were weapons hidden everywhere in Iraq. Letting the old Iraqi army go home without disarming them had made sure that every home had a machine gun and every block had its own artillery. That didn't explain why some D.C. civilian cared about this particular mosque and these particular weapons.

"I called for more troops to secure the position," Smith announced as he handed back her radio. "We should get half a dozen Bradleys and a couple of M1s. Once the armor arrives, we shouldn't have to worry about the pagans any more."

If he had the clout to call in that level of support, Ivy wished he'd done it before he'd gotten Jones shot and put her own men in danger.

She took a deep breath. Tempting though it was, losing her temper wouldn't help.

"Are you allowed to tell me what we're looking for?"

Smith studied her. "Are you a Christian, Sergeant?"

From the two-inch-long cross on his lapel, his super-short blond hair, and the fish-theme on his tie, she'd already figured Smith to be one of the fundamentalist types.

Ivy knew the right answer to that question. She'd been raised Catholic. While she'd dabbled with New Age since, she hadn't totally rejected her upbringing. Besides, admitting her own doubts would weaken her position with her team. "Sure."

"Right. Let's just say we're looking for artifacts of deep religious and historical importance."

"Artifacts?" Only a few seconds ago he'd been talking about weapons. "You're risking soldiers lives to find some old relics?"

Smith frowned. "These 'old relics,' as you call them, just may be the most important objects in the history of the world."

All civilians were crazy, but this was over the top. "Like the Ark of the Covenant?"

"You've been watching too many Indiana Jones movies. The Resurrection replaced the old Covenant with the new. The Ark is now a meaningless symbol of an as-yet unredeemed people."

* * * *

Smith might have a few screws loose, but he delivered on his promises. The Bradleys and Abrams arrived an hour after Jones and been shot. The insurgents sent a couple of mortar shells their way, but faded into the city rather than face them directly. The rebels might not be brilliant, but the ones dumb enough to face ten inches of armor and machine guns that could chew through six inches of solid rock every second had been killed long before.

Smith spent most of that hour thumbing through a pocket Bible. Ivy took one glance over his shoulder and saw that he was reading a Hebrew version of the Old Testament. Impressive--or maybe nutty. Since she'd arrived in Iraq three months ago, she'd tried to learn a bit of Arabic, and she'd studied Latin in school years before, so she had a lot of respect for people who could pick up languages. Still, reading a Jewish book in Iraq was asking for trouble. Smith didn't seem to care.

The armor deployed, blocking access to the mosque complex and shooting a few more holes in the ruins. Smith placed one of his bookmarks, closed his Bible, and slid it back into his pocket.

"I hope you're satisfied. It's way past time to move." He took a wipe from his pocket and daintily washed his hands as if he was getting up from a picnic or something.

"I still don't know what we're looking for," she said. "What sort of artifacts do you expect?"

"The artifacts are my job. I'll tell you what you need to do and you follow my lead. Just trust me."

Trust him? As if. Still, she didn't have much choice. Her orders were to support this civilian and that was what she intended to do, even if he insisted on making her job as difficult as possible.

She'd fingered Smith to be a holy-roller, the big cross on his jacket and fish symbols on his tie being just the start of the giveaway. But she was still surprised when he opened a briefcase and took out a fifteen-inch long wooden cross.

The Bible here was bad enough, but at least Moslems saw it as a holy book. Was he trying to get them killed?

"Sir. If the indig learn that you've brought a Crucifix into a mosque, there'll be more problems. Big problems. Too many of them already think this war is an extension of the Crusades, another attempt to convert them."

"The time for conversion grows short and most of these people are have chosen damnation. But fear not. If we find what we're looking for, there won't be any more problems from the camel jockeys."

Ivy didn't find that attitude helpful. But Smith didn't ask her opinion and she kept it to herself.

Grasping his Crucifix by the crossbeam, Smith began a slow search of the grounds, holding the long end toward the ground, exactly as if the cross were a divining rod.

She might not be the best Christian in the world, but this use seemed close to blasphemous to her. Ivy was also pretty sure Father O'Brien back home would not have approved. She was also pretty sure Smith didn't care about her opinion, or Father O'Brien's.

It was mid-afternoon, and the temperature was at its highest, but Smith didn't even bother taking off his tie. Ivy trailed along wishing she dared strip off some of the armor that protected her but also left her steaming like a potato in aluminum foil. Even though she was drinking as much water as her stomach could hold, fingers of dehydration crept through her body.

Smith hadn't touched a drop of water since their Humvees had arrived at the bombed-out mosque. He'd seemed completely cool and collected--until he started his bizarre dousing.

The cross vibrated in his hands as Smith walked. Although the air was so dry and dusty it sucked the moisture from Ivy's skin faster than she could sweat, oily glistening beads popped out on Smith's forehead— and stayed there.

"So much power around here. It's amazing," he muttered.

He reached the very center of the ruined complex, kicked away the beautifully carved calligraphy on a surviving section of stone and stopped, the bottom of his crucifix pointing straight to the ground.

Beneath his black suit, muscles she hadn't guessed he possessed strained against the pull of the cross.

"It's here." He barely breathed the words. "It's here. After all this time I've found it."

It was possible Smith was crazy. On the other hand, Ivy had grown up in rural Pennsylvania where dousing was still used to locate wells. Using a cross to douse seemed blasphemous to her, but apparently it wasn't to Smith. And it certainly looked like the cross was reacting to something.

Although the Tigris River wasn't too far away, she doubted he'd found water. He hadn't come all this way to help the locals by digging a well.

"Widen the defensive perimeter," he snapped. "Give me your radio again. I need more equipment."

She glanced up at the swollen ball of the sun, desert dust painting it a dull red. "It's getting late, sir. Perhaps we should come back tomorrow."

"And let the pagans come in and steal it when we're so close? I don't think so. We're working here until we recover it."

She suspected that 'stealing' wasn't the right word. After all, most of the insurgents were locals. If anything, Smith was the thief, trying to steal something that had been sealed inside their mosque.

Still, she had her orders. And the Army, even the National Guard, has nasty ways of dealing with people who don't follow orders. "Right, sir."

She handed over the radio and got together with Captain Zack Herrera, the man in charge of the armor company Smith had called in. They'd have to split up the job of keeping the mosque sector secure. Since Smith kept her radio, she got Herrera to order up night vision equipment for her team. They'd need it if they had to stay onsite through the hours of the dark, when the local policemen hid away or changed their uniforms and the insurgents ruled the streets.

She'd seen the Captain on base when he'd first arrived from the states, newly promoted and looking like a kid. Three months later, Herrera had aged ten years. Baking in the desert sun had given his face character, wrung out any baby-fat from his body. Some forgotten firefight had given him a scar that cut across his face barely missing his left eye.

He looked good. Not that Ivy would consider dating a soldier. She intended to serve out her stint, go home, and hope the Guard let her out when her term expired.

From what she'd heard, though, Herrera wasn't bad for an officer. He hadn't lost a single soldier since he'd taken over his company. Easier for armor than for infantry, she guessed. Her own Captain was good, but her Company had lost two dead and more wounded that she could count in the three months since they'd been rotated back to Iraq for their third tour.

"Who is this Smith guy, anyway?" Herrera asked.

She shrugged. "Hotshot from somewhere in the government."

"You know he's asking for trouble digging around at a mosque site. It's Sunni. Even so the Iraqi government will object. If it turns out the civilians called in the airstrike just so Smith could dig around, we're in worse trouble."

Ivy sighed. "Tell me about it. Smith says he's getting some equipment but he didn't mention any extra firepower. Can you call in reinforcements?" A Captain could do that a lot more easily than a Sergeant.

Herrera shook his head. "I tried. HQ says this is Smith's operation. He decides resource callup. You might suggest it to him, though. He listens to you."

* * * *

The man known as Smith pulled a handkerchief from his suit jacket and wiped his forehead. He'd imagined this day starting way back when he'd been a kid in Sunday School staring at pictures of the Lord Jesus on the Cross. Unlike so many others, he'd never given up, never lost the dream. Now, thanks to decades of hard work by himself and plenty of others, he was on the verge of success.

Sergeant Newland headed back from the Abrams Battle Tank where she'd been flirting with a dark-skinned Captain, and Smith carefully composed his face. Although most Mexicans were Catholic, real Christians continued to work hard to spread the true word to those corrupted by the Roman Whore of Babylon. Maybe the Captain was one of the lucky ones who had escaped the Pope's grasp. Christian or not, though, Smith didn't approve of mixing the races and Sergeant Newland's Nordic-blond hair and blue eyes awakened a protective chord inside him.

"Everything under control, Sergeant? I should receive the excavation equipment within the hour."

"Excavation? If it needs excavation, surely it can wait until tomorrow."

Her blue eyes searched the horizon, studying the ugly desert sun as it descended toward night. Even under the bulk of her body armor, Smith couldn't miss the movement of her breasts, the rounded shape of her rear. Temptation.

"The forces of Satan are most powerful at night, but we must fight them nevertheless."

She gave him a strange look and he cursed the insane liberal political correctness that didn't even let the military databases hold vital information like religion. He'd picked the female, despite her sex, because she looked Germanic and came from rural America, as he did. Newland had assured him she was a Christian, but Satan was the father of lies.

"Be prepared to guard against the pagan attackers," he told her. Satan and his demonic host would dearly love to attack as well, but Satan had no power over those who have accepted the Word. Especially not if this place was truly sanctified by what Smith, and the entire Foundation, had been seeking for so many years.

"Captain Herrera suggests that you authorize additional troops, sir."

He considered, then shook his head. He was taking too many chances as it was. Jones had failed him and Sergeant Newland already knew too much. He had ample authority to do whatever it took to do his job, but too many unexplained disappearances could cause problems back home.

"We'll have to make do with what we have on the ground. I'll arrange air support on alert in case the Satanists try a mass attack."

"Right, sir. What else do you need from me?" She looked disgruntled, but she was ready to follow orders. As was proper in a woman, of course.

"Have you ever worked a jackhammer?"

He meant it as a joke. She was a woman after all. Instead, Ivy nodded. "Summer job for the city one year in college. Worked the road crew."

"Great. You can break through the masonry here. He gestured to where he'd doused the source of power. "The jackhammer should be here soon."

It'd already taken longer than it should have—they'd known there might be excavation involved since before the war began. Eventually, though, one of the big Foundation helicopters floated down, its huge rotors sending clouds of dust into the sky, its black matte paint a shadow of darkness against the dusk.

Bright searchlights flashed down as the helicopter neared the ground, blinding anyone who might have been looking through night vision equipment while dust blew everywhere.

"A pillar of smoke by day," he murmured. "And a tower of fire by night." It wasn't blasphemous to see the hand of God in the activities of the Foundation.

"Huh?"

He'd forgotten the woman. That wasn't like him, even if she was merely a female.

"Just admiring the way the chopper is setting down," he explained.

The Foundation had sent equipment, but some of the men with it were mercenaries rather than of the faith. Not even true Foundation men could be completely trusted—not with this treasure. They unloaded the jackhammer and the mini-bulldozer he'd specified, but then he sent them back into the helicopter, leaving himself and the Sergeant to do the heavy lifting. After all, the Bible had said that a single man, beaten and wounded, had carried this treasure once. Girded by the strength of his faith, Smith could do no less.

He handed the jackhammer over to the woman and then took control of the mini-dozer, using it to clear away the pagan rubble from the exact center of the mosque.

"You want me to just punch a hole in the paving stones here?" Newland asked.

He nodded. Why did people have to have everything explained to them?

"I hope you know what you're doing."

He'd had his own doubts when the Foundation had sent him into Iraq more than a year before the invasion. What he'd discovered then had convinced him, and convinced the Foundation Elders, that this was no goose-chase. The artifacts his teams had already uncovered were the real thing—and the ultimate prize would be no less. And it was so close he ached with need to touch it.

"Just do it."

Sergeant Newland finally started hacking through paving stones and mortar that had been placed six hundred years earlier, during the reconstruction of the city after Hulegu Khan's pagan Mongol armies had delivered a fierce blow to the pagan Moslems. That war between Satanists had been a glorious opportunity for the West to fight back, to free the Holy Land from pagan control.

Christendom, under the misrule of the Popes, had squandered that opportunity. As they'd squandered so man others, including the British occupation of Iraq eighty years earlier. Just as this Christian invasion of Iraq, and the most complete Christian conquest of Babylon since the days of the Roman Emperor Heraclius, would be squandered if the Foundation were not successful.

Smith kept one eye on the Sergeant as he completed clearing the area, shoving away each heavy paving stone as she broke up the mortar holding it in place.

Unlike many of the American women he'd seen on this campaign, the Sergeant modestly kept her clothes on, the bulky armor partially disguising the deceitful curves and charms her body certainly held. But he knew they were there.

Smith never lost sight of the true enemy, the ultimate center of true Satanism. Satan might be referred to as 'he,' but the core of his worship had always come from followers of the mother-whore goddess, Ishtar—an evil faith in eternal enmity with the one true God, an abomination that had originated in this very, wholly damned, country.

"Something down here." The Sergeant stepped back from the hole she'd created, pulled off her helmet, and wiping sweat from her eyes.

"What sort of something, Sergeant?"

"Hollow spot. Big. Maybe a crypt. Did those old-time Moslems bury their dead in churches like Medieval Christians?"

He neither knew, nor cared. What he did know was that his dousing Cross hadn't pointed him to some Pagan's skeleton. "Let me shine some light on it."

He drove the mini-dozer all the way the edge of the hole and turned on the headlights. The sun had finally set, plunging the city into a darkness lit only by occasional distant flashes that could be heat lightning, but that Smith suspected were something more ominous. Satan had guarded his stolen treasure for nearly a thousand years. He would recognize the threat to His power, see the coming end to His time of rule over this Earth. He would do what He could to stop the Foundation. And His power, that of a mighty angel, could not be dismissed.

"Can't see anything," the Sergeant reported. "Looks like just a couple of old beams and more rocks."

Cold sweat poured from his body. "Tell me about the beams."

"Big ol' hunks of wood," she reported. "Both notched, for joining, maybe." She paused a moment. "Hey, know what it is? It's the two sections of a Cross. What would Moslems be doing with a Cross buried under the foundation of one of their oldest mosques?"

What indeed?

Smith stepped down from the mini-dozer and dropped down into the hole next to the woman.

This close to her, he couldn't avoid breathing air she had contaminated. A normal person would smell of sweat after a day in the hundred-and-thirty-degree sun. But Sergeant Newland smelled of some exotic perfume, just as the Priestesses of Ishtar had adorning their bodies at this very spot, thousands of years ago--at the cost of their souls.

"Don't touch it."

He lowered his head in prayer, then reached a hand to caress the holiest object in the world.

Whatever the ancient Hebrews had believed, God did not dwell in a gopher-wood box carried through the desert—as in Indiana Jones's Ark of the Covenant. God had lived, died, and been reborn on this wood, though. This artifact, like the pagan Atlas, had carried the weight of the world on its shoulders, had seen the sun darken at the Son's sacrifice, had watched as the Demons of Hell celebrated the brief damned moment when they had been allowed to believe that death could triumph over eternal life.

Smith had achieved the goal of his life. He had found the One True Cross.

He reached his hand for the crossbeams, touched the spot where the Lord's hands had once been held, and felt the surge of power well through him.

"Stand back, Sergeant. I'll lift it out."

"War booty is my guess, sir," the Sergeant said. "Something the Medieval Arabs captured from the Crusaders or whoever else they were fighting, maybe. Here, let me give you a hand with that."

"Don't touch—" but he was too late. Once again, that damned curiosity and willful disobedience of women, the sins that had led Eve to entrap Adam with the apple, proved to be Satan's path to a place He could never reach without human contrivance.

"Wooh! Some kind of electrical charge or something. What's that about?"

Too late. "I told you to back away, Sergeant. But since you insist on interfering, you can help me lift The Cross from its temporary grave.

"You don't think this is..." the Sergeant essayed a chuckle. "I mean, there's no way it could still be around."

The ugly sin of Pride tugged at him, tempted him despite the many hours he'd spent at prayer. Smith wanted to tell Newland how his own research had traced the Medieval accounts of how the Crusaders had lost the rediscovered Cross to Saladin, of how Saladin had taken it back to Kurdistan, his home, before losing it in the supposedly honorable pagan's failed siege of Mosul.

Smith was not immune to the power of Pride, but he was armored by his faith, and fully aware that the creeping fingers of Lust had something to do with his desire to impress the female.

"It certainly would be a miracle if the True Cross had survived the millennia," he observed dryly. "Now lift."

The cross was surprisingly heavy. Without the energy he gained from the artifact itself, he doubted he would have been able to lift it, even with the woman's help. But then, his Lord had been vastly more than human and even He had fallen under its weight.

One of the tanks flashed its searchlight past him and he suppressed a curse—taking the name of the Lord in vain had been one of the hardest sins for him to break.

Could the tank crew have recognized what he held? He couldn't be certain. The Foundation had made their requirement clear. Until the time arrived, there would be no witnesses.

He set the ancient relic in the cart behind the mini-dozer, then jumped back into the hidden crypt and lifted the crosspiece.

"Felt heavier than I'd think wood would be," the Sergeant said. "Father O'Brien will be fascinated when I tell him about this, though." She unbuttoned a couple of buttons on her uniform blouse and swabbed between her breasts.

Smith felt the tightness of temptation in his groin. Satan was fighting dirty now that His back was to the wall.

"Get behind me, Satan."

"Huh?"

He thought fast. "Sergeant. Insurgents. Watch out."

She spun around, her automatic rifle coming up against the perceived threat.

He'd pray over her later, hoping that the Lord would accept her sacrifice to His greater glory.

Drawing the knife from the pocket where he kept it always, he drove it into her back.

It bounced off the body armor.

He blamed the distraction that brief sight of her exposed chest had caused in him for the stupidity and poor-aim of his attack, but he reacted instantaneously, redirecting the energy from the knife's bounce to drive it upward, toward the carotid artery in her neck.

He'd been through the CIA schools. Before he'd been given this assignment, he'd trained in every weapon, every method of killing. And he was filled with the grace and power of the savior.

"Lord, aid me as I smite your enemies," he prayed.

His sharp knife parted her skin as easily as if it had been cotton candy, exposing tendons, veins, and arteries.

He jumped back as blood spurted from her neck. Sergeant Newland was dead already, although she was still standing. It would just take a moment for the message to reach her body.

Reacting on training, instinct, perhaps strengthened by the demonic power of Ishtar, Sergeant Newland spun around, the muzzle of her M16 flashing death in a broad circle of automatic fire.

One bullet from that vast swarm caught him in his stomach, its power throwing him back, as if he had been caught up by a giant hand and discarded as wanting.

But even Ishtar cannot control a corpse for long. The sergeant stumbled and fell, her body splashing blood like a drunkard spilling cheap wine.

Smith looked down and saw the hole in his midsection, then felt his mind begin to drift. He'd done his best, been a soldier in the army of the Lord. Satan had taken him down, but Smith felt no sorrow. He was assured of his place, certain of the Lord's promise of eternal life. Surely the Lord would accept him despite his many failures. Amen.

Chapter 2

Captain Zack Herrera had been facing away from where Smith and Newland did their excavation, using the tank's sophisticated night vision equipment to watch the subtle movement of the locals as they crept around, tried to approach the bombed-out mosque without coming in range of the Abrams' deadly machineguns.

The sudden burst of an automatic weapon sounded too close, but didn't have the characteristic low rattle of the Kalasnikov.

"Soldier down." His gunner, Billy Jensen's voice bumped up an octave. "Jeez. Looks like Newland and Smith both."

An Iraqi sniper could had gotten past the perimeter. With only Zack's company and the few soldiers in Newland's squad available, their perimeter had been porous at best. But something about this didn't smell right and he'd heard only the rattlesnake snarl of an M16.

"Full reverse," he ordered. "Other units, cover our vector. And button up Newland's infantry. We may have to make a run for it."

Almost invisibly in the moonless darkness, the chopper's cannon traced the path of his tank. What the hell?

"Sonders, see if you can raise the helicopter on wireless. Tell them I'll blow their cannon right off the chopper if they don't point it the other way."

"Yes, sir."

An Abrams can move when it needs to, and it only took the massive engine's turbines a few seconds to bring him alongside the bodies of the two Americans.

"Searchlight," he ordered. It would make them a target for every insurgent within ten miles, but he needed to see and he couldn't believe what his eyes seemed to be showing him.

"Off," he ordered a second later. He didn't know what it meant, but he didn't need a million candlepower to see the carnage.

Newland lay across a couple of huge logs with her throat slit. Smoke still trickled from her M16. And Smith held a bloody knife in one hand and his guts in another.

The civilian had killed her, but she'd gotten last licks in before dying. What the hell was this about?

"Unbutton. I'm going outside."

"Captain, the chopper started its rotors and they're still targeting us. Not sure I like the looks of it."

It didn't make sense, but then, nothing about this mission had made sense.

"Put them in the sights of the 120 millimeter and let them see how they feel about turnaround. And for God's sake, button up again once I'm out."

"Right, Sir." The idea of shooting back cheered Jensen right up.

Herrera knew it was hopeless, but he jumped out of the tank and knelt down by the CIA agent, pressing his fingers to the man's neck.

Nothing.

"Call for another Medevac," he shouted. "We've got at least one dead."

He was moving toward Sergeant Newland's body when all hell broke loose.

The huge black helicopter lifted about five feet off the ground and fired at his tank.

The explosion blasted over the tank, shook the remains of the old mosque like an earthquake, and knocked Herrera to the ground.

But an Abrams is a hairy beast and Jensen had been watching for exactly that move. The tank's 120 fired back almost instantaneously and the helicopter went down in a ball of fire that made the earlier searchlight glare look like nothing.

The second explosion shook the mosque like a dog shaking fleas and knocked Herrera the rest of the way to the ground. If he'd been on the other side of the tank, unprotected by its huge bulk, he would be a dead man. As it was, he was shaken, disoriented, and pissed.

Herrera pushed himself to his knees, then realized he'd been pushing on something soft.

"What happened?"

It took a moment for reality to penetrate. Dead women don't talk, right? Which meant Newland wasn't dead. What had appeared from a distance to be a huge slash across her neck was simply a scratch.

Or was it. The pool of blood around her didn't come from any scratch. To all appearances, she'd bled out. But she was alive, and talking. The situation was clearly impossible.

Before he could answer Sergeant Newland, the tank's hatch popped open. "Captain, we've got trouble. Our IFF shows multiple aircraft incoming. They're signaling Friendly, but the signature doesn't look right for Air Force." Sonders was practically babbling now. "I think we may have some more where this black helicopter came from.

Herrera thought fast. Whatever he decided, there would be no going back. He didn't need to be a genius to know that taking on the CIA or whatever other secret government agency was behind Smith and his black helicopters was a fool's game.

"Understood, Sonders. Good shooting, Jensen. Cancel that Medevac order and clear out. I want the entire company to head back to base at full speed. And for God's sake take Newland's squad with you. Don't stop for anything but a valid chain-of-command order."

"What about you, sir?"

What about him? When you grow up in south Dallas, the Army was one of the few options that take you away from street gangs, drugs, or a lifetime of menial work. If he stayed with Newland, he would be pissing away everything he'd spent the past ten years working for—and would probably spend another ten years or so in the stockade for desertion as well.

But he was an officer, and someone in covert ops had knifed a soldier while he'd been on guard duty. He wasn't going to let anyone finish what Smith had started.

"Let whoever does the post-op know that I ordered the shot that downed the chopper. My responsibility. Now move."

As his tank company roared into the night, he bent down to pick up the wounded woman.

She pushed his arms away. "I'm all right. What's going on?"

"Your CIA friend went off the deep end. Tried to kill you. You must have got him before he could finish the job. Now we've got to get out of here."

"Okay. Help me with this." She gestured at the wooden joists she'd fallen upon when Smith had killed her.

"We don't have time for construction debris. We've got to go underground before the insurgents put on a show of force."

"I don't know what's going on, but I do know that Smith tried to kill me over what you're calling construction debris. According to him, it's The Cross."

He must have looked as confused as he felt because she shook her head impatiently. "The True Cross. The one Jesus was crucified on. Not symbolically but literally. I don't know if that's true, but it's clearly important. We need to get it to safety."

Safety was something Herrera suspected would be the last thing they'd find around here.

Newland stood, exactly as if she hadn't just been lying their with every drop of blood in her body spilled on the foundation stones for the old mosque, then lifted up the crossbeam as if it weighted only a few ounces.

"We can hide in the ruins back there. Bring that other piece."

Without waiting for him to answer, she set off at a jog.

Zack eyed the twelve foot long piece of timber. Herrera was as good a Catholic as the next Latino, but he expected the artifacts of the Saints and Angelic Hosts to be in churches where they belonged, not lying on some remote battlefield.

He picked up what Newland claimed just might be half the True Cross and was amazed that it seemed practically weightless. So much so that he was able to grab Smith's body and his briefcase and carry those as well.

From the evidence of the wounds, he'd assumed that the agent had been the one who'd flipped out. Now that he'd heard the Sergeant, he wondered if he'd made a truly monumental mistake.

* * * *

Ivy headed toward the sound side of the mosque complex where a couple of outbuildings were more or less intact.

Her mind whirled with impossibilities but she'd been long enough in Iraq to know that survival came first. In Iraq, understanding what was going on rarely happened anyway.

Running full speed, she hit the door to what looked like it had once been a supply shed and smacked it open, then put her M16 on her hip and stood guard.

Captain Herrera was lugging not only the main piece from the Cross, something she and Smith had both struggled to lift, but also Jones' corpse and his briefcase.

"What did you bring <u>him</u> for?"

"You want to leave his body there for the insurgents to put on T.V.?"

20

Herrera shoved the broken door shut behind him.

She hadn't realized she was poking her rifle into his chest until he used one finger to push it out of the way, then set down his cargo.

"All right," he collapsed onto the earthen floor. "I'm going to assume you know what you're doing. So tell me what you know. We'd better pool our knowledge if we're going to stay alive."

She considered, nodded. She didn't know any secrets. She had no idea why her squad had been assigned to work with Smith and Jones in the first place, how he'd guessed that what he claimed was the True Cross would be here in Mosul, or why he'd decided to try to kill her. But she was interested in learning what she could. Because there was one thing she was certain of. Given the way theater command had responded to Smith, what he was doing was approved at high levels within the government. Which meant the woman who had killed him was likely to be in a heap of trouble.

"I don't know much," she admitted. "Smith hand-selected me and my squad—you know women don't normally fight combat missions--but he didn't tell me anything about the mission. I certainly didn't have a clue what he was looking for until I saw this." She gestured toward the two timbers that made up the alleged True Cross. "He used a smaller Cross from the briefcase like a dowsing rod."

Herrera shook his head. The Captain was a good-looking guy, maybe an inch under six feet with a nice build on him and intelligent brown eyes. The burning helicopter provided enough light for her to see him clearly even without the night vision gear that had never arrived.

"Maybe we should look in the briefcase and see what else he has there," he proposed.

"Might as well." They couldn't get in more trouble than they were already in.

While Herrera fiddled with the locks to the case, Ivy ran her hands along her neck. A new scar was crusted with blood but there was no pain. Indeed, she felt better than she could remember.

"You didn't give me morphine, did you? And how did I heal so fast?"

"As far as I could tell, you were dead." Herrera snapped open the briefcase.

A smile trembled on her lips as she waited to hear the punch line. Yeah, right. Sure she was dead.

Herrera didn't seem to be in any hurry to deliver, though. Instead he flipped through sheets of paper and carefully drawn maps.

"How's your Arabic?"

"Pretty bad. I learned enough to recognize bomb warnings." She

21

paused. "Uh, what exactly did you mean about me being dead? I don't think that's funny."

Herrera glared at her. "No joke. You looked dead. From the blood spatter, I'd say Smith cut your carotid artery and bled you out completely. Training and reflex action allowed you to shoot him but you were already dead by the time that happened."

She swallowed hard. "That's impossible."

"Of course it's impossible. Just like it's impossible that the True Cross has survived for two thousand years and we just happen to come across it. I'm telling you what I saw."

He continued flipping through papers from the briefcase while he spoke.

Since Herrera had the briefcase, Ivy steeled herself and searched Smith's body.

It was nasty work—the M16 bullet had tumbled as it had penetrated his gut. Although the entry wound was tiny, the exit wound in his lower back was bigger than both of her fists. Blood, piss, and feces all blended into his clothing. Herrera was right about the insurgents crowing over his body if they'd found it, but she couldn't help wishing the captain had left it outside anyway.

It stank and it gave her the creeps.

Fortunately, Smith carried his wallet in his suit pocket and her bullet hadn't hit it.

She flipped it open. Sure enough, his I.D. was made out to a 'John Smith,' who lived, if the military I.D. could be believed, in 'Anytown, USA.'

A thick wad of hundred-dollar bills, a couple of thousand worth, filled the cash section of the wallet. At the bottom, wedged in between some of the hundreds, she found a small smartcard with the cryptic label, Property of The Foundation.

"Ever hear of something called The Foundation?" she asked.

"Funny that you say that." Zach had unfolded a huge map of Iraq and he handed it to her, pointing his hand to the legend. "Looks like this Foundation has better intelligence on Iraq than the military is giving to us poor soldiers."

The Foundation was printed in some sort of holographic text at the bottom of the map's legend.

"Oh, and there's some cash here," Herrera mentioned. "A bunch."

"How much?"

"You thinking about stealing Smith's money?" He looked uneasy.

Well, she felt worse than uneasy. She wasn't a lifer. She had plans for her life, plans that the National Guard call-up had put on hold rather than canceling. But if she was right about what was going on, all of those plans were flushed down the toilet now.

"One of us had better start thinking," she reminded him. "Figure it this way. We've got a civilian who can call in air strikes. A civilian who just happened to be at the right place the morning after a late-night air strike on a mosque that might have been a hideout for insurgents, but also might just have been a building he wanted leveled. If you think he was just a loose cannon, that he wasn't following orders of someone back in D.C., then you're more I than I would have guessed. And if he's part of some Foundation, then there are going to be others who knew what he found, folks are going to come looking for it, and who aren't going to want any witnesses around to confuse the issues."

Herrera nodded slowly. "Stealing a dead man's money feels nasty, but I agree. We've got to get out of here. We can't trust the military, we can't trust our government, and we certainly can't trust the insurgents. But if we run, what are we going to do with the, uh, artifact?"

It was a good question. They could just leave it. Smith had asked if she was a Christian and had seemed happy when she'd told him she was. Based on that, she didn't guess the Foundation was an atheistic organization out to destroy Christian relics. But then again, the Foundation had cold-blooded killers like Smith. If it was responsible for bombing mosques that weren't being used as insurgent bases, then it was also responsible for heavy Iraqi civilian and U.S. military casualties, as well. They might be Christian, but she just didn't trust them with the kind of power that The Cross held—power that had, if she could believe Herrera, literally brought her back from the dead.

Not that she could really believe Herrera. There had to be some confusion. Battlefield stories could never be taken at face value.

"We'll take it with us. I figure we've got two hours for whoever runs The Foundation in D.C. to wake up in the morning, read over the transcripts of whatever reports Smith was sending, and then mobilize half the Army to come pouring in to pick up the Cross. If we're still here, we'll be written up as unavoidable casualties in another great victory over the insurgents."

He nodded slowly. "There is one problem."

"Getting out of an unfriendly city, surrounded by insurgents and unable to trust our own side, all the while carrying a ten foot-long chunk of wood. That problem?"

Herrera shook his head. "I was thinking about getting past the insurgents out there now."

"You're the Captain. Should be a piece of cake for an officer like you."

* * * *

Okay, a plan to get past the dozens of insurgents converging on the ruined mosque now, get out of insurgent-dominated Mosul, cross a few hundred miles of CIA-dominated Iraqi Kurdistan, then somehow go somewhere where this Foundation, whatever it was, couldn't catch them. All in a day's work, right? At least his armored company had distracted the aircraft. Now that really would be a party.

"Captain?"

"Damn it, Newland. I'm not a Captain any more. Call me Zack."

"Sure, Zack. You might want to hurry that plan up. Looks like some of those insurgents are coming our way right now."

Herrera didn't know much about escaping the CIA or miracles, but he knew plenty about fighting insurgents, and even more about surviving urban gangs, which was pretty much what most of these insurgents were, anyway.

"Arrange Smith like he's crouched down in the corner," he ordered. "Just in case, don't let him touch the Cross."

He glanced out the door to make sure they had time. Sure enough, a team of four insurgents was going through the mostly shattered outbuildings. They'd bust down a door, fire off a clip of Kalashnikov cartridges on full automatic, then search. That kind of sloppy operation would have gotten him failed out of Officer Training School faster than shit through a goose, but he wasn't going to complain.

"Now what?" Newland demanded.

"Get behind the door. Keep your rifle ready but don't fire it unless you have to. An M16 sounds just enough different from the Kalashnikov to bring every insurgent in fifty miles swarming."

She nodded and moved. She'd lost her helmet somewhere and her golden hair stuck out like one of those cartoons where a character sticks their fingers in an electrical socket. To Herrera, she looked good. Hell, she looked like an angel. Sure he'd always been a sucker for the blonde, blue-eyed thing. Right now, though, he appreciated the fact that she'd follow orders without asking questions even more than he did her physical appearance.

The hard rattle of Kalashnikov fire sounded closer. "One shed over," he murmured.

She nodded and he realized he was talking for his own benefit, to keep his adrenaline level from raging out of control. He'd always been an armor man, even back when he'd been enlisted, before he'd opted for officer training school. He was used to having a few tons of steel between himself and the enemy. Even in the Abrams, things could get hairy. But he had a lot of respect for people like Newland, people who relied on light body armor and prayer to stay alive.

He picked up a two-foot-long hunk of rebar from the clutter on the shed floor and took his own position near the door, thankful for the shed's flimsy particle-board walls. If they'd been in one of the stone buildings in the old mosque itself, the bullets would ricochet and kill everyone inside, like his own shots had on his first tour in this war when Saddam's National Guard had dared face his team from inside stone fortresses.

His heartbeat sounded loud in his ears and he willed himself to breath slowly, silently.

A booted foot kicked open the door Newland had already damaged, and the rattle of automatic rifle fire came immediately afterwards.

Smith's body jerked as dozens of bullets riddled his corpse and the odor of death filled the small shed.

Two tours of duty had given Herrera enough Arabic to understand the shouted celebration. They thought they'd killed an American.

All four of them piled inside to check out the body. As the fourth entered the small shed, Herrera went into action.

He quietly struck the rearmost of the insurgents in the back of his head.

The insurgent slumped and Herrera caught him and tossed him back to Newland, trusting her to set him down silently.

The second of the insurgents was no harder, but the third must have heard something. He spun around, his Kalashnikov already blasting.

If the rebel had waited to shoot until he'd seen Herrera, Zack would have been a dead man. Fortunately, he didn't. The weapon's recoil forced its muzzle upward and Herrera was able to duck under the stream of bullets, smash his hunk of rebar into the rifle, and then a knee into the insurgent's groin.

He followed with a palm-thrust to the guy's head and then turned to deal with the fourth.

He would be too late, of course. No soldier, no matter how ill-trained, would be caught that unaware.

But Newland hadn't just been standing there. She must have moved almost as soon as he had. Now she cradled the last insurgent in a headlock that he still struggled against.

Herrera raised his length of rebar but Newland shook her head. "Two seconds and he's out. We don't have to kill them, do we?"

Killing them would be smart. If they left them alive, there would be witnesses. The insurgents hated Americans, but that didn't mean they wouldn't take their money. Sooner or later, word would get back to the Foundation that two Americans had survived the helicopter crash and had taken the supposed Cross.

But Herrera didn't always do the smart thing. He'd fled the slums of Dallas because he hadn't been smart enough to join a gang and kill in cold blood. He wasn't about to start now, even if these insurgents would have cheerfully killed him.

"We'll tie them up and gag them. It should give us enough time to get back to base." He doubted they spoke English and most were unconscious, but he wouldn't bet his life on them not understanding what he was saying. And the word Base was one that had become part of a common vocabulary.

Fortunately Newland caught on. "It shouldn't be too hard to get past this group and call for a helicopter rescue."

"Exactly."

She gestured at the insurgents' clothing. "Maybe we should take some of their clothes to slow them down even more."

"Good idea." They could disguise themselves as insurgents, letting them get through the current mob, at least.

She wrinkled her little pug nose at the stench—obviously none of these insurgents had access to laundry facilities—or probably any running water. But she got to work stripping off outer garments.

Three of the four men they'd disabled wore ordinary clothing. Stained trousers that might once have been part of an Iraqi military uniform but were now part of the ubiquitous attire of the Iraqi man on the street. Loose shirts with stained pits and grime that looked like it had started setting during the first Gulf War rather than the second. The fourth wore the desert robes of a tribesman.

"Intelligence would like to know about this one," Newland observed as she yanked off the man's desert robes, then took off her own belt to tie his wrists and ankles together.

"Maybe our reinforcements will get here in time to apprehend him."

He added blindfolds to the gags Newland was tying. He didn't want them to see him and Newland putting on disguises.

Fortunately, Herrera wasn't a giant. Still, he was taller than any of the insurgents they'd captured. He yanked the shirt off the largest of the four, stripped down to his t-shirt, held his breath, and pulled on the sweaty garment.

"You might want to hide that." Newland gestured at the St.

Christopher medal his mother had pressed on him when he'd been sent to Iraq in his first tour.

He considered it, then stuffed it in a pocket. They were going to need St. Christopher's help if they were going to get out of Mosul alive. He wasn't sure he could believe what he thought he'd seen, but he'd been an alter boy and believed in ordinary miracles. He'd no more leave St. Christopher behind than he'd spit in the holy water.

"The Army should attack in about six hours." He spoke slowly, using the best Arabic he could muster. "If you haven't been apprehended by then, let the other men know they need to get out of here. Otherwise you'll be bombed straight to paradise."

The insurgents would be overjoyed to kill Newland and himself, but he didn't want their deaths on his conscience. And they would be on his conscience. Because he believed Newland was right. This Foundation, whatever it was, had called in an air strike on a mosque not because it had been filled with rebels, but because they wanted it leveled to the ground to ease their search for the Cross. He didn't like the locals, but he could sympathize a bit with their situation. If someone bombed his church back home in south Dallas, he would have wanted to make them pay, too.

Newland had pulled on the desert robe and was swatting the headwrap against an iron bar. "Trying to get rid of the fleas," she told him when he gave her what must have been a puzzled look. "I won't get all of them, but I'm not looking for perfection."

He took a look outside. "You'd better hurry. We're about to have company. Again."

Chapter 3

The nomad's wool robes and headgear stank and were rich in fleas, but Ivy was glad for the disguise. With his olive skin and black hair, Zack could pass for a local in the dark. Nobody was going to mistake a blond woman for anything but the foreigner she was.

Fortunately, she was tall for a woman and many of the locals were short. If she remembered to walk like she had a poker up her butt, she might be able to pass as male for long enough to get out of this place. They might be jumping from a frying pan into the fire, but for right now, she'd settle for jumping anywhere.

The Captain passed her one of the Kalashnikovs and took another for himself.

She knew the weapon was just part of the disguise, that if she had to shoot, she was already dead, but being armed made her feel more confident. She stuffed an extra magazine into a pocket of the pants she wore under her desert robes and made sure the clip was full before nodding. "Let's go."

They lugged the Cross out of the shed and left it leaning against the rubble of the mosque.

It only took a minute of searching to find a couple of crossbeams in the ruins that looked as if someone could have mistaken them for The Cross, and they dragged those to the crypt where Smith had located his treasure. The Foundation wouldn't mistake those for the True Cross, but she could hope they might think that Smith had.

"Now what?" she breathed as they laid the second of the beams to rest.

"The insurgents didn't walk here. So we find one of their vehicles. Maybe we'll be lucky and they won't have left a guard."

They were lucky to be alive now, even if she ignored Zack's claims that she'd been dead. But relying on luck wasn't in Ivy's training. Unfortunately, she didn't have any better ideas.

Sure enough, they found a truck parked half a block from the mosque complex. Typical of the luck—all bad--they'd had up until then, a couple of guards remained onboard, smoking cigarettes as they waited for the return of their colleagues.

For just an instant, a heavy flash of other-sight lowered itself on her. Bombed-out buildings stood as hollow shells of what had once been vibrant businesses and apartments. Here and there, kerosene lanterns cast small patches of yellow light into the night like camping fires set by barbarians residing on a conquered city. Mosul, formerly Nineveh according to be briefing her unit had gotten before they'd shipped there, had been a major city a thousand years before Rome had been founded. The heavy hand of war had beaten entrenched civilization back to barbarism.

She blinked and the city swam back into focus. It wasn't changed, really. The shattered buildings remained. But it was just a city. In that momentary vision, it had stood for more, as if the entire world had become a war-zone, the heavy tramp of occupying boots not just crushing Iraq, but destroying civilization throughout the world.

"Ready?" She sensed Zack tensing beside her but the truck was parked in the middle of the street. Although the guards weren't especially alert, there was no way they could approach unnoticed. If Zack got brave and rushed them, he'd get shot. Ivy didn't like the situation they were in, but she liked it a lot more than she would if she were alone.

She reached into one of her pockets and pulled out a chunk of the roll of cash she'd taken from Smith's wallet. "Let me handle this."

"But…"

She didn't give him time to voice his objection. Instead she spread the money, flashing that wad of hundreds where the guards could see them and where, hopefully, her blue eyes might be hidden from their gaze. There were some blue-eyed Arabs, of course. But they were rare enough to be noticed, and she didn't want these guys looking at anything but the money.

Money has a compulsion all its own. A few thousand dollars could buy a new truck, let an insurgent forget about being a rebel and think about running a business, getting a wife. In occupied Iraq, money was hope and life. Nobody asked too many questions about money.

One of the guards shouted something to her, but she couldn't make out the words. She waved the cash again, then deepened her voice. "There's more."

She spoke in Arabic. Her accent wouldn't be right, but there were plenty of foreigners, mujahidin, in Iraq. Strange accents wouldn't be completely unknown and her desert robes marked her as an outsider.

From the look the guard gave her, she guessed her accent was beyond strange. Still, the money held him hypnotized for just long enough.

She tossed it into his face, then grabbed him and yanked him out of the truck.

The second guard started to go for his Kalashnikov, but stopped abruptly when Zack jammed his own rifle in his face.

"Out," she ordered. "On the ground." Her Arabic was plenty good for those expressions. American soldiers had to give that command dozens of times every day as they manned the checkpoints around the tortured country.

The Arab's eyes were filled with hatred but he obeyed, joining the man Zack had already dumped on the ground.

"When we leave, take the money and run," Zack told them. His Arabic was a lot better than hers. "The other rebels will kill you for losing the truck if they find you, so hide from them and from the Americans. They'll kill you too."

"Na am fahamt," the first guard said, or close enough. Yes, I understand.

She patted them down, took an ancient revolver, which looked like it might be a souvenir from the war against the British, and tossed it into the cab. "Let's go." She kept her rifle on the two men while Herrera fired up the engine, then, as he started rolling back toward the mosque, she jumped into the back.

Back at the mosque complex, it took less than a minute to load up the Cross. Even that was far too long because a couple of insurgents started shouting at them, probably wondering why they had brought the truck onto the scene. The shooting didn't stop until one of the insurgents they'd knocked unconscious stumbled out of the shed—wearing his underwear.

* * * *

"That was fun."

Newland's eyes snapped with humor and her peaches and cream complexion glowed with health.

They'd managed to get out of Mosul, avoiding both insurgent and U.S. checkpoints, driving at speeds that ranged up to a hundred and fifty kilometers per hour, and into the Kurdish countryside that surrounded the mostly Arab city of Mosul.

"What next, Captain?"

"Zack."

"Whatever. You going to answer the question?"

He rubbed his eyes. The sun was breaking over the horizon and he hadn't slept in about thirty hours. He guessed Newland was no better off.

"We find someplace to hide for the day. The Turkish border is only about a hundred miles away, but that hundred miles is filled with CIA-trained militias. If we make it that far, then we've got a border to cross."

"Why Turkey?"

"Would you rather go to Syria? We've got to get out of Iraq and Turkey is the only country around here where Americans won't stand out like sore thumbs. It's also got enough nationalistic tendencies that the CIA at least has to lay low there."

He turned off Iraq Highway 2 into what looked like an ancient ruin but turned out to be an abandoned farmhouse.

The roof had fallen in, but it was summer in Iraq. It wasn't going to rain and the stone walls would provide shade and some protection. After getting some sleep, they'd be better prepared to make the run for the border.

"We'd better turn back into Americans now, too," he told her as he carried Smith's briefcase into the ruin. "Because around here, they kill Arabs even faster than they kill Americans. I guess we can pretend to be CIA."

"It's encouraging to be so loved," Newland said. She stripped off the sweaty robe and tossed it on the ground. "Hate to admit it, but fleas and all, that's going to be a better mattress than the stone floor.

She yanked off her armor and leaned against the stone wall of the abandoned and bombed out farmhouse.

"You figure we can make it?"

He was glad she spoke because he'd been distracted by the curves beneath the army t-shirt that she'd stripped down to.

He shrugged. "Not dressed like that. I doubt the CIA has any female field agents in Kurdistan. But if you go male, we might be able to. Even if some of our friends back in Mosul decide to become informants, but what could they tell? That we said we were going back to base? That we stole a white truck? Want to guess how many battered old Renault trucks there are in Mosul?"

She shrugged her shoulders, looking about as far from being male as anyone Zack had ever seen. "I can do the male thing."

"Then I figure we can get out of Iraq."

She looked at him. "Okay. Then what?"

He sighed, then stood and looked out at the highway, maybe a quarter of a mile away.

With sunrise, the locals would be moving around. There would be traffic on the road, but not much.

In the distance, a battered jeep cut off the road and headed into the hills.

Iraq was supposed to be the location of the Garden of Eden, the birthplace of Abraham and Jonah. But up here at least, it was desolate hilly country.

"Once we're out of Iraq, I'm clueless. If we can believe what Smith told you, we've got one of the most historic artifacts in history in the back of a farm truck. We already know that the U.S. government is going to do whatever it can to get the Cross from us. From the way Smith turned on you, I'm guessing they won't want witnesses. If we're lucky, they'll disappear us to some CIA torture camp. I don't think we'll be that lucky. They won't want us to talk to anyone."

Newland ran her hand over the scar on her throat when he mentioned Smith. Zack didn't have problems buying into the miracles in the Bible, and from the Saints. But he had a lot more trouble seeing miracles happen with his own eyes.

"Sorry I had to remind you about that, Newland."

She shook her head. "If I have to call you Zack, you can call me Ivy. And the way I figure it, the U.S. Government doesn't have any special right to the True Cross, if that's what it is."

He was perversely glad that she'd invited him to use her first name. "I'd have to agree with that. If anyone has a claim to it, it's the Church."

"Maybe that's what the Foundation is. A Church."

He hadn't thought about that but it made sense. "Maybe. But what kind of church would it be? I'm thinking we need to give it to the Church that's been around since the last time The Cross was in public. The Church that traces its roots back to the apostles."

"Orthodox? That why you want to go to Turkey, Zack?"

"The Greeks might have owned the Cross for a while, but the last Christians who had it were Crusaders. They would have been Catholic. I'd admit I might be prejudiced since I'm a Catholic myself."

Everyone in Iraq remembered the European Crusaders as if they'd just been through a generation before instead of hundreds of years earlier. Saladin was a hero to Turks, Kurds and Arabs. Even Saddam had claimed some sort of descent from him. And he'd been the one who'd captured the real True Cross.

"Speaking of crusades, if The Cross got turned over to modern-day crusaders, it could really bust things open. The entire Middle East would become even more of a battleground than it is now." Ivy shuddered. "I wonder if that's what my vision was supposed to mean."

"Hmm?"

"Back there." She waved in the direction of the city, a cloud of smoke and the distant crunch of explosives marking it on the horizon. "It seemed like I could see the whole world stretched out. And it was all like Mosul—bombs and fires and death."

Zack wasn't a philosopher and had never put much credence in visions--except in ancient visions by saints, of course. But now, all the rules were getting torn up.

"I'm pretty sure nobody is going to send crusaders in here."

"Oh, yeah?" Ivy looked around. "What, exactly, do you think we are, then? Christian occupiers in the heart of the Moslem world, that's what. One thing I agree with. The Catholic Church is a better bet than the Foundation. The former Pope spoke against this war. I figure the new one wouldn't turn the Cross over to crusaders, whether they're us Americans or anyone else."

Newland was right. The modern Catholic Church wasn't going to call for any crusade against the Moslem world. "So we somehow get the Cross to Italy and turn it over to the Pope. No problem, huh?"

As if.

* * * *

Ivy woke up suddenly. Although she couldn't see anything out of the ordinary, the artifact hummed with a strange harmonic, sending subsonic disturbances that had blasted her from her sleep.

"We've got to move."

"Huh?" Herrera was awake, but he seemed groggy, almost drugged.

"Grab the Cross. Move."

Most of the guys Ivy knew would have argued. Herrera picked up Smith's cash-filled briefcase, the assault rifle, and his section of Cross then jogged toward the truck.

That didn't feel right. And Ivy's hunches had kept her alive before. "Leave the truck."

"But we'll never make it to the border without transportation."

"Run."

She grabbed the crosspiece and took off, heading straight up into the mountains. It wasn't the shortest way toward the Turkish border, but it felt right. Today, she intended to follow her gut.

A sudden wiggle tore the Cross from Ivy's hands. She dropped into a narrow gully washed into the hillside by a bigger rainstorm than she'd seen since she came to this desolate country. Zack joined her, ducking deep into the wash. He looked at her quizzically, obviously trying to figure out whether she'd gone crazy.

"I felt some kind of warning from the Cross," she explained. It sounded idiotic, out loud. Even if the Cross was supernatural, why would it waste its time warning her? She was just a National Guard Sergeant who was at least as woo-woo as she was Christian. Why not warn Herrera. From the way he talked, he had to be a lot better Catholic than she was.

"If you're wrong, no harm done. If you're right, I'm grateful," Herrera said. He peered over the edge of the gully, looking for any enemy.

It took her a moment to realize that the hum she heard wasn't all coming from the Cross. A small plane flashed overhead and circled around the farmhouse.

"Predator," Zack whispered.

The Army was stingy with these unmanned flying weapons. There had been plenty of times Ivy wished she'd had better intelligence from above, someone looking down and spotting insurgents before they started shooting—it had been a wish that had never been realized. Clearly someone in charge thought finding the Cross was more important than saving a few uniformed lives. Ivy wasn't sure they were wrong.

The drone circled the abandoned farmhouse again, then a white flash temporarily obscured it.

She barely made out the streak of light that plunged from the drone —into the truck that had carried them so faithfully away from the burning city.

A second flash and the abandoned farmhouse where they'd hidden disappeared into rubble.

The drone continued to circle, watching perhaps, to see if there were any survivors. The missiles made it more likely that the drone was CIA rather than military since the army used its Predators mostly for surveillance rather than attacks.

Ivy swallowed hard trying not to vomit. She'd known they would be hunted, but knowing and seeing were different.

"Crap." Zack pointed to the west where twin lines of dust rose toward the sky.

"Oh, great. Looks like we're about to have company."

It figured that the CIA would attack first from a distance, then send in resources to pick through the pieces. Unlike the army, the CIA couldn't stand the heat of real battle.

"Think we should move?" she asked.

Herrera glanced at the Predator, then at the approaching Kurdish militia.

"If we stay here, we're dead anyway."

She picked up the crosspiece and set off up the wash, trying to take advantage of what cover this land offered.

Fortunately, there was a fair amount of it.

Low shrubs, scattered windswept olive trees and multiple rocky outcroppings made their journey higher into the Kurdish foothills a challenge, but at least it would be largely inaccessible to the wheeled vehicles the Kurdish militia and their CIA sponsors used.

At first, Ivy thought carrying the Cross would slow them. Even the shorter crosspiece she carried had to weigh fifty pounds and the bulky timbers were awkward, with a tendency to dig into her shoulders. As they struggled deeper into the mountains, however, she realized that she wasn't growing tired as she normally would. Could the Cross provide energy to her? She wasn't prepared to believe that, but she could no longer doubt that something weird was going on.

Whoever was operating the Predator kept that drone circling over the farmhouse until the militia arrived, then set it off in widening search patterns. It hovered over the gully where she and Herrera had hidden, then continued on.

"Maybe it can sense the Cross," Herrera suggested.

Ivy nodded, then flung herself down in a rare patch of grass. "Maybe. Or maybe it's something a lot more mundane."

"Like…"

"Like the briefcase." She took the case from Herrera, jerked it open, yanked out the cash and papers, then stared at the Cross that Smith had used to douse for the True Cross. "Can you think of any reason we should take this with us?"

Zack took the dousing cross from her. "Find more holy artifacts?"

"You're joking."

"Only partially. This land is full of Biblical history. Mosul includes the ancient city of Nineveh where Jonah lived and where the ten lost tribes were taken after the destruction of Israel. Further south is Babylon where the Bible was actually compiled."

He waved a hand toward the snow-covered peaks ahead of them. "In the mountains not far from here is the peak where Noah's ark came to rest. Peter preached all around here before coming to Rome. We're only a couple of hundred miles from where Saul was transformed into Paul. Fifty miles past that and you're in Nazareth where our Lord was born.

Just imagine what we could find. Wit a relic-finding tool that actually works, we could unveil some of the most important mysteries in the history of the world."

And it could get them killed. "I've got all the relic I need."

Zack set aside the douser. "I guess you're right. And you're also right that it would also be a good place to hide a tracking device. So, this Cross stays, along with the case itself."

"Just a second." Ivy pulled out her commando knife and slit at the leather inners of Smith's briefcase.

A handful of gold coins and a plastic bag with a few sheets of paper inside rewarded her effort. "I thought Smith was sneaky enough that he'd have something hidden. Too bad we didn't have time to search his body more completely."

"I don't think I could have made myself slice him up with to find a few more gold coins." Herrera looked around, scooped the papers and money into the ample pockets in his uniform pants, and stood. "We'd better get a move on."

Five minutes later, another missile flash told them that they'd made the right call. That peaceful glade where they'd dismantled Smith's briefcase erupted into an inferno. Of course, making the right decision only meant that they were temporarily still alive. Alive but stuck in an inhospitable mountain range, surrounded by people whose dreams for independence completely relied on the CIA, and hunted by a mysterious Foundation that seemed able to use magical means to hunt for the Cross.

It wasn't a happy situation.

* * * *

Zack's foot skidded from beneath him as he hit a patch of loose rock that growing shadows of twilight had hidden from his tired eyes. They'd been on the run for hours now, but they hadn't thrown off their hunters. With nightfall, they would be at an even greater disadvantage compared to the militiamen who had hidden in these mountains for decades in their eternal rebellion against the central authorities in Baghdad, Istanbul, Damascus, Constantinople, Rome, or Persepolis.

Running wouldn't help. They were just as likely to be running toward their enemies as away from them. If he and Ivy were to survive the night, they would need help.

The sun descended abruptly behind tall mountains to the west. They'd been going uphill for hours, climbing toward the mountains that formed the border between Turkey and Iraq. High as they were, it was still hot, but Zack guessed that it would cool off quickly now that the sun had set. Unlike the Iraqi lowlands, the thin air of the mountains would hold little warmth.

A soft curse told him that Ivy too had stumbled in the increasing darkness.

"Getting too dark to see," she admitted. "I'm not crazy about nighttime mountain climbing."

Zack wasn't either. But he was even less comfortable with getting blown up by a Predator missile. And every time they'd stopped for more than a couple of minutes, they'd heard the distinctive whine of the remote controlled drone.

"I'm open to suggestions."

"We need help. Another truck, maybe."

He knew that. What he didn't know was how to get it. "While we're wishing, why not ask for an Abrams. That way, I could knock out those Predators before they could get a shot off."

"Okay, so that wasn't helpful." Ivy paused. Even in the growing darkness, he could tell she was squinching her nose in thought.

"How about if we pray."

"I'm not much on praying. Asking God for personal favors has always seemed selfish."

"Yeah. Well, it couldn't hurt."

"I guess."

Ivy went quiet as they trudged along, using the last moments of twilight to gain a bit more distance.

Lord, he prayed silently. *I don't know what I'm doing, but I know I need help. Anything you can spare would certainly be appreciated.*

It wasn't much of a prayer, and he certainly didn't get a sense that anyone up there was listening. But it was the best he could come up with.

"There's someone ahead."

He froze. He couldn't see through the trees, but the attenuated scent of burning wood told him Ivy was right. Someone was nearby.

"We do need help," she reminded him.

"Whoever is up there is either part of the militia, in which case they'll turn us over to the CIA, or they're innocent civilians, in which case we'll probably get them killed."

"There's a third alternative. Maybe they're the answer to your prayer."

He didn't think the Lord worked that way. But then, it seemed he was learning things every moment.

"We might as well check. If we just stumble on, sooner or later we'll fall off the mountain."

It grated against the code of machismo his father and uncles had beaten into him as a child, but he let Ivy, with her more sensitive nose, take the lead as they searched for the fire.

He wished he had been able to rig up some sort of carrying device for the Cross. Carrying the massive nine-foot timber took both of his hands--which meant he had to keep his confiscated assault rifle slung over a shoulder, inaccessible if he needed it on a moment's notice. But he hadn't thought he'd need a carrier when they still had the truck, and he'd been on the run ever sense.

"It looks like some sort of cave," Ivy whispered after they'd stumbled through the darkness for at least twenty minutes.

He was standing a few feet from her and he could barely hear her words, but apparently she had spoken loudly enough to alarm whoever was ahead of them. Someone dumped something into the fire, eliminating the red glow that provided the only illumination and sending an herb-rich scent toward them.

He inhaled—recognized the distinctive scent of cannabis mixed with cooking herbs and spices that reminded him of the incense used in the south Dallas church where he'd had his first communion.

Stars blurred, seemed to lurch across the sky. His knees wobbled and he fought for his balance.

"I think…"

Blackness plunged over him before he could tell Ivy what he thought.

Chapter 4

"You bear a heavy burden." The voice was that of an old woman, but she didn't look like an old woman. Instead, the face of a monster, lit by a flickering red fire, peered at Ivy.

They were in a cave, but rich carpets lined the floor and walls. An altar, with a strangely shaped figure in blue and gold that could only be the Virgin Mary, adorned one wall. A fire, flames moving in slow motion, smoldered between Ivy and the doorway.

She attempted to push herself from the stone floor but gave it up as a bad job. "Am I dead?"

"Perhaps." The figured moved closer and Ivy recognized the monster shape as a mask. If this was hell, it was a cheap Hollywood version. She couldn't imagine that Satan's imps needed demon masks.

"You drugged us, didn't you?" Ivy couldn't see Herrera but some part of her sensed him nearby.

"Your emotions were too strong, were resonating with the, ah, object. The hunters could pick up on those vibrations. Without meaning to, you were calling them to you. We found a way to take you far away from that."

The woman's voice was strange, each word cutting into Ivy's consciousness and leaving its imprint, but not sticking. She could have repeated the woman's meaning, but not the words themselves. "Are you speaking in English?"

The woman laughed again, her voice ageless. "There is only one true language, the language of the Angels. Those who speak it can be understood by anyone, and can understand anyone. Because it is the true language, what is said in it is true, or becomes true. Some people call this magic."

In her drugged state, the woman's explanation made sense to Ivy, although she suspected it wouldn't when she came down from whatever this person had dosed her with.

From somewhere distant, she heard Herrera groan and thrash around. Soon he quieted.

"Is he all right? Where is he?" Why had she regained consciousness while the larger male had not?

"This is not a place where males are welcome. His sleep protects him from forces he could not understand, forces that would destroy first, then discriminate."

But Zack wasn't the only person who needed protection. Ivy wasn't certain how much time had passed, but surely she'd been unconscious for more than a few minutes. The CIA trackers would have had plenty of opportunity to strike. This woman couldn't realize the danger she had put herself into by bringing them into her cave.

"You'll be in danger if you're found here with us," Ivy said.

"I have already explained that this is not a place that welcomes males. Your hunters are all male. They will not find you. Not here. And not tonight."

As if some crazy hillside shaman would know about the type of electronic surveillance the CIA had available to it. "You don't understand. They have been able to track us everywhere. I think the Cross is sending out some sort of vibration they can pick up on."

Oops. She hadn't meant to mention the word <u>Cross</u>. For one thing, most Kurds were Moslems. For another, the CIA had probably notified everyone in Kurdistan to be on the lookout for a Cross. Even an isolated hermit would have gotten the word by now, if that was what this woman was.

"It isn't only a Cross, you know." The demon-masked woman brushed her hand against the artifact. "It is the One True Cross, the Cross of Jesus's passion. But the wood was holy before it was a Cross. In times ancient even before Moses, it was a tree, planted by Adam and the all-mother Eve from a seed from the garden itself. When the Queen of Sheba went to Solomon, she found these very timbers built into a bridge, recognized them, and brought the news to the King. When Solomon built his Temple, he built them into the structure, understanding in the wisdom that the great Queen had shared with him, that it would become a critical part of Prophesy.

"Power has steeped into this wood from the moment of divine creation herself. Of course those who seek after power are called to it. Did not El Shaddai himself warn that the tree of life would grant vast powers to man? Powers so great he expelled them from the garden, the mother womb, to prevent them from reaching them."

The old woman, or monster, or whatever, tapped the crosspiece which gave out a ringing chime, like a bell.

Ivy wasn't sure what to make of the woman's claim that she spoke some true language, but she found she could not doubt the woman's strange claims. Smith had somehow found the one True Cross. And now, she and Zack were charged with an artifact of such power that God himself had feared it.

The CIA would definitely want something with that kind of power.

"All of that may be true," Ivy said. "One thing for sure, the CIA can track it. They'll try to blow you up with their missiles, and they'll send in their pet militia."

"Not here," the woman repeated. "Here you are safe. Safe from the human searchers, at least."

The old woman's assurance wasn't as comforting as Ivy wished it had been. "So who are we in danger from?"

The woman gestured at her fire and a swirl of smoke rose from it, the tendrils taking bizarre shapes of half-human animals, tortured women, and horn-headed demons. "There is much to fear."

I am so drugged. Ivy forced herself not to react. The woman couldn't know what she was seeing, could she. Ivy didn't believe in magic. Except what, other than magic, had been happening to her?

"Can I ask you a question?"

The woman smiled. "You just did."

"Was I really dead?"

The woman stared at her, round human-style eyes below the strangely shaped eyes of the mask.

"Yes. And may be again. But the tree of life remains strong."

"Ah." It could be a threat. But the way Ivy figured it, if the old woman had wanted them dead, she could have killed them while they'd been unconscious. Which meant she probably wasn't an immediate physical danger.

"You fear me, but you ignore the demons? They are the real threat. They and the men they ride."

"Are you telling me that the people chasing us are in league with demons?"

The woman considered, then muttered something.

The language was the same as she had been using, but suddenly it was incomprehensible to Ivy although each word hung on the air like a precious gem, beautiful, distinct, filled with power.

As they watched, smoke from the fire reformed into the shape of a group of men sitting around a table. The old woman watched intently for a moment, then waved her hand.

The smoke vanished completely, the fire abruptly gutted down to a few glowing embers.

"They call themselves the Foundation, do they?" Her mouth seemed to have a hard time shaping itself around the English word.

Ivy nodded. "We think so. We don't know much. Just what Smith said, and what we've learned from his papers."

"Yes, the Foundation. A reasonable name for them. They seek to found something new, something complete, something even beautiful in its own way. They are not knowingly evil. In fact, they claim the side of those who would bring virtue to triumph. They are militant in the host of your Christian God."

There was more meaning there than Ivy could stop to analyze. But if the Foundation were on the side of good, then maybe leaving the Cross somewhere for them to find would be the right thing to do.

"So you're saying we should turn the Cross over to them?"

"I spoke of their intent, what they hope to accomplish, not of the path they actually take. Does not your Jesus remind you that goals are not the most important thing? By their fruits, you shall know them."

Ivy wasn't sure the old woman had the Bible's meaning right, but she agreed with the sentiment. Smith's casual decision to assassinate her had made the Foundation's standing clear. Whatever side they wished to be on, Ivy didn't like them.

But that didn't mean this woman was any better. The way she spoke of your Jesus meant she was no Christian, either of Foundation or of Catholic background. Neither was she a Moslem. No Moslem would tolerate that icon in his presence.

"Okay," Ivy said. "So, tell me what you think we should do."

The old woman fingered her mask. "What do you want to do?"

Ivy thought about it. "Stay alive."

"Alive? Is that all? And the burning city? You'd do nothing to prevent the spread of destruction from the navel of the world throughout its extremities."

"How did you—" Ivy stopped herself. The instant Smith had doused the True Cross, Ivy had left the world of the mundane. Why shouldn't this woman know what she had seen in her visions?

"Obviously I'd like to stop that kind of destruction as well."

The woman shook her head. "It is not so obvious. The burning city does not happen by itself, or through some supernatural force of Yahweh, or the Son, or the Goddess, or the Adversary. It is people who bring it about. It can only be people who prevent it. So, pursue your goal. Continue your search. Keep the holy timbers safe and with you. But do not, I think, take them to Rome. There are those in the Roman Church who maintain the hidden faith, but they are weak in Rome." Her voice was fading, as if she were walking away from Ivy although she seemed no more distant. "Venice," she whispered. "Byzantium first. There is something in that city that you will need. And then Venice. In Venice you will find those who can help you. Venice, city of the last Crusades. Venice."

* * * *

"Who were you talking to?"

Ivy opened eyes she hadn't realized were closed and looked around.

The woman was gone although her last word continued to reverberate through the cave. Venice, Venice, Venice.

"The old woman," she told Zack.

"What old woman? You were babbling, but there was no one else here."

Although Ivy would have sworn she hadn't slept, the gray light of morning penetrated the mouth of the cave.

She looked around and saw nothing was as it had been.

Rather than rich carpets, stones and ancient straw lined the cave's floor. Lichen and moss, and not tapestries, decorated the walls. The niche where the Madonna had presided was empty and covered with dust.

"She drugged us," Ivy guessed. "She must have made me see things that weren't there."

"Maybe." Zack rolled to his knees, then cursed softly. "What the hell —"

He pulled a broken bit of clay from where he'd set his knee on it.

A hint of color so faded and pale it seemed more than a memory than actual pigment promised that it had once held a design. Something about one curve seemed familiar, although it was merely a piece of dried clay, hardly something she would have seen before.

"Can I see that?"

He handed it over. "What do you think it is?"

It crumbled slightly as she touched it. Ancient as it was, though, it held a warmth like what would come from human touch.

"It's a mask."

Despite the residual warmth, no one had worn this mask the previous night, or any night for thousands of years. Time had eroded away the hard-fired colors until only a trace of the demon remained. No wonder

43

the woman hadn't been worried about being found by the CIA. The CIA was hardly a powerful force in ancient Babylonia.

"You know the saying about being careful what you pray for?"

He nodded. "I take it you got something different from what you'd expected."

"We're still alive," Ivy reminded him. "And we've got a goal. Venice."

"Venice? I thought we were going to Rome, to the Church."

"She told me Rome would be a mistake. Venice."

"I'm not so sure." He stared at her but she didn't back down. "Still, I guess we can decide that once we get off the mountain. If we get off the mountain."

"We will."

"You sound more sure than I am."

"Look around you, Zack. Check out the cave carefully. What do you see?"

He did as she urged, humoring her, she knew.

"It's just a cave."

Maybe she would doubt again. But that would be later, after the fresh memory of a visit from a priestess who had been thousands of years dead before even Peter walked these mountains.

"This cave has been a holy place. A temple. When we prayed, it answered."

He looked confused. "I certainly didn't pray to any mythical god."

"Goddess, I think," Ivy said. What had Sister Paraclete told her when she'd attended Catholic School in Pennsylvania, at a time when there were still a few nuns among those who taught? Something about the old religions. "I think I met someone from a time when the Queen of Heaven wasn't just Mary, mother of God, but the great Goddess herself."

"You can't believe that stuff," he insisted, his voice tinged with fear. "If there's one thing the Bible is clear on, it's that Goddess worship is wrong."

She didn't want to get into a theological debate with him. "Maybe. But she reminded me of something important."

"Why am I sure you're going to tell me?"

"She said, by their fruits you shall know them. She saved us last night, hid us out of sight from the CIA and let us rest. That doesn't sound like evil to me. She's going to save us again today. We're going to make it to Byzantium, and then go on to Venice. That doesn't sound evil, either."

Zack shook his head. "My priest always said that the Devil could quote scripture. We'd be crazy to go to Byzantium. Besides, it's Istanbul now."

"She called it Byzantium. And that's where we need to go first. There's something we need to learn there. It's connected to the war in Iraq, and connected to what the Foundation is trying to do."

* * * *

Zack collected his Kalasnikov, then hefted the Cross timber over his shoulder. There was no point in trying to argue with Ivy about this. Besides, it didn't matter. They weren't going to get out of these mountains. The solid stone walls of their cave had probably blocked out whatever signals the CIA was using to track them. If they stayed, though, they'd starve. And once they left it, the CIA Predators and the Kurdish pesh merga would be after them again.

"Let's go."

Ivy nodded and grabbed her own equipment. "Ready."

Neither of them should have this much energy. They hadn't eaten in close to forty-eight hours and had spent most of that time on the run. He should be weak, blistered, and ready to quit. Instead, he'd never felt healthier. Not that he would turn down breakfast if anyone offered one to him.

Ivy trotted out of the cave as if the crosspiece weighed fifty ounces instead of fifty pounds and scanned the area.

"You see something?" He'd been listening for the telltale whine of the Predator or the sudden silence that might indicate a party of men approaching but had detected no signs of them.

"Just looking for our way off the mountains."

"Our way off is attached to the bottom of your legs."

Ivy frowned. "I don't think we'll make it all the way on foot. Besides, we're in a bit of a hurry. We need to find out who's behind the Foundation, what they're trying to do with the Cross, and what people in the Catholic Church know the real secrets."

"You're still suffering from those drugs."

"What drugs? Do you see any remnant of a campfire? You remember seeing that as we approached, right? So, where is it? I'll tell you, we were sent back more than a thousand years into the past. We were safe last night because we weren't here at all. Or rather, we were here, but not now."

"You're been reading too many fantasy books, Ivy. There's got to be a scientific explanation for what's happened." He couldn't explain what had happened to Ivy on the Cross, but that didn't mean he was prepared to believe in magic, time travel, and pre-Christian priestesses.

She shrugged. "There's a lot going on that doesn't fit any science I've ever heard of. That doesn't mean it isn't happening."

He couldn't argue with her. He stopped wanting to when they came across the battered Jeep five minutes later.

"Our way off the mountain," Ivy said. "Right on schedule. I wish I knew her name."

"The Jeep's?"

"Very funny. The old priestess's. I'd thank her now."

"One thing for sure, this jeep doesn't belong to a pre-historic priestess. If we steal it, we'll as good as send a notice to the world that we were here."

"The pesh merga know we're here. On the long-shot this doesn't belong to the guys hunting us, go ahead and leave them some money. A couple thousand sounds like a fair price. This thing is pretty beat up."

Unfortunately, they had no choice. Walking through the mountains would take weeks—weeks they didn't have with Kurdish militias and the CIA on their trail. "There must be a road nearby. That Jeep didn't climb the trails we've been following."

Ivy loaded her Cross section into the Jeep. "Want me to drive first?"

"I think I can manage."

She smiled coyly. "There is one thing. Do you know how to hotwire a car?"

"I grew up in south Dallas."

"Good. Because I have a feeling we have about five minutes before the militiamen who left this car here head back. And I'd like to be gone when they do."

Zack peeled a stack of hundred-dollar bills from Smith's stash and laid them under a rock.

Jeeps hadn't been designed with security in mind and it only took him a few seconds to yank the ignition wires out, slice through the electrical cable with his fighting knife, and spark the engine into a sullen roar.

"Straight ahead," Ivy ordered.

They flashed past a trio of militiamen, their CIA-supplied jungle-camouflage uniforms a poor choice in the rocky gray mountains.

Ivy waved at them and shouted something about getting supplies.

One of them, a kid who couldn't be more than sixteen, waved back, his eyes obviously taking in the curvy blonde.

The others weren't so completely fooled, but by the time they had recognized that it was their Jeep heading toward Turkey, and that these just might be the people they were hunting for, Zack was hundreds of yards past them, accelerating quickly.

A few M16 rounds clanked off the Jeep's mild steel body, but didn't penetrate anything critical.

"Piss-poor anti-Jeep weapon," Ivy grumbled. "I wish I knew why the Army standardized on that piece of junk."

"Write it up to another miracle," Zack said. "Like finding the Jeep. Someone up there was looking out for you and knew you'd need to face weapons with no penetrating power."

"Very funny."

He reached into his jacket and pulled out the papers he'd collected from Smith's briefcase. "Why don't you take a look at these and see if you can figure anything out. We've been so busy since Smith killed you, neither one of us has had a chance to think."

She accepted the papers and nodded. "My money says they'll confirm everything the Priestess told me."

"Why don't you look rather than jump to conclusions."

"It seems to me that you're the one who's not being open to possibilities. If you believe the Cross brought me back to life after Smith slit my throat, why can't you believe in a three thousand-year-old priestess?"

It was a fair question—but one he didn't particularly want to face. "I'm still having a hard time with the Cross thing, but I was raised right. If we're fighting against the Christians and being helped by demons, what does that make us?"

"According to Sister Paraclete, the Bible is a bit ambiguous on other gods. We're not supposed to worship them ahead of God, but that doesn't mean there aren't others, or even that it isn't okay to respect them as long as you don't put them first."

Zack had never met Sister Paraclete, but he was pretty sure she would have been run out of his Parish on a rail.

"Read the documents and see what you can find," he growled. He shifted into four-wheel drive, splashed through a mountain creek, and headed up the side of a mountain.

* * * *

They almost made it.

Zack figured they were within five miles of the Turkish border when Ivy grabbed his arm. "Stop the Jeep and run."

He jammed on the brakes and spun out the Jeep, then reached for the Cross.

"No time for that. Move."

He followed Ivy as she jumped from the still slowly moving vehicle and ducked under a small stone bridge that might have been built over two-thousand years earlier by Alexander the Great's invading armies, or possibly last year by an ambitious shepherd.

"What—"

A missile's shriek put an end to his question. He closed his eyes, but even that didn't block out the white-hot incandescence of the fireball.

He ducked into the shallow stream of water and held his breath as long as he could.

Ivy's blue eyes appeared blank when he came up, and her blond hair had been singed.

"Are you all right?"

"Ohmigod, I can't see. We're trapped on a goddamned mountain and I'm blind."

They might survive her blindness, but panic would kill both of them. She'd been so brave for so long, he'd almost thought she was superwoman. Seeing her like this made her like her more, but it could also get them killed.

"Your blindness is probably temporary. Were you looking at the explosion?"

"Maybe you should leave me." she ignored is question. "Continue on to Istanbul and Venice and see what you can learn."

"What for?" He gestured to the burning Jeep, forgetting she couldn't see. "They destroyed the Cross."

Ivy shook her head. "Do you think it would have survived the millennia if it was that easy to destroy? Why would the Moslems have hidden it rather than destroying it? It was the ultimate sign of their enemy."

He could think of plenty of reasons. After all, Islam teaches that Jesus was a great Prophet, even that he was born of a Virgin. Ivy seemed more and more to be living in wishful thinking, just as she'd believed they could escape the CIA's hunters thanks to a drugged dream.

"I'll get it," she told him. "I can see well enough for that."

She was out of the stream and walking toward the burning Jeep before he could react.

"Get down, Ivy. The Predator is still up there."

"A Predator is the least of our problems. We need to keep moving. The militia will be here soon."

She walked into the fire.

His muscles clenched as he listened for her scream. Of all of the ways to be injured, burning is the most painful. And the Predator's missile was ignited with phosphorous, burning even hotter than the gasoline from the Jeep.

Her pants brushed against a chunk of burning steel and smoldered, but Ivy kept walking, knelt by two lumps that, impossibly, glowed black into the white inferno of fire, and carried them out.

Gasoline burned on the surface of the ancient timbers, but the wood itself seemed unaffected. From the depths of the flames, Ivy looked straight at him--and smiled. She could see again.

He caught his jaw before it hit the ground. She'd walked through flamed unharmed, and her eyesight had been restored.

He hugged her quickly, using the occasion to check her out, make sure she was all right.

Other than some damage to her uniform pants, she seemed fine. Which was more than he could say for himself. Zack was a mess.

He had to accept that the artifact was powerful, capable of protecting itself and healing those who possessed it. No wonder the U.S. military and the mysterious Foundation wanted it.

Ivy's delusional belief that she'd been contacted by an ancient priestess still bothered him, but he could no longer doubt that they had found the one True Cross. Ivy had been blind, but now she saw. She'd walked, like Shadrach and his friends, into an inferno yet not been burned. Only the True Cross could work the kind of miracles he was seeing. Only the True Cross was likely to generate the kind of interest, to the extent of redirecting the war in Iraq, that the CIA and the Foundation was showing.

Zack wasn't prepared to believe that anyone in league with the Devil would be able to carry the Cross, or that the power of the Cross would heal anyone evil. Which meant that Ivy was special. But special or not, he hadn't a clue what to do about it. It was his job as an officer to an enlisted soldier to keep her alive. It was his obligation as a man of faith to help her in her quest.

"I guess we should keep heading for the border," he said. "Maybe we'll be safer there."

"Maybe." Ivy handed over the heavier main section of the Cross, then headed north, toward the border. "I'm afraid the papers from Smith's briefcase didn't survive the fire. They flared up."

"Probably flash paper."

She nodded. "Anyway, I did read some before we got hit, but not enough."

Speaking of getting hit, the CIA had strayed very close to the border in their attack. This part of Kurdistan had far more Turkish presence than it did Kurdish pesh merga. Zack wondered if that meant the CIA or its clients would follow them into Turkey. Would the U.S. risk an international incident with one of their few allies in the area just to stop himself and Ivy? Based on what he'd seen so far, Zack decided they probably would.

He should have been depressed. He'd lost his job, his future, and his life wasn't worth spit. But the touch of the Cross restored him.

One bit of good news was--he could no longer see the Predator. Either its remote control pilots had believed their job was done when they'd launched the missile, or they'd returned it to home base for more ammunition. Either way, he and Ivy had a temporary respite. The CIA and the Foundation had proven they were capable of following them. Without the Predator, though, they should have a harder time pinpointing their location to the Kurdish militiamen. Once he and Ivy got away from the huge pillar of smoke that marked their current location, at any rate.

He used the stream to wash burning gasoline from his Cross section and then hefted it. "Then let's see how far we can get before they find us again."

He broke into a jog, slowed by the awkwardness of the long timber he carried over his shoulder but not by the weight, which seemed to shrink as he grew more fatigued.

The Turkish border would be well guarded. Independence-minded Kurds living within Turkey had been a thorn in the Ankara Government's side for decades and the increasingly self-governing Kurdish portion of Iraq created nothing but worry for the Turks. But he and Ivy were well away from the traveled roads.

Lines drawn on maps didn't mean much in the high mountains. The Turks would use satellites and surveillance aircraft to spot large-scale incursions, but a pair on foot might slip past without being noticed. Unfortunately, so could the small groups of Kurdish militia who'd be chasing them. Of course, the CIA had probably supplied the Turks' satellites and surveillance aircraft in the first place. Zack was certain they would have put in place backdoors to ensure the Turks wouldn't spot anything the CIA wanted to keep secret.

Hours later, hunger pangs reminded him that he hadn't eaten in days. His lungs ached from the thin mountain air was surprised to notice the growing darkness as the sun plunged behind the high hills.

"We've got to stop for the night," Ivy said. "I've got a feeling there's someplace designed as a refuge around here." She paused as if casting about for direction, then turned from the northerly direction they'd been following and headed almost due west.

He followed her, his doubts not supplying any alternative. He knew she'd never been to Turkey before, but she'd led him into the mountains, found the narrow passes that had hid them from the returning Predator, avoided any hint of human habitation.

Stone walls marked the outcropping of a type of civilization.

"There are people here," he whispered. "Even if these are Turkish Kurds, they'll be in contact with the Iraqi Kurds from across the border."

"I don't think this place is occupied by Kurds." Ivy gestured toward a building that blended in with the gray slabs of mountain stone.

A sound of bells, church bells, confirmed her guess.

"Christians?"

Ivy shrugged. "Seems like they're everywhere. The only question is, will they help us?"

It was a good question. Made even better by the distant sound of the Predator as it sought traces of them and their cross.

"I guess we'll have to ask find out," Zack said, resigned to taking the risk.

Ivy sniffed the air. "You think they have something to eat?"

Chapter 5

The Predator wafted out of sight.

"Whatever vibes it's picking up from the Cross get confused by the Monastery," Ivy guessed. "Let's see if they'll let us inside before it comes back."

Zack glared at the vanishing drone, clearly torn between their knowledge that the U.S. was trying to kill them and his patriotic fear of letting what could be a powerful weapon fall into any hands other than those of his own country.

"We aren't going to give the Cross to these people," she reminded him. "We're just asking for sanctuary. Isn't that what churches are supposed to provide?"

He set the Cross section on the ground and shrugged his shoulders. "Some churches, Ivy. I don't know anything about this church. One thing for sure, they aren't Catholics. I don't even think they're supposed to be allowed here."

She didn't care if they were Snake Charming Pentecostals, as long as they weren't part of the Foundation. If she and Zack didn't get help, they weren't going to make it much further.

They waited for a break in the chanting and then Ivy knocked on the wooden door to what she guessed was a sanctuary.

The bearded man who opened the door frowned at her and muttered something in a language that wasn't English, Arabic, or anything else she recognized.

"Do you speak English?" she asked.

"¿Usted habla Español?" Zack added.

"English," the man grated. "Some." He wore what looked like an old poncho over his shoulders except it draped all the way to the ground and was tied at his waist by a rope. From the oversized crucifix around his neck, Ivy realized her guess had been right. They had stumbled upon a group of Christians in the middle of Moslem Turkey.

"We were lost in the mountains," Ivy explained. "When we saw your Church, we hoped you'd let us take shelter here, just for the night."

His blue eyes widened. "This is a monastery," he said. "No women."

He started to shut the door but Zack put in a boot before the monk could slam it closed.

"Look, we're not asking for anyone to violate their vows or anything. We just need a place to sleep. If you've got a shed or a barn, that would do."

The monk's face darkened and he looked like he was going to try to take Zack's foot off with the door, but another monk, this one wearing something similar to the robes old-fashioned priests had worn in Ivy's church years ago, stopped him.

"Let me handle this, Brother Eudor."

Brother Eudor wanted to argue, but a stern look from the priest stopped him. "Yes, Father Stefan."

The priest looked at Zack and Ivy, his glare only slightly more welcoming than Eudor's.

"The Monastery is available only to those seeking the truth through prayer." He paused, shaking his head slowly. "Years ago, before the Greeks were forced from Anatolia and the slaughter of the Armenians, we had more visitors. The visitor buildings are old and crumbling, but they should provide better shelter than the mountains themselves. Let me take you there, then we'll see about getting you some food."

Stefan's crucifix bobbed on his chest as he led them away from the church toward what Ivy had thought was only part of the mountain.

"You must be lost indeed to end up in our mountains," Father Stefan told them in practically accent-free English. "We get a trickle of visitors from Russia and Serbia, but I don't remember ever hearing of an English."

"We're quite lost, and a long way from Istanbul," Ivy admitted. Stefan would probably guess they were Americans and that they'd come across the nearby border from occupied Iraq, but she didn't want to get into a discussion of whether they had deserted. Or why.

"It would be harder to get much further from Constantinople than you are now," Stefan agreed using the traditional Greek name for that ancient city. Not the ancient word Byzantium that the priestess had used, but the name that under which it had been the center of the civilized world for a thousand years after the fall of Rome.

"I will have one of the brothers bring you food and blankets." He looked at the Cross sections that Ivy and Zack had been unsuccessful in carrying inconspicuously. "Are you on some sort of pilgrimage? Although our monastery is very old, it is largely contemplative and we don't have the type of relics that bring many worshipers. Certainly not those who follow the Western rites. You do follow those rites, don't you?"

"Yes, we're Catholic. And we are on a sort of pilgrimage," Zack said, stretching but not quite breaking the truth.

"I see." Stefan clearly didn't see, but Ivy wasn't going to enlighten him.

The priest nodded and turned to go, then stopped. "Oh, there is one thing. As you may have picked up from Brother Eudor, we are quite strict about sexual relations here. Although I'm sure you are being chaste during your pilgrimage, I'll still have to insist that you use separate chambers during your stay. You may eat together, if you wish. Or Zack may eat with the brothers."

"That won't be a problem, Father," Ivy said. Zack hadn't shown any sexual interest in her at all. Maybe he was gay, or had a girlfriend or wife at home. Or maybe he was just a good guy who recognized that they were already in a world of trouble and didn't want to add sexual issues to the list. Then again, maybe a couple of days without a shower, makeup, or a comb for her hair had turned her into something that could churn any male's stomach.

"I'll leave you to your prayers, then," Stefan said. He lit a small oil lamp and then left, his sandal-clad feet slapping against the stone floor.

"He doesn't believe us," Zack whispered.

"Would you?"

"Not really."

A young monk carried in a pair of blankets and a large bowl of some sort of meat stew. He blushed when Ivy tried to thank him, then almost ran for the safety of the main monastery.

"You'll probably be the center of a couple dozen fantasies tonight," Zack told her as he reached for the steaming stew.

"If I am, they'll probably be fantasies about a snake-headed gorgon." She grabbed the stew bowl from him and sniffed it cautiously.

"You think they're going to try to drug us? Come on, Ivy. These are priests. Even if they aren't Catholic, they're still men of God."

"The Foundation people are religious too. Smith was always muttering about Jesus and the trumpets of the end time. What's that prove?"

Zack didn't answer, but didn't look convinced either.

Ivy sniffed the stew again and learned exactly nothing. She'd watched enough detective movies to know that the smell of bitter almonds meant arsenic, but other than that, she wouldn't recognize a poison if one bit her in the butt.

"I'll eat some first," she finally suggested. "If I fall unconscious, you could lug me out of here. I'd never be able to carry you."

"Hey, I've just been going for forty-eight hours without eating. Why not wait even longer? It probably wouldn't kill me."

"Good." She took a bite. "So, how do you figure a bunch of Christians got stuck up here in the mountains.

Zack watched her spoon as it moved from the bowl to her mouth and swallowed. " Turkey was Christian once. Remember, Peter and Paul both preached in Anatolia. Some of the great synods of our faith were gathered here in what is now Turkey but was then the Eastern Roman Empire. I think these monks are carrying on a tradition that was already old when the Seljuks tore this part of the Anatolian peninsula from Byzantine rule almost a thousand years ago."

She took another bite. "You really know about this stuff, don't you?"

She could have sworn he blushed. "I've always been interested in history, especially Church history. My mother wanted me to be a priest."

Hum. That might explain his lack of interest, too.

"So you think they'll help us."

"Unless they realize what we have here and decide the Cross is a call for a new war to throw the Turks out. There have been at least three wars between Greeks and Turks since the end of the nineteenth century."

She couldn't remember Smith killing her and dumping her body on the Cross—but she had felt that surge of healing and power when she'd picked it up in the inferno left by the Predator's missile. That sort of power would be a temptation even to the most reclusive. Maybe these monks would decide that the Cross was their sign for an uprising to restore Christian rule to Constantinople.

* * * *

Zack watched Ivy eat, his mouth watering from the scent of lamb and Greek spices.

Ivy was being paranoid about Priests poisoning them, of course. Given what they'd been through, Zack couldn't blame her. After all, who would have thought the U.S. Government would make war on its own soldiers?

Ivy stopped when she'd eaten exactly half of the stew and then pushed over what was left. "Hasn't killed me yet. It would probably be smart for you to wait longer if you can, but if there's poison in it, it isn't fast acting." She grinned at him. "One thing, though. If I start barfing, you might want to stop."

"Good thinking. And I don't think I can wait any longer." He dipped the black bread the monks had provided into the yogurt-flavored stew and then savored the spicy tang.

He'd been running on empty for days now and his eyes were already flickering when he finished the last bite.

He yawned, then chuckled to himself when Ivy let out an extremely unladylike snore.

"Guess that means this cell is yours," he told her sleeping form.

He draped one of the blankets over her and, taking the other, headed toward his own chamber.

Halfway there, he decided the walk wasn't worth it since there was only a stone bed if he made it. His head nearly conked the ground as he collapsed in a corner in the hallway outside Ivy's cell.

A dim awareness shouted a warning. He wasn't just tired. He was drugged! Ivy had been right.

* * * *

"Wake up! Danger!" The voice echoing through Ivy's head sounded like a beautiful angel as it pulled her from a sexy dream about her, Zack, and a tropical island somewhere.

She tried to open her eyes and failed. Either she was still dreaming or she'd lost all control over her body.

Panic swept over her and she had to bite back an attempt at screaming. She'd been in the Guard long enough to know that panic killed.

A flickering light shown red through her closed eyelids and she hoped she really was dreaming. It didn't seem likely when she heard the whispered male voices.

She couldn't understand the words, of course. She'd never had occasion to study Greek or Armenian or whatever. Still, she could only think of two reasons why the monks would be coming for her in the middle of the night. Either they wanted her body or they wanted the Cross.

Neither was acceptable.

She gave up on opening her eyes figuring that she might have an advantage, however, small, if the monks believed she was asleep. Instead, she commanded her fingers to clench.

For the longest time, it seemed even that simple exercise was beyond her. Then, operating with an impossible lag, her muscles responded.

Progress. But she wasn't going to win any fights that way.

From the scent of garlic in the air, she knew that several men had entered the small chamber where she'd eaten her dinner. Obviously she'd been right about them drugging her food. Equally obvious, Zack hadn't waited long enough before eating. Awake, he wouldn't have let attackers in without a fight.

The Cross had restored her life and restored her vision when she'd been blinded by the Predator's missile. Maybe it would work against poison too.

She ignored the nagging possibility that using the Cross for personal healing might be blasphemous and commanded her hand to stretch across the stone cot she'd slept on and touch it.

One of the monks must have seen her movement. He snatched the blanket wrapped around her and dumped her on the floor.

Okay, that settled it. They were after the Cross rather than her female body.

Sharp pain from being dropped onto a stone floor cut through the drugged fog, but not enough. There were too many of the monks and there was no way she could fight them all. These men might spend most of their lives at prayer, but they also built the stone walls, herded their goats, and climbed up and down hills even bigger than the Pocono Mountains back home in Pennsylvania.

Since they knew she wasn't sleeping, she risked opening her eyes.

Father Stefan was bent over the two sections of Cross, studying it carefully.

He said something to the monks with him and Ivy caught Zack's name among the unfamiliar Greek words. Three of the monks headed out, but that left three more, plus the priest.

Unfortunately, the odds didn't figure to get any better.

Ivy seemed to be moving in slow motion as she rolled her way into one of the monk's legs, not coincidentally also freeing herself of the encumbering blanket.

They hadn't expected that. The monk she hit fell, his head cracking hard against the stone floor. One down. Three to go.

Father Eudor kicked her in the ribs, hard.

She had seen the kick coming and was already rolling away from him, but that only dampened the impact. The drug continued to hamper her reactions. She hadn't been tagged by a kick that slow since she'd been a green belt years before.

"Don't try to fight us." Stefan brandished a heavy walking stick. "It's obvious that you're archeological treasure-hunters, taking advantage of the situation in Iraq to loot an ancient crucifix from one of the dwindling churches there. It is our duty to stop you and protect the precious treasure."

Which is why he'd decided to take matters into his own hands rather than notifying the Turkish police? Ivy didn't think so.

Apparently he didn't think his words were convincing either. Without waiting to see if she would surrender, Father Stefan swung the staff at her.

Willing each muscle into action and thankful for the pain which at least partially cut through her drug-induced lethargy, Ivy rolled away from Stefan's strike—and into the Cross.

The Cross's power swept through her body, washing away the effect of whatever drug the monks had added to the stew, filling her with energy and strength.

She back-somersaulted, jumped over Stefan's low back-swing, rebounded from her landing to bounce a front kick into Eudor's knee, but then stumbled when the first monk she'd disabled reached out a hand to grasp her foot.

"Enough of this nonsense," Stefan said. He raised his staff for a killing blow.

"Exactly." Zack punctuated his statement by chambering a shell into his Kalashnikov. "Now back away from the woman and the Cross."

"We have thirty monks here," Stefan warned him. "What are you going to do, shoot us all?"

Zack grinned and slapped his automatic. "You make it tempting, Father. But no, I suspect your monks would stop attacking after I kill only five or ten of them. I'm not sure I could bring myself to kill the survivors when they were running away. I like to think I would, though, if you hurt one hair on Ivy's head. Who'd like to be first to die?"

Stefan paled. "Graverobbers."

"We're not—"

"He's not interested in legalities," Ivy told Zack. "He wants the Cross for himself."

Stefan glared at her. "As if a mere woman could possibly understand the meaning of our lord's sacrifice. Daughter of Eve, mother of sin."

"Either rush us or shut up," Zack said.

They shut up.

"In that case, I think we've overstayed our welcome. Perhaps you have a car or truck we can use to depart more quickly."

Stefan laughed. "You're mistaking us for a group with money. If we had worthwhile relics, we'd get pilgrims and be able to afford vehicles. As it is, we walk."

Ivy's heart dropped. The CIA was still after them, the CIA-sponsored Kurds would have contacts for hundreds of miles within Turkey. And now any Christians in the area would be hunting for them, too. There was no way they were simply going to walk out of this.

Zack's eyes narrowed. "Somehow, I just don't believe you. Even a self-reliant monastery needs contact with the outside world. And you need the ability to bring in food you can't grow and maybe to sell your surpluses. You have some kind of transportation."

Stefan started to bluster but Ivy could tell he was prevaricating.

"Didn't anyone ever tell you that telling a lie is a sin?" she demanded.

"I have no need for religious instructions from a female."

"Better instruction from a female than from a Kalashnikov, don't you think?" Zack reminded him. He was yawning and a bit unsteady on his feet, but to Ivy, he looked like a miracle.

"Show us what you've got. After surviving your poison, I'm not feeling especially kindhearted. Or patient."

"It wasn't poison. We never intended to harm you," Stefan said.

"Right. That's why you dropped me on the ground and took a couple of swings at me with your stick," Ivy said.

"We have a right to protect ourselves from grave robbers."

"And we have a right to get out of here. Now show us what you've got."

* * * *

"This is kind of fun, isn't it."

"If you're into torture," Zack grumbled. Unlike her, he'd come down from the monk's poison naturally and was suffering a nasty drug-hangover.

"I haven't ridden a bicycle since I was a kid. I think maybe I'll take it up when I get home."

"We've got to get home first. Even then, I don't think they allow bicycles in the stockade where they'll probably put us for desertion."

"I think getting my throat cut counts as an honorable discharge."

Zack considered a comeback, then decided his attention was better spent worrying about avoiding the potholes that seemed to cover as much of the road as the asphalt did. Besides, he didn't want her to think he was flirting with her. Which, bottom line, he was.

Dawn was barely peeking her fingertips over the horizon, but they'd already pedaled for miles and Zack was hurting.

In the end, Ivy had made him pay the monks for the two three-wheeled bicycles they'd taken, as well as for slicing up the tires of the other two bikes that were the monk's sole transportation.

With luck, they would be well out of the area before the monks could contact the authorities—or talk to anyone in the Kurdish underground. Of course, Zack wasn't counting on getting lucky. They certainly hadn't had much luck since they'd gotten away from the insurgents.

At least the three-wheelers made it possible for them to carry the Cross sections. And, although they had to get off and push when they were going uphill, they could rest on the long downhill stretches and pedal along at a good speed on the rare but welcome flat areas.

The monks had reluctantly turned over an old map of Turkey and pointed them in the direction of the nearest highway, and he and Ivy were making their way west, away from the Iraqi border, away from the heart of the Kurdish underground and their CIA sponsors, and generally toward the Mediterranean coast and Istanbul.

Ivy's drugged dream about a Priestess had pointed them to Istanbul. But Zack was tired of letting others jerk him around. The Priestess, the CIA, the Foundation, the monks, and the Kurds had been dictating their direction, forcing them to react. So far they'd been lucky not to get killed but that was about all they'd been doing. They'd managed to stay ahead of the men sent to kill them and Stefan's monks had been unarmed and over-reliant on their drugs. But Zack's officer training made one thing clear—if you're just reacting, you're losing. They needed to take the initiative.

"We need a plan."

"How about planning to keep pedaling," Ivy suggested.

"Not bad as a start." Constant movement and hiding in other religious areas like the priestess cave and the monastery seemed to make it tougher for the CIA to track them. The bicycles made movement easier than it had been on foot. And Turkey was filled with religious sites reflecting its historical role as a crossroads between east and west. Turks had build mosques here for hundreds of years. For a thousand years before that, Greeks, Armenians, and others had built Christian churches. For three thousand or more years before that, Greeks, Hittites, Thracians, Assyrians, and pre-exilic Jews had built their own temples. The entire countryside would create a confusing baffle of religious noise.

If they were lucky, all of that camouflage would give them a little time.

"But just running from the CIA and their Foundation bosses isn't going to do the job," Zack continued. "We need a real plan, some firm objectives."

"The Priestess told me what we need to do. We've got to go to Byzantium and then to Venice."

"And do what? If we bring the Cross into Istanbul, one of two things is going to happen. Most likely, the police will spot us and decide, like the monks, that we're stealing archeological artifacts. Even if they don't recognize this as the True Cross, they'll see that it's old and think we've looted it from an ancient Church. If that doesn't happen, some local religious leader will send a mob after us for defiling Moslem land with our Christian idols."

Ivy set her jaw stubbornly. "Turkey is supposed to be a secular state."

"Yeah, and America is too. But walk into a restaurant and announce that Mohammed, peace be upon him, could take on Jesus with one hand behind his back and chances are that you'd get pounded."

"The Priestess said we could find the secrets and we've got to do it." Ivy was talking to him like he was a stubborn child who refused to see what was perfectly obvious.

He sighed. "I'm not arguing against the objective. We do need to find out the Cross's secrets. We need to learn why the Foundation wants this thing, what they're intending to do with it, and how we can keep it from falling into their hands. But objectives aren't plans. We need tactics and strategy to get us there."

"Sounds brilliant, general. The only problem is, we don't know enough to make plans. We don't know the enemy, don't know the territory, and we don't know the consequences of our actions."

He considered, then nodded. "We should have pumped the Priest for information about the Cross when we had him."

Ivy brightened. "Okay, so that's our first step. We know we're supposed to go to Byzantium. So, when we get there, we find a priest and ask him what's so important about the Cross. Besides its historical significance and the fact that it can heal wounds and bring people back from the dead."

"That isn't enough? Think how easy it would be to justify wars if we could just use the Cross to heal up anyone who got hurt or killed. Those Foundation people could get away with attacking anyone who didn't agree with them--so long as no Americans came home in wooden boxes. Isn't that why most Americans oppose war? The deaths and injuries to our own people?"

Ivy pedaled slowly up a slight rise. "I think there's more than that. From what I got from the Foundation papers I read before the Predator blew them up, I don't think they cared about healing powers. They called it the key. They seemed to mean to do something that would make the whole world take notice."

Unfortunately, those papers were lost so they couldn't figure out what that meant. "So our plan is, we disguise the Cross, and then we talk to a priest about what makes it tick and what a group of nutcases could do with it." It didn't sound like much of a plan to him.

"Not just any nutcases. Nutcases able to give orders to the U.S. military and to the CIA," Ivy reminded him.

"Yeah, those are the ones."

* * * *

They were hungry and tired and the sun was setting by the time they rolled toward Simak, about sixty miles from the mountain monastery

Still deep in the heart of Kurdish Turkey, Zack wasn't surprised to see a couple of Turkish Army jeeps and an Armored Fighting Vehicle in the town.

That was better, Zack supposed, than Kurdish pesh merga who were completely controlled by the CIA. Not much better, though.

"Doesn't look like a tourist destination," Ivy said.

Zack looked down at the town from the low rise they'd spent the past ten minutes pushing their bikes up.

About all you could say for Simak was it was a town on a crossroad.

The town's center consisted largely of one-story stone buildings with a couple of multi-story commercial buildings rising up like skyscrapers. Further from the town's center, old stone structures blended with newer wooden buildings.

Ivy gestured at a deteriorating barn. "What do you say we hide the bikes and Cross here and head into town to see if we can get some food and maybe buy a truck?"

As plans went, it wasn't much. But according to their map, Simak was the biggest town within a hundred miles of the monastery. Presumably the locals would recognize the distinctive three-wheeled bicycles from the monastery and be suspicious of a couple of foreigners who showed up riding them. And while Zack hadn't thought the Cross sections looked like much, it hadn't taken long for Father Stefan to recognize them as something significant and historical—although even he hadn't guessed that they were the original True Cross. Hiding them made sense.

The only problem was, once they stopped moving, the CIA would spot them. They couldn't just hide it in a barn, they needed to hide it someplace with religious camouflage.

He explained that to Ivy.

"Yeah, got it."

She closed her eyes and exhaled, her face casting around as if she were using some sense on the outside of her eyelids. "I'm going to see if

I can hunt up a safe place."

"Oh, great. Magic." He did not believe in magic. Still, that didn't mean Ivy couldn't find an old holy site. After all, this part of Anatolia had been civilized since the Hittites, at least. Had, in fact, been the center of the discovery of iron and the launch of the modern age. The chances that there were old temples, ruined churches, or even abandoned mosques around were very high indeed. Any of those could send signals that apparently baffled whatever the CIA used to track the Cross.

"You don't have to believe in it, just follow it. This way." Ivy gestured to a dirt trail that led off what passed as the main highway—a road that hadn't seen fresh asphalt for a couple of decades at least.

The path was rutted with old wagon tracks and, after a few minutes of struggle, he gave up on pedaling and got off to push his bicycle along it.

* * * *

Ivy closed her eyes again. Her proximity to the Cross, or maybe her bizarre resurrection through the Cross had awakened a sense she hadn't guessed any human could have. She could feel the Cross's power, red and strong. Power pulsed from it like blood being pumped from a huge heart. Other influences, like the monastery they'd visited the previous night or the ancient cave-temple sent out their own emanations. The Monastery had been red. The Temple-cave a peaceful dusky blue. The CIA must have tools that detected the same waves of power although Ivy doubted they used the same color-coding that her brain did to label what she sensed.

Clearly the power from the mosque in Mosul had been enough to hide and disguise the characteristic emanations from the Cross for the centuries it had been buried there. Now, besides the pulsing red glow of the Cross, she felt yellow vibrations of something old and uncomfortable nearby.

Behind her, Zack trudged quietly. His doubts were a pale green haze over him. Despite all he'd seen, despite his Catholic faith, he didn't really believe in their Cross or in the powers she was discovering. He thought of the True Cross as simply another relic to be venerated in church in America—objects with no special power of their own but with some holy significance that somehow connected them to the power of God.

But that was wrong. Whether the Priestesses story of the wood from the Cross having been a part of the tree of life itself was true, or whether it had gained powers through the death and resurrection of Jesus, its powers were real and frightening. She'd proven it held the power to heal. In her heart, she feared its power could be used for things more dangerous than simply healing. And the Cross wasn't alone in holding power. Mosques, the Orthodox monastery where they'd spent the previous night, the temple to the Goddess, and whatever they were approaching all held their own peculiar, but powerful energies.

With her eyes open, she couldn't see the glows. When she tried to navigate using her new ability to sense power, her eyes shut, she tripped all over the ground. So she stopped frequently, reoriented herself on the yellow glow that she hoped could disguise the Cross, and continued on.

After a few minutes, the ugly yellow glow was so close she felt that she should be able to touch it. But, with her eyes open, she could see nothing but the fallow land of a hayfield.

She closed her eyes one more time and oriented herself on the dark yellow surge of power, then opened them and walked straight forward.

Nothing.

That was odd. She closed her eyes and the glow had moved. Or maybe she had changed direction without meaning to.

"There's nothing here," Zack protested.

"That's where you're wrong, Captain. I don't know what it is, but there's definitely something here."

She tried again, this time, keeping her eyes closed. At least she didn't veer. Instead, she bounced off the yellow glow as if she'd hit a glassy-sided wall.

"Something is keeping us out," she confessed.

"Out of what?" He waved his hand across the apparently empty landscape. "There's nothing here but hayfields."

A sheep butted its head against Ivy's bicycle but must have decided it was inedible because it wandered off.

"And sheep," he added.

She noticed that the sheep avoided the flow of yellow power.

It would have been handy if Zack could see what she saw. But if it took killing and resurrection to open his eyes, she didn't want to take the risk. What if the Cross only healed some of the people who died on it? What if she'd used up its last shot?

She waved him to silence. "Let me think."

He nodded, then leaned against his bike. It had been a long day and he had to be at least as tired as she was.

She closed her eyes again, studying the jaundiced glow to see if she could spot any breaks in the smooth dome-like construct.

At first, she saw nothing. But as she looked more closely, she saw a faint discoloration where the Cross was closest to the yellow.

That gave her an idea. Maybe the Foundation document that had referred to the Cross as the key had been literal.

"Pick up the cross," she commanded.

Zack obeyed, humoring her although the green haze of his doubt intensified around him.

"Trust me on this, Zack. Just close your eyes and walk straight forward."

He tried to follow her directions, but veered to his right, sweat glistening on his face.

"Are your eyes really closed? Ten degrees left, Captain. And put the Cross out in front of you."

His muscles shook as if he were struggling with an impossible weight and beads of sweat ran down his face, but he made the turn.

The end of the Cross penetrated the yellow glow—and vanished into an orange hole.

"Open your eyes."

He stared. "That's impossible. It's like something swallowed half the cross."

"I'm pretty sure the Cross is intact." Wouldn't that be a kick in the rear, though? Suppose, after all they'd been through, she managed to stick the Cross into some sort of satanic meatgrinder and ended up with sawdust?

He set his end of the cross down and wiped the sweat from his eyes. "This would be a perfect hiding place."

She nodded. "Unless someone has a douser, they'd never find it."

"There's only one problem," Zack said.

"Yeah?"

"If we hide the Cross in there, how are we ever going to be able to get in to retrieve it?"

Chapter 6

Ivy took Zack's hand in her right hand and brushed her left hand against the Cross.

She closed her eyes and stepped forward.

The malignant yellow glow resisted, but she pushed harder. It yielded slowly, like a mountain of Jello, as the Cross lent its power to her own strength.

"Wow! I can't believe this." A boyish excitement pushed all fatigue from Zack's voice.

She opened her eyes to a completely transformed landscape.

Where moments before there had been nothing but a hayfield and rocky outcrops, now a perfectly preserved structure rose above a stone courtyard.

A gargoyle-like statue leaned out over the wooden doorway, the head that of a bird and the body that of a man. The statue reminded Ivy of an Egyptian exhibit she'd once seen in a museum, but the bird's expression was colder and crueler than anything she remembered.

"It's got to be an ancient temple," Zack breathed. "Do you have any idea how archeologically important this could be? A perfectly preserved temple that's thousands of years old."

"Compared to what?" she asked. "I mean, if you're talking about historical importance, I think the True Cross is a pretty hard act to follow."

He grinned. "Can't argue with that. But this is pretty cool too."

The black stones of the temple were intricately carved with a frieze that started at the bottom and continued all the way to the top of the ten-foot-high structure.

"Maybe not so cool. This stuff is nasty," Zack reported from where he had bent to examine the sculptures more closely.

Ivy didn't know what she was expecting—maybe kamasutra-like sexual instructions. Instead, the temple wall was carved with hundreds of miniature statues of humans being slaughtered—and eaten by animal-headed gods.

"People have believed in some pretty sickening things," she observed.

Although the temple was intact, there was no evidence that anyone had been inside the temple for ages.

A thick layer of dust lay on the temple steps but there were no spiderwebs. Maybe the ugly yellow barrier kept out even insects.

Inside the temple, another sculpted depiction of the god with a human torso and a hawk head stood, his muscular arms holding a basin that drained into his open mouth. A long flint knife lay on his basin. And it was definitely a him. The god's enormous erection made that clear.

Richly colored paintings on the wall depicted naked priests using that knife, or one just like it, to butcher a series of children.

The god was turned on by drinking human blood. Very nasty.

"Lots of old religions centered on human sacrifice," Zack said.

She'd almost forgotten about him and Zack's voice startled her.

"So maybe it's a good thing this place is sealed away."

"People don't worship gods like this any more," Zack reminded her. "Even by the time Homer wrote, almost three thousand years ago, human sacrifice was seen as perverse." He paused for a moment, "in this part of the world anyway. This place must be really ancient. More than three thousand years old, for sure. Maybe lots older. I don't see any signs of metal at all. Neolithic."

"It may be old, but the power is still here," Ivy reminded him.

The hairs on her arm stood abruptly as a chilling idea crossed her mind.

"What do you figure the odds are that we just happened to stumble on the only hidden place like this?"

Zack didn't even pause to consider. "About zero. There have to be thousands of places like this. Although you do have to remember that we're in a particularly ancient part of the world. In other countries, there might be fewer things like this."

"And the Cross is the key to opening them all." She sagged against a wall, then recoiled as the hideous yellow power clawed at her. "If someone could unlock the power that is keeping this place hidden, they could do almost anything."

Zack nodded slowly. "The ultimate weapons of mass destruction. Maybe Colin Powell and those guys weren't lying after all about what was hidden in Iraq. Not completely."

"Maybe."

The air inside the temple seemed suddenly stale to her and Ivy stepped outside, back to the stone courtyard surrounding the temple.

"Okay," she said. "We'll bring in the bicycles and the longer Cross section. We'll leave the cross-piece hanging out a few inches so we can get back in. I know it's taking a chance, but we'll have to hope nobody can spot it. I think this place's power glow will shield it from any CIA sensors. That's what the orange color was all about."

He gave her a funny look and she had to remind herself that Zack couldn't see the power. It was frighteningly real to her.

"What if you're wrong?"

"If I'm wrong, we're dead, Zack. Is that what you want me to say? Because it's true. But if we just wander into town and walk up to the Turkish Army with pieces of the True Cross and a couple of bicycles we stole from a monastery, we'll be just as dead. We don't have a lot of choices here. One way we're taking a chance, the other way there's no chance at all."

"I'm not arguing. I just don't like it."

She didn't feel great about it, either. She hoped there wasn't any leakage of the temple's power. Letting that sick yellow glow out would probably hit this part of Turkey like a plague.

"Let's head into town and see what we can get, then," she said. "I'm ready to take a bath and discard these bloody clothes."

"We should leave the Kalashnikovs here," Zack reminded her. "I don't think the Turkish Army would be any happier than the Dallas Police seeing someone walking around with a machine gun."

She hoped he couldn't see her flush in the twilight. She'd completely forgotten her weapon and had been ready to leave it strapped on her back.

"Right." She stripped off the assault rifle and leaned it against her bicycle, careful not to let it come in contact with the temple itself. "Are we ready now? Because this temple is giving me a headache you wouldn't believe."

* * * *

Simak wasn't much, but its coffee shop had a single room for rent, and it served a sort of falafel sandwich that was the best thing Zack had ever eaten.

He had to claim that he and Ivy were married before the coffee shop proprietor agreed to rent them that room—and didn't miss the doubt and lust in the man's eyes as he stared at Ivy. Considering that she was still blood-soaked and filthy from days of wandering through the mountains, Zack could only conclude that they didn't get many blondes in this part of the world.

At least no one would mistake them for soldiers. With his three day beard and Ivy's uncombed short hair, they looked more like hippies in search of the perfect drug deal than they did like members of the world's greatest fighting force. Even the ratty remains of their uniforms, mixed with the few pieces they'd saved from the insurgent gear they'd stolen, added to the stoned-loser look.

After a quick shopping trip garnered them a bar of scratchy soap and some used clothing that smelled clean, they headed for the room they'd rented.

Zack really wanted a shower, but settled for soaking in the diminutive bathtub in the bathroom down the hall.

He had to replace the filthy water three times before he was clean enough to dry off. Then he dressed himself in the rough but clean wool pants and heavy cotton shirt he'd bought and knocked on the door to their room.

"Finished," he admitted. "The bath is all yours."

"Good. How's our money holding out?"

"I've got a few thousand left. Plus the gold coins."

"Good. If we can buy a truck, we should be able to move more quickly."

"Take your bath and we'll talk about it." Now that they had a safe hiding place, Zack's military instincts were telling him to lay low, resupply and recuperate, and let the hunt die down. Ivy seemed ready to push ahead, but pushing without a plan and without adequate preparation was asking for failure.

His face must have given his thoughts away because he saw Ivy biting her tongue to keep from snapping back at him. She grabbed the bundle of clothing and her towel and headed down the hall.

Zack considered flopping on the lumpy bed, but the leer from the coffee shop owner kept coming back to him. Instead, he forced himself to his feet, followed Ivy down the hall, and parked himself outside the bathroom door.

Ivy could take care of herself, but there was no lock on that door and Zack figured the police wouldn't be sympathetic if he had to explain why Ivy had murdered their host.

A couple of minutes later, large brown eyes and a mop of dark brown hair peeked up from the steep stairway leading from the coffee shop downstairs. "You are needing something, perhaps?"

It wasn't the proprietor but his teenaged son.

"Everything's under control," Zack said.

"Ask him about a truck," Ivy shouted from the other side of the thin bathroom door.

"Right. My uh-wife and I are wondering if anyone in Simak has a truck they're interested in selling. I'll give you twenty dollars if you find one we can afford." Plus whatever commission he could wangle out of the seller.

The young man studied him. "Euros would be better than dollars. And are you sure you only want a truck? I can find you Hashish. Plenty."

Well, Zack had been right about the disguise. Nobody thought they were soldiers. "I'd rather have Euros myself, but what I've got is American dollars. And we're not interested in drugs."

"No alcohol here."

Now that he knew he couldn't get one, he craved a beer more than he could imagine. "What we need is a truck," he repeated. "Not expensive, though."

"Fifty dollars and I'll see if I can find." The kid held out his hand.

"Fifty dollars if you find one that we can afford. I'll pay you then."

The kid's grin let Zack know he'd been suckered. Well, it wasn't the worst thing that had happened.

That grin widened considerably when Ivy stepped out of the bathroom wrapped in nothing but a towel.

Zack was used to seeing Ivy in baggy military pants and the armor-encrusted tunic. Not that he was unaware of Ivy as a female, but that awareness had always been somewhere in the back of his mind rather than a conscious thought. He'd never feel that way again.

The small towel the coffee shop proprietor had supplied covered her strategic areas, but just barely. She was tall for a woman and there was definitely a lot of leg going on there.

Both the kid and Zack puckered their lips to whistle, but Zack managed to stop himself before he actually let out any noise.

No such luck from the kid.

"If you two perverts would get out of my way, I'll put some clothes on," Ivy snapped.

"I was just guarding—"

"Good. Keep on guarding." She walked down the hall, gave the kid a hard stare until he blushed and looked away, then slammed their bedroom door.

"Your wife, she is quite, uh, glamorous," the kid observed. "Is that right? Glamorous? Movie star?"

"Glamorous, yes. Movie star, not yet, kid." But the discoverer of the True Cross was likely to be quite a media favorite when word got around. Who knew, maybe Ivy would make it to Hollywood and become an actor.

"I go look for a truck." But the young Kurd remained in place, as if glued to the floor where he sat, waiting for another vision.

It took Zack a few seconds to figure out the problem. The kid was embarrassed to stand up because his arousal would be sticking out like that bird-god statue's.

He pretended he had to look at a faded print on the wall so the kid could leave without being ashamed. "I appreciate your help," he called to the kid's retreating back.

"I'm very a big help. Maybe you give me one hundred dollars. Fifty U.S. dollars are not so much. Only thirty Euros."

"Fifty dollars." Zack wasn't going to get suckered again.

He waited until the kid nodded and vanished before softly knocking on the door to the room he and Ivy shared. The kid might not think anything of it, but the proprietor would get suspicious if he learned Zack was waiting out in the hall while his supposed wife was getting dressed.

* * * *

Ivy planned on getting about twenty-four hours of sleep. She'd recognized the predatory look in Zack's eyes as well as those of the young Kurdish man who'd offered to help find them a truck, but she figured she could trust Zack to keep his pants zipped. He certainly hadn't caused her any problems before. Then again, before she'd had her bath, she reeked enough that she would scare a skunk.

"Do you think one of us needs to stay awake?"

Zack glanced at the thin door. It didn't have anything as sophisticated as a lock and wasn't strong enough to resist a kick even if they used a chair to prop it closed.

"I don't—"

Whatever he did or didn't became irrelevant because the hard knock on the door cut him off.

"Police. Open."

The proprietor's son, apparently drafted into translation duty, looked visibly nervous as three Turkish soldiers shoved him into their room and followed.

A Sergeant barked something at the young man. He wasn't speaking Kurdish, which made sense. The Turks probably didn't trust local Kurds

71

given their continuous low-level conflict against Kurdish insurgency.

Fortunately, the multi-lingual young man seemed to understand.

"He wants to know if you're English."

"American," Zack answered.

The Kurd translated and got a growled response.

"He wants to know where is your baggage. Your passports. They think you are carrying drugs."

Since the Kurd had offered to find hashish for Zack, that wasn't a bad guess. Ivy remembered an old movie about Turkish drug prisons and was glad Zack had turned down the offer.

"We lost our bags," Zack claimed. Probably smarter than telling the truth.

Zack's translated answer provoked a heated discussion amongst the three soldiers.

"They want you to go with them," the kid finally reported. "They're going to take you to their headquarters in Batman. Many kilometers away. They say maybe you are drug smugglers, maybe someone they have been told to look for. You want me call American Embassy?"

From the young man's nervous expression, he feared the soldiers almost as much as Ivy did.

"No Embassy," she said.

He gave her a strange look, almost as if they were somehow allied. "You come back, I have truck," he said.

Ivy didn't think he was translating. She also didn't think she'd be coming back if these soldiers had anything to say about it.

"Thanks."

He blushed and hung his head, unwilling to meet her eyes. Turkey wasn't supposed to be as conservative as a lot of the Middle East, but here in the eastern part of the country, looking a woman in the eye was still a bit more daring than this young man could quite bring himself to do. Not that he'd minded looking at her legs when she'd come out of the bathroom.

The soldiers hustled them downstairs, away from the lumpy mattress that had felt like paradise during the few moments when she'd actually been able to lie down and enjoy it.

They left the young Kurd behind. Ivy hoped that meant the Army had its own translators in Batman, wherever that was. The alternative was worse.

"Buck up," Zack advised. "We're innocent of any drug charges. They'll have to let us go."

Ivy didn't think so. Her time in Iraq had made her painfully aware of how little it takes to become a suspect, and how difficult it is for the system to let go once it has you in its grip. And the Turkish system definitely had Zack and Ivy in its grip now.

The soldiers bypassed the World War II vintage jeep she and Zack had noticed when they entered Simak and led them to a panel truck with bars in the windows.

"They must have sent for this the minute we walked into town," Zack whispered as the soldiers patted him down, took his commando knife, and then shoved them aboard. "Because it sure wasn't here when we arrived."

The rear hatch closed with a solid clang and the three soldiers headed for the comfort of the cab.

Moments later, the engine fired up and the truck slowly gathered speed as it left the cobbled roads of Simak and hit the rough asphalt pavement of the Turkish highway.

"Okay, Mr. Plan-man, it's time for you to come up with something to get us out of this." Ivy shut her eyes and watched the distant glow of the old temple fade from the horizon.

They'd jumped out of the frying pan and into the fire. She didn't know whether the soldiers would turn them over to the CIA for torture, or handle the torture themselves, but it didn't really matter. Unless she and Zack figured something out in the next couple of hours, their lifespan would become measured in minutes and in pain rather than in years.

Chapter 7

"If we ever needed a key, now would be the time," Zack said. "Although I don't suppose they would have let us bring the Cross along."

"Don't joke about this stuff." Ivy sat on the floor, trying to hold on as the truck made its way through hairpin switchbacks and splashed through small mountain streams that either hadn't ever been bridged or where bridges had long since been washed away.

"Why? Is something worse going to happen to me?"

A tear glistened in one of Ivy's eyes and he instantly felt like a complete heel for his response.

"Sorry."

"It's all right. I'm just scared."

After fighting the Foundation, the Iraqi insurgents, the CIA, the Kurdish militia, some crazed Orthodox monks, and now the Turkish Army, Zack couldn't blame her for being scared.

He took off his belt and looked at the buckle. Unfortunately the belt was of the military variety, with no tongue he could yank off to pick the lock. Still, it was metal. He smashed the buckle against the truck floor until the little roller piece came out. It would make the world's worst lock-pick, but he couldn't just sit and do nothing.

Ivy noticed his feeble efforts just about the time the truck hit an especially large bump and the buckle bit slipped out of his hand and vanished into the dust behind them.

"Damn." Now he was still locked in and his pants would fall down.

"What are you doing?"

"What I'm trying to do is take advantage of skills learned in my misspent youth and pick the lock to this place. What I'm actually doing is banging up the knuckles on one hand and holding my pants up with my other."

She perked up. "You know how to pick locks?"

"If I had the picks I had back in south Dallas, I'd have this door opened in twenty seconds."

"Really? What kind of tools do you need?"

"Ideally? Professional locksmith quality picks would be perfect. In a pinch, a couple of nice hunks of spring steel would do the job. I've proven a one-inch-long round piece of tin won't do the job, though."

"Oh. Turn your back for a minute."

Zack started to ask her if she'd gone crazy, then decided not to bother. Given what was going to happen to them when they reached the Army interrogation center, insanity might be the best way out for both of them.

He did as she asked, and stared out the barred window at the back of the truck.

"Okay, here."

She handed him her bra.

The fabric still held the warmth from her breasts and carried the scent of clean woman.

His brain instantly went into short-circuit mode. "Listen, I like you and everything, but I don't think this is the--"

"The underwire, idiot. It's made out of springy steel."

Smooth work, he assured himself. Not only had he missed the obvious, Ivy probably thought he suffered from delusions.

He turned away again, mostly to hide the flush on his face. He used a sharp edge from the carcass of his smashed belt buckle to slice the two thin wires out of Ivy's bra and handed the ruined bit of fabric back to her.

"What am I supposed to do with this?"

"Put it on. It's better than nothing." For him if not for her. He didn't have time to think about Ivy's breasts unbound.

"You're a strange man, Captain."

"You don't know the half of it."

The underwires were a bit slender and flimsy for the size of the lock he was dealing with, but he had time. Zack managed to get the truck's rear hatch opened within a couple of minutes.

It would have been smart to wait until they slowed for something, but Zack had a sneaking suspicion that even on this old truck, an open door would signal an alarm. At least they weren't on a freeway. The truck's top speed going up through the Turkish mountains couldn't have been more than twenty-five kilometers an hour and they weren't going top speed right then. "Jump," he ordered.

Ivy leapt off the truck and he followed as soon as she was clear.

The ground came up and hit him hard but he managed to protect his head. Still the impact had him seeing stars.

"Come on, we've got to move." Ivy must have landed better than he had. She was dragging him off the road before he recovered.

"Where to?"

"Back to Simak. Back to the Cross."

"The entire Turkish Army is going to be looking for us now."

"Everyone in the world is looking for us. Why should the Turkish Army be different? Besides, would you want to abandon the Cross after all we've been through?"

"It didn't hurt anyone when the Kurds left it in Mosul for seven hundred years."

Ivy shook her head angrily. "That was before the Foundation came looking for it. They aren't going to give up, Zack. It might take them a few months, but our hiding place isn't perfect."

Unfortunately, she was right. "We'd better stay off the road, then. Because I have a feeling we're about to have company. A lot of company."

* * * *

The distance that they'd covered in less than an hour in the Army paddy wagon took close to twenty-four hours to retrace on foot.

The Turkish Army had plenty of experience tracking small bands of Kurdish guerillas in the area and used that experience to hunt for Ivy and Zack. Their low-flying helicopters and the ambushes they set up on fords and bridges crossing the fast-moving mountain streams were bad enough.

The dogs were worse.

Three times, she and Zack waded miles in impossible streams, climbed out on low-hanging trees, and tried to escape the scent-sniffing animals. Each time, the lead they gained was temporary. The Turks knew those tricks. Zack's urban background was no help at all, and Ivy's small-town Pennsylvania upbringing wasn't much better. Nobody had used tracking dogs in her neighborhood since it had been a stop on the Underground Railroad a century-and-a-half earlier.

Every muscle in her body complained, wanted to surrender and get this over. But surrender was no option. If they'd gone peacefully to Batman, maybe they could have persuaded the Turkish authorities that they were no threat. It wasn't likely, but it had been possible. With their breakout, they'd given up that option. If they were captured, the Turkish Army would be so certain they'd found drug smugglers that she and Zack would spend the rest of their lives in some Turkish prison—unless the Turks handed them over to the CIA.

"How hard would it have been for me to grab a GPS before I bailed out of my tank?" Zack complained. "I don't even know where we are any more. For all I know, we passed Simak hours ago."

Her second sight didn't help, either. But Ivy was pretty sure they hadn't gone far enough.

"It doesn't matter. The longer we stay free, the wider the Turks will have to spread their net and the more likely they'll be to miss us."

He grabbed her arm as she stumbled over a rock, then froze.

"What?"

"I smell someone."

Ivy couldn't smell anything other than herself. She'd had that wonderful bath, but one thing they'd forgotten to buy had been deodorant. It was an error she swore she'd never repeat."

"That's me, you idiot. I smell like a horse."

"I don't—"

"Stop, please."

The coffee shop owner's son stepped from behind a tree. "No more talking. I have found you when the others couldn't."

She couldn't see his cocky grin, but she could hear it in his voice. She relaxed, inhaled, prepared to launch herself at the latest threat.

The hard ratchet of a shotgun cartridge being seated stopped her. The sound came from behind her. They were surrounded.

"If you think you're going to get a reward, don't count on it," Zack warned.

"The talking is dangerous. You must shut up. You will please to follow me. We have kilometers to walk."

Ivy looked toward Zack but didn't see any inspiration there. "Guess we have no choice."

"Talking is bad," the kid repeated. "The Turks have sensors. Hear long distances."

Great. With her big mouth, Ivy had probably been leading the Turkish Army around like a dog pulling on a leash.

She forced herself to follow the kid as he climbed higher into the mountains.

Another of their captors sidled up to her after they'd walked a few minutes. "Take," he whispered. He nudged something into her ribs. That it brushed against her boobs might have been an accident. She didn't think so.

She resisted the urge to hit him. Whoever the kid was with, they weren't going to turn her over to the Army. For now, at least, they were the best option she and Zack had. She forced herself to remain calm and took the hard object he'd shoved into her boob.

She wasn't sure what she'd been expecting, but a plastic bottle filled with water and a handful of dried apricots were better than a feast. It had been hours since they'd left the last stream and her throat was about as parched as the mountains.

She drank deeply, then passed the water bottle over to Zack.

He nodded his thanks and she realized that she could see his gesture. Darkness was graying into dawn.

"Hurry," the kid urged.

The fiery aurora of the sun barely peaked over the horizon when the kid dropped out of sight in front of her.

She stopped abruptly, but the guy behind her, the one with the shotgun, shoved her, hard.

Her feet slid out from under her and she scooted down a steep, but fortunately not too deep, hole on her rear.

"Talk now," the young Kurd announced as she landed with something of a splat—and Zack fell on top of her. "This cave is safe."

She inhaled and understood why he knew about such a perfect hiding place. Black bricks of hashish, hundreds of them, lined the stone walls of a cave which was partly natural but that showed the marks of human expansion.

"We seem stuck spending our lives underground," Zack complained.

"The last time we were safe was in that cave in Iraq. I'm not going to kick."

"So, kid, you and your buddies are in the hashish business," Zack observed. "I guess you showing us this means you aren't going to turn us over to the Army. But what are your plans?"

"I am Cejno. A man, not a kid," the kid reported. "My friends and I, we sell such hashish to the Americans in Iraq. Good soldiers like a smoke sometimes. It's," he wrinkled his forehead, clearly looking for the right words, and settled on, "it's the prime shit."

The kid with the shotgun, and Ivy could now see that all five of the men who'd found them were teenagers, toked up a small pipe and proceeded to enjoy some of that prime shit.

"Congratulations on your entrepreneurial zeal," Zack said.

"Thank you." Cejno didn't seem to hear Zack's irony. "But we are looking for the business expansions. More markets for our product."

"And you think we might be able to help you with that?"

Cejno nodded soberly. "Rich tourists, maybe American. Maybe

English or German because the Army is looking for Americans. Such tourists can travel places a poor Kurdish man would be a questionable. No? And here are you, looking for a truck. It is meant to be."

Ivy sank to the stone floor. She'd thought things were already as bad as they could get. Getting drafted into an amateur drug smuggling operation was the one complication she hadn't envisioned.

"What do we get out of it?" Zack demanded.

"You escape the Army. Very important, no? And you are looking for this certain truck. A truck can be found. You need papers? We have a friend provides papers. You need much money? Once we reach Istanbul and hand the hashish over to our friend there, he does pay you for the driving. Of course, you will also have a pleasant native guide to help you with your travels through historical Turkey."

"Can we decide in a few hours?" Ivy asked. "We need sleep."

Cejno grinned. "Sleep. Sure. Feel free to slip into something comfortable. My friends and myself will avert our eyes, surely, if you wish to wear less."

Surely not.

"I'm not going to slip into something comfortable but I do need rest. I can't remember the last time I got more than a couple of hours of sleep."

Cejno said something in Kurdish and the kid with the shotgun rummaged around in a box and came up with a couple of blankets.

"Here, sleep. We cannot move until it is night again, anyway."

Ivy thought about asking for something to eat first, but her head hit the blanket before she came up with the words.

* * * *

Twelve hours of sleep should have helped.

They didn't.

Ivy groaned softly as she tried to stretch the kinks out of her muscles.

Eight young Kurds were playing some sort of game that involved slapping cards on a makeshift table and roaring at each other.

Zack watched the card-players from a seat on a crate of hashish. More importantly, he was eating.

"Food," she groaned.

"Sorry, all gone."

"You know I'm going to have to kill you for that."

He laughed. "You wouldn't have liked it. Dried apricots and some sort of sheep jerky. Good thing I finished it."

"Sounds like heaven. Gimmee, dead man."

He handed her a rope of the meat and a paper tube filled with fruit and Ivy sank back into her blanket and blissed out. Her stomach rumbled in surprise that it was finally getting fed, but she told it to settle down. Who knew when they'd get their next meal?

* * * *

At twilight, Cejno led them out of the cave. They'd crated up a lot of the hashish and everyone had to carry some of it. Zack and Ivy hauled a forty-kilogram box up the steep entrance to the cave, and then they set off with Zack walking in front and Ivy bringing up the caboose.

About a mile from the cave, they stumbled onto a narrow dirt road off the main highway. Cejno proudly led them to a shiny Mercedes Benz conversion van with German tags.

"Such a perfect, isn't she?" Cejno effused. "We'll load up and get started. German tourists seeing their poor Moslem neighbors in Turkey. Very broadminded."

Zack was tempted to leave it at that, but he knew Ivy would never agree to leave her precious Cross. "We've got something to pick up first."

Cejno shook his head. "The Army took everything you'd left in your room. Even your money. No hundred dollar finder fee for Cejno."

Zack shrugged. When the CIA heard about the money, they'd know where he and Ivy had holed up and would send their black helicopters to help out the Turks—whether the Turks wanted CIA help or not.

"We hid something outside of town," Ivy said. "It's important. Real important."

"And we need to work on the disguise a bit," Zack added. "We aren't going to fool anyone into believing we're rich tourists if we're still wearing clothes like this." In fact, they looked convincingly like drug smugglers—exactly the wrong impression if they were going to be driving a van filled with maybe two hundred kilos of processed hashish.

Cejno got into a fast, hand-waving, Kurdish-language conversation with the other drug smugglers.

"They say you want to get your guns, steal the good stuff," he finally reported. "I tell them you are my friends, but they remain suspicion."

Zack would have been suspicious, too, if he'd been asked to risk a hundred thousand dollars worth of hashish and a pretty nice vehicle on a couple of AWOL soldiers who had just broken out of Turkish questioning.

"We can't steal your hashish," Ivy reasoned. "It would be too dangerous for us to try to sell it and we don't have your contacts. Remember, the authorities are looking for us."

Cejno looked relieved and got into another animated conversation that Zack couldn't understand a word of. For all the good it was doing him, he could have skipped his Arabic lessons and spent his spare time playing computer games like most of the rest of his armored company did.

"Sahmar's sister does the haircut. She helps you look German," he finally reported. "How distance to your hiding place?"

He lightened up when they explained it was only a couple of kilometers outside of Simak. "We stop there after we turn you into perfect German tourists. Now get in the truck. Mr. Zack, he will drive. Miss Ivy will sit in the middle. I ride the shotgun."

The other drug smugglers vanished back into the woods or into the back of the van with the hashish. Zack, Cejno, and Ivy got into the front seat.

Cejno took a call on his cellphone and routed them around one Army checkpoint, then pulled into town in front of a small shop labeled with a painted sign showing a pair of scissors.

Sahmar's sister, Mijgul, took one look at them and shook her head. "Who cut your hair? Butchers?"

Zack couldn't disagree. Being a Captain, he'd long since left the buzz cut of the new recruit behind him, but he kept his hair short. Ivy's hair had been spiky after her bath but now was just matted and dirty. When he'd first seen her, he'd thought she looked butch, but either he'd gotten used to the look or it had grown on him because she looked good to him. Hot, in fact.

"They need to look different. German tourists," Cejno said.

"I know that. But you give me nothing to work with." She grabbed at Ivy's blond hair. "Ruined. You let this grow out for some months and then I'll give you a real cut."

"We don't have months," Ivy said.

Mijgul gave the universal sigh of the artist forced to work with inferior materials. "I will do what I can. No promises."

What she could do turned out to be pretty good.

Zack had never tried to analyze it, but Europeans and Americans have a slightly different look. Mijgul dunked Ivy's head in a bowl, shampooed her hair while Ivy blissed out, and then went to work with her scissors. A black dye completed the transformation from a spiky blonde to a spunky brunette with a definite European look.

"Now you." She narrowed her eyes as she stared at him. "You have darker skin, like a Kurd or a Turk, not like a German. This I cannot avoidance."

"Maybe I'm a surf bum," Zack suggested. "Dark tan from all those days catching waves."

"Yeah, it could be so. I make you one of those. But still German, or maybe Swiss. A French or Spanish surfer bum would have the longer hair."

Zack closed his eyes when she dunked his head into a bowl of water, shampooed him so hard he figured he would be lucky to have hair left at all, then smeared him with some sort of chemical.

"My friend brought me these," she said after she'd rinsed out his hair and attacked it with her scissors. "Perhaps they will fit."

She handed over a contact lens box.

He put in the no-prescription tinted lenses, then stared at himself in the mirror.

He looked horrible. He also looked completely unlike Captain Zack Herrera.

She'd bleached the tips of his hair and lightened the rest so it looked brown rather than black. The contacts turned his eyes deep blue. A pair of black linen pants and a natural wool sweater completed the look.

If his friends from South Dallas ever saw him looking like this, he'd never live it down.

"You do look different," Ivy commented.

"Perfect," Cejno crowed. "The European, no?"

Given the microdress Mijgul had found for Ivy, Zack didn't think Cejno had seen him at all.

"No one will recognize either of you. Now we leave, head for Istanbul."

"Now we pick up our, uh, item," Ivy corrected.

"But that will only take a moment."

"I hope you're right."

* * * *

For the first time since she'd left the priestess's cave back in Iraq, Ivy felt a sense of, if not confidence, at least potential.

She'd made major steps toward catching up on her sleep, had eaten enough to stave off starvation, gotten a new look and a classy European wardrobe, and she was going to get to drive a Mercedes to Byzantium where the Priestess had told her to go. She, Zack, Cejno, and the Cross would be traveling in style.

"There is nothing here but hay fields," Cejno argued when Zack turned onto the road they'd ridden down as she'd been searching for that evil yellow glow. "No place for hiding of loot."

"Trust us," Zack grated. "Ivy, I could use some help navigating. Everything looks sort of the same."

She closed her eyes and felt for that arcane energy—and found it exactly where it had been.

"Straight ahead," she told him. "It's just over that rise."

Straight ahead meant leaving the road and Zack bumped the Mercedes over a field, then stopped abruptly. "Holy Jesus."

She inspected the ground with closed eyes. "We're not there yet. Another two hundred meters, I'd guess."

"I sure hope you've brought us to the wrong place, Ivy."

She opened her eyes, and wished she hadn't.

Two days before, they'd hidden the Cross in what had then been a perfectly ordinary hayfield with perfectly ordinary sheep wandering around.

Now, the fields were gray with death. Grass had died in a ring that extended hundreds of feet out from the yellow glow of the temple. A few battered sheep corpses lay on the ground, their guts scattered and bones gnawed. Even with her eyes still open, the shimmering outline of the temple was almost visible.

The monster glaring at their truck had only a distant relation to any sheep. For one thing, its teeth had grown into fangs. For another, its hooves had sprouted long claws.

A sense of wrongness swept over Ivy like fog over a Pennsylvania mountain.

"This is my father's field," Cejno's eyes looked as disturbed as Ivy felt. "What have you done to it?"

"It's one hell of a good question," Zack said.

"We've got to yank the Cross out," Ivy said. "The Cross must have created some sort of leakage where the orange glow is. The Temple's power is doing this."

"I will wait here in the truck," Cejno reported. "You get your baggage if you can. I'm not afraid but I don't like the look of that animal."

Ivy didn't either.

What had once been a sheep snarled at the truck, long canines glistening red with blood.

She held out her hand. "Give me your gun."

"You'll leave me here and steal my truck."

"You know we're not going to steal your truck. I don't want that monster running loose. What do you think it could do to Mijgul if it came across her in the fields?"

Ivy didn't think she'd mistaken the way Cejno had stared at the pretty Kurdish hairdresser. He might lust after American women famous for their supposed sexual appetites, but what the young Kurd really wanted was the girl next door.

He swallowed hard, then pulled a handsome automatic from his pocket.

She inspected it. It was a Beretta 9mm. A nice piece of equipment. She thumbed out the magazine, checked to see that it was fully loaded, then slapped it back into place.

Zack cleared his throat. "Maybe I should—"

"I'm infantry. This is my job."

She slid over Cejno, opened the passenger-side door, and stepped out.

The sheep that had been on the field when she'd been there a couple of days earlier had been slow-moving and lethargic creatures. This animal, the one survivor of the small flock, was a blur of motion— heading straight for her.

She sank into a two-handed firing position and fired twice, hitting both times.

The bullets' impact knocked the monster back on its butt, but it was up again in less than a second, and charged straight at her.

Too bad Cejno hadn't loaded with silver bullets, she thought. She fired again and again, methodically making sure she got a good aim for each shot as the monster absorbed the punishment and kept coming.

It leapt toward her from about five meters away. From her studies of the martial arts, she knew it had made a mistake. It was committed now —unless it surprised her again and somehow grew wings. Of course, if you're a sheep-turned monster who shrugged off bullets, you just might be able to afford to make some mistakes.

She dropped flat on her back as the beast leapt toward her, then fired her final two bullets into its gut as it sailed over her, its front claws and teeth ripping for where her throat would have been if she'd stay standing.

The bullets' momentum lifted the animal higher and flipped it on its back.

It landed hard and for just a moment, Ivy felt a trickle of hope. What animal, even an animal empowered by the evil Temple's occult glow, could survive ten bullets in its brain, heart, and gut?

The answer, it turned out, was this meat-eating sheep.

It gasped for breath, as if the wind had been knocked out of it by the fall, but it struggled to its feet.

The bullets should have ripped huge holes through the animal. Even if it could stand, it should be gushing blood from both entry and exit wounds. Instead, its thick wool seemed to have been transformed into something a lot more effective than the Kevlar the Army used for its armor.

"Oh, shit," Ivy said. She took off toward the Cross.

Chapter 8

"Get in the car." Zack had joined Cejno in shouting at Ivy since her first shot had deflected off the transformed sheep's reinforced skull.

In her battle-frenzy, though, she had clearly forgotten that she had allies, had a place of refuge. She ignored Cejno's advice and started running across the field, away from the doubtful safety of the van.

The transformed sheep shook itself off, snarled, then clawed at the ground, tearing it up like an angry bull.

Waiting was its mistake. If it had acted at once, it might have chased Ivy down before Zack could react. But its pause gave him the moment he needed.

He shifted the heavy van into four-wheel drive and floored it.

A full-grown sheep might weigh a hundred pounds. From the hard impact jolt when he hit it, this abomination had to weigh more than five hundred.

The van shuddered as it collided with what had once been an animal but was now a monster. Zack held onto the steering wheel and kept driving, making sure that both front and back wheels passed over the thing.

Then he reversed and ran over it again.

He avoided its head. Ivy had already proven that its skull was harder than a steel jacketed bullet. Besides, its fangs looked sharp enough and tough enough to rip the van's steel radials to shreds. Its tough fleece could keep bullets from penetrating, but he suspected it didn't have much structural integrity. It wouldn't protect the creature's internal organs from two tons of Mercedes Benz squishing down.

He put the van in drive again and rolled over the former sheep's ribcage a third time.

"I have heard of such a monster only in the oldest legends my great-grandmother used to tell. We thought she tried only to frighten the children." Cejno's voice was shaky. "Killing this thing, you have done something very good."

Zack nodded, but didn't stop until he'd run over the thing a dozen times.

When he decided the monster was sufficiently two dimensional, he drove the conversion van toward where the tip of the Cross extended from—nothing. At least nothing he could see.

"Where is Miss Ivy?" Cejno demanded. "Could another of these monsters have eaten her?"

Zack could only hope that scattered sheep corpses and the blood on the beast's teeth and fleece had been evidence that only one monster had survived the battle for supremacy. If there were more, that was very bad news for their future, and for this part of Turkey.

Ivy answered one of the questions as she popped into visibility, one Kalashnikov strapped around her shoulder and the other in her hands, ready to fire.

She checked out the dents in the van. "Did you kill it?"

He nodded. "But bring along the rifles. With the luck we've been having, we're going to need all the firepower we can get."

She slung the Kalashnikovs behind the front seats, then yanked the Cross pieces out of the Temple.

Cejno gasped as Ivy did what could only appear as a magic trick—pulling long sections of timber from nothing.

It was magic. Increasingly, Zack was forced to concede it wasn't a trick.

Zack shifted the van into park, popped the rear hatch, and helped Ivy load the Cross.

"Someone might have heard the gunshots," she said. Let's get out of here."

Zack didn't wait to be asked a second time.

* * * *

Fortunately, Cejno's partners kept him informed about police and army roadblocks and the van had a GPS loaded with detailed maps of eastern Turkey, because they had to detour frequently. By escaping their paddy wagon, they'd raised the Army's state of readiness by two notches.

It took them a couple of days to make it out of Kurdish highlands and to the Mediterranean coast where, Cejno insisted, they could blend with the rich European tourists.

"Do you speak any German?" Ivy asked Zack as they neared the outskirts of Anamur. It would help.

He shrugged. "I was stationed in Mannheim for a few months. I picked up a little German. My accent is horrible."

"With a lot of luck, we won't have to convince any real Germans. I might be able to order a beer but that's the extent of my German so I'll play dutiful wife who lets her husband does all the talking."

"Wouldn't be any German wife I've met."

And she wasn't good at dutiful. "Maybe the Turks won't know that."

"Let's hope not. We've got to go in. We need supplies. And I'm desperate for a shower and a bed to sleep on."

"What about it, Cejno?" Ivy demanded. "We don't have any money. Do you have enough to put us all up in a hotel tonight?"

The young Kurd blushed. "I may have some American hundred dollar bills."

Ivy suppressed a laugh. So the Army hadn't gotten all of their money after all.

"In that case, maybe you can rent us two rooms. Zack and I could use a bit of privacy."

Cejno stuttered something and turned an even darker red.

"I couldn't hear that, Cej."

"I think such would be the good idea. The two of you have not had much chance for the, uh, making of baby"

"We have been busy," she admitted.

Zack's knuckles had whitened a bit on the steering wheel but there was no way he was getting off the hook. They were committed to playing the husband and wife thing in public. If Zack wanted to back out now, that was his tough luck. She wasn't going to spend however long it took to get across Turkey with Cejno thinking she was available.

Anamur was an attractive coastal town with a couple of beachfront hotels.

Zack picked the more run-down of the hotels on the theory that it would cost less and be less likely to be filled with actual Germans flush with the high value of the Euro.

The shower, room service, and a nap were definitely what the doctor had ordered and Ivy promised herself she could luxuriate for a while, soak up a bit of bliss after all they'd been through.

About four hours after they'd arrived, though, she felt an itch to flee.

"Grab the keys, Zack. We've got to move."

He was on his feet in less than a second. "You sense someone homing in on us?"

She shrugged. The feeling wasn't quite the same as when that

Predator had nearly blown them up. "Can't tell. But something is telling me I need to be somewhere, and that this hotel isn't it."

"Let's get Cejno. He won't be happy if we drive off in his van and leave him behind."

An unhappy Cejno wouldn't turn them over to the police. But he probably would notify his contacts in the Turkish underworld. Ivy wouldn't have bet a nickel that the Turkish drug smugglers weren't infiltrated by the CIA. Not that getting tortured by the Turkish Mafia for stealing a vanload of hashish would be much better than being tortured by the CIA for stealing the True Cross.

Cejno wasn't happy anyway. He had just discovered pay-per-view and had tuned into an Italian movie where slightly overweight and significantly over-endowed women ran around looking for reasons to lose their bras and flash their tits.

It didn't look like much of a movie to Ivy and the soundtrack was horrid, but Cejno was enthralled and she noticed even Zack's eyes quickly got glued to the set.

"I'll buy you some DVDs when we make it to Byzantium," she promised. "Both of you."

"Istanbul," Zack corrected.

Cejno shook his head sadly. "My father is a good Moslem. He would not allow such material into his home. And I think perhaps Mijgul would not like to see this either."

"You think?"

Cejno missed the sarcasm. He considered, then shook his head sadly. "I am quite certain."

"We need to move," she said. "Now."

"The hotel will charges me for this movie yet I have seen only a small piece."

"Hey, we're near the ocean," Zack said. "Lots of German girls go topless. Maybe we'll see something even better than the movie."

That cheered Cejno up and he grabbed the keys he'd taken from Zack—unaware of Zack's talents as a car thief—and tromped down the two flights of stairs to where they'd left the van.

The Cross was undisturbed, and Ivy let out a breath she hadn't realized she was holding.

"West," she said when Zack had started the engine and looked at her for direction.

She'd opened her mind to her senses when she'd gone looking for a hiding place near Simak—and found that nasty temple. She wasn't looking now, though, but the power was still pouring through her, guiding her as they traveled the coast road along the Mediterranean.

"Perhaps such a bikini would look attractive on Miss Ivy," Cejno suggested when the road took them close to the beach and the young Kurd spotted a blond girl wearing a thong that Ivy wouldn't have been caught dead in.

"Perhaps Cejno should keep his dirty mind to himself unless he wants to have his balls extracted," she said.

"Play nice, children."

"And keep your eyes on the road, Zack," she fired back. "I don't want to end up in the ocean because you couldn't help looking at some bimbo."

About six miles outside of Anamur, they rolled up to the broken stone wall surrounding an abandoned city. Flickers of power, mostly red and blue, arose from buildings that looked as if they had been left untouched for hundreds, maybe thousands of years.

"What the heck is this?" she demanded.

"An old city?" Cejno guessed.

"Good thing we brought our native guide. I'd never have been able to guess that."

It had once been a huge place. Crenellated stone walls surrounded the city: in places pristine, in places shattered by time or ancient battle. A long row of arches stretched to the nearby mountains showing that an aqueduct had once brought fresh water into the city. Houses and larger buildings crowded up against the walls and stretched block after block inside.

"Keep driving." Her voice was barely a whisper.

"This is so cool," Zack said as he eased off the brakes and approached the walls. "The entire city is just sitting here, not covered by mud or anything. If we had anything like this in America, there would be a line ten miles long to see it and you'd have to pay fifty bucks to get inside."

Cejno shrugged. "We have plenty of old things in Turkey. We need more new things."

The coastal road veered away from the abandoned city, but Ivy gestured to go straight, onto a gravel road that might, possibly, have been the remains of a road the Romans had built before Peter and Paul had walked these pathways spreading the word of the miracle on the Cross.

The pathway led through what Ivy thought had once been city gates but might have been a breach in the walls that invading armies had used in some ancient sack of the city.

Both inside and outside the walls, olive trees and scraggly bushes grew among the ruins of what had once been houses, an amphitheater, and Roman-style baths.

In a few places, the Crescent moon of the Moslem faith had been hacked into the stone over older signs of fish and the Cross. These, in turn sometimes obscured still more ancient signs of the various pagan faiths that had mingled in this crossroad to the world. Ivy couldn't tell if the most recent marks had been made by Turkish tourists the previous week or by invading Arabic armies in the years after Mohammed's death when it looked like the armies of the Jihad would sweep the remnants of Rome before them and conquer all of Europe as easily as they'd conquered North Africa, Persia, and the northern half of India.

The gravel path Zack drove on ended, with only footpaths extending in three directions before them. "End of the road, Ivy. Is this a tourist outing, or do you have some particular destination in mind?"

"I'm sorry I disturbed your nap, Zack. But I trust my feelings."

Zack had the grace not to argue with that—her feelings had kept both of them alive during the past week.

"Perhaps I should walk to the beach," Cejno offered. "I maybe could learn something there."

What he was likely to learn was whether pretty northern-European tourist girls would go for a drug-smuggling Kurd. Ivy couldn't guess whether they'd be interested but she didn't figure that, like him or not, any German girl was going to turn him over to the police. Unlike Americans, most Europeans had a relaxed attitude toward drugs.

"Go," she said. "Be back in an hour."

"But if I—"

"One hour," she repeated.

"You're a bit rough on the kid," Zack observed as Cejno high-tailed south the quarter mile or so from the abandoned ruins to the nearby beach.

She ignored him. Cejno had saved their life from the Turkish Army, but that didn't mean it was her job to get him laid.

"Help me unload the Cross. We'll have to go on foot from here."

He stared at her for a moment, his weirdly blue eyes giving him an almost evil look. "Right."

The compulsion abandoned her as soon as she touched her section of the Cross, as if its power could not penetrate through the energy field the Cross itself generated. But when she closed her eyes, the blue energy glow was easy to spot.

"This way."

Zack followed her down a narrow alleyway past tumbledown houses, through the remains of a substantial cathedral whose walls resonated red with the Cross, and then finally into a narrow grotto-like structure.

Although its roof had fallen centuries before, the overhanging walls provided some protection from the elements and, aside from a thick layer of dirt on the floor, it was surprisingly clean. Where the remains of the roof had gone, Ivy couldn't guess.

Zack knelt down and brushed at the floor until he revealed a complex Roman-style mosaic. "Hey, check it out. This should be in a museum."

She studied the intricately worked image of a naked woman stepping from the sea. It could have served as the inspiration for the famous Botticelli painting of Venus in a half-shell.

But Ivy didn't think it belonged in a museum. It belonged here, where it was.

"It is pretty amazing that no one has scooped that up to decorate their patio back home in Nebraska or something," she said.

"Is this where we are supposed to be?"

She nodded. "It feels right."

"So, what do we do?"

That was the question, all right, but now that she was here, she had no idea about what came next. She put down her Cross section to see if its energy field was blocking out any psychic suggestions.

The Cross's red glow interacted with the blue of the long-abandoned temple, bathing her in a healing purple aura.

Zack jerked at the heavy thunk of wood against stone. "You sure that's a good idea? Last time we touched the Cross to a Temple, some really evil things happened."

"Does this feel dangerous to you, Zack?"

He shrugged. "I'm blind to whatever messages you get, Ivy. And if I could pick those signals up, I wouldn't trust them. Who says feelings can't lie?"

He was right, of course. They'd already proven that ancient power locked up for hundreds, or even thousands of years could be dangerous. From what had happened near that temple in Simak, whoever had locked up those evil powers had known what they were doing—and their handiwork shouldn't be disturbed. In fact, she and Zack had gotten lucky. Bad as things had seemed with that monster-sheep, only a remote hayfield and some sheep had been sacrificed. What if that evil force had caught a carnivore like a wolf? What if humans had wandered into that power and been transformed? What if the temple had been in the middle of an active city rather than a deserted field?

Still, she needed to do something here.

"Give me your section," she said.

He shrugged, then passed over the long beam of the Cross.

* * * *

She didn't have a clue what she was doing.

Although Ivy had been raised a Catholic, as he had, Zack felt certain her church, and her upbringing, had been vastly different from his own. His grandmothers and his priests preached the warnings of pagan churches, pagan beliefs. Hers probably emphasized the Good Shepherd aspects. And Zack had seen enough lately to know that the warnings reflected real dangers.

Still, dying on the Cross had transformed Ivy. He couldn't doubt that she saw things, knew things, which no human agency could explain. Despite his priests' warnings, he couldn't believe Ivy had succumbed to any sort of satanic spell. She was trying to do what was right.

But that didn't mean she couldn't be making a horrible mistake.

Ivy laid the long section of the Cross on the ground facing north/south, the tip almost at the head of the mosaic goddess, then stepped back, studied what she'd done, and made a microscopic adjustment.

Although the Beretta hadn't done much against the sheep-monster, Zack suddenly wished he'd thought to bring one of the Kalashnikovs with him rather than leaving them in the van where they couldn't help anyone.

"Can I—"

She gestured him to silence and then set the cross-piece at right angles the long piece, in the center rather than at the end so that it made a sort of compass diamond.

Zack had thought he was immune to the sensations Ivy experienced. He couldn't detect the colors Ivy saw, but something hit him like a hard kick in the gut.

The force was internal rather than something physical, but it still bent him over, rocked him back on his heels. "Wow!" He shook his head hard to clear it.

"Do you have any idea what the hell—"

His mouth fell open, his question only half-asked when he got a good look at Ivy.

She looked the same, but also completely different.

She was still the tall, more muscles than curves, woman she'd been since he'd first seen her in the killing zone in Mosul. But now she radiated a sexual appeal that any Hollywood movie star would have given her firstborn child to achieve.

"There was power there that had been locked up too long," she said. "It needed to be set free. Don't worry, I don't think we're going to see any transformed animals here."

"You're beautiful," he breathed.

She squinted at him. "Huh?"

He stepped closer to her. "I don't know how I could have missed it before, but you're, like, a sex goddess."

"Zack, get real."

He got real. He wrapped his arms around her and kissed her.

For a second, he thought he'd misread the situation, that she was going to resist him. It would have broken his heart if she rejected him because she was the ultimate woman. Ivy embodied what he'd searched for until he'd become convinced it was a myth, one of those fantasy dreams that keep men from accepting what they have, leave them miserable no matter what they found. But Ivy was real.

And she was going to reject him.

To his surprise and pure bliss, she didn't.

Her lips, soft and warm, met his.

Her kiss was sweet wine, intoxicating, powerful, filling him with a rush of emotion he didn't want to analyze, only savor.

"I don't understand what's happening," he admitted when he came up for breath. "I've never wanted anyone like I want you right now."

He kissed her again, let his arms roam down her back, enjoying the sensual delight of the hard muscles of her shoulders and the firm roundness of her bottom.

She kissed him back, then slowly pushed him away.

"I don't think this is a good idea, Zack."

Talk about a mistake. It was a terrific idea.

"Why?" He brushed a knuckle against her cheek. Simply touching her sent a wave of power through him, made him feel like he could climb a mountain naked, stand at the top, thump his chest and challenge the gods.

"You feel the power of the temple, not anything that comes from inside yourself. I was wrong about there being no transformation. Remember that sheep that changed into a monster? That's you."

He shook his head. "I'm not a monster, Ivy. I've just had my eyes opened. How could I have missed seeing that you're an angel?"

"I'm not an angel, and you're not yourself. Come on, Zack, wake up."

If this was dreaming, he didn't want to wake. Still, he wasn't going to argue with her. How could he argue with the perfect woman?

"Help me with the Cross, Zack."

"Huh?"

"We've got to get back to the van. I've got a nasty feeling that whatever happened here is sending off alarm bells in Washington, or wherever it is that the Foundation has its headquarters."

Zack wanted Ivy, wanted to have sex with her, make babies with her, sacrifice himself for her. But he also needed to protect her. If she thought there was danger, that was good enough for him. He reached down and grasped his section of the Cross.

The instant he touched the iron-hard wood, he realized what he'd done. "I just made an idiot of myself, didn't I?"

An idiot? He'd almost raped her. It was odd that he hadn't really noticed how attractive she was, but there were a lot of attractive women in the world—and he'd been raised well enough not to go around attacking them just because he thought they were sexy.

"Yeah. But then, so did I." Ivy grasped her own section and looked around the temple. "But we'd better get our butts in gear while we still can."

Despite the weight of timber on her back and the broken ground they had to cross, Ivy broke into a run as soon as they had cleared the temple.

Zack glanced back and almost tripped in a double-take. The dusty mosaic glowed like new. It was probably a lighting effect, but the temple walls glistened with what looked like fresh whitewash. And he'd been sure the roof had fallen in: it now seemed intact.

"Hurry, Zack. We don't have long."

Chapter 9

Ivy shoved her section of the Cross into the back of the van, grabbed the keys from Zack's hand, and opened the driver's door. "I'll drive. See if you can spot the kid."

Zack looked like he wanted to argue but simply nodded.

She shoved the shifter into reverse and gave the big Mercedes gas. She didn't want to believe the CIA would launch missiles against an archeological site as valuable as this, but she'd been underestimating their capacity for pure nastiness ever since she'd come to Iraq.

"He's over there on the beach," Zack reported.

"The kid?"

"Yeah, Cejno."

She leaned on the horn, then shifted into four-wheel drive and pointed the van toward the beach.

"If we get stuck, we're dead," Zack reminded her. "Sand is tricky."

"We're in a hurry."

"We won't go faster if we can't move."

She leaned on the horn again.

Cejno looked up, then laughed and waved.

She rolled down her window. "You've got thirty seconds to get in the van, kid. If you don't make it, we're leaving without you."

He waved again, gave a hand up to an attractive and completely naked middle-aged woman, kissed her on the cheek, then ran to join them.

"I don't know what happened to me in that temple," Zack said as they waited for Cejno to join them. "All of a sudden, I saw the true you for the first time. I mean, you were still Ivy, but everything about you was perfect and I'd never realized—"

"Shut up, Zack. You're not making me feel any better. That was a temple of Aphrodite. She's the love goddess, you know, Venus to the Romans. We used the Cross as a key again and unloosed the power that had been bottled up inside it for centuries. Naturally you'd have a sexual reaction."

She didn't want to think about her own reaction. Because she hadn't suddenly seen Zack as different and perfect the way he claimed he'd seen her. He'd been exactly the same person, but she'd still kissed him—and enjoyed the kiss.

That she'd taken advantage of Zack's magic-induced confusion to kiss him senseless made her feel a bit like a pervert.

Fortunately, Cejno joined them in the front seat and quickly dominated the conversation, providing at least a bit of distraction from her shame.

"It was amazing." Cejno was so excited, he had problems keeping his volume down. "I was on the beach and there was this woman. She was French, I think. Very pretty. Did you see how pretty she was? All of a sudden, she wanted me. We could hardly understand each other because her English is worse than my own, but no talking was to happen. I had no idea how it is with a woman, really."

He looked away from them. "I talk the big story, and no doubt you find me very sophisticated. But in my city it is not so easy to find a girl whose father and brothers will not be guarding over her all the time."

"So you had a good time?" Zack suggested.

Cejno brightened. "Oh, my, yes. A very good time."

"I just hope she doesn't get pregnant." Ivy wasn't getting into this male sex-bonding thing.

"She looked a bit old for that," Zack said.

Like that would matter. "Aphrodite is the goddess of fertility. Have you ever thought about why the Bible is full of stories about women way past childbearing age having babies in the Bible? Power over fertility is important, is a manifestation of deity."

"Aphrodite isn't real," Zack assured her. "And those Bible stories aren't about Aphrodite or any other fertility goddess. They're about the Lord."

"There is no God but God," Cejno, the not-so-good Moslem agreed.

"Maybe." But Ivy wasn't convinced. Something had happened back in the ruins. The more she learned, the more there seemed to be a connection between the Cross and all sorts of ancient and long-buried religions.

For the next few minutes, she concentrated on keeping on the road while putting as much distance as she could between the three of them and the Temple she'd opened.

Zack scanned the horizon in what they both hoped was a bit of pointless paranoia—until he suddenly froze.

"You might want to give it a bit more gas."

"What do you see?"

"Looks like a navy fighter squadron."

Which meant Americans. At least she didn't think the Turks had aircraft carriers.

They were in the Mediterranean theater now, which meant they might be out of range of spy planes and black helicopters based in Iraq, but they were close to home base for the U.S. Navy Sixth Fleet. Like the rest of the U.S. military, it had been denuded to help support the Iraq war, but it was still among the largest force concentrations in the world.

"Maybe sending that temple-opening calling card wasn't the smartest thing we've ever done," Zack suggested.

"If it had anything to do with Monique, it was very smart," Cejno argued. "Very very smart."

"Even if it ends up killing you?"

Cejno shrugged. "Who cares? I can die now: now that I have lived."

Ivy would never understand men. She figured that was a sign of her intelligence.

The Navy fighters circled over the abandoned city, but they didn't bomb anything. Whoever was flying those fighters probably didn't want to have to explain to the Turkish authorities why they'd destroyed a priceless cultural artifact.

That didn't mean they weren't going to investigate, though.

Helicopters move more slowly than jet fighters, but their van was still in the hills overlooking the abandoned city when three of the lumbering beasts crawled over the horizon and headed directly toward the temple.

Ivy veered to the side of the road looking for a turnoff where she could safely close her eyes and use her newly developed senses to find a hiding place.

"Keep moving," Zack said.

"They'll spot us."

He shrugged. "Maybe. But do you really think the Foundation has Cross-finding equipment on every ship in the fleet? I'm betting it will take a little while for them to get it here. And we're better off putting some distance between us and them than just sitting here and waiting for them to show up with all of their forces."

She'd just been thinking about how irrational men could be, but she couldn't argue with Zack's logic. Besides, even if he were wrong, it wasn't as if they could hide forever.

* * * *

They were a hundred kilometers up the coast from Anamur when Ivy screamed and clutched her head.

Zack grabbed the steering wheel as the heavily loaded van veered off the road. Wrenching it from Ivy's unresisting hands, he managed to mostly avoid a scrub tree that grabbed at them, sacrificing a few paint shavings in return for staying alive.

He yanked up the emergency brake and finally breathed again when the van crunched to a stop.

"What was that about?" he demanded.

Ivy opened her mouth, but not to answer. A gob of blood gushed out.

Before they'd discovered the Cross and the Foundation had forced them to run, Zack had been on his fourth tour in Iraq. He knew was first aid. What he didn't know was how to deal with serious internal injuries.

He was going to have to assume that whatever had hit Ivy was something he knew how to deal with.

"Out," he told Cejno.

"Where should I—"

"Get some water from the back. And some clean rags if you can find any."

Cejno nodded, happy to be given a task.

Zack wished someone would tell him what to do, take this responsibility from him.

Ivy's pulse was fast, fluttering. She murmured something, but she appeared unconscious, unresponsive to his words or touch.

He rinsed Ivy's mouth out with water Cejno brought him and made sure her windpipe was clear. He knew how to do a pocket-knife tracheotomy, and he'd try it if he had to, but he wasn't sure his patient would survive the exercise.

Ivy moaned as he shifted her on the van seat, but she didn't say anything coherent or regain consciousness. The tracheotomy was out, but that didn't give him any answers.

"Hospitals would ask many questions," Cejno told him as he passed Zack another bottle of water. "They would demand to see the passports."

If it came down to a choice between that and letting Ivy die, he'd take his chances with the Turkish medical system. He hoped that wasn't a decision he'd have to make. Ivy wouldn't thank him if he got her turned over to the CIA torturers.

One possibility no first aid class had ever mentioned was putting her back on the Cross. It had saved her at least once already. But he knew so little about how it worked, what its risks might be, and whether using it might have sent the signal that the Navy had used to home in on the Temple back in Anamur, that he was reluctant to do that as long as Ivy didn't seem to be getting worse. He'd try it before he resorted to the hospital, though.

"Those men in evil helicopters. Perhaps they do something that hurts Miss Ivy," Cejno said.

It was as good an explanation as any. It would also mean he'd underestimated how long it would take the Foundation to respond to sighting the Cross, or perhaps he'd never shaken them as completely as he'd hoped. Either way, the search was back on, in spades.

Which meant they couldn't stay here like mice frozen by the hypnotic gaze of a cobra.

He gathered Ivy up in his arms and carried her around the van to the passenger side. "Lay down the passenger seat," he told Cejno. "We're going to keep moving."

"Is that safe for Miss Ivy?"

"Better than sitting here."

After making Ivy a pillow out of a couple of blankets, rejecting Cejno's offer to ease her pain by feeding her a bit of hashish, and inspecting the van's underpinnings for broken transmission or oil lines, Zack reversed back to the highway and headed west.

By European standards, Turkey is a good-sized country, one and a half times as large as France. By American standards, it was maybe the size of Texas, but with a population much larger than that of California.

Using decent freeways, they could have crossed it in a long day.

But while Turkey does have superhighways, Zack didn't trust them. It would be too easy for the military to put roadblocks across the major arteries. He guessed that the Navy hadn't positively identified their van as holding the Cross, but they probably had photographed all of the vehicles in the area of the temple. Within hours, the the Turkish authorities and an official suggestion that each of them be inspected.

Since they'd left the heavily Kurdish territories, he couldn't even rely on Cejno's contacts for updates on where the roadblocks might be located.

Fortunately, as he veered away from the coast, he and Cejno were able to spot a series of small roads, some paved, many not. With a bit of help from the GPS, He picked one that seemed to lead in the right direction.

There were probably a million such roads in Turkey. It would take incredibly bad luck for them to stumble across a military checkpoint as long as they stayed off the beaten path.

* * * *

Ivy emptied her Kalashnikov into the monster, but her bullets seemed to pass through it like a sword through the fog.

It reared closer, its breath foul, stinking of rotten flesh and fresh blood.

She considered fighting but her courage failed. Instead, she turned and ran.

Tried to run, anyway.

Her feet couldn't grip the ground. With each step, she slipped back almost as much as she moved forward. Terror swept over her and she could do nothing to control it.

The monster didn't have any problems with his chase, though. He came closer until she felt the heat of its breath against her neck and naked back.

She redoubled her efforts to run, but now her legs wouldn't move at all. Something wrapped around them, constrained them.

The monster's tentacles, she realized. How could she have missed seeing those?

She was going to have to fight after all.

She tried to turn, but even that was beyond her.

"I'm not going that easy, you son of a bitch," she screamed.

"Hey. Are you all right?"

Zack. He was here too? Why wasn't he doing something to help her? Could they have gotten to him, converted him? Was he too one of her enemies?

"Come on and fight me, bastard."

Something struck her shoulder, gripped her, shook her.

She lashed out with a palm thrust and connected with something.

"Jesus."

Good. It might kill her, but at least the monster would know it had been in a fight.

"Wake up, Ivy. You're having a nightmare."

Nightmare? She didn't think so. Her eyes were open. She could see the monster, feel the tentacles around her.

Just to prove it, she opened her eyes—again.

"Oh."

Zack leaned over her. One of his eyes was puffy and red, showing signs of what she suspected would become a monster of a shiner before

101

long.

"Was that me? Sorry I hit you. I must have been dreaming after all." A horrible thought hit her. She'd been driving. "Did I fall asleep at the wheel? Is everyone all right?"

"You didn't fall asleep. Something hit you all of a sudden. You went unconscious and bled like a pig."

That didn't make much sense. If the Foundation could reach out and disable her, she had to believe they would have done more than send her into a nasty nightmare. But she didn't have time to worry about that now. "Okay, so where are we?"

"We're getting near a town called Yaylaalan."

She tried to remember what she'd seen of the map of Turkey they'd studied earlier that day—or the last day she'd been conscious anyway. "Is that on the coast?"

"Maybe thirty kilometers inland," Cejno said. "We thought it wise to get off the coast road. The Army will be looking for us there."

There was that. It seemed that no matter what they did, the CIA and the Foundation always found them. Of course, her trick with Aphrodite's temple hadn't helped.

"So, why are we parked by the side of the road?" If there was one thing they'd learned for certain, it was that the CIA was better at spotting them still than when they were moving.

"You started thrashing so badly you hit me a couple of times," Zack admitted. "I was afraid you were going to make me drive off the road."

"Is that what happened to your eye?"

He rubbed it. "That was a few minutes later when I tried to wake you up. Do you have any idea what happened? Do you think the Cross's cure could be wearing off?"

Since she'd been dead before the Cross had 'cured' her, she had to hope that wasn't it.

"Who knows? Anyway, I'm not going to clobber you again so let's get going."

Zack headed for the drivers side and Ivy shook her head. "Maybe I should drive."

"You almost killed us last time you tried that."

"I really think I should drive."

"Listen, you got sick, bled all over the place, and then had a nightmare you couldn't wake up from. You can drive some tomorrow, after you've had a good night's sleep and something to eat."

Her stomach churned. "I've got a feeling, Zack."

"You also had a feeling you should go into that temple. I'm not sure we can trust your feelings to keep us safe, Ivy."

She felt a painful emptiness when she thought about that temple to Aphrodite. She still thought she'd done something important and powerful, although she wouldn't argue that it had been smart. And she guessed she shouldn't argue with Zack about that, either. It wasn't as if he was going to change his mind.

Still, her body remained tense as Zack rattled the Mercedes along a road that had certainly been paved once, but could hardly be considered paved now.

They were in the mountains again. Although the sea was only a few miles distant, low shrubs and the occasional grazing goat had replaced the beach-going tourists and the denser populations of the Mediterranean coast.

When Zack had insisted on taking the wheel, she'd felt uneasy, but the pressure on the inside of her brain abruptly multiplied into a huge headache. "Stop." She could barely make the words out as a whisper.

"There's a crossroad in Yaylaalan." Zack's voice held pity and annoying condescension. "We can decide on our directions there."

"Damn it Zack, don't humor me. Turn this crate around. Now."

Fortunately, he listened this time, hitting the brakes despite the disbelief written all over his face.

Unfortunately, he'd waited too long.

"I think we have the company," Cejno said.

Ivy's instincts might have warned them away from the Turkish Army roadblock. Once they'd been spotted, though, she would have wanted Zack at the wheel. He'd been armor and it showed.

He leaned his skid into a turn, abruptly reversing direction without fully coming to a stop and headed away from the roadblock even faster than he'd approached it.

"Guess you were right," he growled. "Sorry."

"I would have settled for being wrong and safe."

"If I lose the hashish, the drug makers will kill my parents," Cejno wailed. "This is very quite horrible."

Zack turned onto a dirt road, then shifted into four-wheel drive and wallowed along a dry creekbed until he came to another dirt road.

He followed that until he came to an apricot orchard, then went off-road under the trees.

"Here's where we bail." He switched off the engine and reached into the back for his Kalashnikov. "Let's get the Cross."

"But what about me?" Cejno demanded.

"What do you want? You can come with us if you want to. But if our theory is right, they'll be tracking the Cross, not the van."

"But they will recognize the van. The Army will know what to stop. Even if they don't find you, they will find the hashish. And they'll keep it for themselves."

Zack shrugged. "I owe you, Cejno. You saved our lives and I'd save yours if I could. But right now, I think the safest thing is for you to lay low for a couple of days. Find an abandoned barn or garage to hide in. Call your friends back home to come and give you a change of license plates and maybe a new paint job for the van."

Cejno nodded. "This is a good plan. Then I can meet up with you when you are safe."

"We owe you too much already, Cejno."

"We are friends, no? Of course I will help you get to Istanbul."

He nudged the GPS system, scrolling across the map of Turkey. "We meet in Isparta. In one week. I shall find you outside the central mosque. There is always a mosque."

Ivy nodded. "A mosque would give us some cover. If we make it, we'll be there. Good luck, Cejno."

"You as well have good luck, Miss Ivy. I hope Allah will speed your journey." Cejno shoved a packet at Zack, waited until Zack and Ivy had taken their sections, and then grasped the keys from Zack.

* * * *

Zack hefted his section of Cross, watched Cejno head off toward the north, then turned deliberately west. "It's just us again."

Ivy nodded.

"Did I tell you I was sorry I didn't trust you?"

She shrugged. "Who would?"

He didn't have an answer for that, so he walked along with her, first on the road and then, when a sheep-trail headed off the road, he followed that.

It had been a horribly long day, but Zack was still surprised when the glare of the setting sun partially blinded him.

"We need to find someplace safe to rest," he said.

"I haven't had much luck with that."

He shuddered when he remembered that monster sheep. "We're still alive."

She had to think about that before finally nodding. "Guess that's one way to look at it. I'll see if I can sense anything."

She stopped walking and closed her eyes.

Zack studied her. The strain of their disastrous adventures was telling on her. She hadn't had much excess weight to start out with and now she looked gaunt rather than merely slender. Still, her face demonstrated a strength more subtle than the purely physical.

"Pretty much straight ahead," she said, finally opening her eyes. "We can follow this path. It looks like it will lead us somewhere."

Night came quickly in the hills of southern Anatolia. Stars were beginning to creep out when he finally saw the lights.

"There are people here," he whispered. "They'll turn us over to the police."

Ivy shrugged. "Turkey isn't like Texas, Zack. There are people everywhere."

That wasn't especially reassuring. Still, the last time he'd overridden Ivy's judgment, he'd driven into an Army checkpoint. He gritted his teeth and forced himself to walk forward.

The village wasn't much. Maybe twenty houses, a couple of small shops, and a tiny mosque.

Ivy headed straight for the mosque.

He grabbed her arm. "We can't go in there."

"This isn't Mecca," she reminded him. "And it's not Iraq where clerics use their mosques to arm their militias. A Mosque is like a church. Most of them welcome everyone."

Still, he was relieved when she leaned her Cross piece against the outside of the mosque and sat down on it. "At least it doesn't look like rain."

He edged his own section next to hers. "Why don't we take a look at whatever Cejno thought we needed to have?"

What Cejno thought they needed turned out to look pretty useful. There was the blanket he'd wrapped Ivy in, a thin wad of hundred dollar bills, and a water bottle. Nothing to eat, unfortunately, and Zack was hungry, but the water helped.

He shared the bottle with Ivy, then wrapped the blanket around both of them. Away from the coast, and in the altitude of the hills, it got cool in the night, even in August.

Ivy resisted a bit when he moved closer to her so they could share body heat.

Her fear and discomfort with his proximity was his own fault, he knew. He'd been an idiot to let himself get carried away in the temple.

"You know they're going to catch us sooner or later, don't you?" Ivy finally relaxed enough to let him near to her.

"We've stayed ahead of them so far."

"But we haven't done anything. We're running around without a plan and they are triangulating and narrowing down the kill zone."

"We're heading to Istanbul and then to Venice?"

"Those seem like impossible dreams to me."

Zack had never been to Venice, but he'd seen pictures and movies. From them, he had the idea of a sort of fairy tale city, all canals, ancient palazzos, and singing gondoliers.

"We'll make it."

Ivy laughed. "I know I'm just an NCO, Zack, but you don't have to give me the officer pep-talk."

He took another sip of water, then leaned back against the mosque's walls and closed his eyes. He didn't have much hope either, but they were still alive and still free. Considering the alternatives, he couldn't complain.

Chapter 10

The monster swept a clawed hand at her face and Ivy held up her sword in response. But it wasn't her sword: it was the Cross.

The monster's foot struck the cross and vanished in the glare of an explosion.

She jerked awake.

"It was just a truck backfiring," Zack said.

"Huh-uh. My dreams are trying to tell me something. We've been so busy running that we haven't really thought about what's going on."

"We know what's going on. The Foundation wants the Cross and is willing to kill to get it."

"But we've learned more than that. We know it's the key." She stood, yanked the blanket away from Zack, and folded it into a pad that she could rest the Cross section on.

"For what that's worth." He looked around. "Let's get going."

With the sun's light peaking over the horizon, a call to prayer sounded from loudspeakers within the mosque.

"Don't move." Zack whispered directly in her ear, his lips so close they tickled against her lobe.

As if she would. He'd spent more time in Iraq than she, but it didn't take long to realize that many Moslems were extremely devout. Strolling around during morning prayers would make she and Zack about as popular as a Moslem walking into a Catholic church and washing his hands in the holy water.

The town came to life when the prayer ended. Farmers kissed their wives goodbye and headed for the fields, a shopkeeper pulled open the corrugated metal opening to his shop, and a couple of women headed there, one of them with a clutch of eggs in a basket, the other with an empty basket.

"Let's see if we can buy something to eat," Zack suggested.

A voice spoke inches behind them and Ivy almost jumped out of her skin. She grabbed her Kalashnikov and spun around.

The mosque's imam smiled, holding his hands in a peaceful gesture.

Ivy felt like an idiot. She slung the rifle behind her back and gave a martial arts bow. It was the least she could do for taking advantage of his mosque's hospitality the previous night and then threatening a holy man with a weapon.

He said something else but Ivy could see his words meant as much to Zack as they did to her—which is to say, nothing.

"Do you speak English?" she asked.

He shook his head. He probably understood enough to recognize the word and that was about it.

Zack tried German with no better success before finally launching into Arabic.

The imam smiled. "Yes. Of course I speak Arabic. Would you and your wife break your fast with me?"

Zack nodded. "We would be honored."

That brief conversation had stretched Ivy's Arabic, but Zack seemed comfortable. And the imam didn't speak as quickly as the Iraqis had. Which made sense, she realized. Arabic wasn't his native language either. But as a Moslem, and a religious leader, he would have had to learn it to read the Koran, just as Catholic Priests learn Latin and Jews learn Hebrew. It was easier for her to understand another foreign speaker of Arabic than it was to understand native speakers.

"Our Army is looking for you," the imam said after they'd all finished their first cup of coffee. It was, Ivy decided, probably the best coffee she'd ever tasted, thick and dark and so bitter it gave her a delicious shiver.

"They may be," Zack admitted. "But we have done nothing wrong. Nothing but flee for our lives when they were threatened."

"The Army says you were smuggling drugs. And I see you are armed."

Ivy closed her eyes and studied the imam's aura. He radiated a pink glow of contentment, faith, and goodness.

"Tell him everything," she said in Arabic. "I trust him."

The imam smiled at her. "Trust is often better than mistrust."

That hadn't been Ivy's experience, but she didn't disagree out loud.

Zack gave her a doubting look, but for once he didn't argue. Instead, he quickly summarized their discovery and their flight.

She hadn't expected the imam to believe them. To her surprise, he took in everything Zack told him and nodded.

"May I see the Cross?"

With their agreement, he bent over the two pieces of timber, spoke a prayer so quickly that Ivy could catch only a few words, and then rose. "This is a holy object indeed."

"For our religion," Zack said. "Not for yours. Didn't Saladin drag it through the streets of Jerusalem like garbage behind his horses?"

The imam shrugged. "Is that what your legends claim? I wasn't there, but perhaps it is true. In warfare, people lose sight of what is important and seek to cause pain. Even men who have become heroes may do so. But Jesus, peace be upon him, is not the sole property of the Christian faith. He is a prophet, acknowledged by all Moslems. While Moslems do not fetish relics the way some Christians do, this is still a holy object." He paused and wiped sweat from his forehead. "I do worry, though, about this pagan temples. Tell me more."

Zack struggled with the words, and Ivy wasn't much help. How do you say 'mutated sheep monster' in Arabic? He made Ivy give her own descriptions of how she had seen the temples as a sort of color—yellow for one and blue for the other.

"And my Mosque," the imam gestured at the walls to his small building. "Does it have a color as well?"

"You know, that's the strange thing. It's red. Which is the same color as the Christian monastery and the remains of that cathedral we found in the abandoned city."

"Not so strange. Allah is our word for the one God. The God you call Jehovah and that the Jews call YHWH. Perhaps red is the color of Allah."

* * * *

The imam insisted that they move into his clean home, bedded them down for twenty-four hours, then took Ivy for a long tramp through the hills around his village.

Nine thousand years of civilization had dwelt on these hills, he explained. Hittites, Assyrians, Phoenicians, Thracians, Trojans, Armenians, Kurds, Greeks, Persians, Macedonians, Romans, Byzantines, Seljuks, and Ottoman Turks had all lived, built, worshipped, and died here.

The imam seemed as interested in Ivy's views of Christianity as he did in her ability to see the power traces left behind the worship and sacrifice of thousands of years of civilization. Her Arabic improved dramatically under his patience.

"This Foundation is intent on finding the Cross," he observed.

"They've chased us for hundreds of miles."

"Mesopotamia is full of ancient holies. If the Cross were just one more, I wonder if they would be so intent."

Ivy shrugged. A couple of days of good meals and plenty of sleep had let her regain her strength. "They seem able to order the U.S. Army and CIA around. With a few hundred thousand fighting men and women, plus a thousand or so aircraft, they can go after more than one relic at a time."

"True." The imam picked up a small rock—one carved, Ivy noted, into a rough shape of a pregnant woman. He examined it briefly, then put it down carefully but quickly, as if afraid it would burn his fingers. "But they call the Cross 'the key.'"

"When I read that in their papers, I thought at first it meant the most important. But after what happened at the temples, I think I know better. The Cross can unlock certain powers. Of course nothing says there can't be other keys."

"Like the sword of the Prophet, peace be upon him," the imam laughed. "True. But think of this. What is the Cross?"

"A piece of wood. I have heard that the wood came from the tree of life."

The imam smiled at her. "Exactly. I don't know if that is literally true. Perhaps your American scientists could do DNA analysis and find if the wood came from something unique in our world of suffering. But after the Prophet Jesus, peace be upon him, was sacrificed on the Cross, it became special, even if it wasn't before. It became a link between life and death, between the world of man and the world of Allah."

Ivy wasn't going to argue religion with him. But just knowing that the Cross was important didn't seem too helpful.

"I am troubled by the Priestess," the imam said when he realized Ivy wasn't going to say anything more. "And by the story of the Temple of Aphrodite."

There was no reason for Ivy to get defensive. She was a Catholic, not a follower of Ishtar or Aphrodite. Still, the hairs on the back of her neck stood in reaction to the imam's cautious criticism.

"Both the cave and the temple were places of refuge. Unlike that place in the mountains, I didn't feel any danger there."

He nodded. "The Prophet, peace be upon him, warns against the worship of false gods. Think what happened to your young friend and that French harlot. And I suspect that there is more to your story that you did not tell. Perhaps something happened to you and your young husband as well?"

Ivy blushed. She did her best not to think about Zack's strange reaction to the unlocking of Aphrodite's temple, the way he'd kissed her.

"I fear that you have been unleashing demons into our world," the imam concluded.

If she hadn't seen that sheep-monster, Ivy would have argued with him. As it was, she couldn't.

"There are those of the Christian faith," the imam went on as if she'd answered him, "who claim that Islam hides its own goddess worship. That the crescent moon is a symbol of the goddess. That the Kabala stone itself is the ancient throne of Ishtar on earth. Such beliefs are wrong, of course, but I have heard people proclaim them."

"Zack knows a lot more about this religious stuff than I do," Ivy said. "Maybe you could have this conversation with him."

"But Zack is not a Saint," the imam corrected her.

Ivy couldn't help laughing. "I know my Arabic is rough, but I didn't know it was that bad. Because I'm no Saint."

"You were dead and you live again. You see the divine with your eyes closed. You have spoken to a priestess dead for thousands of years." The imam shook his head slowly. "Ivy, of course you are a Saint. That doesn't mean you are perfect, of course. Only Allah is perfect. But you are special, touched by Allah in a way that I have trouble understanding."

"You're not the only one."

* * * *

Ninety years of avoiding militarily enforced secularism in Turkey had given Moslem religious leaders ample training in moving undetected through the country.

After four days of rest, recuperation, and interminable discussions with the imam about faith, God's role in religions that faded long before the Prophet walked the sands of Arabia, and Ivy's role and duties in being a Saint, the imam equipped them with false papers, transformed them into a mythical Romanian couple visiting Turkey on their honeymoon, and handed them off to the imam in the next village to the west.

"I don't know any Romanian," Ivy had reminded the religious leader when he handed her the passport.

His white teeth glistened through his long beard. "No one in Turkey knows Romanian: that's the beauty of it. If anyone questions you, use your Church Latin. It's close enough to fool anyone here. Just don't go to Romania. Neither your papers, nor your Latin, are that good."

A series of midnight transfers, rides bundled in secret compartments under cars, trucks, and farm wagons, and the occasional guided hike through unmapped mountain passes avoiding Army checkpoints, brought them to Isparta, a good-sized city that seemed anchored on the production of roses.

The Isparta Mosque was ancient and far grander than that in the first village where they'd huddled while waiting to be discovered by the military, but the imam of this Mosque seemed in awe of the time they had spent with their imam.

"He is famous as a holy man," he explained in pretty good English. "For him to name you a Saint is exceptional, almost impossible. Traditional Moslems do not venerate Saints of any kind."

"That's what I told him," Ivy said. "I'm no angel."

The imam considered that, then smiled. "Modesty is a positive trait, but it is not necessary for a Saint to be unduly modest. Still, I have taken the liberty of creating for you a list of Mosques along your way. Mosques where our brother's words will be heard and respected." He handed her a fairly thick stack of paper, still warm from his laser printer.

"Are any of these in Istanbul?"

"Oh, yes. Steer clear of the larger Mosques, of course. They are too closely tied to the government. Those who hold to the right path are often pushed into smaller venues. Visit the Blue Mosque if you want to be inspired by architecture. Visit a more humble Mosque if you wish enlightenment."

Ivy figured she could use some enlightenment. "Thank you."

He bowed. "Thank you, Ms Ivy. And thank you for bringing your artifact to our city. Islam does not worship objects the way your Catholic Church does, but I cannot deny its holiness."

"Has anyone heard word of our friend, Cejno?" Zack asked.

The imam nodded and gestured to his cell. "He is only moments away, stuck in a bit of a traffic jam that will also delay the police from following too closely. By the time you step outside, he will be in sight." He hesitated for a moment, then blurted out his question. "It is presumptuous, but perhaps I could be given the honor of helping you carry this historical artifact of the Prophet Jesus, peace be upon him."

Zack looked at Ivy for guidance, but she could think of no reason not to let the imam help. He had thousands of followers within shouting distance. If he intended to steal the Cross, he could have done so. For that matter, since the Cross had spent nearly a thousand years under a Mosque, the Moslems might have as good a legal claim to it as anyone.

"We can use all the help we can get."

"Thank you." He reverently lifted one end of Ivy's Cross section as she picked up the other. Another imam from his Mosque nodded to

Zack and, with his permission, helped him lift the large balk of timber.

"Your young Kurdish drug smuggler should be coming now."

Sure enough, Cejno rounded the corner to the Mosque just as the imams helped Zack and Ivy carry out their Cross sections.

The Kurd gaped and practically ran into a flower cart when he saw the religious leaders helping, but he managed to brake to a stop. As Zack had suggested, the van had been transformed into a mottled brown and its license plates changed, but the irrepressible Kurd's smile was unaltered.

"I had thought to never see you again, my friends," he shouted. "What a happy day. Let us make on our journey."

Moments later, they'd secured the Cross, and, with just a bit of discussion, Cejno turned the wheel over to Zack.

"If you feel anything, any danger at all, please let me know," Zack told Ivy. "I promise I'll listen this time."

It turned out, though, that they only had to listen to the sound of Cejno's cell. Each morning, a different imam would call with the day's route, possible roadblocks, and friendly places to stop for food or rest.

Their trip really did seem to become a holiday as they made their way through the beautiful lake region around Isparta, to Denizli, Salihli, and Izmir, and then up the Adriatic coast.

* * * *

Zack had been in plenty of historical cities. In two tours in Iraq, he'd been to Baghdad, Mosul, and the ruins of Babylon, Nineveh, and Ur. In Europe, he'd seen London, Berlin, Paris, and the remains of the trenches that had once crossed France and Belgium. But Istanbul was different. The past seemed closer here, as if they might turn one corner and see Janissaries drilling: another corner and run into a mob of blues and greens on their way to the hippodrome for racing and riots.

The domes and minarets of the famous Blue Mosque shadowed what had been, for a thousand years, the largest and most powerful church in Christianity—the Hagia Sophia—the Church of Holy Wisdom. Only during the Renaissance had the Pope finally built today's St. Peter's Cathedral in Rome and exceeded the massive structure originally built by the Roman Emperor Justinian. The Topkapi Palace, home to the Ottoman rulers when they'd threatened Europe, conquered Africa, and dominated Asia, still stood atop the ruins of the earlier Roman Imperial palaces and government quarters.

"Wow," Zack said.

"I have to make contact with my, 'uh, friends," Cejno said. "Perhaps you would not like to be a part of this drug business."

Zack didn't want to be a part of it. He thought the U.S. laws against pot wasted a lot of resources that could be better spent on controlling terrorism and helping the poor, but he'd had enough drug-abusing soldiers under his command to know that hashish can impair judgment as badly as alcohol can.

Still, Cejno had risked his life for them. The least they could do was pay him back now.

"Do you think there's going to be trouble?"

Cejno laughed. "There are plenty of Kurds here in the old capital. They would not allow me to go unavenged if something were to happen to me."

"In that case, why don't you drop us off at one of the Mosques on our list," Ivy said. "I have this tingle that tells me time is running short."

"A tingle that like that?" Zack gestured to the harbor where, amidst a long line of cruise ships, a U.S. Navy aircraft carrier was dropping its anchor.

"I hadn't gotten that specific," Ivy said. "But now that you mention it..."

They exchanged phone numbers and e-mail addresses with Cejno, promised to stay in touch in the future and made Cejno promise to come and visit them in America if he could, but leaving his drugs back home. Then they unloaded their Cross sections and packs stuffed with food and Romanian gear, and watched him drive away.

"Think we'll see him again?"

Ivy considered. "I wouldn't be surprised. Wait a few years and we might see him on the cover of Newsweek."

"Drug smuggler of the year?"

"I was thinking, President of Turkey. Didn't you notice the way he wanted to talk to everyone, learn their names? He's a born politician."

"Could be a good thing. Having a Kurdish President might help reduce ethnic tensions in Turkey."

The local imam must have been warned that they were coming. He rushed out of the Mosque and almost dragged them into a nearby apartment that, he said, had been set aside for their use while they were in Istanbul.

"My brothers tell me that you are looking for secret wisdom while here," he said in English. "I must warn you that there is no true or certain knowledge outside of the Koran: outside of the words of the blessed Prophet Mohammed, peace be upon him."

There didn't seem to be any way to answer that, so Zack smiled and nodded politely. He also managed to stomp on Ivy's foot when it looked like she was going to start an argument.

"Perhaps we merely follow a round-about path to that certain knowledge," he said when it looked like Ivy was going to explode anyway.

The imam nodded as if he'd said something intelligent. "Let me show you the apartment."

The apartment was built into a building that had been old when the Turks had conquered the city. Deep inside the city walls, it was a three story stone building, retrofitted with plumbing and covered with a slate roof that Zack didn't guess had been updated since the last Sultan had been sent into exile.

"Perhaps you are fatigued after your travels," the imam said. "I shall return after some two hours."

He bowed, then left.

"What do you think? Are you tired?"

Ivy looked exhausted. She closed her eyes and, without warning, seemed to sag.

Zack barely caught her in time to keep her from hitting the floor.

* * * *

The colors of power nearly blinded Ivy.

Their blasts physically buffeted her. Even with her eyes open, she could sense the deep resonance of the Blue Mosque and the Hagia Sophia, both repositories of centuries or millennia of prayer and worship. Underlying them, deep and tricky, trickles of older power, some disguised, some filled with ancient evil, set her hair on edge.

She swayed, suddenly dizzy, then felt the warmth of Zack's arms as he caught her and gently set her on a chair.

"Are you all right?"

"Istanbul is tearing me apart."

"It's an old and holy place. This was the largest city in the world for hundreds of years. And under both Emperors and Sultans, it combined political with religious leadership. Both the Byzantines and the Ottomans were more than secular rulers. They tried to create real holy empires—god's kingdom on earth. Caliph as well as Sultan."

She must have looked a bit blank, because he explained that the Caliphs had been the early leaders of Islam after Mohammed, combining both secular and religious authority.

Ivy nodded and tried to relax but she wasn't fooling anyone. "So all we have to do is explore one of the biggest and oldest cities in the world for, uh, something. Even better, we don't know whether that something is a person or an object, or whether we'll recognize it when we find it.

Good thing we don't have any real challenges, isn't it?"

Zack grinned ruefully. "Considering the odds against us making it this far, I'd say we already know how to do the impossible." He paused, thinking. "You know I've been correcting you every time you say Byzantium, but I wonder if your Priestess was really confused. Maybe she was trying to send a very specific message. Something that could help us with just that problem."

"Like?"

"Well, Istanbul is the modern city. Constantinople is the city as it existed in medieval times, from the fourth century until maybe the nineteenth. Byzantium was the name of the ancient Greek colony that Constantinople was built on."

She yawned despite herself. "How does that help? It's all the same city."

He shook his head seriously. "Think about it like tree rings. Istanbul is millions and millions of people of today. Its suburbs stretch out into Asia and Thrace, way beyond the old city walls. In Byzantine times, when it was Constantinople, there might have been a million people living here, but they had to stay inside the walls. They got invaded too often to want to build too much outside. But the early emperors built new walls to enclose a lot of what hadn't been part of Byzantium proper. The old Greek city would be deep inside the old city walls. That's a much smaller territory to cover."

"Makes sense. But it doesn't tell me what we're looking for."

Zack shook his head. "You're the saint, Ivy. I'll leave the holy stuff to you."

"But you're the history buff. I didn't even know there were multiple walls here."

"You'll find whatever we need," he said. "Try to remember exactly what the Priestess told you to look for. In the meantime, we'll play tourist. I've always wanted to visit Istanbul."

The feeling of countless years of prayer, sacrifice, worship, good and evil bore down on her. "I don't think we have long, Zack. I think if we don't find what we're looking for in the next forty-eight hours, it's going to be too late."

They grabbed quick naps and were showered and ready to go when the imam showed up to take them to dinner. He brought along with a couple of kids who would have been alter-boys in Ivy's church growing up. She didn't know if Moslems had altar boys, but figured these kids would play a similar role, whatever they called them.

"We need to hide the Cross," she told the imam when he tried to usher them out of their apartment.

"No one will bother it here," he assured them. "We have people watching."

If she hadn't seen the U.S. aircraft carrier in Istanbul's huge harbor, she might have been reassured. "It needs to be hidden inside a holy place."

He looked uncomfortable. "A Mosque is not a proper place for an artifact that does not relate to Islam."

"The first imam we talked to told me that Jesus is a prophet in your faith."

"Peace be upon him," the two altar boys piped.

The imam rubbed his hands through his greasy beard. "This does not seem right. Still, I will defer to the friend of my friends, even if he is from the country."

Since she was getting what she wanted, Ivy ignored the snobbish attitude.

"Perfect. Zack and I are starved. Where should we eat?"

The imam knew a nearby place that served great food. He led them there, then ordered for all of them.

"I brought the boys because they can show you around tomorrow," he explained once they'd eaten enough to stave off the worst of their hunger pangs. "It is better to have someone who knows the city with you. There are some in Istanbul who prey on tourists rather than find honest work."

For just a moment, she let herself imagine a night in a bed. Unfortunately, that dream would have to be deferred again. The sense of time pressed on her like lead weights. "We're in a hurry. What about tonight?"

"I thought it best for you to sleep tonight. The city is safer during the day. There will also be many sailors from your U.S. Navy on shore leave tonight. They will be out in the bars drinking and whoring and looking for trouble."

And looking for Zack and Ivy. Ivy could only hope that their disguises would hold.

"It's hard to explain, but we're short on time."

Zack warmed her heart with his unquestioning support. "We'd understand if the young men aren't able to help us tonight, but we need to be out."

"But none of the attractions will be open," the imam argued. "You can't see a Mosque at night. The palace complex will be closed. The museums will be closed. If you want alcohol, we can have that sent to your room. Although our religion forbids alcohol for those who follow our faith, the secular government allows it. You don't need to go out to find whatever sin you seek."

"We're not looking for that type of sin," Ivy said. "But we need to find something quickly."

The imam shook his head, then spoke in quick Turkish to the altar-boys. "Nesip will help you tonight." He pointed to the older of the two boys. "Tolga will help you tomorrow if you want to see any of the true sights of our wonderful city."

"We really appreciate this," Zack said.

It was nearly sunset by the time they'd finished eating. The imam hurried off to his Mosque for the after-sundown prayers. Tolga bowed and headed for his home. Nesip, a handsome boy of maybe fourteen, took charge.

"I can take you to places where you will see extreme perversions. Woman with a snake. Much alcohol and hashish smoking." His dark eyes flashed with delight. He thought he was in for fourteen-year-old-boy-heaven.

Chapter 11

"Places of extreme perversion wait those who come to Istanbul. Very much fun."

Ivy suppressed her laugh. Is that what the imam had told him? She'd known he hadn't bought the Saint line some of the other imams had foisted on her, but she hadn't realized that he was that much of a doubter.

"We want to go to the old section of town," Zack said.

Nesip grinned. "Excellent thinking by the Mr. Zack. There is indeed much sinfulness here. For we already are in this old section as promised."

"The really old section," Zack amended. "Where the city was before Constantine."

Nesip shrugged. "But that is the museum area. There will be nothing to see. All is closed for the night."

"That's still where we have to go."

Nesip rolled his eyes. "Then there is nothing for it but that it will be done. Come. We will catch such taxi."

Old Istanbul wasn't that big. Once Nesip had secured them a taxi, it took them only about ten minutes to travel from their restaurant to the old Roman center of the city, near the tip of the peninsula that, according to Zack, had once made Constantinople a nearly impregnable fortress, protected by sea on three sides.

In the harbor beyond the still-standing ancient sea walls, ships moved, their lights blazing against the dark water. As it had been for thousands of years, Istanbul was still the crossroads to trade between north and south, Asia and Europe.

Nesip argued with the taxi driver when he tried to overcharge them, got twice as much change back, and then led Zack and Ivy down a narrow footpath to a broad stone roadway.

119

"This is hippodrome, famous for the Nike riots that nearly overthrew the Emperor Justinian." Nesip went into tour-guide mode. "Such riots between chariot factions much like football riots, yes? Here on one end of great hippodrome is Egyptian obelisk of Tutmosis. On the other is a stone obelisk built by Greeks. Once this Greek obelisk was covered with bronze and was very beautiful. Later, janissaries would climb it as part of their training. Now it's not so pretty."

Ivy couldn't argue the sights weren't impressive. As large as a Nascar track, but almost two thousand years old, the hippodrome glistened with remnants of power. Ancient trees that had seen the fall of the Sultan, the invasion by the Greeks in their failed attempt to create a new Greek empire, and the rise of the modern Turkish state lined the broad stone track. Around the hippodrome, churches, mosques, and even older ruins of ancient temples glowed with magic.

"Some day I'd like to return and hear all of this historical details," Ivy admitted. "But now I need quiet."

"But the imam tells me I am to be your guide. How can I guide you if I cannot speak?"

"I'll ask you questions when I need answers. Believe me, I need answers."

She closed her eyes and oriented herself by the colors of power.

Even without the distraction of mundane reality, the city was overwhelming. The close-by Hagia Sophia sent red pulses of light into the heavens like an enormous laser show. From what Zack had told her about that building, it had been a church for a thousand years and a mosque for four hundred after that. But that ancient monster of a church had been built on the site of older churches still. And underneath the Christian and Moslem constructions were remains of a temple of Apollo. Well over two thousand years of worship powered the vast dome and high-reaching columns of the church.

The Hagia Sophia was far from alone. Only a few hundred meters from the massive cathedral, the Blue Mosque rose even higher into the night sky, its red glow reminding Ivy of an open hearth furnace where molten iron is transformed into hardened steel. Ivy didn't recognize the other buildings, but the energy said that many of them had been, or still were places of worship.

All of which meant she was in trouble. She couldn't call in the Air Force the way Smith had, leveling ancient holy places so she could search the wreckage. And she suspected the really ancient churches would have guards who would stop her from just digging around.

"She said we were to find something we will need here."

"The priestess?" Zack asked.

Nesip made the sign of the evil eye. "There are no priestesses."

"There were priestesses once. I think we are supposed to find something here that will help us when we go on to the next city." It wasn't that she didn't trust Nesip. Still, the fewer people who knew their next destination was Venice, the safer she'd feel.

"Maybe we're supposed to find the nails from the Cross," Zack guessed. "Supposedly Saint Helena brought them to Constantinople after she recovered the True Cross. One was put into the Emperor's crown and another into his horse's bridle. I'm not sure what happened to the other, or others. Anyway, later they were supposed to have been brought to Western Europe. I suppose those relics could have been forgeries, though. I mean, how would you know you had the right nail?"

How would you know you had the right Cross? By what it did, of course. Same with the nails. Ivy didn't know if the nails were still hidden somewhere in the city that had once been the second Rome, but even if they were, that didn't seem quite right.

The sense of time, of urgency, pressed down ever-harder. With so many sources of power all around them, she wouldn't have time to investigate each. And if whatever they were looking for were hidden and disguised inside one of the many churches or mosques, they could look forever.

"Maybe you could douse," Zack suggested. "Like Smith did with his cross."

Ivy shook her head. "Bad idea. First, there aren't many people around, but there are some. Even here, if I start waving a cross around, it'd probably start a riot. Turkey is supposed to be secular, but that doesn't mean that most of its population isn't Moslem. Second, I'd still need to know what I was looking for. Otherwise, I wouldn't be able to orient the douse and I'd find anything ever associated with any religion at all. And third, there have to be Foundation agents around. They'd pick it up in a second if I pulled out a cross and started dousing."

Zack wouldn't give up. "The priestess must have given you some hint."

She shook her head. "I think we're supposed to figure it out on our own."

"Great. Someone up there thinks we're on a heroic quest. So of course we have to be tested. It would be too easy to just give us the information we need. I got enough of that in the military. You'd think surviving the past couple of weeks would have been enough test."

He wasn't attacking her, but it almost felt that way and she got defensive. "Yeah? Well, if I was in charge, I'd say just give it to us. Since that isn't going to happen, we'll have to keep on working at it."

Zack grunted. No help there.

"Okay, Nesip," she said. "You can help with this too. What kind of religious artifacts would there have been in Istanbul?"

Nesip considered, then shrugged. "The Ottoman Sultans became Caliphs many hundreds of years ago. Surely they bring important artifacts here. But why would they have become lost? All are in the Topkapi Museum."

"Great. We're only being chased by the CIA, the Foundation, the Turkish Army, and the US Navy now. Let's break into a museum and add the local police and Interpol," Zack said.

Ivy considered. "It's nothing Islamic. That doesn't feel right. Remember, this was a priestess. I'm thinking something female."

Nesip made another of his evil-eye gestures.

"What's the matter? Don't Moslems have female saints?"

"Mohammed, peace be upon him, was the last prophet. Islam has no need for saints of any kind, male or female."

Ivy wasn't sure what that made her. Unnecessary, or not a saint at all. "I still think it's something related to a woman. Didn't an Empress find the Cross? Maybe that's related."

"Yes, Saint Helena. She was the Emperor Constantine's mother."

"So she's the saint. Maybe there is some artifact of hers. Something related to the Cross."

The call for evening prayer went out and Nesip knelt in worship leaving Ivy standing there like a heathen.

What possible artifact of some long-dead Empress could remain more than fifteen hundred years after her death?

"Documents," suggested Zack, when Nesip finished his evening worship. "Saint Helena had the Cross for years. She might have figured out how to use it, left directions behind. Constantine supposedly used the Cross as his emblem in battle, and never lost. Maybe they learned the magic. I mean, it's pretty obvious it didn't work for the Crusaders, so there's more to it than just waving the Cross around."

Ivy started to answer, then froze. "Full tourist mode, Nesip. Go."

"Although the Blues and Greens were affiliated with chariot teams," Nesip lectured, "they also had political, social, and religious aspects. Thus, the greens believed in the wholly divine nature of Christ, the so-called Monophysite heresy, while—"

"A little late to be out touristing, aren't you?"

Ivy pretended she hadn't noticed the half-dozen sailors approaching.

Each wore an 'SP' armband, signifying that they made up a Shore Patrol, supposedly keeping U.S. sailors from offending the host country.

They had no legal authority in Turkey, of course. No right to arrest anyone who wasn't part of the military.

She didn't think they'd care about that if they were under orders from the Foundation, though. Of course, if they found out she and Zack were AWOL from Iraq, they would haul them in for desertion.

"Please to join the tour," Nesip offered. "Only twenty Euros, for the each of you. I will share with you such stories of the ancient Greeks with their famous orgies and the decadent Ottomans with their harems and thousands of beautiful concubines."

"We are happy to have this company," Ivy agreed. She was doing her best to adopt a Latin accent, whatever that was. Since she didn't know any Romanians, she figured that was as close as she could get. "Especially as you are Americans, are you not. My husband and I have discussing move to America of the future but it is difficult to receive the papers. Are you knowing how to file such?"

The SP sergeant stared at her, then at the blue-eyed, surfer-haired Zack. "No, we don't want to listen to some wog tell us about dead Greeks. And we don't want more wogs coming to America. Get lost."

"Perhaps I will be showing you the famous and quite antique Blue Mosque," Nesip offered. "So named for the handsome blue tiles that decorate it throughout. Your shoes will have to remove first, out of respect."

"Blow off," the sergeant said. "We've got work to do."

"Perhaps we should go home to bed," Ivy said. Around the hippodrome, other black-clad SP units seemed to be setting up a loose perimeter. "Before we're completely cut off," she whispered to Zack."

* * * *

"We need an English-speaking priest," Ivy decided. "Someone who knows about the city and what might be here."

They'd gotten outside the informal boundary the SP was establishing, but not before they'd spotted some black-suited spook types. More guys who sent shivers through Ivy and reminded her of Smith. Like the Cross and the Islamic mosques, these men glowed with the red color of their faith, but that faith didn't comfort Ivy at all. The kind of Christianity that would slaughter a soldier just because she witnessed the Cross was different from anything she thought deserved the name.

A few of the black-suited Foundation-men even had crosses out and were dousing. Apparently they didn't care about the feelings of the local Moslem population. Which shouldn't have been a big surprise to Ivy.

123

After all, they'd bombed an ancient mosque in Mosul just to get to the Cross.

"Looks like we missed our chance," Zack said. "Even if we knew what we were looking for, we'd be outnumbered. And they seem to know what they're after. At least you were right about it being an object, not a person."

He could be right. Certainly rummaging around the ancient quarter of the city while the Foundation men were in control bordered on foolishness. But Ivy couldn't dismiss the Priestess's charge. Until she knew they'd missed their chance completely, she needed to do what she could to discover the object.

"These Christian men would cause arguments," Nesip suggested. "If word spread among the young and fervent, they could be forced from the city with much violence."

Ivy shook her head slowly. Tempting though it would be, she didn't want a bunch of banged up sailors on her conscience. They were just doing their jobs, after all. Worse, she wasn't going to let a bunch of Nesip's friends get hurt. Because if the Foundation really was in control, they wouldn't hesitate to order the SPs to fire.

Provoking a diplomatic incident between her country and one of its oldest allies, getting a bunch of kids killed, and still not finding whatever she was looking for seemed the most likely outcome.

"Let's just see if we can find a priest," she repeated.

"You do remember what happened the last time we ran into Orthodox priests," Zack said. "They might have sent word here. After all, Constantinople still is the official center of the Orthodox Church."

Ivy wasn't going to forget the monastery and the monks' attempt to steal the Cross, but she needed help and couldn't see any alternative than taking a chance.

"There's got to be someone. Some scholar. Someone who would know what might have been hidden. If we knew what we were looking for, we'd have a chance."

Nesip brightened. "We can visit this coffee shop. Quite nearby, truly. Plenty of young people come there."

"Are any of them priests?"

"No priests, I suspect."

"Then—"

"But it is an Internet connection. I ask my friends. On-line chat. Someone will know some priest, perhaps."

It wasn't a great idea, but Ivy couldn't think of anything better.

The coffee shop sat on the boundary of the famous Istanbul bazaar

—a square mile of tiny shops selling everything from cheap tourist trinkets, to pre-Roman artworks, to the occasional assassination.

No lights shone from the coffee shop's windows and no sound penetrated over the rumble of traffic and the whisper of voices as shopkeepers replenished their stocks and prepared for the next day's shopping.

"Looks closed," Zack said.

"Of course," Nesip said. "How could it look otherwise when the police are anxious?"

He knocked on the heavy iron-bound door, waited, then knocked again.

After perhaps a minute, a tiny peephole opened and someone inside shouted something in Turkish.

Nesip answered, ignored the obviously negative response, and rattled something. "I am telling them of your troubles and of your fame with the imam," he explained.

Finally, the door swung open for mere seconds and they were rushed into the shop.

Despite outside appearances, it was open and doing a fair business. Black crepe paper taped to the windows gave the large room a wartime look, and a couple of old men wearing fez and smoking bongs looked like they could have stepped in from the nineteenth century.

The scents of strong coffee mingled with the sweet smell of hashish.

"Internet," Nesip told the shirtless bouncer who'd finally opened the door for them.

The bouncer flexed his muscles, then finally gestured toward the back.

"I will contact my friends," Nesip promised. "You may order some coffee. If you wish drugs, the men with the pipes could possibly help you."

As he turned toward the computer, someone grasped Ivy by the shoulder.

* * * *

She didn't have her AK-47, but she spun, ready for a fight.

"Miss Ivy, how wonderful to find you here."

Cejno looked cool. He'd abandoned the baggy pants and hand sewn off-white shirt he'd worn when he'd been driving with them and wore a thin-lapelled black suit and dark sunglasses.

"I have found my business contacts, as anticipated, and done considerable trading."

"What are you doing here, Cejno?"

"I have been making deals," he proudly proclaimed. "My friends were right about Istanbul. These rich Europeans visit here and pay more than even American soldiers in Iraq. They have nice Euros, so much more better than the dollar."

Ivy suspected she should be glad. The more dope sent toward Europe, the less that would flow to the troops in Iraq, and the fewer would be stoned out of their brains when insurgents attacked. Still, her involvement with a drug-smuggler continued to trouble her.

If Cejno noticed her concerns, he didn't let on. "You are continuing your quest, is it?"

"We're looking for a priest," she said. "Know any?"

He wouldn't, of course. He'd only arrived that day, as they had.

To her shock, he grinned. "A priest? I know a most excellent priest. Oh, yes. You want him here?"

Did she? Suspecting he was pulling her leg, she decided to put him to the test. "Sure."

He pulled out his cell, dialed a number, then spoke a few words—in Greek.

"He say he come here to meet with you," Cejno reported as he closed his cell and refastened it to his belt. "He think maybe I cut him a better price if he does me mighty favors."

"Wonderful. I'm sure a hashish-abusing priest is exactly what we need."

Zack managed to get the attention of a male waiter and ordered four coffees and Ivy took the opportunity to look around.

Like everything in this part of Istanbul, the coffee shop looked as if it had been there forever.

Wooden pillars held up a wooden ceiling, both of which had blackened from centuries of smoke.

Intricate carvings decorated the pillars and the walls. Many were in Arabic calligraphy, almost certainly going back to the pre-Ataturk days. Greek script might have been left during the Greek occupation—but might, perhaps signify that this building had once been a Byzantine wine-shop. The few notes in the modern Roman-Turkish script were almost apologetic by comparison.

Ivy guessed that all the inscriptions, whichever the language, proclaimed either subversive political messages or prayers to various gods.

In darkened corners of the shop, Turks, Arabs, and Europeans sipped coffee and read flimsy newspapers that proclaimed the coming revolution. In this crowd, atheistic Communist revolution mingled easily with theistic Islamic revolution. From time to time, oddly matched pairs would join, whisper dark conspiracies to one another, then separate again, like lovers exchanging secrets under the watchful eyes of jealous spouses.

Nesip emerged from his computer-daze just as Zack finally persuaded the waiter to bring his coffee paraphernalia to their table.

Ivy had thought Starbucks went overboard in their presentation of a simple beverage. Compared to what she saw in the Turkish coffee house, the Starbucks ritual was nothing.

First, the waiter measured out a dose of beans, which he proceeded to hammer into a powder. Once the coffee was pulverized to his satisfaction, he poured the dustlike grains into a tiny pot he called an ibrik. He held the long-handled ibrik over a flame, then added what looked like enough sugar to clog arteries just as it neared a boil. Each time the coffee foamed, he poured off the foam into tiny coffee cups, then returned the ibrik and the remainder of the coffee to the flame.

"This had better be good after all this production," Ivy whispered to Zack.

"This will be the best coffee you have ever tasted, Madam," the waiter assured her in perfect English. He carefully poured four tiny demitasse cups of the blackest coffee Ivy had ever seen, then stepped back from the table, crossed his arms across his chest and watched.

"He's waiting for your approval," Zack said.

Feeling suddenly large and clumsy, she picked up the small paper-thin porcelain coffee cup and sipped.

Hot and strong, the coffee's bitterness cut by the sweetness of sugar, she could almost feel the caffeine entering directly into her bloodstream. No wonder the Turks, whose religion forbid alcohol, made such a ritual about their coffee. This was powerful stuff.

"Good," she managed.

The waiter nodded, mollified, then vanished.

"I don't think little bitty cups like this are going to catch on at home, though," she told Zack. "People in America like to super-size."

"Speaking of super-sized." He gestured at the door where an enormous man was entering.

"Father Galen." Cejno was on his feet, shaking the massive priest's hand. "Come meet my friends."

Father Galen eyed the chairs at their table suspiciously until the waiter appeared with something reinforced. Then he sat down heavily at the head of the table, looking, for all the world, like a put-upon king in his black robes. "I understand you need a priest. You wish to be married, is that it?"

If his mother ever found out she'd spent weeks on the road with Zack, she would be horrified they weren't married. But Ivy didn't have time to think about that.

"Bad guess, father," she said. "Have you ever heard of something called 'The Foundation?'"

"There was a famous Science Fiction novel by that name. By the Russian author Dr. Isaac Asimov. Quite excellent, really. I suspect he must be Orthodox, as are most Russians."

"I'm thinking about something a little more here and now. This particular Foundation appears to be a U.S.-based group with considerable authority even over the armed forces. We don't even know if it's a governmental organization or a private group."

Father Galen made a major production of a shrug. As he raised, then lowered his shoulders, waves of fat rippled down his torso, then rippled up again. "America is home to thousands of religious beliefs. Recently they have become more involved in the political process. As I understand it, many have influence in your government. This is not new. In Europe, religion has long been involved with politics. In Germany, there are the Christian Democrats. Here in Turkey, the Welfare Party has a Moslem agenda. Of course, in Greece, the Church is central to our political life. Even the Greek Communist Party has great respect for the Church."

All very interesting, but not especially helpful. "So you've never heard of a Foundation?"

He shrugged. "I confess that my memory is imperfect." Father Galen had the good grace to look a bit embarrassed. "Many of my fellow priests are more diligent than I. My faith is strong, but I'm not good at spending long hours at study."

Since he was an acquaintance of Cejno, Ivy had a pretty good idea how he did spend his long hours—and what gave him the munchies that had led to his massive size.

"I don't suppose you'd have a guess about what kind of religious artifact might have been lost in ancient Constantinople, then?" She didn't hold out much hope. He'd already let them know he wasn't the studious type.

He gestured to the waiter, who carried over a large plate of cakes and set it in front of the priest. Ivy hadn't even known you could order food here. It was the kind of detail Father Galen would know.

"Religious Artifact?" Small bits of cake sprayed as he spoke. "Constantinople is full of artifacts. Constantinople was Christian when the pagans still paraded in Rome."

"I'm thinking of something relating to a woman. Perhaps Saint—"

Father Galen held up a hand. "Constantinople has also been called the City of Mary. Although the Protestants accuse Catholics of undue adoration of the virgin, it was with the Orthodox that Marianism first took hold. For five hundred years, Constantinople was safe under the protective veil of Mary, Mother of God."

Ivy almost smacked her forehead. The Virgin Mary was a lot more obvious and a lot more important than St. Helena. Sure St. Helena was associated with the Cross. But the people most closely related to the Cross were Jesus, the Virgin Mary, and Mary Magdalene.

"Tell me about the protective veil of Mary. Was this a real veil, or is that just symbolic for the fact that the city was just a strong fortress?"

"Not just a strong fortress. Constantinople was a strong fortress of God," Father Galen said. Despite his girth and his assumed drug habits, the man was clearly a committed Christian. "For a thousand years, after the fall of the Western Rome, we protected the barbarian west from the despotisms of Asia. Without us, Europe would be Moslem now."

"But the veil. It wasn't an artifact, a relic?"

"Ah, but it was." Father Galen stuffed another cake in his mouth, chewed once, then swallowed. "The veil of the Mother of God was the most holy symbol of the city. According to legend and church doctrine, the Emperor paraded the veil on the walls of the city the very night before the Turks finally broke through the pitifully few last defenders and sacked the city. It was terribly real, wonderfully holy."

"And what happened to it then?"

"It is said that Mary herself came down from the heavens and recovered her veil, as this City of God would require it no longer."

He ate another of the small cakes. "Constantinople was an experiment," he explained when he saw that Ivy was still listening. "For a thousand years, the Orthodox strove to create the Kingdom of God here on Earth. Not by waiting for a mysterious rapture, but by living in a Christian way, with a Christian Emperor. The Emperor's title was Autocrat, Equal to the Apostles, and it was quite literally meant. Greek Emperors summoned the great councils of the Church, councils that still bind your Catholic Church, and many of the Protestants as well. The bishops and priests argued, but the Emperor decided. For hundreds of years, a Roman Pope could only be elected with our Emperor's approval."

He actually wiped tears from his eyes. "Now, the Church in Constantinople is poor. Even the other Orthodox have their own concerns. Few send money to us and, of course, the Turks expelled most of the Greeks from Anatolia, a land where they had lived for three thousand years or more. But once, we were the city on a hill, the strong shield of the west, the one beacon of civilization while Europe descended into barbarism. And the veil of the Mother of God was our symbol."

* * * *

The Veil of the Mother of God. It sounded like something out of a secret codebook.

"What could it do?" Zack asked. "Did it have special powers? Could it really defend an army or a city?"

Father Galen looked at him like he'd peed in the communion bowl. "This is a holy object, but it is only a thing. Objects can be adored to help the faithful focus their attentions on the holy. They themselves must not be worshipped. Objects don't have power."

Which didn't answer Zack's question. He wondered if the Foundation agents knew a more complete answer.

"Are we certain that the Virgin Mary came down and recovered her veil?"

Father Galen pursed his lips in distaste. With his fat cheeks, doing that made his nose almost disappear in rolls of fat. Which meant he couldn't do it for long without cutting off his breathing. "Some say that the veil was taken to Russia where many of the faithful fled after the fall of the City. Others believe it was taken to the Catholic west and is now hoarded amongst the secret treasures of the Vatican. The story of Mary recovering it could be apocryphal. Although if it was not true, why has the veil not been found and shown? It has been almost six hundred years since the Turks violated the center of western civilization, after all."

He ate another cake, this one pensively, actually taking the time to chew three times before swallowing.

"When the Greeks occupied Constantinople after World War I, many thought that the veil would be recovered, that the time for a new greater Greece had arrived, that we could claim our place as one of the powers of Europe. But that was not to be. Surely, if Mary had not taken the veil back to heaven, they would have discovered it then."

* * * *

Father Galen's words were almost like a light bulb going off in Zack's head. It was hard to imagine two symbols most closely connected to the wars between the Christian and Moslem worlds. The Cross had been found by the Byzantines, stolen by Persia, recovered by the Byzantines, taken by the Arabs, recovered by the Crusaders and used by them as their battle standard, before finally being captured by Saladin. And this Veil of Mary had apparently been used in a similar role by the Orthodox—and, according to Galen, at least, could launch the Greeks into a war against the Turks.

Armed with the recovered Cross and Veil, could the Foundation be contemplating a new crusade? Given the problems the U.S. was already having in Iraq, only a complete idiot or a fanatic would want to launch a more general war between Cross and Crescent. As they'd proven in Iraq, winning isn't the problem. The problem is what to do once you've won. The Foundation wasn't made up of idiots, but it did seem to have its share of fanatics.

"Let's just assume for a moment that Mary didn't take the Veil back to Heaven," Ivy said. "And assume that the Russians and the Catholics didn't get it either. Where would it be if the Greeks had hidden it, waiting, perhaps, for the day when the city would become Greek again?"

Father Galen glanced at Ivy, then back at the last of the cakes on the plate. He pushed the plate away as if he were making a huge sacrifice. "Who knows? Perhaps it was looted by the Turks. Perhaps it was destroyed in the fires the Turks set when they rampaged through the city raping our women and murdering our scholars and priests. Perhaps it was buried in a grave."

"You're Greek, right father?"

Father Galen glared at Ivy. "Of course I am Greek. But I am not from Greece. My family has been Greek and in Constantinople for more than a thousand years. Although the Turks persecute us, some of us who will not flee, but will remain to remind the world that Constantinople is a Greek city, a holy city, the Second, perfected, Rome."

"Right. So, where would you have hidden the veil? Think hard. Someplace the Turks wouldn't have looked, right. Someplace that only another Greek would guess."

He squinted at Ivy. "I tell you this and then you steal it? How does this help my people?"

Zack figured it was time for him to break in. "Did you notice anything strange when you were outside, father? Maybe you saw the dozens of U.S. sailors with Shore Patrol insignia. But they aren't patrolling the harbor bars the way a Shore Patrol should. They're wandering around the oldest parts of the city, probing, poking, looking for something. One thing you can bet. They aren't doing it because they want to help the Greeks. I don't know exactly what the Foundation believes, but I do know one thing. They aren't Catholics, and they aren't Orthodox, either."

Father Galen sighed. "If the veil is hidden, it has survived detection for over five hundred years. Why should a group of uneducated sailors succeed where holy fathers have failed?"

"The hunters aren't just sailors. They know where to look, and they use the Cross like a dousing rod," Ivy said. "I've seen it work."

Zack wouldn't have guessed it possible, but Father Galen exploded to his feet, shoving the table away from him and catching his balance by leaning on one of the carved support columns so hard that the entire coffee shop shook. "They are using the Cross, the symbol of Christ's suffering, to work magic? We cannot allow this blasphemy."

Zack caught the priest by the cassock, then wished he hadn't as the big man leaned his four hundred pounds against Zack's battered body. "Careful, Father. If you try to stop them, they'll kill you. They don't care about human life. Probably they figure God will sort it out. But if you help us, we might be able to find it ahead of them, keep it from whatever they plan to use it for."

"I will talk to my fellow priests," Father Galen promised. "I have young Cejno's number. I shall call you in the morning and let you know what we have decided.

Chapter 12

The eastern horizon didn't even hint at dawn when someone started hammering on the door to the apartment Ivy shared with Zack.

She pulled herself out of bed and stumbled to the entryway. Cejno peered into the apartment eyehole, probably trying to catch a glimpse of her running around naked. His brief experience with the French woman apparently hadn't satisfied Cejno's curiosity about the female form.

The hashish smuggler exploded into the apartment as soon as she opened the door. "Father Galen says the priests will help you. He says their Patriarch has heard of the Foundation."

"What did he hear?" Zack demanded.

Cejno shrugged. "He's heard of them and he wants to help you. Is that not enough?"

"Great. Does he say anything about where we should start looking?"

Cejno looked at the floor. "Father Galen says the priests will study their church records. Although the Turks destroyed some and the Venetians others, they have records that go back long before even those in the Vatican."

"Just what we need. A bunch of priests sitting around reading old books. If those books said anything about where the veil was hidden, someone would have found it by now. Which means we're on our own," Ivy concluded. "Give me ten minutes to get showered and we'll head out and see what we can find."

"Father Galen also asked me to tell you that the Americans are still everywhere."

"Are they digging?"

"I have not heard that."

"Good. Why don't you see if you can round up something for us to eat while Zack and I get ready?"

Cejno nodded and headed out the door.

"Mind if I go first?" she asked Zack when she saw him outside the bathroom.

He shook his head. "I have a bad feeling about the Bishop's reaction, though."

"Why's that? He's going to help us. Didn't you see how Father Galen reacted when we told him how Smith used his crucifix as a dousing rod?"

"So how do you think he's going to take it when you use the True Cross as a door opener?"

Ivy hadn't thought about that. To her, it wasn't the same. The Cross wanted to be used as the Key. But she could see how a priest might not see things that way.

"We've got to go with the allies we can find." She stepped into the bathroom and turned on the shower. Even a lukewarm scrub would feel good. If she ever got back to America, she planned on soaking for a week.

Father Galen met them at a pastry shop and proceeded to impress everyone by buying two-dozen cream-filled pastries and eating them all.

"We have found no indication that the Veil was hidden," he admitted. "But we are quite certain that the Veil now in Russia is not the one that we held here. This does not mean the Russian one is inauthentic, of course. Mary may have had more than one garment."

"Got it," Zack said. "So if it's hidden, you don't know where?"

"Correct."

"How many people can the Patriarch spare to help our search?" Ivy took one of the pastries and bit into it. The chocolate and cream concoction probably had five hundred calories all by itself.

Father Galen looked embarrassed. "I am that person."

"So, it sounds like we're outnumbered. We'll have to outthink the Foundation people." Which wouldn't be easy. The Foundation had obviously been researching the artifacts for years. "If you were a Byzantine Greek and the Turks were about to take over your city, where would you hide the veil?"

"In the Great Church," Galen said without pausing for thought. "The Hagia Sophia had already been the center of our faith for a thousand years."

"Too obvious."

Unfortunately, Ivy agreed with Zack on that one. Besides, if it were hidden in the Hagia Sophia, the Foundation would get there first. "When the Turks conquered Constantinople, the first place they went was the Hagia Sophia. The defenders would have known that. So, where else might they have tried?"

"The Great Palace, I supposed. Perhaps the church of the Twelve Apostles, or of Saints Sergius and Bacchus. Of course, there were hundreds of monasteries within Constantinople during those days. It could have been taken to any of them."

"Where was it kept before the siege?"

Father Galen rolled his eyes. "That I do not know. Doubtless there was a church built to hold it. Perhaps the Blachernae Church."

Galen seemed more interested in the future than in the past, as long as the future looked like his idea of the idealized past. Well, Ivy couldn't hold that against him. Lots of people thought that way.

"If it's in a church, the Foundation will find it. Tell me about the Great Palace. Is that what they call the Topkapi Palace?"

Father Galen laughed. "The Turks wish it were so. No, the Great Palace was a whole city for the government of the entire world. Built by Constantine, it was much larger than Topkapi. Indeed, a major piece was recently found well outside the Topkapi."

"So, if the veil was taken to the Great Palace, it could be pretty much anywhere in the old section of the city?" Zack said.

"But of course. This was a city within the city."

"Is there anyplace sacred to Mary? Maybe the legend of Mary coming to earth and retrieving her veil was meant metaphorically, or even as a clue."

Father Galen crossed himself—it wasn't quite the same sign her Catholic priests used, but it was similar, just as his robes were different but similar. "That is an interesting thought. There are many sites in the city sacred to the Queen of Heaven."

"Which would be the oldest?"

Father Galen looked at Cejno. "Perhaps I could have just a small amount for the pipe. Thinking is heavy work."

Cejno shrugged. "All of the hashish is dispersed, Father. I merely stay here to help my friends."

"Ah, well. I feared it was to be so." Father Galen removed a tiny pipe from a pocket he had hidden somewhere in his robes, sniffed at it, then put it back without lighting. "In Constantinople, the 'oldest' can be very old indeed. Many of our churches were built on Greek temples. Although it is not always political to remember this, the pagans once had their own Queen in Heaven."

Ivy felt the same surge of rightness she'd felt when she'd been dragged into the temple of Aphrodite in Anamur. From what she'd seen of Smith and read in the Foundation papers before they'd been destroyed in the Predator attack, the Foundation seemed to be made of exactly the kind of Christians who would deny the earlier heritages and the truths that had shaped their faith. "So, what place was sacred to those pagan goddesses?"

Father Galen looked at Cejno again, but without much hope. "Who can say? The Hagia Sophia was built on a pagan temple. Even Christian Emperors saw themselves as conservators of the Greek culture and collected statues and other works from the pagan Greeks."

They were no better off than they had been when they'd started this adventure. Ivy refused to give in to despair.

"Which of the Greek goddesses would have been Queen of Heaven?" Zack asked.

That wasn't a bad question, although Ivy suspected that the truth was complex. Just as Catholics insisted on the separate yet indivisible nature of God, so Ivy now understood that the separate goddesses of the pagan Greek faith were not completely separate individuals but could also be seen as aspects of one Goddess. The legend of Aphrodite, Hera, and Athena seeking to be selected as most fair might also relate to the aspects of the Goddess—virgin, mother, and crone. Bits of mythology that had never made sense to her before suddenly fell into place with new insights.

"Probably Hera."

"And is there a site most associated with Hera?"

Father Galen raised his eyes. Not to the heavens, Ivy realized, but to the counter. He'd finished his pastries and was seriously considering buying more.

"There was a famous statue of Hera once," Cejno said. "Part of the Hippodrome. It was stolen by the Catholic invaders."

"Stolen and destroyed," Father Galen said.

Great. And now Catholic invaders were looking to steal the veil of Mary. No wonder the Orthodox were suspicious.

"The Foundation guys have already been over the ruins of the Hippodrome," Zack reminded them. "If it's there, they've got it."

Nobody else had any ideas and Father Galen had pretty much cleared out the pastry store so they agreed to meet again for lunch at a nearby restaurant and went their separate ways.

* * * *

"You've got a plan, right?" Zack bought coffees from a sidewalk merchant and they were pretending to be tourists along the wall that had protected Greek Constantinople for so long before the great Turkish cannon, Basilica, had crashed through the ancient gates and doomed the city to Turkish rule.

"Let's just say I've got an idea."

Although the city walls were over fifteen hundred years old and had been prayed over by countless defenders and invaders alike, they lacked the distinctive colors of power that Ivy thought she would find. Apparently there was more to the magical powers than just prayer. Perhaps there needed to be an enclosed area to hold that power inside rather than let it leak out. Or perhaps the walls, important as they were, were simply not regarded as holy objects. She was pretty sure it wasn't the violence those walls had seen that kept magic at bay. That yellow temple to the hawk-headed god they'd found in Kurdistan had seen plenty of violence, of human sacrifice, yet it still reeked with power.

"I thought it possible that there would be some trace of the veil's power in the last place where it was positively known to have been," she admitted. "But I'm not seeing anything."

Zack looked concerned. "Do you need to connect to the Cross again? We haven't touched it in twenty-four hours. Could you be losing the sight?"

She couldn't help laughing. "Trust me, that isn't the problem. All of the power in this city has nearly blinded me to ordinary sight. But I'm not seeing anything here."

"What color are you looking for?"

"It would be red, wouldn't it? That's the color of Christianity and Islam."

He nodded. "But Mary's traditional color in church art is blue."

Blue was also the color of the temple of Aphrodite she'd unlocked. "You know, Zack, I think you've hit on something. Let's get going."

She bought a tourist map, then flagged down a taxi and ordered the driver on a long trip through the alleys of old Constantinople.

As she'd told Zack, the city was a mosaic of power. Colors radiated from mosques, churches, city parks, scattered ruins, and, in one case, an apparently empty spot in the sky fifty feet above the nearest building.

Most of the power gleamed red—the heritage of nearly two thousand years of rule by Christian and then Islamic empires.

But there were other colors. Yellow glowed sullenly from doorways leading down into subterranean hiding places. Orange brightened the rooftops of truly ancient buildings that still bore telltale marks of the Bull's horns. Green glistened from grottos and treed parks. And blue tantalized and teased from a few churches, from ruined temples, and from behind the walls of the Topkapi Palace complex.

Zack marked up the map with Ivy's descriptions and also kept up a running description of the numerous sailors and accompanying black-suited Foundation types wandering through the city.

After an hour, he slapped his forehead. "I can't believe I just noticed this."

"What?"

"Wherever you spot a blue power source, there seems to be a group of sailors and SP forces nearby. That hasn't been universally true of the other power colors, although there are plenty of sailors around some of those, too."

Which meant the Foundation had set a trap for them.

"Let's go meet the guys for lunch," Ivy said. "There's something going on here we haven't figured out yet."

* * * *

"They're guarding the sites while they bring in their detectors," Father Galen said when he'd finished putting down most of a side of beef and an entire chocolate cake. "They must have followed the same logic you did, decided that the veil would be hidden in a place sacred to the Queen of Heaven, and identified those spots. But they wouldn't dare just start digging. Our Turkish government may roll over for the Americans, but this would be too much, even for them. I would have heard if they'd started digging and I haven't heard anything. This can only mean they haven't found anything."

He punctuated his speech with a long draught of beer.

"If we can guess which of the ten spots Ivy found is the right one," Zack said, "we might be able to get there before the Foundation's diggers. Even so, they'd be on us before we could recover the veil."

A sense of unease had been percolating through Ivy since Zack had recognized the Foundation men scattered near the blue power sites. The priest's words finally gave her the missing pieces.

"We aren't ahead of them. They're ahead of us. They aren't waiting for permission to dig, they're waiting for us to walk into their arms."

Father Galen smiled and shook his head, then waved to the waiter for the desert tray. "How could they be waiting? And why? If they know how to find the veil, they would take it. What could be more holy? What could be more important than the very veil of the Mother of God?"

Zack shook his head slowly. "I think Ivy has a point. Has the Patriarch learned anything more about the Foundation?"

Father Galen gave another of his massive shrugs. "He contacted one of his fellow students from the old days, a Russian Bishop. The Russians have more experience with the radical Protestants because some groups of them have been trying to convert the Orthodox of Russia since the fall of the Soviet Empire. Anyway, his friend says The Foundation is an offshoot of one of those radical Protestant groups. The Russian spy agency, the SVR, says the Foundation has gained influence in U.S. government circles. But no one seems to know what their beliefs are, what they seek, or whom they proselytize. Indeed, they seem only to approach those who are already believers and already secure in their power. It is a mystery."

"Extreme Protestant groups deny the special position of Mary and hold it blasphemous that we Catholics and you Orthodox call her Queen of Heaven," Zack pointed out. "So, why would they be looking for the veil?"

"But she was selected for the most holy—"

"I'm not arguing with you," Zack interrupted. "I'm just telling you what they believe. And if they don't believe in Mary, why would they care about her relics?"

"Power is power," Ivy said. "I don't believe in the hawk-headed god we ran into in Kurdistan, but I wouldn't want to see him again, either."

Zack nodded. "Good point, and I wasn't thinking that way. But think about this. The veil has been here for hundreds of years, right?"

Ivy started to see where this was going. "Right. What are the odds that they decide to come looking for it exactly the day we arrive in Istanbul? They aren't looking for the relic. They're still looking for the Cross. By tracking us, they could tell we were heading toward Byzantium and guessed we'd try for the veil. They've set a trap for us."

"Cross? You have the Cross?" Father Galen's fat jowls quivered. "The True Cross is found after all these centuries? Truly this is a miracle, a sign that we may be entering the last days."

He heaved himself out of his chair, shoved the table out of his way, and embraced first Zack, then Ivy. "You must show it to me. The Patriarch himself will wish to see this." Tears ran down his cheeks and he pulled a green handkerchief from a hidden pocket and blew his nose with it. "Where is it hidden? Is it quite safe? Do you truly believe these men would use force to seize the holy symbol of our Lord's suffering? Surely they are Christians, even if Protestants."

"That's a lot of questions," Ivy said. "And the short answer is, yes, it's hidden. And yes, they would kill, have killed, to get it."

"I must tell the Patriarch. Every priest in Constantinople will wish to see it. Every lay Christian. This may be the new beginning for our Church." He blew his nose on the handkerchief, then waved the rag in the air. "The Turks have not been kind to we Christians who stayed after the forced repatriation of Greeks. Although the treaty between Greece and Turkey expressly called for protection of Greeks living in

Constantinople, we have been reduced by pogroms and violence. Now, only a few thousand of us remain. But the recovered Cross justifies our faith. We shall have new converts. Whatever the oppression, Greeks will return to the land of their parents when they hear that the Cross is found, was returned to Constantinople."

He reached to pull Ivy into another slobbering hug, but she stepped back in time to get away from him.

"If we put the Cross on display, the Foundation will find it and take it."

Father Galen laughed. "How could they, if it was guarded by priests and preserved in the sanctuary of the Cathedral?"

"They bombed an ancient mosque in Mosul and killed an American soldier to take it before," Zack answered. "I doubt your aging priests would offer it much protection."

"Perhaps I can offer a suggestion," Cejno put in.

Ivy had almost forgotten the young Kurd was still with them but she had a lot of faith in his political instincts. "Yes?"

"Each of you has a problem. Your problem is, you want to take the veil, but it is guarded. Father Galen's problem is, he wants to touch the Cross and show it to the Patriarch. Perhaps the solution to each problem lies in the other."

"How, exactly?" Ivy asked.

"What could distract this Foundation of you Americans? What could give you and Mr. Zack the time you need to snatch the veil without being disturbed? I tell you truly, a parade, a procession, with enough people that it would push the Foundation men out of position. And who could make such a parade? Only the Patriarch himself."

"So, we let the Patriarch see the Cross and he gives us a noisy and pushy parade," Zack repeated.

"There are only a few thousand of us remaining in Constantinople," Father Galen said. "Most are old, too old for a parade." He gave a longing look toward the kitchen, then shook his head. "I cannot eat now, I must work. We will need more Christians, but it could work," Father Galen said. "If we promised a viewing of the long-lost veil, we could get pilgrims from Thrace and beyond."

Ivy's first reaction was an emphatic no. She'd been in school with fanatical Protestants who viewed everyone who disagreed with them as scum. She didn't think the Foundation would have any particular moral qualms about killing Orthodox pilgrims. Even if they did have time to bring in pilgrims from the Orthodox world.

"Sounds dangerous," Zack said.

Father Galen smiled. "I insist that we make this parade happen. How could it be dangerous to join our fellow Christians in worship?"

Ivy had an uneasy feeling they'd soon discover the answer to Father Galen's question, and they wouldn't like what they found.

* * * *

It took six hours to gather thousands of pilgrims.

The Patriarch made calls to his fellow church leaders in Greece, Serbia, and Bulgaria as well as a few of the nearby Greek islands nominally under his direct control. All of those neighboring nations had large Orthodox populations and a traditional relationship with the Patriarch of Constantinople.

After making the phone calls, the Patriarch joined Zack, Cejno, Ivy, and Father Galen outside the apartment they'd been given by the imam.

The Patriarch wasn't as old as Ivy had guessed he would be—maybe because her expectations had been created by the ancient Pope—but he looked serious and worried. He would be embarrassed if Ivy and Zack were pulling a hoax.

The Patriarch shook hands with everyone, gave Cejno a stern look that indicated he knew more about the hashish-smuggler's business than anyone was admitting, then demanded to be shown the Cross.

The imam was not happy to see the Orthodox leader show up at his mosque. "This is a house of prayer, not a hotbed of conspiracy."

The Patriarch replied to him in Turkish, finally quieting his objections before actually entering the mosque.

Ivy was relieved to see the Cross, safe in a storage room, shoved against the wall as if it were a couple of hunks of timber left over from a reproofing. Although Zack had been wrong about her need to touch the Cross to see the colors of power, seeing it, touching it, always provided her a sense of healing and strength.

The Patriarch must have felt a taste of the magic himself, because he immediately knelt before the object and prayed silently for nearly an hour before finally reaching out a tentative hand and touching the longer section, searching for the spot where the head of Jesus would have rested.

"It is truly a miracle," he announced. "The discovery of the Veil will be another miracle. The world is filled with change. Sometimes I wish I had been born at an easier age, but life has never been easy for the Orthodox, standing as we do at the fulcrum between east and west, between Christianity and Islam. Between Europe and Asia."

He tracked down the imam who was stomping around outside his own mosque, and rattled at him in Turkish for another ten minutes.

141

"Good," the Patriarch said in English. He turned to Ivy and Zack. "Ugur will see that our parade is not disturbed by an Islamic mob. In fact, Ugur will speak to some of the hotheads and encourage them to march beside us, adding to the confusion for your Foundation men."

"How did you talk him into that?" Ivy demanded. The imam hadn't seemed especially positive to her.

The Patriarch shrugged. "I told him about the Foundation and the bombed mosque in Mosul."

Chapter 13

A couple of days of research and more taxi reconnaissance narrowed down the possible locations for the veil.

There was an ancient spring that completely glowed with the blue power of the female, and there was a spot about thirty feet above the ruins of the Hippodrome that shined with a similar magic. One was the spot of an ancient church. The other had once been occupied by an enormous statue of Hera, that other Queen of Heaven.

They'd have to try both spots.

Meanwhile, pilgrims poured into Istanbul.

The patriarch led the procession himself. It would end, somewhat provocatively, at the enormous doors to the Hagia Sophia Cathedral. Provocatively because the Hagia Sophia had spent five hundred years as a mosque and still carried the Crescent on its highest spire rather than the Cross, which had been put there in a time when the world was still Roman and first becoming Christian.

Zack and Ivy joined an American tourist group being shown around the ancient Hippodrome an hour before the parade was due to arrive.

"There's the truck," Zack observed, barely flicking his gaze toward their first target.

Cejno parked the Turk Telekom truck on the side of the road, about twenty feet from a small group of uniformed U.S. Navy SPs and three black-suited, pale-faced men who glistened with the red glow of their certainty in the Christian faith. The young Kurd hopped out and placed orange construction cones around the truck, closing one lane to traffic, then returned to his truck and lit a cigarette and opened his newspaper. He looked so exactly like the stereotype of a government employee earning his paycheck by sitting on his rear that Ivy had to suppress her laughter.

After another twenty minutes of fascinating lectures on the history of the hippodrome, a hubbub went through the tourists. Everywhere Ivy looked, tour guides were on their phones, or trying to hustle their charges out of the area.

Ivy simply ignored her guide's efforts, until he shrugged his shoulders and left, taking the rest of the tourists with him.

A few moments later, the Patriarch marched in, leading thousands of the faithful and surrounded by jeering Moslems.

The Orthodox Christians carried relics on elaborate palanquins. Several lifted huge Crosses that looked superficially even more impressive than the True Cross in the Telekom truck. Robed and bearded priests mixed with jean-clad teens. Dark-haired mothers herded young children along the parade route.

Ivy shook her head. Children! She hadn't thought things through. She and Zack were soldiers. They'd signed up for danger when they'd agreed to take the government's paycheck. But those young mothers thought they were just here to celebrate their faith. Instead, they'd walked into the lion's den without even realizing it.

And the only things they could do about it was find the veil and then get out of Turkey before things got even worse.

Taking advantage of the distraction, Ivy and Zack slid into the back of the Telekom truck and Ivy stepped into orange Telekom coveralls, finally plastering a yellow hardhat over her hair.

Loud shouts from outside the truck distracted her from the next step, which was to climb on top of the truck and ascend to the mysterious blue glow that hung above the ruins of the ancient Hippodrome.

For a moment, Ivy wondered if the imam had broken his promise. The Turkish youths who surrounded the parade seemed angry and, although she couldn't understand the words, they definitely didn't sound polite. But then she recognized the imam in the crowd and saw he was directing the jeers—and making sure only his trusted and designated few went close to the parading Christians.

The Moslem Turks weren't especially friendly toward the Greek and Slavic marchers but, as the Patriarch had predicted, the long-warring factions could reach agreement when they faced an even greater common threat--the Foundation.

The Foundation agents and SPs tried to stand their ground as the procession filled the streets, but the relic boxes, cross replicas, and palanquins took up too much room.

The Orthodox shoved their way forward, using the boxes as tools to clear their way, pushing the Americans away from their post and dispersing them.

The Moslems took over from there, knocking radios away as Foundation men attempted to call for backup and shoving them further from the blue glow.

"Here goes nothing." Ivy lifted her Cross section through the roof of the Telekom truck, climbed into the cherrypicker, and hammered the control lever to raise her up. She hoped the Cross section would look like a piece of a telephone pole to anyone glancing her way, although someone looking closely would notice a peculiar lack of phone lines overhead.

The cherrypicker seemed to move in slow motion as it lofted her upward. Her skin crawled and she felt the weight of dozens of Foundation killers' eyes on her body. Now that she was lifted above the crowd, any Foundation sniper could take her down.

Over the sound of the praying mob and the shouts of Turkish youths, she made out a few words of English. The sailors and Foundation agents might not be able to reach her, but they'd certainly recognized her: they'd be calling for backup. The young Turks might distract some of them, but Ivy knew that others would get through on their radios or cells no matter what obstacles they faced.

The cherrypicker finally lifted her to the blue area and she forced herself to ignore the danger below—and pay attention to what could be an even greater danger here. The Foundation agents and sailors could only endanger her body—messing with strange religions could endanger her soul.

Unlike the temple to the hawk-headed god, the blue glow didn't push Ivy away. Nor did it welcome her. It simply parted like a fog around her.

She crossed her fingers and brought the Cross section up until its red glare touched the blue, sending a purple sheen as far as she could see.

She directed her cherrypicker through the portal she'd opened. And looked.

Her mouth dropped open.

Hera was enormous. Her head alone was taller than Ivy. The goddess reclined comfortably as she surveyed her realm. Although Ivy knew there was no physical statue of Hera here, the goddess's body seemed more solid than the misty vision of the parade or the road below.

From what Zack and Father Galen had told her, Constantinople had been a Christian city almost from the beginning. Maybe so, but Hera had absorbed considerable power to so dominate this spot where thousands of Greco-Romans had wagered on chariot races, plotted the defense of

Europe against Pagans, Zoroastrians, Arians, and Moslems.

The lifelike statue was so overwhelming that Ivy had to remind herself of her mission. There was no hiding place for a veil here. Their first, best guess had been wrong. If they missed on their second guess as well, they would be in trouble. The Foundation wasn't likely to let them pull the parade stunt twice.

She pushed the lever to descend but was still within the nimbus of Hera's statue when the first bullet whizzed by.

She flashed back to the months she'd spent in Iraq, constantly under fire, never certain whether the next civilian would be begging for food or wired with explosives.

But these weren't Iraqi insurgents shooting at her. They were fellow Americans. And if the firing was the result of a Foundation decision, rather than an overwrought Foundation agent reacting to his frustration, they were in more danger than she'd imagined. Their plan had counted on the Foundation wanting to capture her so they could discover the location of the Cross. Shooting to kill was a whole 'nother problem.

She shifted her Cross section so it would lead her—the last thing she needed was to be stripped out of the cherrypicker as it hit the wall of the statue's nimbus. As before, the Cross opened a portal in the ancient holy site and she was free.

Free to be shot at.

She could barely make out the sound of firing over the noise of the crowd. Fortunately, there didn't seem to be any Foundation snipers. At the ranges they were shooting, and with the jostling, handguns would be inaccurate.

She jerked the control levers on the cherrypicker, trying to make herself a more difficult target and shouted down to Cejno to start driving.

"The truck won't go into gear when the cherrypicker is in the upward."

Great. She needed to ride it all the way down.

The imam's bullyboys concentrated on the gunmen, knocking them down, blocking their clear shots. Ivy looked down and saw she had only a few more yards to the relative safety of the truck.

She was going to make it. It would take a miracle for one of the gunmen to actually hit her at that range, with all of the action going on around them.

That's what she assured herself a couple of seconds before excruciating pain exploded through her leg.

She looked down, then wished she hadn't. Blood spurted from her calf and bone chips littered the front of the cherrypicker where a nearly spent bullet had flattened against the steel.

"Oh, shit."

"Come on, Ivy. Finish coming down. We can help you."

Zack's voice barely penetrated her thoughts. Despite the strength lent her by the Cross, pain cut through rational thought like a chainsaw.

Still, she was a soldier and her officer had given her an order. She jerked the down lever once again before slumping into unconsciousness.

* * * *

Ivy's blood fountained from her leg and the Cross section she carried wobbled from her grip, then tumbled toward him.

Zack caught it, shoved it through the truck's skylight, then reached for Ivy.

She slumped against him and he lifted her out of the cherrypicker's basket and down into the truck.

Her lower leg was shattered and blood sprayed from severed arteries like a garden hose gone berserk.

"Just like back in Iraq," he muttered to himself.

He pressed a spare shirt against the wound. Ivy might lose the leg, but that wouldn't kill her. Loss of blood or shock would kill her and that's what he needed to prevent.

"Drive," he commanded Cejno. "The cherrypicker is in place."

"Shall I go to the second location?" Cejno called from the cab.

"Forget that. Ivy needs a hospital."

"Hospital very dangerous. They ask many questions about gunshot wound."

Zack didn't doubt that. He also didn't care. What was important was saving Ivy's life.

"Got to find the veil," Ivy gasped.

"Screw the veil," he said. "It's an old piece of cloth. You're what's important."

"Romantic but stupid. Better to die now than be tortured to death by the Foundation."

They didn't know the Foundation would torture them. On the other hand, they did know that the Foundation would kill without scruples, and that the Turkish government would turn them over to the Foundation if they caught them. The Turkish government had to be aware of what was going on here in Istanbul. There was no other way they would have permitted these mobs of Shore Patrol sailors to wander the streets of their nation's largest city.

"Try the Cross," Cejno suggested. He grinded the truck's gears as he revved the engine, inching his way through the parade crowd.

Zack didn't think the Cross was going to do the job here. Ivy had been carrying her section of Cross when she'd been struck and the bullet had still ripped a big hole out of her leg. Still, he had the worst of the blood flow controlled. Prayer and a liberal application of the Cross seemed as good an idea as any.

He tied his shirt around her wound, then shifted Ivy so her leg rested propped on the two sections of Cross.

She sighed, then fell back into unconsciousness.

"Well, that didn't work."

"I drive to the second checkpoint," Cejno announced. "Should be able to arrive just as parade hits for maximum safety."

"The Foundation will know we're coming. They'll have been warned about this truck and they'll be shooting to kill."

"I shall pray they fail."

"Even if they don't kill us, so what? I can't see the magical blue barriers or whatever they are. The Cross doesn't respond to me. I'm just here for the ride. And Ivy isn't in any shape to go opening portals."

"It shall be as Allah wills it."

That might be true, but Zack didn't find a lot of assurance in that. While he believed that God cared about him, he didn't think God was going to protect him from his own stupidity.

Cejno didn't seem to be listening, though, so Zack went back to taking care of Ivy.

She was frightfully pale and had lost nearly as much blood as she'd lost when Smith had slit her throat, but she was still breathing. As hot as it was in the truck, Zack didn't have to worry about exposure.

"Just hang in there," he whispered to her. "Somehow we're going to make this right. Maybe the Patriarch can smuggle you to a doctor we can trust."

Ivy's blue eyes opened briefly and she stared at him without positive recognition, then closed her eyes again.

Well, that was effective.

The truck made flapping sounds as it ran over the last of the traffic cones Cejno had set out to make it look like he was on official business, and Cejno honked his horn as he weaved through traffic.

A couple of stars in the windshield showed that the Foundation guys had found their range. Fortunately, they were high and Cejno was short.

The hashish smuggler was on his cell as soon as they'd pulled out of the worst of the crowd. Clicking it off, he leaned back toward Zack, taking his eyes off the road despite the notorious drivers of Istanbul. "Father Galen says all is taken care of."

"He got a doctor lined up?"

Cejno wrinkled his forehead, then glanced back at the road barely in time to avoid smashing into an oversized tourist bus. "He said things is taken care of, that's all. Now I must pay my attentions to the driving."

Cejno looped around the city for a few minutes, running a red light to shake off a motorcycle that had followed them from the Hippodrome before finally pulling the Telekom truck into a treed lot a few hundred meters from where Zack had marked the next blue zone.

They'd planned out the parking spot and were largely hidden from where the Foundation goons were waiting. But someone on the other side was watching. The minute Cejno pulled in, a couple of black-suited Foundation Agents headed toward them, one talking on his cell and the other with his hands conveniently tucked into his jacket.

Zack recognized that look from his gang days. The agent could shoot through his jackets without having to reveal their weapons, meaning Zack would have exactly no time to get a jump on them.

"I think we have about thirty seconds before we're in range," Zack whispered.

"Open the back hatch. It is time to bail."

"I'm not leaving Ivy." If he had any brains at all, Zack would take Ivy and abandon the Cross. If they let the Foundation have their treasure, Zack felt certain the Foundation agents would forget about he and Ivy. It wouldn't be worth their while to pursue vindictive revenge against the woman once they had what they were looking for.

Ivy didn't open her eyes, but she shook her head.

"We need the Cross. We can't let them have it."

She was right, although her mind-reading trick was more than a little disturbing. They'd seen too much of what the Foundation would do, how it behaved, to think they could be trusted with something that could open the doorway to power like that which had transformed a sheep into a man-eating monster.

"I'll take care of it," he promised as he gathered her into his arms.

"Father Galen has a treat for the Foundation men," Cejno promised. "It cost me plenty. Watch."

As the Foundation agents stepped closer, a thick cloud of smoke emerged from manholes and sidewalk grates around them. The Foundation men froze. More started running their way and one pulled a mask over his face but most seemed unprepared for chemical warfare.

Zack sniffed the air. "What is that?"

"Concentrated hashish smoke. We thought it might mellow them."

The Foundation hitmen might worry about losing their jobs for testing positive to cannabis, but Zack thought it would take more than a few quick tokes of smoke to mellow that crew out.

"It will also obscure their vision," Cejno added. "Go."

Zack gathered Ivy and the two cross sections and lugged them from the truck.

"Put her here." Father Galen was beaming at him. A group of eight pilgrims carried a shoulder-born float, draped with crosses. Other pilgrims were quickly arriving, filling the gap between their truck and the Foundation agents.

"What is that?"

"It's a palanquin. We use it to carry relics in procession. Surely the Cross and the saint are relics.

"Saint?"

"Saint Ivy. We've learned from our Moslem brothers that Ivy was killed and brought back to life by the strength of the Lord. Like Lazarus. If that doesn't make her a saint, what could?"

Father Galen's smile faded when he got a good look at all of the blood on Ivy's leg.

"Is she dead?"

"Not yet."

"Then load her up. We've got to get out of here."

The pilgrims filled the area between the truck and the hitmen, but Zack didn't think they'd hold up the determined agents for long. From the way the crowd moved, it looked as if the Agents were using force to shove their way through. A bunch of pilgrims, however inspired by their religion, wasn't going to do much more than slow the trained killers.

Turkish policemen, unseen before then, had started to appear as well and they joined in shoving pilgrims away, out of the Agent's path, clearing a firing zone for the Foundation killers.

For just a moment, though, the smoke, truck, palanquin and other relics obscured the Agent's view. Zack took advantage of that moment to lift Ivy into the palanquin, then put the Cross sections in on either side of her.

"We shall take Ivy to safety. You and Cejno should escape now."

Which meant they were abandoning the quest for the veil. There would be a lot of disappointed pilgrims, but Zack wasn't one of them. Saving Ivy and keeping the Cross out of the Foundation's hands were what mattered to him.

* * * *

Ivy hurt.

Her leg throbbed and her body felt as if she'd been at the receiving end of a severe beating.

It wasn't hot enough to be hell and she didn't feel good enough to be heaven. She must still be alive.

"Time to wake up," Father Galen said.

"What happened?"

"The Foundation agents shot you. But we're at the grotto. We need you to open the hidden way to the veil."

Something about that seemed wrong. "Didn't you tell Zack you had given up on the veil?"

"If he chose to understand my words that way, I am not responsible."

Yeah, right.

Still, she had come to Istanbul to get the veil. Unless the Foundation managed to finish killing her, she was going to keep on trying.

"Okay. Let's go."

Her leg had stopped bleeding, but it still didn't seem capable of bearing her weight. She leaned on Father Galen as she lugged her Cross section toward the deep blue glow of the grotto.

"There was a church here once." Father Galen sounded like he'd seen it, although there were massive trees growing there—trees that had to be generations older than the priest. "Like so many others, the Turks destroyed it."

"I thought the Ottomans allowed their subject people to keep their religions." Ivy had a vague memory of covering that in high school Western Civ. If only Zack were here, he could tell her. He seemed to know all that stuff.

"Tolerance wasn't a highly developed concept back then. You have to remember that the Spanish forcibly converted or expelled their Jews about this same time. By the standards of their time, the Turks were models of moderation. But that says more about the standards of the time than about the Turks. Uh, are we there yet?"

"Just about."

The blue glow held the distinct form of an early medieval church. It lacked the flying buttresses and airy height of the great Gothic Cathedrals of France and Germany, but it projected a solidity and faith that remained even after the church's physical destruction.

At the nave of the invisible church, a spring bubbled from the ground, creating a thin trickle of water that flowed downhill, toward the nearby sea.

For a city so frequently under siege, a fresh-flowing spring would have been a treasure indeed. Around the spring, the faint tracings of an earlier temple glistened the same blue shade as the church. Other ghostly walls showed still more generations of worship. Despite the time they'd spent in this part of the world, Ivy still had problems really grasping how long humans had inhabited these hills and grottos, how many centuries of worshipers had consecrated generations of holy buildings. Compared to Byzantium, Philadelphia was a flash in the pan.

One church had been built on the ruins of another, which in turn had been constructed on even more ancient foundations. All shined with the blue glow Ivy equated with the faith in the Queen of Heaven, although the Queen might have been worshipped under different names.

Ivy touched a hand to the blue glow of the outer church and felt a tingle as her fingers passed through the glow. But they didn't really enter the church. Instead, they remained in normal space.

No change there. She still needed the key, the Cross, to open the gates between the normal world and that strange world where the past lingered on, and where magic and power lay waiting to be tapped.

"I'm going to have to lean on you," she told Galen.

"Good. But move quickly. We threw the Foundation agents off track with the switch, and many of them followed Zack and Cejno, but some are starting to return. And they've called in reinforcements from the police and from their other agents around the city."

She nodded, then used him for support as she pressed the Cross piece to the closed doorway of the immaterial church.

It penetrated easily, even more easily than it had done when she'd entered the area holy to Hera. Either the Cross was somehow learning, gaining power, or maybe she'd changed. Each time she crossed between the dimensions, the barriers seemed weaker.

With the Cross halfway between the physical world and the spiritual world, she let go of the Priest and, hand on the Cross, stepped across.

"Ivy, I can't see you."

Father Galen's voice was excited.

She couldn't blame him. While the discovery of the True Cross was a wonder, seeing a woman step through an invisible wall and vanish was the kind of thing that could reinforce faith in even the strongest doubter. She suspected Father Galen could break free of hashish now that he had been given a true vision.

Without the priest to lean on, Ivy's right leg couldn't support her. She half-hopped and half limped toward the inner temple.

She left the Cross behind her, guarding the portal between mundane and holy, so she reached out her hand and touched the inner temple's door.

It felt as solid as fresh-cut wood and barely resisted when she pushed it open.

Even though it was bright day outside, the thousands of burning oil lamps around it seemed to outshine the mundane light of the sun. In the very middle, surrounded by the glow of magic and oil lamps, stood a low altar of polished stone.

Unlike the altar to the hawk-headed god they'd found in Kurdistan, no sacrificial knife or thick-crusted blood lay here. Surrounded by flowers, a gossamer strip of silky fabric draped over the four-horned altar.

The old story of Mary returning the veil to her own place had more truth than anyone had guessed.

Reaching out and physically touching the holy object somehow seemed even more profane than carrying the Cross. Ivy glanced at her hands to make sure they were clean, that she hadn't carried in the filth of the mundane world to pollute this holy object, then reached out to the altar and picked up the veil.

It was longer and wider than she would have guessed from its thin shape. The material seemed to be silk, or perhaps a linen so fine it could pass for silk. Bright eight-sided stars of silver and gold ran down each side, making the deep sapphire blue of the fabric even more jewel-like.

Its touch sent shivers through her body. For just a moment, she saw through Mary's eyes as Roman soldiers brought Jesus's body from the Cross. Even older visions, of ancient cities and blue-clad priestesses mingled in, hinting that Mary was a part of an ancient tradition.

"Ivy. The police are beating the pilgrims. They'll be on us soon. You must come out now." Father Galen's voice sounded desperate.

Ivy took the veil, then hobbled back to where the Cross sill penetrated the ancient blue walls.

"Hand it to me," Galen urged. His face and hands shimmered through the barrier and she guessed he was holding onto the Cross section.

"I'll hide it."

That sort of made sense. Ivy passed the veil to the waiting priest.

As he touched it, his face lit. "Oh, holy."

Before she could react, say anything, his hands and face disappeared —followed by the Cross. She made a grab for it, held onto it briefly, but her loss of blood had made her too weak. The crossbeam was jerked out of her hands, and it disappeared beyond the misty blue wall.

"Wait. Father Galen!" Didn't he realize she needed the cross to exit this dimension? Then, with horrific certainty, she realized he did.

He'd done this to her on purpose. Worse, he'd deliberately sent Zack and Cejno to their deaths.

Ivy was trapped in the other world—a world without food, without any contact to her everyday Earth.

Without Zack.

Chapter 14

Trapped.

She should have recognized the fanatical look on Father Galen's face. She should never have handed over what he clearly saw as a symbol of rightful Greek ownership of this ancient city.

Recriminations didn't help, though.

Ivy fought the urge to surrender, to sink to the ground and let the power of the invisible church creep over her, subsume her into its embrace and make her a part of something that had endured for hundreds of years while the city outside, the ordinary world of man, hurried by.

But surrender, even surrender to a force that seemed benevolent and loving, wasn't in her. Growing up in the shadows of old Appalachian coalmines, Ivy had learned to fight before she'd attended kindergarten. She wasn't going to stop fighting just because she was locked inside a prison whose walls were not stone or iron, but hundreds of years of faith and prayer.

She closed her eyes and made herself remember exactly where the Cross had penetrated the church wall. Surely some residual weakness would remain.

It made sense, but if there was any breach, Ivy couldn't feel it and certainly couldn't push her way past.

"Think, Ivy," she murmured to herself. "You're a woman. That means you get to outsmart problems rather than bull through them."

One thing the National Guard taught was that the obvious solution was generally the right solution. And the obvious way to get out of a church was to use the doors.

The doors in the little temple in the middle of this larger church had opened easily enough. Would the larger doors on the outside of the church?

She limped over, inspected the latch, threw it, and then opened the doors.

Sunlight flooded in. "A lot of worry for nothing."

The first step was easy. The second step was harder. The third was impossible. The blue glow gave, but like elastic, the harder she pulled against it, the more firmly it pulled her back in.

With her wounded leg, Ivy wasn't up for tug-o-war. She went back into the church and sat on the base of one of the tall Doric pillars that supported the imposing dome overhead.

The talent the Cross had given her really was amazing, she mused. Archeologists and historians would probably pay big bucks to learn about the various layers of the old church—and to get a second look at a building that had been destroyed when Columbus was still wearing short-pants.

She got a start when a Turkish policeman, nightstick in hand, burst through the blue haze of the Church's walls and stepped directly toward her.

"I was just resting," she said in English. "I got a little overwhelmed by all of the things to see in your city."

He ignored her.

"Interesting," she breathed.

The policeman looked around. Some part of him must have sensed that something wasn't right, the type of feeling Ivy's grandmother had claimed was someone "walking over your grave." Then he shook his head and walked on, his feet sometimes sinking beneath the stone floors of the church and sometimes floating a few inches above it.

Ivy hobbled after him, then reached her hand to touch him.

Her hand and arm passed right through him.

Okay, she really was on a different plane or dimension. That made as much sense as anything. The question was, if she stayed close to him, overlapped with him, would she be able to follow him out of the church and back into the world of the mundane?

She didn't have a lot of other thoughts and this one seemed worth a try.

She stepped even closer, until their torsos actually overlapped.

The cop yanked out his handgun and spun around. Clearly he'd sensed more than a vague feeling. Equally clearly, he couldn't see anything because he growled what could only be a Turkish curse, shoved his handgun back in its holster, and strode from the church like a man who wants to get away from a graveyard but doesn't want anyone to know he's frightened.

Ivy's bum leg made it hard for her to keep up, but she forced down the pain and stumbled after him—and slammed into the stone wall of the church as the cop walked straight through it without even noticing it was there.

"Oh, hell," she moaned. "I am so dead."

* * * *

Cejno and Zack used the cover of thousands of pilgrims to stay down, get away from the rampaging cops, and finally duck into the massive Istanbul Bazaar.

Cejno insisted on paying as they both bought a change of clothing—Cejno unzipping the Telekom coveralls he'd worn to put on a western-cut shirt and cowboy hat and Zack a pair of tan slacks and a shirt that looked like it had already seen more than one owner but was at least clean.

Strengthened by a package of dried apricots, Zack was ready to get back to work.

"Where do you think Galen would take Ivy?" he asked.

"Father Galen is not the kind who is easily dissuaded," Zack said. "I think we should find the parade and assume ourselves into it."

It took Zack a second to figure out what Cejno meant, but it was as good a plan as any. The parade had been scheduled to end outside the Hagia Sophia, so they could go there.

At least the Turkish police and Foundation agents would have to be careful there in an area where a thousand videocameras would be filming at any given moment. The Turkish police might not like Greek pilgrims, but they wouldn't want to spoil their city's appeal as a tourist destination by slaughtering a bunch of them either.

"Right. Let's go."

Pilgrims filled the square in front of the Hagia Sophia and a determined line of cops guarded the cathedral's enormous doors, presumably to prevent any attempt by the Archbishop to reclaim the ancient structure as the center of his see. That really would create a riot in this ninety-nine percent Moslem nation.

As the Patriarch led the assembled pilgrims in prayer, Zack and Cejno pushed their way to the front, ignoring angry murmurs and excited hand-gestures from those they disturbed.

"He is saying they have found something wonderful, a true miracle," Cejno whispered. Apparently the kid spoke Greek as well as Turkish, Kurdish, and English. Zack felt like a provincial American.

"The Cross?"

"Perhaps. That doesn't feel—ah—"

The 'ah' was because Father Galen appeared from somewhere behind the Patriarch with a heavy relic box in his arms.

"It's got to be the veil," Cejno announced unnecessarily as the Patriarch lifted the box's lid and raised a long strip of fabric into the air.

The hush from the crowd wasn't that of reverence, but of question. They'd come all this way to see some old piece of fabric? Clearly they'd been expecting something more dramatic. The head of John the Baptist, maybe, or the crown of thorns.

But when the Patriarch announced that they had rediscovered the very veil of the Virgin Mary, protected all these years from looters and invaders, the crowd went wild.

"He's inviting them to return to Constantinople," Cejno translated, "to become a part of this most cosmopolitan city. I think they will like it better if he tells them to go and burn some automobiles."

Zack couldn't disagree with that. But he was getting an increasingly uneasy feeling. Father Galen had at least implied that he had given up on his quest for the veil and that he would take Ivy for help. If he'd been lying about one, he might have been lying about the other as well. Either way, where was Ivy?

He shoved his way through the increasingly dense crowd that gathered to get a closer look at one of the most holy relics of Christianity.

The relic was odd, he thought. Sure it would have been strange if Mary had crosses on her veil. For one thing, the Cross hadn't been adopted as the symbol of the religion until long after Mary's ascension into heaven, and Mary was often associated with stars. But he would have expected six-pointed stars of David rather than the eight-pointed stars actually embroidered into the veil.

Also, while medieval paintings might portray Mary as a Queen, crowned and sceptered, she was still the carpenter's wife, carpenter's mother, wasn't she? So, where had the gold and jewels come from?

"Pretty nice," Cejno said. "The sainted mother of the Prophet Jesus, peace be upon him, is well respected in the Koran."

From what Zack could see of the Patriarch's face, he had some of the same questions Zack did. Of course, the answer was probably that the simple garment of a carpenter's wife had been decorated and made more ornate over the centuries it had been a worshipped object. Six-sided stars of David would not have been used because of the antipathy that had existed between the Christian and Jewish faiths in the middle ages. The five-sided star had sometimes been associated with magic and paganism.

He couldn't remember anything about an eight-sided star. Could they have picked that to avoid confusion?

The crowd thinned out as Zack headed for Father Galen rather than for the relic itself.

"Where the hell is Ivy?" he asked without preamble.

Father Galen jumped. "Ah, Zack. I thought you were going into hiding."

"And I thought you had given up finding the veil. I guess we were both wrong. Now, do you want to answer my question, or should I just tear that answer out of you?"

"Saint Ivy was transformed into the heavenly domain," Galen reported with a solemn face. "I witnessed this myself."

"She's dead?" He was glad he wasn't armed because he would have been tempted to start shooting.

"I did not say that. She passed beyond the veil of the mundane, was translated into the separate world of the holy."

"Translation, you left her in the grotto?"

"She was badly injured, Zack. To bring her back to this world of suffering would be no kindness."

"I'm not interested in kindness. In fact, I'm thinking of ripping your throat out. So, why don't you tell me where you've hidden the Cross and I'll go fetch Ivy?"

"Alas, she took the Cross with her. She handed me the veil, then pulled the Cross after her."

Zack considered. He knew the priest was lying. He also knew that Father Galen was safe now, surrounded as they were by thousands of pilgrims who were aching for a fight and would be just as happy to turn on a western Catholic as they would on a Turkish Moslem.

"I'm going to get her out," he said. "And when I come back, I'm going to collect the veil. So, if you're lying, you'd better start running."

"But..." Father Galen sputtered for words. "But I'm a priest."

"You're also a hashish-smoking weirdo. I'd trust your Patriarch, but I'd only trust you about as far as I could throw you." Considering the bulk of the priest, that wouldn't be far. Still, he was ready to try.

"Will we be able to get in without the Cross?" Cejno asked as Zack turned on his heel and shoved his way away from the Hagia Sophia and toward the grotto where Father Galen had abandoned Ivy."

"If Father Galen wasn't lying, she'll have the Cross with her," he said.

"Of course Father Galen was lying. Didn't you see the way his eyes flickered?"

Zack had missed that. "I'll tear him apart later."

"He means well," Cejno said. "But his vision is small. He wants Greeks to return to Constantinople. Nothing seems more important to him."

"If the Foundation gets the Cross and veil, who lives in Istanbul is way down our list of worries."

"For us, yes. I think Father Galen would turn the rest of the world over to Shaitan himself if doing so would return Constantinople to Orthodox rule."

"If we can't save Ivy, he just might have turned the world over to Shaitan."

* * * *

After her failed attempt to follow the policeman, Ivy rested, letting the blue power of the otherworldly church soak into her tired and injured body, trying to stay calm.

Surely Father Galen would return. Although he was absorbed in his belief, he wasn't a cruel man, and he was a priest.

Instead, as the pilgrims left, Foundation Agents, easily visible by their black suits and the red glow of religious fervor that surrounded them, trickled back into the area of the old church.

Several wandered through the territory of the church, but Ivy was careful not to repeat the experiment she'd tried with the policeman. The policeman had sensed something. She suspected that the Foundation agents would know exactly what they felt—and have weapons that could reach across the barriers that kept her enclosed and made her invisible to ordinary sight.

Although she couldn't make herself touch them, she did hobble toward the nearest one—and then froze when he reacted.

She'd been trained in firearms when she'd gone through basic in the National Guard, and she'd brushed up a lot when she'd gotten word her unit was being shipped to Iraq, but not even her drill inspector moved as quickly or made the gun as much a part of his body as did the agent.

His lips moved as he shouted something out to his fellow agents and they started to converge. One of them reached into his ubiquitous black briefcase and a chill ran down Ivy's back.

Before the Agent withdrew his crucifix, though, the whole group cocked their heads. Several pulled out cells, and started listening.

She strained her ears and could almost make out the words. Although she had no skill at lip-reading, she thought she recognized the shape of the words veil and Cross.

Abruptly the entire group of agents took off running in the direction of the Hagia Sophia.

Being abandoned had never felt better.

Ivy leaned against the insubstantial wall and closed her eyes. Impossible though it seemed, her leg was healing. Either the Cross, which she knew Zack would have put her on, or the power of this ancient and long-vanished church, was accelerating nature's healing power. The matter needed to replace the big hunk of her leg the Foundation Agents had blown away seemed to be coming from other parts of her body. After a few months of Iraqi heat, she'd already been too skinny. Now, she felt emaciated.

Starving to death in this peaceful prison was starting to seem more likely than dying of blood loss and shock.

That wasn't an improvement.

She closed her eyes to rest for a few minutes, and to think about what she could do next.

She didn't even notice Cejno and Zack when they first entered the grotto.

Their conversation barely seeped through the dimensional barrier. Their bodies were insubstantial shadows rather than complete people.

When Zack called her name, though, his meaning penetrated where sound alone could not.

She stumbled to her feet. "I'm here, Zack. Did you bring the Cross?"

He cocked his head as if he'd almost heard her.

She ran to him, threw her arms around him—and watched as they passed through his body without any resistance whatsoever.

"I'm here," she repeated, shouting this time with her lips only inches from his ear—inches and a million miles.

He brushed at his ear as if pawing away a mosquito.

"Damn it, Zack. Get the Cross. You know that's the only way to get through the barrier."

* * * *

"We must go back and get the Cross," Cejno announced. "If she is here, she is beyond the sight of the merely human."

"I don't know how to use the Cross," Zack said. "It's part of Ivy's talent, something she was given when the Cross brought her back."

"Then you must kill me and put me on the Cross. When I am healed, I too may be able to see between our world and the world of Allah." The young man looked horribly pale, but wonderfully brave.

Zack shuddered. "The Cross didn't help much when Ivy got shot. It's too big a risk."

If anyone was going to lay down his life on a long-shot to save Ivy, it was going to be him, not the Kurdish teen who'd already gone way beyond the bounds of hospitality and kindness. "Not that I wouldn't try something if we actually had the Cross."

"I can speak to the imam. The Moslems could riot for real rather than for play."

Zack shook his head firmly. He hadn't quite bought into Ivy's theory that the Foundation was seeking the relics that could provoke a war between the faiths, but he wasn't going to risk launching one himself. Especially with no certainty that it would help Ivy.

"Give me a second, will you?"

It was strange that Ivy, with her casual attitude toward religion, had been tagged as the saint, while he, who had always been devout, was nothing more than her sidekick. But that didn't make his faith any less genuine. He knelt and prayed.

Lord, help me find Ivy now. I need her and the world needs her.

It would have been a good time for a divine revelation. Unfortunately, no trumpets blared, no deep voice thundered instructions, no bushes burned. A bug kept buzzing in his ears, distracting him from his prayer, but he waved it away and really tried to concentrate.

None of it did any good.

He shoved his hands in his pockets and turned to Cejno. "All right, let's go beat up on Father Galen."

"I can offer him more Hashish."

"I thought you were out."

Cejno shrugged. "I did not tell the priest the complete truth when he demanded more. His greed is too vast."

Zack felt a strange shape in his pocket and absently pulled out the St. Christopher medal he'd stuffed there the day he and Ivy had first fought their way free of the Iraqi insurgents. Since then, he'd transferred it from pocket to pocket whenever he'd managed a change of clothing. The modern Catholic Church had stripped St. Christopher of his Saint's Day and relegated him to a sort of ambiguous status, but more traditional Catholics like Zack's mother still swore by the giant's protective power.

If he were going to go beat up a priest, he'd need all the protection he could get. Ol' Chris might not do him any good, but he'd be able to tell his mother he'd done everything possible when he got back to Texas.

* * * *

Ivy's throat was raw from shouting at Zack, her fists bleeding from when she'd tried to touch him and instead banged into walls that Zack simply walked through. She wasn't ready to despair, but she couldn't deny feeling down.

Then he pulled out his St. Christopher medal.

Unlike the rest of the external world, which remained blurred and distant from her vantage point, the silver metal glistened with hard solidity as Zack draped it over his muscular chest.

He'd told her that his mother had given him the St. Christopher as protection during his distant travels. She hoped Zack's mother wouldn't mind if she shared a bit of that shelter. Nobody needed protection more than Ivy did, and she knew of no one on earth who had traveled so far.

The bright gleam of the St. Christopher medal was a ray of hope, but a ray that was getting away fast.

Zack was already near the boundary to the grotto and walking out when he took out the medal. She launched himself at him, grasping for his shoulders with one arm while her left hand reached for the medallion.

Her body slipped through his and she slammed into the hard glowing walls of her prison when her fingertips finally reached the medallion.

"Something's choking me. Cejno, help me get this medal away from me before it tears off my head."

She could make out his words, although they seemed impossibly distant, like an accidental signal picked up by a radio.

"Don't you dare," she screamed. It was a thin lifeline indeed, but if Zack took off the chain, she would be left holding a silver medal on the wrong side of the barrier.

"Ivy? It's almost like I can hear her, Cejno."

Cejno's eyes bugged out over the way Zack's medal hung straight out from his body, defying gravity. As if he hadn't seen a lot of stranger things since they'd been hanging around together.

"Perhaps it is Ivy trying to come through, but also perhaps it is a monster from the other side," the smuggler suggested.

Details of the mundane world were getting clearer. Ivy could hear Cejno as well. Unfortunately, her body still rested where it had fallen on a stone floor inches higher than the dirt where Zack stood, solidly trapped in the walls of power.

"Shout out a warning if it's dangerous, Ivy," Zack said. "Is it you, or a monster?"

"Me, obviously."

"A monster could imitate her voice," Cejno warned.

"I'm willing to take that chance."

Which was a relief for Ivy. But not much of one. Unlike the Cross, which opened a portal from the mundane to the mystical universe of power, Zack's medal had an existence in both the world of the mundane and that of faith and power, but it didn't really open anything.

She'd have to do this the hard way.

She wrapped her fingers completely around the St. Christopher medal and savored the sensation of something solid, earthly, mundane.

Her leg twinged as she built a connection to the darker world outside, and she shivered. Maybe Father Galen had been right and she was best off if she stayed within the protective power of the temple. Maybe her wounds would reopen if she managed to breach the barriers. Maybe she'd cross over and instantly die.

She shoved her doubts away. Dying quickly of battle-wounds was better than a slow and lonely death by starvation.

Since she'd fallen down when she'd grabbed for the St. Christopher medal, the chain around Zack's neck was supporting almost all of her weight. Which meant either the chain would break or he'd choke to death. Neither was an attractive option.

She pulled her feet under her to take the weight off the chain and considered.

She needed to deepen the connection between herself and the mundane world.

Getting closer to the Turkish cop hadn't done her any good at all. Getting close to the Foundation Agents had nearly gotten her killed. Getting closer to Zack seemed simultaneously dangerous and unlikely to help. But she didn't have any choice.

She stepped into him, brought her lips to his, wrapped her right arm, the one she wasn't holding the medal in, around his shoulders. She concentrated every ounce of her energy, every drop of concentration on deepening the connection between Zack and herself.

Her arm passed through his body as if he were no more solid than a fog. Her lips met his and didn't touch. Her tongue tasted nothing but the acidic ozone of mystical energy.

Her plan hadn't worked.

Chapter 15

Zack knew Ivy was at the other end of his chain, hanging on for dear life. He couldn't have explained how he knew, but he was certain.

That was about the only certainty he had. Because his body seemed to be acting up in mysterious ways. One thing that didn't make sense at all was for him to be sexually aroused.

He closed his eyes and strained for any contact from Ivy on the other side of the invisible wall. But straining only made her seem more distant.

Finally, acting against every instinct, he forced himself to relax, using the muscle-by-muscle approach a yoga-loving physical therapist had taught him while he'd been recovering from a Baghdad roadside bomb during his previous tour of duty.

Starting with his toes, he willed each muscle group into submission.

He slowly overcame his soldier-trained instincts to stay alert, to be instantly ready for an attack and made himself open to whatever might happen.

His imagination started playing tricks on him.

Ivy's hand, disembodied and hanging in midair, appeared, apparently solid. But, impossibly, it didn't obscure the shape of the ancient saint, which was completely enclosed within her fist. Then the hand vanished again, leaving him to wonder whether he was fooling himself.

Cool softness pressed against his lips—"an angel's kiss," his mother would have called it. But no face slanted against his own.

A feather's weight pressed against his shoulders, then impossibly entered into his body, pressing through it without disturbing anything but leaving him with a feeling that he had been vulnerable, that Ivy, or the demon if it wasn't Ivy, could have reached in and rearranged things without his being able to do anything to prevent it.

He had to have faith. Faith that this was Ivy. Faith that she'd chosen <u>him</u> as her bridge to the Istanbul of the present and from the lost Constantinople of the Roman Empire. If he had faith, he could only do what she asked.

He tried to kiss her back.

One moment, his lips met a cool fog. A moment later, he was kissing a warm, breathing, and completely delectable female.

He opened his eyes, fearful that his imagination had run completely wild. But she was here, she was real--and she was kissing the daylights out of him.

And now she was going to think him a big pervert for pushing his straining erection directly into her crotch.

"You made it. Thank God. I was worried sick about you." He held her, fearing that if he let him go, she might vanish again, return into the mists that had hidden her from his sight.

She pulled away abruptly. "That was tough."

That wasn't the reaction he'd hoped for. "Sorry."

"Yeah. Me too."

So much for any fantasy that she wanted him. "How's your leg?"

She bent down and pushed on it. "Seems to be healed. This magic stuff is weird and unpredictable, but it has a lot of power."

"No kidding."

Even when she'd moved, she'd kept one hand gripped on Saint Christopher, that hand also resting on his chest. Now she let it go, finger by finger, her face showing her fear that, without the medal, she'd be whisked back into whatever invisible world had kept her trapped.

He'd never forget the grin she gave him when she didn't vanish back into the blue haze or wherever it was she'd been trapped. The imam had called her a saint. With that smile, she could certainly model for any religious painting.

"Father Galen stole the veil from me," she said.

"I think he's got the Cross too," Zack admitted.

Her smile vanished. "Those objects are too dangerous. We've got to get them back and take them to Venice."

Zack nodded. He was way past questioning Ivy's visions now. If she said it needed to happen, he would do his best to make it happen. "I'm open to suggestions."

"We go to the Patriarch," Cejno said. "We tell him Father Galen steal these things. He give them back to us."

It wasn't much of a plan, especially since they didn't know that Father Galen hadn't just been following the Patriarch's orders. But they had to start somewhere. Zack didn't have any better ideas. From the grim look on her eyes, Ivy didn't either.

* * * *

The pilgrims melted away.

They would have rioted for the Patriarch and for the incredible miracle of Mary's Veil, returned after so many hundred years. They would have fought for him, burned for him, killed for him, even died for him. What they wouldn't do was live for him. Not here. Not in Constantinople, the city of so many of their ancestors.

Tears blurred the Bishop's vision as he greeted those who stopped to pay their respects before returning to their homes.

When he'd been a child, not so very many years before, the streets of Constantinople still rang with the musical sound of the Greek language. Back then, church bells competed with the Mosque's calls to prayer. The dream of a cosmopolitan city rather than a wholly Turkish one, a dream that had been sustained by both Roman and Ottoman Emperors, had not seemed impossible.

Back then, his seminary had been filled with fellow students, Greek by culture and language but Turkish by nationality and birth. Then, the young were everywhere. The land of their fathers and grandfathers and countless generations had still been largely Greek.

But that had been before. Before the anti-Christian pogroms that had created fear in a city that had once welcomed everyone. Before steady and insidious pressure to make Turkey a unified whole—despite treaties and agreements. Both priests and parishioners had fled, driven from a city where their ancestors had lived for two thousand years, from a part of the world where Greeks had thrived a thousand years even before that, going back to the days of Achilles and Odysseus. Greeks had survived in this land through Trojan, Persian, Macedonian, Roman, Gothic, Hunish, Arab, Slavic, Bulgar, Seljuk, Ottoman, and finally nationalist Turkish invasion and conquest.

But no more. The dreams were dying. The Miracle of the Veil's return had proven to be more bitter than sweet. Perhaps Mary had been right to take the Veil and hide it. Perhaps he had been wrong to drag it out of its holy resting place for the gratification of a mob and the crushing of his dreams.

"Dream new dreams," his visitors whispered to him. Even priests who had studied with him, here in Constantinople, but who had fled the city in the hard years shook their heads when he begged them to stay.

"Constantinople is lost to us, at least for our generation. Perhaps one day, we shall return like the Jews have to Jerusalem, but our time is not yet. Faith, even with the protective shield of the veil, cannot protect us. The Turks do not welcome us."

It was easy for them to say. They had their parishes, their Greek, Serbian, or Bulgar weddings and babies. They had the resurgent Church in Russia as a solid anchor of support. They didn't face vast but empty cathedrals of faith, the few graying faces of those too old to flee trembling on the edge of their benches as if only waiting to be swept into the arms of the Lord.

The Patriarch had no new dreams to dream; he had only his old dreams, dreams his father had whispered to him when he'd come home drunk, telling him of the war, of betrayal by the French, the incompetence of the Greek Generals, but that some day, Constantinople would stand at the head of a renewed Greek nation, would lead the world from the darkness of their dangerous days.

When he'd dared touch the True Cross, then again when Father Galen had handed the veil to him, the Patriarch had believed that those old dreams would come true.

The last of the priests who'd been visiting him left and the Patriarch wiped his eyes, gathered the wine glasses, and rinsed them off in his sink, smiling to himself as he imagined his housekeeper's face if she saw what he was doing.

So be it. He was the servant of the servant.

The creaking sounds of the old building didn't surprise him. Constantinople has a revered place among the Orthodox Bishops, but his Church lacked the strict hierarchy of western Catholicism. Respect flowed upward from the many Orthodox churches around the world, but little money came with it. And the few hundreds of the faithful remaining in the ancient city couldn't afford the maintenance all of the Church's structures required. He spent what money they had on Churches, on the poor and aged. Little had been spared for his personal comfort.

He started, though, when a shadow moved against the wall.

"You have stolen what is ours."

He whirled around to see the people whose gift had made his dream seem within reach.

The woman's pants had been ripped and a solid sheet of dried blood covered the torn fabric and had soaked through her once-white athletic shoes. The man looked angry and he certainly looked as if he knew how to handle the submachine gun he carried as lightly as a toy. Father Galen's torturer, the young Kurdish smuggler, lagged behind them.

"I don't understand." He considered offering them wine, but they didn't seem in the mood for conversation.

"Where is my Cross? Where is my Veil?"

"Both remain within the protection of the Holy Church. Where else should such precious objects remain?"

"They are not yours, your Grace. We need them back if we're going to prevent something horrible."

The woman had changed. A priest learns to recognize the eyes of someone who has peered beyond the ordinary world and gazed too deeply on the holy. There is a reason why the Lord shrouds so many of his mysteries from casual view. Her tall and slender form had gone gaunt, but she stared at him with neither anger nor mercy. So the angel set by God to stand guard at the Garden of Eden must look. Wisely did the angels tell the shepherds to fear not, for the face of an angel inspires both awe and dread.

"Father Galen told me you had given the Cross and Veil to us," the Patriarch said. "If he was lying, of course you shall have them. I hope, though, that once you have finished, you can return the Veil to Constantinople. It has been a symbol of our city for a thousand years or more."

The woman considered, then nodded. "If it can be done, it will be done. But I need them now."

He glanced at his watch. He should be in bed. It was after three in the morning and he was expected to perform mass in a few hours. But a man does not ask questions or complain of the hour when an Angel of the Lord visits him and tells him to rise.

"We'll go to Father Galen now and recover the relics."

"That is a wise decision," Ivy said.

* * * *

It was about time something went right.

The Patriarch seemed subdued, but the red glow of his faith still surrounded him.

Ivy was ever-conscious of power now. Back in eastern Turkey, she'd had to shut her eyes to see its outlines. Now, she sometimes had to concentrate to see the real world through the bright glare of the holy and anti-holy.

The Bishop led them through narrow alleyways to a two story stone building that stood out from all of the similar buildings around it only by being a bit more dilapidated, then pounded on the massive doorknocker.

It took a good five minutes before a priest finally opened the door, an angry scowl on his face.

The scowl vanished when he saw who was knocking. "Your All Holiness!"

169

"Bring Father Galen to me."

"At once, your All Holiness. Will you and your guests wait here?" He ushered them in, giving Ivy what looked like an unfriendly gaze. She knew that the Orthodox allow married priests, but this one still seemed uncomfortable with the presence of a woman.

Or maybe it was the Kalashnikov around her shoulders.

The priest shot another look at her, then squeaked out of the waiting room and backed up the stairs.

He reappeared moments later, sweat glistening on his forehead. "Father Galen is not here, Your All Holiness."

That couldn't be good news.

"We will inspect his apartment," the Patriarch announced before Ivy had a chance to react.

He swept forward, not giving the priest a moment to complain or come up with a reason why something like this was simply not done.

Ivy tagged along, her hands relaxed but ready to swing around the assault rifle if anyone made a suspicious move.

A row of identical doors lined the second story hallway. Only one of these was opened. Without hesitation, the Patriarch led them to it, then stepped inside.

"Father Galen does not usually leave his room in such a state," the priest explained as they stared at the ransacked closet, the open chest of drawers, and the books spilled from a large bookcase. "I cannot understand what possessed him."

Ivy could guess. "He was packing."

"But he hasn't asked his superiors for permission to travel and his vacation isn't scheduled for months," the priest argued.

She shrugged.

Ivy wouldn't have guessed that greed would have motivated the fat priest, but the monetary value of Mary's Veil and the True Cross would have to be measured in millions, if not billions, of dollars. With the possible exceptions of the Ark of the Covenant and the Holy Grail, these were the most holy artifacts in the Christian religion.

"He is a faithful member of the Church," the priest protested.

"All our faiths are continually tested," the Patriarch reminded him. "Mine has been tested severely over the past twenty-four hours as I realized that not even the return of Mary's Veil would bring our people back to the holy city. Father Galen is not the strongest vessel, although I have always believed him to mean well. Gather all of the priests you can and follow me to the treasury."

"It might be dangerous," Zack said.

"No one ever claimed that the Lord's work must be easy."

He set off at a clip that Ivy thought admirable.

* * * *

Constantinople had been looted by the Catholics during the infamous Fourth Crusade, and by the Turks when the Empire had finally fallen. Ivy would have guessed that the city's conquerors would have left the Church's treasury bare.

She would have guessed wrong.

The Patriarch punched a combination into an electronic lock as sophisticated as anything Ivy had seen in any U.S. bank and stepped into a huge warehouse that glistened with gold and with every color of power.

"When the Roman Emperors created Constantinople as the New Rome, they moved many of the Eternal City's ancient treasures here," the Patriarch said when he saw Ivy's interest. "We hold in our treasury the ancient gods from the thousands of cities and tribes the Romans conquered, as well as objects remaining from the destruction of the Second Temple in Jerusalem and many relics of the prophets and disciples of our Lord. We protected many of them from both Franks and Turks."

"Where are the Cross and Veil?" Zack got to the point.

The Patriarch led them to a second vault, then froze when he saw that its door was ajar.

He struggled to push the armored steel door open until Zack lent his muscle.

The vault stood empty.

"When the pilgrims refused to stay, I was horribly disappointed," the Patriarch said. "That must have been a test of faith for Father Galen as well. A test that, tragically, he seems to have failed."

"Where would he have taken them?" Zack demanded.

The Patriarch shrugged. "I cannot believe he would simply sell them. Perhaps he intends to use them to set up a heretical church of his own. Maybe he thought to smuggle them out to our sister church in Rome, or the wealthy Orthodox Church in Russia."

"Whatever he plans," Ivy said, "he won't make it far. The Foundation learned of the Veil and it must have realized we'd sprung their trap. They'll be over Galen like flies on, uh, honey."

"When the Foundation finds him, they'll kill him," Zack added. "These are not nice people."

"Perhaps we should notify the police," the Patriarch said. "They might be able to find Father Galen before the Founda—"

"Your police are working with the Foundation," Ivy interrupted.

"We've got to go after him ourselves."

She looked at her watch. It was after three in the morning. The Foundation wouldn't let a little thing like darkness get in their way, but their agents had been working all day and would be nearly as tired as she was. It was possible that they hadn't immediately picked up on Galen's theft. If he'd left in the middle of the night, he might have gotten a jump on them. He might be able to stay ahead for a few hours. Time enough to catch up with him--maybe.

"If Galen stays in Istanbul, the Foundation will find and kill him. If he's not a complete idiot, he knows that and he wouldn't leave without a plan, some sort of bolt-hole he thinks is going to get him out of this with both the relics and his life."

In her opinion, whatever Galen's plan might be, it didn't stand a chance. The Foundation had shown an unhealthy ability to track down the Cross wherever it went. And Galen was an obese and sedentary Priest, not a battle-hardened soldier like Zack or even herself.

The Patriarch nodded. "Perhaps. But how does this help us?"

Cejno shuffled his feet. "I could, perhaps, contact some of my friends. But they will want money."

Now it was Ivy's turn to get nervous. In her bank account back home she had a couple of thousand dollars. She didn't think that was the kind of cash Cejno's "friends" would be interested in. For that matter, she doubted if they would take an IOU. Zack was probably a bit better off than her—a Captain's pay is significantly better than an NCO's, but that still didn't make him a moneybags. And recently, Cejno had been subsidizing them.

"We'll get them money somehow," Zack promised.

"Remind them that the Foundation Agent I killed had a briefcase full of hundred-dollar bills," Ivy said.

Zack turned on her, horror showing on his face. "You're talking about murder. Setting Americans up as targets."

"I'm talking about saving the world from something more horrible than Hiroshima."

* * * *

Zack sighed. He was tired and it was only going to get worse.

With a loan from Cejno, flush after his hashish sales, the remaining hundred dollar bills Cejno had returned to them, and an offer of ten thousand Euros from the Patriarch, they put together a reward for the underworld. Enough, they hoped, to be interesting.

The reward taken care of, the Patriarch commanded a small army of priests to search the neighborhood churches and cathedrals for any evidence of Father Galen. Zack, Ivy, and Cejno took responsibility for the seamier side of the city.

"Father Galen isn't an idiot," Zack said. "He would have joined with some of the pilgrims and headed back toward Greece or Bulgaria. You saw all of the crucifixes and icons they carried. I'd think all that stuff would provide a sort of religious radar cover for whatever the Foundation uses to track the Cross."

Cejno had shaken his head. "He will try to get hashish first."

Which was why they were standing outside of a highrise condo complex where the average monthly apartment rent was probably higher that what Zack made in a decade.

"I don't sense anything," Ivy admitted.

"Would you? I mean, through the walls and everything?"

"Maybe. I'm still learning how this second sight works. I don't know how long the Foundation has been working on this, but I'm guessing they have a lot more practice than I do."

Maybe. But what they were very unlikely to have was someone who had been brought back to life by the Cross or who had held the Veil of the Virgin Mary in her hands.

"We go up and pay a visit on my friend," Cejno suggested.

"How do we get past security?" They could possibly break into a second story apartment, then use the elevators to head up to the tenth floor where Father Galen's pusher lived, but the odds of getting caught were pretty high.

"Trust me," Cejno said.

He waved them to come after him and tromped directly into the marble and plush carpet security lobby.

The guard looked up from his desk, then gave a double-take when he saw the submachine guns over Ivy and Zack's shoulders.

The thick armored Plexiglas separating him from the visitor portion of the lobby muffled his voice, but not enough. He was practically screaming at Cejno.

Cejno opened his wallet and showed the guard the thick sheaf of U.S. Hundreds and 500 Euro bills and proceeded to give the security guard what Zack guessed was a lecture on his need for a bodyguard.

The security guard considered, then shook his head, shaking it more firmly when Cejno offered him one of the five hundreds. He did look longingly at the large lump of hashish Cejno added to the bribe, but finally shook his head again. Letting an armed squad into his building would cost him his job and a cushy job like that had to be worth more than a few hundred Euros and a good high.

"Have him phone your contact," Ivy broke in. "It's not like we want to hurt the guy. We just want to make him rich."

Cejno's face showed he hadn't even considered that idea. Zack hadn't either. He'd been assuming they would have to trick the dealer into giving up his customer. But if he knew Father Galen was heading out of town, he wouldn't have much residual loyalty to him anyway.

Cejno passed the thought to the guard who picked up the phone and then grabbed the hashish lump from the security opening before Cejno could get it back.

"I leave it there of purpose," Cejno whispered, in English. "He feels better, get the jump on us."

After a few minutes on the phone, the guard buzzed them through and they rode the elevator to the dealer's apartment.

* * * *

Zack had expected nice. He hadn't expected to be whisked into the world of the Arabian Nights or the land of Odysseus's Lotus Eaters.

The elevator opened directly into a huge chamber carpeted with what looked like antique Persian carpets. Beautiful women, mostly dark-haired, but some blonde or redheaded, swirled around in skimpy silk pants and halters. The hemp smoke was almost thick enough to get Zack high just by breathing.

A cosmopolitan group of Europeans, rich Americans, and Arab princes smoked oversized water pipes, played cards, drank single malt whiskey, and allowed the beautiful women to distract them occasionally.

A young Turk in an Italian suit that probably cost five thousand dollars gave Cejno a nod and said something in Turkish.

"Speak English," Cejno suggested. "My friends are limited in their education."

The elegant Turk bowed to them. "Welcome to my home," he said in perfect English. "I hope you don't plan to rob me with those guns. You would never leave the building alive."

Zack shook his head. "We're looking for friends, not enemies."

The Turk's smile gleamed white. "You have definitely come to the right place. We are all friends here."

"We're looking for one particular friend," Ivy said. "Someone I think you know. Father Galen. He's an Orthodox priest."

"I rarely give my friend's names away, even to other friends." He looked like he sincerely regretted not being able to help. He also looked like he'd already be heading back to an overly buxom blonde if his attention hadn't become fixated on Ivy.

What Zack noticed, though, was the slight emphasis on the word 'rarely.' He hadn't said never.

"Galen's life is in danger. His dope-buying days are over if we don't get help."

"Everyone wants to help Father Galen. I suspect that some of those who say they want to help him may be lying."

"Has someone else been looking for the priest?" Zack knew he should fake indifference, but he couldn't. If this drug dealer had sent the Foundation ahead of them, they were in serious trouble.

"Perhaps. And perhaps their financial incentive was more generous than the puny reward I understand you can offer."

That should have been obvious. Of course they'd never be able to outbid the Foundation. From everything they'd seen, the Foundation as good as had access to the printing presses back in the U.S. Mint. They could only hope the priests found something on their end because the underworld was a dead end.

Ivy, however, didn't give up easily.

"You're a Moslem, aren't you?"

He shrugged. "I'm a Turk. Of course I'm a Moslem."

She shook her head. "A real Moslem. You believe. You've done the Hajj. You mean it when you pray."

"How could you know that?"

"Miss Ivy is a Saint," Cejno said. "She has the second sight."

The Turk lost that dreamy lusty look in a hurry. "All right. This is true. I am a believer. But your Father Galen means nothing to me. I am not obligated to favor one group of infidels over another."

"How would you feel about a war between Moslems and Christians?" Ivy demanded. "A war launched by Christian extremists and aimed at destroying the entire Moslem population."

"Allah will prevent it."

"Do you Moslems have a saying about Allah helping those who help themselves? Does Allah want you to just let it happen and force him to step in? In the story of David and Goliath, David picks up five stones. He's going to give it his best shot, not test God by picking only one. Maybe you're Allah's way of preventing this war."

The drug dealer's face grew first red, then deadly pale under Ivy's attack.

As she trailed off, he turned to Cejno.

"She is a Saint? This is not a lie?"

"More than one holy imam has so asserted."

"Then I will do what I can to help. Unfortunately, I fear it is too late. I gave the CIA men what they wanted to know hours ago. By now, they will surely have Father Galen in their custody."

"If they catch him, they'll kill him," Zack said.

Chapter 16

Istanbul is one of the world's great natural harbors. Standing at the junction between the Black Sea and the Mediterranean, Europe to the west and Asia to the East, and with the Suez Canal only a few hundred miles to the south, Istanbul rested, as it had for thousands of years, at the crossroad between cultures, continents, religions, and worlds.

That's what Zack explained to her. To Ivy, it just looked like there were a whole bunch of ships there, everywhere all around because the core city was a peninsula practically surrounded by water.

The drug dealer, whose name turned out to be Mustafa, after the famous creator of modern Turkey, drove them across the Bosphorus Bridge, back to Asia. A dozen bodyguards, including three of the beautiful women from the party now dressed in practical commando clothing, followed Mustafa's Mercedes in tiny Opals.

Father Galen had been smart enough to know the Foundation would be watching official border crossings. He'd gone to Mustafa for advice on smuggling himself, and his stolen relics, out of Turkey. Mustafa had given him the name of a tramp freighter.

A couple of hours later, he'd shared the name of that steamer to the Foundation Agent who'd visited his home, somehow getting through the security system that had stopped Zack and Ivy. Finally, he'd provided that information to Zack and Ivy.

The Foundation Agents had paid Mustafa fifty thousand U.S. dollars, in sequentially numbered hundred dollar bills, for the information. Zack and Ivy didn't pay anything. Ivy's insight into Mustafa's character had proven enough.

"I'd hide for the next few weeks," Zack said when Mustafa mentioned the amount of money he'd extorted out of the Foundation. "I wouldn't be surprised if they decide you know too much, and try to clean up their mess."

If Mustafa hadn't been having a party with some of the jet set of Europe and America, Ivy guessed they would have cleaned things up right there rather than wasting their money.

"Perhaps it is time to visit my suppliers in Kurdistan," Mustafa agreed. "I hear the mountains are quite beautiful this time of year."

"I think you will need only a few of your most attractive bodyguards," Cejno effused. "We can have a very nice vacation. Very restful."

"What about Mijgul?" Ivy reminded him. "I don't think your girlfriend would take kindly to the competition."

Cejno reconsidered. "Perhaps the female bodyguards should stay in Istanbul."

They slowed down as they approached the wharfs. Dawn peered over the horizon and was reflected back by dark waters.

"Looks quiet," Zack breathed.

Ivy let herself hope they'd beaten the Foundation Agents here and could get in and off without anyone getting hurt. Surely it would take the Foundation a while to get their assets in place. It had been pure luck that Mustafa had been willing to launch himself into their adventure.

She could hope, but she wouldn't count on it.

"I'm going on board the ship. Zack, stay hidden and be ready to provide me cover if anyone spots me. I'd recommend that the rest of you get out of here if you don't want to be caught in a crossfire."

Mustafa shook his head. "That a Saint recognizes my faith is a great day in my life. I am not a very good man and have often run when I should fight. This time, I stay and help."

"It's dangerous."

He reached into his glove compartment and pulled out a solid black automatic—a nice Glock. "Have you ever met an old drug dealer? In America, you may have them. Here in Turkey, we die young. Why not take a chance when I can do something good rather than only evil?"

Males. "Right. If you, Cejno and your bodyguards will provide cover, then I'll go in with Ivy," Zack said before Ivy could argue any more. "Let's move."

"I'm on point," she insisted.

"Fine."

She moved.

Crates of supplies, pallets of freight, and a couple of rusty and warped containers that looked like rejects from the regular merchant service gave them plenty of cover as they approached the old freighter.

The small ship was so covered in filth and rust that Ivy couldn't even guess what color it had once been. No flag flew anywhere onboard. A pump poured a steady stream of rusty water into the Marmara Sea.

Two gangplanks provided access to the ship, but Ivy ignored them. Instead, she swarmed up a line that tied the ship to the wharf, entering at the bow.

Zack waited until she was on board, his Kalashnikov silently fanning the deck, and then followed while she covered him scanning for any hint of movement on the deck.

Ivy hadn't spent much time around ships, but something seemed wrong. Why weren't there sailors on deck? Surely they should be loading and unloading. Even if most of their merchandise moved at night, wouldn't they pretend to be legitimate?

Mustafa, Cejno, and the bodyguards were almost invisible as they covered the ship's gangways, hiding themselves in the clutter of the wharf. They were willing, but Ivy wondered how much actual damage they could do with a collection of overpriced handguns. Maybe she should have swapped weapons with Mustafa, giving him a gun with some range and firepower. But she'd made her decisions and it was too late to change them.

Zack climbed over the bow and kept moving, leapfrogging her hiding place next to a small crane.

He crouched next to a stack of ropes and waved her forward. She moved, leapfrogging him in turn as each provided cover for the other, protected each other, worked as a team.

She wasn't a professional soldier, had once looked forward to getting back to real life, but she was glad she'd had the chance to experience the teamwork and co-dependence that the infantry creates and requires. Like a circus trapeze artist, she was willing to let go of her connection to safety and fly, knowing that Zack would be there to catch her.

She skidded to a stop when she saw Zack wasn't giving her cover. He was looking at a lump on the ship's deck.

With an abrupt change of focus, she realized that the lump wasn't the pile of trash she thought she'd seen. It was a body.

"Murdered," he whispered. "His throat was slit."

She swallowed hard, then nodded. "No wonder it's so quiet. The Foundation got here first."

Zack held up his hand, dripping with the dead man's blood from where he'd tried to find a pulse. "Maybe. But this body is still warm. He hasn't been dead much more than five minutes and nobody has left the ship in that time. They're still on board."

For a moment, the soft swish of bilge water being pumped into the sea was the only sound Ivy heard.

Then she noticed the stream of blood from the corpse into the scupper. "That isn't rusty water, it's bloody water being drained. We're on a slaughter-ship."

He nodded. "Maybe. And maybe we should get off and rejoin Cejno and Mustafa. The Foundation Agents are going to have to get off sometime and we can trap them when they come."

She considered. She'd seen too much death when she'd been in Iraq and didn't have any sick compulsion to see more now. Unfortunately, the easy way was too risky.

"They may plan on helicopter evacuation or to head out to sea. The Navy is only a few miles away, you know. We've got to stay on board until we know their plans."

"You're right. Damn."

She liked the fact that he didn't argue with her, didn't try to hold to positions that weren't right. Most of the guys she'd known over the years would assume she was wrong just because she was a woman.

"I'm moving toward the stern."

He nodded and Ivy checked to make sure no Agent head had popped up from below the decks before sprinting to the next cover.

Another corpse, his face distorted by a second grin cut into his throat, met her in what seemed to have been a smoking area. A cigarette butt still smoldered on the deck.

She felt for a pulse with one hand while waving Zack forward with the other.

No pulse, but there was movement. A large freight hatch groaned, then slowly opened.

Zack hit the deck about ten meters short of his next hiding place, rolling away from the hatch as he brought his Kalashnikov into firing position.

"What should we do with the priest?" The distinctly Midwestern America accent left no doubt in Ivy's mind that they'd discovered Foundation Agents.

"This thing weighs a goddamn ton."

"Adams, you're on report. I've spoken to you about that language."

"Sorry, Jones."

It wasn't the same Jones who'd gotten wounded in Mosul, Ivy saw. Apparently they weren't very imaginative with the names.

"We going to take the priest on board the carrier?" Adams asked.

"Not sure the choppers have that kind of heavy lift capacity."

"Smith says to kill him," Jones ordered. "Then pour gasoline on him and throw the veil on top. We definitely don't want to encourage any sort of Mary fetish, and the bosses can't use that kind of power."

"You've got it."

A muffled squawk told Ivy that Father Galen was still alive, at least for the moment.

She waited until they'd lifted both sections of Cross onto the deck and prodded Father Galen up after before gesturing to Zack to stay under cover and then stepping out, her AK-47 aimed directly at the Agents.

"Thank you for returning our items, gentlemen. And we'll take the priest off your hands as well. His superiors have been looking for him."

Jones met her glare with a cool stare of his own.

"You know, Sergeant Winters, you had a great opportunity to walk away." His hand gestures were probably supposed to be invisible to her. They weren't.

She fired a short burst over his head as a warning that she'd seen through his game. "Stay nice and close together, gentlemen. When I get nervous, I start shooting. Next time, the shots won't be high."

"You're engaged in treason against your nation, Sergeant Winters." Jones's voice was still cool, seemingly unaffected by the bullets that had just whizzed a couple of feet over his head.

"America needs the Cross," he continued. "There are those who claim that no weapons of mass destruction were hidden in Iraq. But they are wrong. The Cross was hidden. Just as we knew it would be. Compared to the power of the Cross, all the nuclear arsenals in the world add up to nothing."

"Pretty handy for you that the U.S. invaded Iraq, than, huh?"

Jones grunted out two ha's. "Handy? Not at all. We spent years preparing the nation to do the Lord's mission."

Ivy didn't figure Jones was crazy. Maybe he was mistaken about the war being launched just to let some mysterious Foundation grab the Cross. Or maybe he was dead-on-right about who was driving what in America. What she did know was that she couldn't start shooting at a bunch of Americans who were following their government's orders.

* * * *

Ivy distracted the Foundation Agents for long enough to let Zack get under cover.

He had a bad feeling about the way Jones looked at Ivy—it reminded him of the time he'd seen a shark swallow a smaller predator whole. But

Ivy had taken the lead. He'd back her up.

He kept his Kalashnikov at his hip, ready to spray a stream of death at the agents while he let Ivy try to talk her way out of trouble.

The Foundation Agent was smooth. He played Ivy like a piano, appealing to her patriotism, her sense of duty, her Christian faith. He didn't bother talking about little things like why he'd slaughtered an entire ship full of sailors or why, if they were such good Christians, they planned to kill a Christian priest like Father Galen.

After what they'd been through, Zack would have guessed Ivy was immune to that kind of persuasion.

Apparently he was wrong again.

"Do you really want the True Cross to stay in the hands of the infidel Moslems, available for them to use as a weapon against the democratic west?" Jones's voice was smooth, soft, creating doubt where only certainty had existed. "We wouldn't allow them to hold nuclear weapons, would we? The Cross is far more powerful than a bomb. You must understand that. After all, you've been in its presence for days."

Ivy's eyes drooped and she lowered her assault rifle.

Jones signaled Adams who dropped Father Galen, pulled a long knife and stepped toward the unmoving Ivy.

Zack's brain told his finger to squeeze the trigger, but nothing happened.

Then he understood. Jones wasn't being persuasive. His talking was only the carrier for his real message. After all the time he'd spent with the Cross, Zack had learned that magic exists, but he still didn't take it into account with his plans. And neither had Ivy.

The Foundation Agent had cast some sort of spell.

If Zack didn't do anything about it, he'd have to watch Ivy die.

That wasn't going to happen.

He told his lips to begin a prayer, thinking the words when his lips refused. "Hail Mary, full of Grace."

By the time he reached the word Grace, Adams had almost reached Ivy.

But he said "Grace" out loud. And his fingers, freed from the spell that had been aimed, after all, at Ivy and not at him, tightened around the trigger.

Adams went down. Jones ducked.

* * * *

One instant, she'd been frozen, unable to do anything but watch the Foundation Agent approach her with a knife that could have been the twin of the one Smith had used to slit her throat. The next, she was free.

She raised her weapon and fired a burst, but Jones had moved impossibly fast. Other than Adams's corpse, a few feet from her where Zack had shot him, only Father Galen remained in sight.

She ducked back herself just in time to avoid being hit by a hail of semiautomatic fire.

"They'll radio for more help. We've got about five minutes before the Navy gets here," Zack said.

Another couple of shots clanged off the ship's steel hull near her, the ricochets spraying her with paint chips and rust. They'd reached a kind of standoff but, as Zack had just reminded her, the other side could summon a lot more help than she could.

That wouldn't help them, though, if their prize had already vanished. And the agents had lifted the Cross to the deck before they'd ducked back for cover.

"I'll get the Cross."

"You'll get shot," Zack said.

"Maybe." But men armed only with knives and pistols tend to duck when someone is shooting at them with an assault rifle.

She fired a couple more bursts in the directions she thought the Agents had shot from, then scooped up the Cross.

"I'll help," Father Galen said. "Thank you for coming to rescue me." He waved the veil like a flag. "Mary must have protected me."

She didn't bother telling him he could have rotted for all she cared.

"Get off the ship," she ordered. "Cejno is waiting."

"Okay." He put his bulk in full forward motion. Even full speed wasn't too fast for the overweight priest, but the ship wasn't that big either.

An agent popped his head up and fired a shot after the priest, but Zack disturbed his aim with a burst from his Kalashnikov.

The priest stumbled when he hit the gangplank but he kept going. Ivy fired another quick burst, then another, until her AK-47 locked. She was out of bullets.

"Cover me."

Ivy scooped up both sections of Cross.

Although the Agents had complained about the Cross's weight, it seemed almost weightless to her.

She didn't dare turn around and head for the gangplank. Instead, she kept moving forward.

Single large-gauge shots sounded like low rumbles over the higher-pitched chatter of Zack's Kalashnikov. The kinetic energy of a bullet smashed the Cross into her side and twisted her around. Once again, though, the Cross saved her—admittedly in a much more mundane way than before. Still, she wasn't complaining.

She leapt off the side of the ship into the waiting green of the Marmara Sea.

Wood floats.

She reminded herself of that as the Cross's momentum pulled her deeper and deeper into the salt water.

White streaks, like laser lightshows, cut through the water—bubble trails left by bullets.

There were more of those bullet trails than she would have guessed possible from handguns. And they were closer than comfortable. Water slows a bullet pretty quickly, but that didn't mean those shots wouldn't kill.

She hoped the volume of fire didn't mean the agents had finished Zack off. She'd never had the chance to tell him how she felt about him, hadn't really figured that out herself, for that matter. But he was the best partner, they the best team she'd ever worked on. If she had to go on alone, she didn't know how she'd make it.

She reminded herself she didn't have time for maudlin thoughts. If she bobbed up like a cork next to the ship, she'd be easy prey for the Agents and Zack's survival would be the least of her problems.

The wood's buoyancy slowly overcame her downward momentum and she headed up. Despite her aching lungs, she resisted the urge to head for the surface. Rather than kick for the air, she angled the Cross sections so their lift would move them forward at an angle, away from the death-ship, then paddled to extend the distance.

Her lungs screamed by the time they finally reached the surface but she'd moved maybe twenty yards away from the ship. It wasn't far, but when you're getting shot at with short-barreled handguns, twenty yards can be the difference between safety and certain death.

She mounted the two Cross pieces like they were a waterlogged surfboard and paddled toward the shore where they'd left the cars.

A couple of splashes persuaded her to stay low, but the shooters gave up on her pretty quickly. Instead, they rushed Zack.

* * * *

Now what?

Zack squeezed off aimed single shots at Agents who popped their heads up above the hatch, but this standoff wasn't going to end in his favor. Within minutes, they would get reinforcements from the nearby aircraft carrier. Even before that, he'd exhaust his thirty-round magazine.

He fired again and heard one of the Agents curse.

184

A few pistol shots sounded from below the decks. They were firing at Ivy out of their portholes and there was nothing he could do about that unless he wanted to go down after them.

Unless he could get them to come after him.

Pretty obviously, these Foundation Agents had received military training. But training isn't the same as being in an actual war, facing actual bullets, getting actual friends and fellow soldiers killed around you.

Zack had been in a real war. That should give him an advantage.

He'd need all the advantages he could get.

He switched the selector to short burst mode and aimed low, trying for ricochets down below the decks. Two quick three round bursts persuaded the Agents to keep their heads down. He broke from cover, backing toward the same gangway Father Galen had taken off the ship.

He'd lost count of his shots, so he switched back to single mode when he hit the gangplank. Time to make every bullet count.

A flurry of bullets from the bow of the ship told him his time had run out. The Agents had found another hatchway and outflanked him.

He fired a couple of times in the direction of the shots, dropped his rifle, and rolled down the gangway.

Maybe they thought they'd killed him. Maybe they were just surprised by his unorthodox tactics. Either way, they stopped shooting for a moment.

He turned his roll into an awkward cartwheel and ended up on his feet, sprinting for the cover of the rusty containers where Mustafa and Cejno were holed up.

"Let's get out of here," he shouted.

The deep thrum of helicopter rotors barely penetrated his awareness. They were still a ways away, but helicopters travel quickly. He was about to have even more unfriendly company.

"I shall hold off the men on the ship," Mustafa volunteered.

"Don't be an idiot. We've got to move."

Mustafa smiled. "Hediye, give Mr. Zack your keys. The rest of you, take young Cejno and make sure he goes back to the east, to his family. I'll take the Mercedes once I've delayed them for long enough."

Zack had little use for heroes. In the Army, heroes end up killing a lot more of their fellow soldiers than any enemy.

"Where's the priest?"

"He got away."

Damn. That meant he and Ivy would have to track him down again. This was getting tiresome.

"He gave this to me first." Cejno pulled a piece of fabric from his pocket. The veil. "Go with Allah, my brother."

Zack shook his head in amazement. He'd been sure the priest would holdfast to his treasure. He'd abandoned his calling, his career, his life for the sake of the veil, after all. Given what Father Galen had done to Ivy, it was hard for Zack to generate much sympathy for the dope-smoking priest. Still, when Galen had seen the real stakes, the real enemy, he'd done the right thing.

Zack stopped arguing and went.

He'd reached the end of the pier when a storm of pistol fire sounded.

There were more Agents on the ship than Zack had thought. At least twenty of them were firing from the deck of the freighter or pouring down the gangplanks.

Mustafa fired calmly, his body in the classic target shooter stance he'd probably learned during his days as a draftee in the Turkish universal military service.

A couple of the Agents went down and Mustafa shifted his position just in time to avoid the Agents' counterfire.

Mustafa's bodyguards popped away at the agents exposed on the gangplanks. Another agent fell, although whether he'd been hit by Mustafa, a bodyguard, or had simply slipped, Zack couldn't guess.

Mustafa fired again, then reached into his jacket pocket for a reload.

An agent caught him in the throat with a knife before he finished.

"Damn."

"He wanted to die a mujahedeen," Cejno said. "Let his death serve a purpose."

Zack looked at the keys in his hand. The Cross was far longer than the little Opal, but it was their best chance.

"Stay alive, Cejno."

"You too, Mr. Zack. Oh, you may need this." He handed over the fat wallet filled with the reward money the Patriarch and Cejno had come up with.

"But—"

"I can make more. Mustafa is not the only hashish dealer in Istanbul."

"What next?" Ivy looked like a goddess as she stepped from the sea, the Cross sections over her shoulders.

"We're taking the Opal and I've got the Veil. Smash the Cross through the back window. It's the only way we'll make the things fit."

She used her rifle butt rather than the Cross to make a hole in the glass while Zack fired up the engine.

He helped shove in the Cross sections, waited until she was seated, then took off.

"Fasten your seatbelt. The Marines are coming and believe me, that isn't good news."

He peeled away from the harbor heading south, along a narrow gravel road that looked like it was mostly tree-shrouded. The helicopters would pick him up with their infrared scopes, but he could hope they wouldn't just start shooting anything with an engine. There was enough traffic that he could hope to get lost.

"Aren't we heading the wrong way?"

Zack looked back. The helicopter about a hundred meters above the death-ship looked like a hungry locust waiting to feed.

"Anywhere away from those guys is the right way."

"We've got to get to Venice."

"We've got to stay alive."

"If we can," Ivy said. "But getting to Venice is more important."

Chapter 17

"How's your Australian accent?" Zack asked Ivy.

She stopped drying herself. "Goodai, mate."

"That was horrible. But maybe it'll be good enough."

"Good enough for what?"

"Americans have mostly forgotten World War I. It was a long time ago, we entered late, and only got involved in the fighting in France. My great grandfather fought there, with Pershing. I barely remember him, but I remember how much he loved France."

"Your point?"

"It was a World War, not just a war in France. An especially horrible part of it was fought near here. Just across those straits."

He pointed the few miles to the hilly peninsula on the other side of the waterway.

"Most of the world has forgotten Gallipoli. But the Australians and New Zealanders remember. They come here in their pilgrimages, the same way some Americans come to the beaches in Normandy."

"Maybe some day they'll come to the deserts in Iraq, too."

"Not if the Foundation has any say about it. I'm not sure what their plans are, but I'm pretty sure they're intent on something that will make Iraq look like a Sunday picnic."

"I take it we're going to Gallipoli?"

Zack shielded his eyes with his strong hand. It was nearly noon and it seemed like they'd been on the move, on the run, forever. Still, his hand was rock-solid, without a bit of the trembling that seemed to come over Ivy and shake her like a child with a rattle.

"I think it's called Gelibolu now. Maybe it was then, too and the Brits just got it wrong. But yeah, that's where we're going. From there, we figure out how to get to Italy."

"Just keep driving."

He smiled. "I guess that'll do it. We've made it through one international border so far. If we can make it across to Greece, getting to Italy should be easy. Lots of shipping across the Ionian Sea."

She heard what he didn't say. "You think getting into Greece will be tough?"

"The Turks and the Greeks have only hated each other for a thousand years or so. I don't think there are going to be any border areas we can just walk across. First, though, we have to figure out how to get across the Dardanelles into Gallipoli."

Figuring out how was easy. A regular ferry ran from Lapeseki on the Asian side to Gelibolu on the European side and Zack and Ivy simply merged into the line of cars and trucks waiting for the next boat.

Given the chickens and goats hanging out of many of the vehicles, the balks of timber sticking out the back of the Opal barely got a second glance from the toll collectors. After a brief negotiation, Zack pulled the car onto the deck of the ferry, turned off the engine, and yanked up the parking break.

"How far do you figure it is across?" Ivy asked after the ferry pulled away from the dock and plowed through the choppy waters of the straits.

Zack squinted at the European shore as the ferry plowed through the water. "Four miles, maybe. At most."

"Good."

"Why?"

She gestured at the sky. "I think we're going to have company."

A navy fighter roared overhead, making a high circle over the ferry.

Zack opened the car door and stepped out.

"Let's be ready to jump if they take out the ferry."

Ivy had to hope, even if the Foundation ordered them to fire into the crowded civilian ferry, that Navy pilot would refuse. She was pretty certain that the Foundation wanted to create a war between Islam and Christianity. In such a war, Turkey would be on the other side. But Turkey had been a part of NATO for half a century and the Navy pilots would know that.

The fighter shrieked overhead, flying upside down and barely above the ferry's radio antenna to get a better view of its target. She caught a quick look at the pilot's face.

Although his eyes were covered by mirrored sunglasses, his jaw was set in fierce determination.

Like a quick strobe, her eyes caught that image, then he was gone. At five or six hundred miles an hour, the fighter would be somewhere over the Mediterranean before it could turn around and head back.

The ferry captain shook a fist at the departing jet and kept on his route. He probably thought this was a routine training flight, a hotshot Navy pilot causing troubles for his fearful cargo. Only Zack and Ivy had any idea how close the captain had come to having his ferryboat blown up underneath him.

Zack muttered a couple of numbers.

"What?"

"Trying to calculate how long before a helicopter can get here."

A chopper full of Foundation Agents wouldn't be so reluctant to shoot, or they might just hold the ferry until the naval taskforce arrived and took control. Either way, a chopper would be a lot more dangerous to Ivy and Zack than was the fighter.

"Well, what do you figure?"

"It's going to be close."

* * * *

The ferry looked like it might be a survivor of the Gallipoli battles, and its ancient diesel engines cranked enough horsepower to push them through the water barely faster than Zack could have swum it.

No amount of his willpower managed to move it any faster.

But they only had a couple of miles and a helicopter would have well over a hundred, assuming the aircraft carrier had stayed in Istanbul harbor. If it had upped anchor and steamed the moment Zack and Ivy had started west, the Agents could be a lot closer.

The navy fighter flew back overhead, then began making long circles high overhead, marking the ferry for whatever was coming.

"You speak English?"

He had been so intent on the jet that he hadn't noticed the elderly woman who approached.

"Yes. Zack Hererra, from Texas."

"Apologies. With your dark hair and all, I thought you were a local."

He guessed it had been a while since he'd had the blond highlights added. "With your accent, I'm guessing you're from Australia."

"You'd be right about that, young man."

"Here to see the memorial?"

"Me mum was pregnant when da' got killed here but I always said I'd come some day. Almost waited too long."

If her father had died in World War I, that would make the woman at least ninety. Zack suspected he wouldn't survive until ninety.

"It was a horrible battle."

She poked him in the chest with a twisted finger. "It was a war. All war is hell. Didn't anyone ever tell you that?"

"But some wars—"

He wouldn't have guessed her lined face could get more wrinkled but it did. "People always say that. Some wars are different, they say. Some wars have to be fought. Maybe they're right. The only problem is, people can always find reasons to fight this war. And both sides are always certain they have the right on their side. The human mind is infinitely capable of justifying evil."

"There's some truth to that." Zack believed some battles had to be fought: he wouldn't have decided to make a career out of the Army if he hadn't. But he recognized he wasn't going to persuade a ninety-year-old woman of anything. Especially not a woman who had lost her father to war before she was even born.

"My mother never married again," the elderly woman continued. "Weren't enough men to go 'round back then. War wiped a clean slate of the whole generation. Just women and children and sheep over most of the country. And cripples. Those lucky enough to come home from the war mostly didn't come home in one piece. Ever see those old newsreels with all the soldiers missing a leg marching together with their crutches? Thousands with no right leg, then thousands more with no left?"

Military medicine had made dramatic improvements since the days of World War I. But with improvements in body armor, injury still often meant loss of a limb or loss of sight. Too many of Zack's friends had been injured in Iraq. "It must have been horrible."

"Now you Americans are running around the world starting wars. Dragging the rest of us into them, too."

Back when he'd fled the streets of Dallas to join up, he would have argued with her, would have told her that America would never launch a war without provocation, without extreme need. But could he really say that any longer?

"As Tolstoy reminds us, 'all that is necessary for evil to triumph is for good people to do nothing,'" he said.

"And you Americans are always so certain you're some of those good people, aren't you?"

She turned on her heel and stumped back to her car.

"That went well." Ivy was laughing at him.

He got back into the Opal. "Yeah. And Australia was part of the coalition in Iraq. Good thing we didn't run into someone from France. They lost soldiers here too, but they don't have to come this far to see their graveyards. Their whole country is covered with them."

The ancient ferry wheezed into its dock a few minutes later and Zack

191

started the car's engine. "Looks like we made it."

"Maybe."

He didn't like the sound of that. "Trouble?"

"There's a whole flock of helicopters heading this way. Looks like the rest of the Navy sailed too because I think I see a couple of destroyers heading this way at a speed that's illegal in crowded waters."

He looked at the line of cars waiting to exit, then at the helicopters.

"Keep your fingers crossed."

Ivy nodded. "Think about where we're going to go if we make it off. Because there's going to be a second invasion of Gallipoli any minute now. And this time, the Turkish military and police are likely to be on the same side as the invaders."

Zack roared off the ferry as soon as the cars in front of him cleared a path and headed for the village of Gelibolu.

Ivy rolled down her window and leaned out, giving him a blow-by-blow of the arrival of the helicopters.

"I wonder why they're not heading straight for us," she said after he'd spent ten minutes trying to get lost in the narrow streets of the town. "We know they have sensors that can track the Cross."

"This place is chock full of war memorials, graveyards and chapels," Zack said. "Lots of prayer. Should be plenty of power spots to disguise us. Can you sense them?"

She went still, examining their surroundings by that inner sight the Cross had given her.

"You're right. Maybe there's enough power here to confuse them for a bit. Let's keep moving."

Zack concentrated on driving, letting Ivy navigate.

She gave him directions using a cheap map they'd bought from a tourist shack and even more often, using her second sight.

Five times in the next couple of hours, she directed him off the road to nearby Mosques, chapels, or the ancient marble bones of what might have been Byzantine churches or possibly the ruins of even older pagan temples going back to the days when Alexander the Great had set off from this region on his quest to conquer the world.

Others had tried to emulate Alexander's quest. Crassus, The Emperor Julian, Richard the Lion Hearted, Barbarosa, Napoleon, Hitler —all had failed in their attempts to impose the sway of the west over the east. Most had been destroyed by that destructive goal.

It occurred to Zack that the Foundation might be following that same dream. Alexander had pulled it off and it was possible the Foundation could match his accomplishments. No one could stand against the U.S. military in open battle. Already, they occupied Iraq and Afghanistan, and had powerful bases in Turkey, Kuwait, Saudi Arabia, and Oman as well as an aggressive and warlike ally in Israel. The True Cross had led the west into battle before. Could a new crusade be more successful?

"There's something weird ahead." Ivy's voice broke through Zack's concentration. "Get ready to slow down."

"Dangerous?"

She shrugged. "Isn't everything?"

* * * *

They'd just passed through the city of Kesan when Ivy spotted the pale lavender power glow.

Unlike the red of the Cross or the blue of the Veil, this power was more dispersed but it was definitely strong.

"Turn right here." She directed Zack into a grove on the side of the road.

"What is it?"

She checked her Kalashnikov. With no bullets left, it might serve as a threat, but she'd learned one thing from her military training—never threaten if you aren't prepared to follow through.

Zack followed her directions, weaving the Opal through the grove until he emerged into a clearing.

Wooden carts, a huge bonfire, and a troop of children practicing acrobatic moves told Ivy they'd stumbled across a gypsy caravan.

"Perfect," she said. "We'll blend in with them."

"What makes you think they're going our way?"

She smiled. "We'll persuade them."

Although the gypsy children pretended not to see them, Ivy noticed they didn't come too close to the car. She was pretty sure there must be adults around too, but she didn't see any. No one lingered around the fire. No mother supervised her children.

They got out, moving slowly. "Hello. Do any of you speak English?"

After a brief discussion, one of the children, a girl of maybe twelve, was appointed the spokesperson.

"Take my picture, then pay," she suggested. "Maybe have fortune said?"

"I have a bad feeling I know my fortune," Zack whispered. "If I'm right, I definitely don't want to find out for sure."

The girl grabbed Ivy's hand, stared at her palm for a moment, then dropped it and screamed.

"They'll probably try to sell you something to eliminate your bad luck." Zack was being cynical. Maybe he'd had bad experiences with gypsies before. To Ivy, they seemed incredibly romantic and old-fashioned.

One thing for sure, she didn't think the girl's scream was anything planned. The other children had huddled around the girl and were speaking a mile a minute, but using whatever language gypsies use when they don't want strangers to understand them.

After considerable screeching and a lot of hand-pointing, a boy of maybe six separated from the group and ran off into the trees.

"Summoning adult supervision," Zack said. "I wonder if we shouldn't get back in the car and get out of here while we still can."

"That might have been wise." The voice was heavily accented, male, and positively threatening, although not as threatening as the over-under shotgun he pointed at Zack. "But it is too late for that decision."

"We are looking for some help crossing the border into Greece." Ivy forced down her fear. "It's important that we get away from here."

"Important to an American does not necessitate important to the Romany."

The girl who'd grabbed her hand ran up to the man, being careful not to step between Zack and the shotgun, and started blabbing something.

It must have been convincing because after twenty seconds of listening, he shifted the shotgun so it pointed at Ivy.

"Who are you and what are you looking for?"

"As I said, we're looking for a way out of Turkey. Into Greece, if possible."

He narrowed his dark eyes into a squint. "Why would a vampire want to go to Greece?"

Where had that come from? "I'm not a vampire."

"Yolanda has the second sight. She says your lifeline is broken in the recent past. You were dead, then alive again. Who else but an undead would have such a line?"

"Are you Christian?"

He shrugged. "I ask the questions here."

"I just wondered because all Christians know the story of Lazarus, how he was dead and then came back to life. I've never heard he was a vampire."

The gypsy squinted. "Did you hear that he wasn't?"

Okay, he had her there. She thought the point of the Lazarus story was just about how Jesus brought him back, not about what happened once he'd been brought back, although presumably he had comforted his grieving relatives and got on with his life. Still, Ivy didn't think the Bible would have played up the story quite so much if he'd come back and started killing and drinking blood.

"Come on. You can touch me. Feel my pulse. Feel that I'm still warm. Oh, and I'll eat something with garlic." What did gypsies eat? Ivy was hungry enough to give just about anything a try, although she might draw the line at human blood.

The gypsy ran a hand through his long greasy hair and then barked a question at the girl.

She nodded cautiously.

"This is beyond me. I will summon the Queen."

Ivy had noticed the second man sneaking up on her from behind. As he reached for her, she shifted her weight and let him stumble past.

Zack's fists knotted and the muscles on his neck tensed as he prepared to go into white knight mode and probably get both of them killed.

"It's okay, Zack. They probably just want to make sure we're not carrying."

The first gypsy nodded. "My friend gets sometimes over-ambitious. Please allow the tapdown."

Ivy anticipated some extra groping, but the quick search was professional and impersonal. "She's clean. And she's warm. Feels alive to me."

"Take her to the Queen."

Hidden in a dry wash a few hundred yards beyond the traditional carts of a gypsy caravan were the modern versions. Truck-pulled trailers, the aluminum dull and pitted, had been pulled in a circle reminiscent of old western movies showing wagon trails under Indian attack. Possibly, Ivy reflected, the gypsies would see themselves as continually under attack, just as the neighboring communities would see themselves as threatened by the gypsies.

The shotgun-wielding gypsy gestured them to open the door to one of the smaller trailers. "In there."

Ivy had collected the veil from Zack, but felt a bit naked with the Cross out of her sight. Still, the lavender haze of the gypsy camp would hide both Cross and veil from the Foundation. If she could win the gypsy Queen over to help them. If she couldn't, physically dragging the thing around with her wouldn't help.

She opened the door and stepped into the unlit interior.

The door slammed into her butt the instant both her feet were inside, shoving her forward and turning the dim interior into complete darkness.

Physical darkness, anyway. Because the power glow was strong inside. Incense smoldered on little alters devoted to otherwise forgotten gods and provided multicolored energy light that her newly developed senses picked up.

Behind her, she heard the sounds of a brief struggle, of fist hitting flesh.

"It's okay, Zack," she called to her partner through the closed door. She sensed that this was a place reserved for women, that Zack would be making a horrible mistake if he tried to force his way into the trailer.

The struggle subsided, although she could practically smell the testosterone exuded by the males outside.

What appeared to be a heap of clothing in the center of the room shifted slightly and Ivy recognized the heap as something human. The Gypsy Queen.

The Queen looked as old as the Australian woman on the ferry, although Ivy suspected the strains of her office and of living on the road, rather than merely chronological years had created much of that sense of age.

"They told me we needed to see you," she said.

"And do you see me?" The Queen's voice was harsh, like a rusty gate that had been too long without oil. "It is dark in here."

Ivy closed her eyes. "You're wearing a sort of poncho with an eight-sided cross pattern and sitting in the middle of the floor. It looks like you've got some sort of pentagram going with a little mount of sea-salt at each corner. I can't see your eyes and your hair is covered by a handkerchief."

Hope sprang up in her heart—the eight-sided pattern reminded her of the stars on Mary's veil.

"Yes, you see something. Give me your hand."

Ivy stepped toward the pentagram, then reached across the faint lines that ascended from the floor into infinity.

Her skin tingled where it crossed the line, but it wasn't painful.

The Queen snatched her hand and studied it carefully.

Only then did Ivy realize that the Queen's eyes had been sewn shut. She was blind. Blind, at least, to the wavelengths which normal humans could detect. Blind or not, though, clearly the Queen could see plenty.

"My granddaughter thinks you are a vampire."

Ivy hadn't thought about it before, but the original Dracula hadn't lived too far from where they were now. It shouldn't be a big surprise that the legends of the undead would be strong in his neighborhood.

"Your granddaughter sees part of the truth and fills in the rest from her imagination."

"That truth being that you are not a vampire but a saint?"

Ivy wished people would stop calling her that. She was a woman trying to stay alive.

"I just got lucky when someone tried to kill me."

The blind woman stared at her. "Show me what you're carrying."

For an instant, Ivy thought she meant the Cross. But the Cross was still outside, in the car. So, she must mean the Veil.

"It's very old."

The Queen gave a choking laugh. "I can be careful."

The Veil's power shined so brightly Ivy had to blink the tears out of her eyes. With her eyes sewn shut, the Queen couldn't do that. She reared back at first, then reached out her hand to stroke the precious material.

"Beautiful."

Ivy nodded, wondering if the Queen could see her gesture.

"Do you know what it is?"

"The Patriarch of Constantinople says that it is the veil of the Virgin Mary."

"Is it?" The Queen snorted.

"So he says. It was hidden for many hundreds of years."

"Hidden, yes. For more years than you can imagine. Mary may have worn it, but it was not Mary's alone, not hers first. This Veil was a secret for centuries before Mary was born. If this was indeed hers, Mary is more than your Christian faith allows you to believe."

She pushed her own poncho forward so Ivy could make out the design. She'd been right—the designs were almost identical to those on the veil. "What do you see?"

"Sorry, Queen. I don't believe that Mary was a gypsy." Since she'd found the Cross, Ivy had been forced to believe plenty of things she had never even suspected, but there were lines she wasn't about to cross. It was a lot more likely that the gypsies had adopted Mary's design than that Mary had chosen theirs.

The Queen snorted. "Of course not. But if she wore that veil, she was more than just a mother."

Mother of God, Queen of Heaven. Yeah, Ivy had been raised Catholic long enough to think of Mary as a lot more than just a mother.

"We need help." Ivy figured it was time to change the subject. "We're trying to get to Greece but we don't have passports and I wouldn't be surprised if the Turkish army wasn't looking for us. As is the CIA."

"I see."

"Will you help us?"

The old woman moved her cheeks in and out. It wasn't an attractive gesture and Ivy made a mental note not to do anything like that, ever-- especially if she one day lost all of her teeth.

"The Veil you carry was hidden well. Our people have walked the streets of old Constantinople searching for power for hundreds of years. How did you find it when we could not?"

Ivy suspected the Queen wasn't changing the subject. This question had something to do with whether the gypsies would help them. "It was not just hidden, it was locked and protected. I had the key."

"Ah, a key."

The Queen brushed away the ward lines and grasped Ivy's arm, her thin fingers cold and rough against Ivy's skin. "A bargain, then. We too have a lost object of power. If your key can recover it for us, we will help you get across the border."

A quick mental flash on the carnivorous sheep made Ivy cut off her automatic agreement. "What sort of object?"

"Does it matter?"

"If it's evil, I won't do it."

"There is already plenty of evil in the visible world. A little more would not add much to the equation."

The Queen was right, of course. The world was already filled with evil. Getting to Venice was important, was worth making sacrifices for. She should agree. She opened her mouth to agree.

Instead, "No."

Well, that surprised her.

The Queen's grip tightened on her arm. "If you won't help us, why should we help you?"

Chapter 18

Ivy stared into the Queen's eyes. Darkness was becoming less and less of a problem. Would she, like the Queen, someday have to sew her eyes shut against the glare of light?

"We're trying to stop a war," she explained. "We've got to get to Venice soon."

The Queen shook her head slowly. "There will always be wars. I must look after my own people. Why should I care when Americans kill Arabs or Turks?"

Ivy's blood froze "How did you know that was what I was talking about?"

The old woman cackled. "I am not so blind that I cannot see something of the future. And a dark future indeed is what I see. Your own Bible tells the story, does it not? Gog-Magog is upon us."

Ivy wasn't sure exactly what Gog-Magog was, but she did recognize the words. Partly from a horrible church retreat she'd been on when a truly weird priest had insisted on keeping the group of teenaged girls up all night long with horror stories from the Bible and partly because she'd seen those words in the papers she'd swiped from Smith—papers that had been destroyed in the predator missile strike.

"What is Gog-Magog?"

The woman shrugged. "A war. Nothing to do with gypsies."

But it was in the Bible. A few more pieces of the puzzle fell together. The Patriarch had said that the Foundation was a group of extremist Christians. And Ivy's own experience said that the extremist Christians tended to love the most horrible of the prophesies.

If they could combine their dreams of Crusade with Biblical

prophesies of a great war, presumably a war they would win, that would seem like a double-win to the Foundation.

As a soldier, it didn't sound so great to Ivy.

"Everyone gets hurt in a war. Even if you aren't directly involved."

"Gypsies are not locked to the land the way you gajikané are. When war strikes, we move away."

Ivy didn't think so, and she didn't think the Queen did, either. Zack could tell her for sure, but she seemed to remember that the Gypsies had been hurt badly by Hitler's genocide during World War II.

"Tell me about the object you want me to unlock."

"You said you would not find it if it were evil."

Ivy studied the Queen. "That was a test, wasn't it? You wanted to know if I had sold out. But I don't believe you would intentionally bring something evil into the world. You'd want it to remain locked where it could do no harm."

"You think you know a lot about me, don't you?"

"Not a lot, but I can read your aura just as you can see mine."

"Ah. And what does my aura tell you?"

"It's lavender, like much of the camp. I don't know what gods you worship, but you aren't a Christian. Nor are you a Moslem. Both Christians and Moslems glow red for me. Except for when they're blue for Mary. But you're not blue, so that can't be it." Although, come to think of it, there was a similarity between Mary's blue glow and the lavender of the gypsy camp. And what logic was there for Mary to be a different color than Jesus?

The Queen gave her a toothless grin. "We do not discuss our faith with outsiders."

"But you want me to find your holy thing."

"If you have the key, we have little choice. The Gypsies need it."

"And I need to know more."

"Very well, I will be frank. Everyone knows the Nazi slaughtered many Jews. But Jews were not their only targets. Hitler had a list of inferior people, people who needed to be exterminated as part of his final solution. Gays, pagans, anyone handicapped. The Nazi killed the Romany as well. Thousands of us: as many as they could catch. What treasures we carried, they stole from us, tried to use in their clumsy attempts to gain power over the other planes. My grandmother was Queen then, and she hid our chalice from them. She used the magic of her own death to wall it away completely. As she was dying, she told my mother that only a dead person could reach in and return it. My mother passed the words on to me, as if it mattered."

The Queen gave a hacking laugh. "When my mother told me that, I thought she meant that no one could ever reach it again. Dead people do not walk, do not grab chalices from where they are hidden, do not return them to the living. Or so I believed. I was wrong, though, wasn't I? Because, behold, a dead person has come to us now."

What were the odds?

Ivy had thought she was in control, making decisions. Obviously there were stronger powers in the universe that were directing her path, or perhaps had directed the paths of the gypsies to meet her.

"And the chalice, it is a force for good?"

The Queen shrugged. "So it was said. It was hidden before I was born."

An uneasy feeling swept over Ivy. She'd found the Cross and the Veil of Mary already. Of the holiest relics of the Christian faith, the only one missing was the Holy Grail. Which was supposed to be a chalice, right? And if she just happened to stumble over the Holy Grail, she'd have to wonder whether there was any such thing as free will at all. It went way beyond coincidence.

"What sort of chalice is it, anyway?"

The Queen gazed at her with her sewn-shut eyes, then cackled. "Just a cup. It came with my people out of India a long time ago. It isn't what you are thinking. Not that cup."

Ivy exhaled a breath she hadn't known she was holding. "All right, I'll get it. Where is it hidden?"

Although, if the Queen announced they'd hidden it back somewhere in Constantinople or Kurdistan, Ivy thought she would have a cow.

"It is not far. I will show you. After sunset. But first, we must disguise you and you must eat."

The Queen rapped on her floor and the gypsy with the shotgun opened the door and peered in.

"Is she safe?"

"She will help us find it."

"Ah."

"But first, more gajikané approach, quickly. Give the man and woman clothing, let them blend in."

He nodded, then gestured for Ivy to follow him to another of the dilapidated trailers.

"In. My wife will help you."

Whether the woman's costume choice helped, Ivy wouldn't guess. Zack seemed appreciative, though, when she emerged twenty minutes later in a swishy skirt that seemed to be made up of men's neckties sewed together at the top but that hung loose after the first few inches around her waist, so her legs were exposed every time she made a step. The off-the-shoulders top left her breasts halfway naked and tied well above her navel. They'd also decorated her with a necklace of fingernail-sized gold coins of every vintage from the Roman Empire to modern South Africa. A greasy kerchief covered her short blond hair.

"A gypsy carries her treasure, her dowry, with her," the shotgun-man's wife insisted. "You have no money, you no gypsy. Need to have sex with lot of men to make this sum of money."

Well that certainly made Ivy feel special.

The makeup had taken even more time than getting dressed, but by the time they let her out of the trailer Ivy was fully vamped.

"Wow."

With his dark skin and hair, Zack didn't have to do much to look gypsy. Black pants, a multicolored striped shirt, and a Greek sailor hat seemed his whole disguise. Until he turned his head and she saw the gold earring.

"Pierced?"

He fingered the large gold ring. "They insisted. I guess it'll heal eventually."

"Leave it. I think it's cute."

He stared at her long enough to make her listen to the words she'd just said. Cute? She'd sounded like a high school girl with a crush.

"You will be quiet," the gypsy with the shotgun said. Although, by now that shotgun was hidden. Ivy wondered what the local police would do if they spotted it.

She suspected that it could reemerge again quite quickly and that, if it did, she and Zack would be in trouble.

* * * *

No matter how they twisted, they seemed unable to escape the Foundation search.

Zack wondered how many Foundation Agents there could be.

Although the gypsy camp was hidden from the road, the Turkish Army patrol headed directly toward them, under the direction of one of the ubiquitous black-suited Agents.

The Agent waved his Cross like a weapon while the Turks pointed real weapons at the gypsies, kicked over their cooking pots, frightened the draft animals, and pinched the women.

"There's something weird here," the Agent announced. "Keep looking."

The Turk shouted out orders to the soldiers, but the only result seemed to be more destruction, more shoving, and a pathetic offer by one of the soldiers to buy Ivy's virtue for a few thousand Turkish Lira. Given the value of the Lira, Zack figured no one was surprised when she shook her head vehemently and spit on the ground.

The Queen waited for about five minutes, then emerged from her trailer.

Ivy had given him a vague idea about what the woman was like, but seeing her in person was positively frightening.

She wore a shapeless black drape that reminded him uncomfortably of what the nuns had worn when he'd been in school. Thick black twine pierced through her eyelids, sewing her eyes shut.

She ignored the Agent, but screamed at the soldiers in a language neither Zack nor the soldiers could understand. They understood enough to back away from her, though.

She had been leaning heavily on a walking stick when she'd come down the steps to her trailer, but she straightened her back and threw the stick in front of the Agent.

He dropped his crucifix and pulled back when the stick writhed and transformed itself into a snake.

"Jesus."

The Queen cackled. "Take your abomination away from here, English."

The soldiers did finally leave.

Which seemed way too easy.

"Why do you think they couldn't find the Cross this time when Smith was able to track it down back in Mosul?" he asked.

He had to watch himself to make sure he didn't just stare at Ivy like a lovestruck high school freshman. The skirt they'd put her in showed more leg than you'd see in a USO show and the top seemed connected by a single button at her breasts that threatened to pop every time she breathed. A rope of gold coins drew his eyes toward her cleavage. Looking at her tangled his tongue up in itself. Looking away from her was just plain impossible.

Ivy leaned toward him, oblivious to the fact that this let him look further down her blouse. She spoke in a whisper, obviously not believing that the Queen's little magic trick had permanently gotten rid of the Foundation Agents.

"There's a lot of magic around this camp, and their Queen seems able to generate some sort of confusion. She knew they were coming but she didn't come out of her trailer until they'd been here a while. In Mosul, Smith didn't have to confront active magic, just the holdover from hundreds of years of prayer and faith, and he started by bombing out the mosque which probably diluted its power. Of course, they may also be scraping the bottom of the agent barrel. Smith was top-notch. This guy looked like a desk-worker, not a field agent." She giggled. "Did you see the way he squirmed when he saw that snake?"

"Yeah, a good trick."

"I thought only Moses could turn a staff into a snake."

"Huh-uh. The Egyptian priests did too. Don't know if you noticed, but our friend the gypsy with the shotgun picked up the snake after he scared the agent. He's their pet."

Zack fingered the heavy gold ring dangling from his ear. It felt strange and not particularly comfortable although, given Ivy's reaction when he'd said he would lose it, he figured maybe he'd better keep it in.

There was no way he was going to be welcomed back into the Army after going AWOL for so long, so he didn't have to worry about the dress code.

"I told them I'd help them find something they magically hid during World War II," Ivy said. "They're waiting until dark."

"Waiting for another visit from the Foundation is more like it," he guessed.

Sure enough, another group of soldiers, this one including three U.S. sailors and a pair of Agents, showed up just before dark.

One of the Agents spent five minutes walking around the spot where Zack had parked their Opal. The car was gone now, probably vanished into a Turkish chop shop for parts, but it, or the Cross that had been in it, must have left some magical residue that Foundation sensors picked up.

The Agents wanted to haul the whole group of gypsies in for questioning. But the Turks continued to demur, possibly, Zack guessed, because they were afraid of gypsy magic—he saw a number of the Turkish draftees fingering evil-eye pendants--and possibly because they just didn't know how to deal with all those gypsies.

And there were a lot of them. From almost the minute Ivy had finished her appointment with the Queen, gypsies had been trickling into the camp until they now numbered better than a hundred.

They milled around, confused the soldier's efforts to count and organize them, started small fires where they burned incense and herbs that Zack didn't recognize but that seemed to confuse the brains of anyone who inhaled too much.

"Gypsies no have Turks with us," the shotgun-wielding gypsy insisted to one of the Turkish officers in English. "None of kidnapping here. We good Gypsies."

"We're not looking for Turks. We're looking for Americans. Deserters."

"Yes, yes. Americans looking. Looking for stealing our women. We know this Americans. They want women but they think payment is of muchness."

His English was better than that, but he obviously didn't think it wise to let on.

Dozens of gypsy children tagged after the Agent, jumping in front of him whenever he held out his crucifix at anything, pretending interest in what he was finding, then holding out a series of pendants and what looked uncomfortably like voodoo curses, offering to sell but also, Zack guessed, confusing the dousing.

"Want sex slave?" the twelve-year-old who'd accused Ivy of being a vampire demanded. "Buy this and no woman can resist of you." She waved a doll with a large penis in his face. "Or no man, of course. I think you maybe like the man better than the woman."

The girl jumped out of his way when he threw a fist in her direction, then unbuttoned one of the buttons on her blouse. "Oh, you like women to hit. I am virgin. Ten thousand dollars and you can have me first. Hit me for five hundred dollars more. Special price in Euros."

"Whore." The Agent shoved at her, then tripped and fell when she slipped out of his way.

"Whore is good, no? Have plenty sex and I make good dowry for handsome gypsy husband some day. You get nice virgin. Clean. Your wife, she understand. Or boyfriend, he no mind just a bit of difference."

The gypsies were playing a risky game, Zack saw. But they had little choice. The Agents knew he and Ivy had been there. They might suspect that the gypsies had sent them on their way, but they didn't know for sure. They would keep looking.

It took two of the gypsy women actually persuading Turkish soldiers to head into the trailers with them before the Turkish Lieutenant put down his foot. He wasn't going to risk losing control of his platoon just because some American civilian was standing around bugging him.

"Then we'll stay, without you," the Agent declared.

"You will not," the lieutenant growled. "America is our ally, not our master. You have no authority in our country without our agreement. I no longer agree to this."

"You're making a big mistake, sand-pounder."

The insult was the final straw. "If you aren't back in the jeeps in one minute, I will take you there myself."

The Agent swelled up like he was ready for a fight, but he was outnumbered twenty to five, not to mention more than a hundred hostile gypsies. "You're going to get busted back to private," he assured the Lieutenant.

"Perhaps so," the Turkish Lieutenant agreed. "Perhaps our government is as venial as you say, playing lapdog to you Americans. Until that happens, though, I suggest that you get into the vehicle." He fingered his holstered sidearm looking like he'd like an excuse to eliminate this problem right there.

The Agent made a few more swipes with his crucifix, smacking it into one of the gypsy children who kept darting around him. The flood of tears from the little girl caused even the U.S. sailors to look at him with disgust.

"Don't go anywhere," the Agent told the shotgun Gypsy. "Because I'm coming back. And next time, you won't get rid of me so easy."

"That'll definitely make them want to stick around," Ivy whispered in Zack's ear.

* * * *

"Now, we recover the chalice. After, you leave," the Queen said.

Ivy nodded. She trusted the Agent when he'd said he would be back. They didn't have long. "That American is going to cause problems for you if you run off. I bet he has some sort of monitoring around the camp."

"I said you will leave. Some of us will stay, including a pale-skinned female who will wear your same clothing. First, though, the key."

They'd had to explain the Cross to the gypsies when they'd taken it out of the Opal and handed over the keys to the vehicle. A little work with carpentry tools and the Cross now appeared to be a couple of beams in one of the oldest of the gypsy wagons.

Since no nail could penetrate the rock-hard wood of the Cross, it only took a few minutes to free it.

"Now, where's the hidden object supposed to be?" In the darkness, Ivy's second sight was more dominant and she could see countless shades of power, blobs of energy that seemed to come from everywhere. No wonder the Agent had been frustrated in his search for the Cross.

The Queen cackled. "In my trailer. You think I would let it get far away?"

Ivy shook her head. "Your trailer is old, but it isn't that old. I don't think they even made trailers in the 1940s."

"You know everything, do you? Follow me."

Ivy gestured for Zack to come with her and carried her section of

Cross into the Queen's trailer.

"I can't see anything. Crap." Zack bent down and rubbed his shin where he'd bruised it on a crouching red cat statue.

"Don't touch things," the Queen demanded.

"Can we have some light for Zack?"

The Queen considered. Finally, she nodded. "Why not. Electric."

She flipped a switch and a couple of globes of pale light gleamed.

Since they were far from the nearest town, Ivy knew the lights were battery powered. Which may have been why the Queen was reluctant to use them. Of course, she also probably gained power over the other gypsies by being the only one who could see in the dark.

"What do you see, twice-dead?"

When she'd been in the Queen's trailer before, Ivy had been distracted by the icons and by the Queen herself. Now, she forced herself to relax, maintained a light grasp on her section of the Cross, and opened all of her senses to the trailer's interior.

The Queen had said that the gypsy treasure had been hidden inside this trailer decades before the trailer could have been built. But was that really a contradiction? Because the gypsies didn't just buy fancy Winnebagos and drive them around. They patched together trailers from the remains of vehicles abandoned by others, and from scraps gathered, or stolen, from non-gypsies. As Ivy let her senses penetrate beneath the surface of her surroundings, she saw that much of this trailer had once been something else. The wooden ceiling beams were not original to the trailer, but they were original equipment on some long-vanished gypsy cart similar to those they'd first approached when they arrived at the gypsy camp. Some of the beams beneath the floor were hewn tree trunks that dated back hundreds of years and who knew how many generations of gypsy transportation.

"You see it, don't you? Even my granddaughter can't see it and she has the sharpest sight in the Romany. But she is young and has plenty to learn no matter how smart she thinks she is."

"You've got hundreds of years of history in this trailer. No wonder everyone is confused."

The Queen gave another of her hacking laughs. "Confused isn't the word I would use. But before a cart is broken up, one of us, those with true-sight, find the parts that have absorbed power and then incorporate them into a new wagon. It has always been that way, and thus, with each generation, we grow in power. Only so can the gypsy survive."

She and Zack had been on the run for less than a month, but that was long enough to give Ivy a taste of what it must be like to be constantly on the move, constantly surrounded by distrust, hatred, and suspicion.

She could hardly imagine living like that for the long term, always prepared to flee, always threatened by the outsiders, always hoarding your treasures and your power—and then bringing children up to do the same thing, generation after generation for hundreds of years.

Then again, if she survived at all, her future would be like that. She hadn't though of anything beyond getting first to Byzantium and then to Venice. But getting to Venice, even if they could accomplish that, wouldn't solve their problem. The Foundation would still be looking for them. Would she and Zack grow old, perpetually on the road, always hiding, scrabbling for a few days of safety before they had to run again? Maybe, someday, she'd look back at the gypsies as having practically ideal lives.

She shook her head to clear it from the depressing thoughts. "What color is your chalice?"

"How would I know? I'm blind. I don't see colors."

"Do you know where, in all of these sources of power, the chalice is hidden?"

"I preserved everything from my grandmother's old wagon. I know it's here, somewhere. I know we need it. It has power."

Not enough power to protect them from Hitler, Ivy knew. But, the Queen had said that Hitler and his Nazis had tried to gather occult powers for themselves. Maybe the Indiana Jones movies hadn't been as farfetched as she'd thought.

"Okay, let me concentrate."

Centuries of magic pressed down on her like a straitjacket, making it hard to breathe. Her instincts were to close herself to the sensory overload and she felt momentary sympathy for the Foundation Agents who had confronted the animosity of the gypsies. Even with the Queen's support, this wasn't easy.

But concentrating was the wrong approach. Only when she let herself relax did she start to feel the reality underlying the trailer.

"Your religion is dualistic, isn't it?"

"Good, evil, balance. Yes."

"And some of you gypsies worship the evil side?"

The Queen shrugged. "Good, evil people like good, evil deities. We Roma are no better than other people."

That went a long way to unlocking the puzzle of the accumulation of magic within the trailer. The lavender glow wasn't monochromatic after all, but composed of a rainbow of colors and powers.

Ivy concentrated on finding the greatest concentrations of power and then picking which of those were oriented toward the side of good. Because it was pretty obvious that not all of the Queen's predecessors had been wholly committed to the good. There was plenty of evil in here, too.

"You must hurry," the Queen insisted. "The gajikané return now. They've left the Turks behind this time and have an aircraft full of angry men."

"How long?" Zack's sudden words made Ivy jump.

"Fast. Maybe ten minutes."

She almost missed it. She'd been discounting evil because she believed the Queen wanted to do good and supported the good side of the dualistic belief system. But death magic is wrapped up in evil, and the former Queen had died resisting the Nazi, a recent embodiment of evil on earth. And that knot of simmering heat in the very corner of the trailer looked nasty enough to be important.

"If you're lying to me about this chalice, I'm not the only one who's going to be sorry."

The gypsy Queen just cackled. "If I wanted evil to win, I would have handed you over to the Americans."

Well, that was a pretty depressing way to think about it.

Ivy closed her eyes and probed with her second sense.

It looked like a smooth ball of orange and purple, but when she reached out her hand for it, she contacted sharp edges—edges she would have mistaken for wooden splinters if she hadn't been relying on her second sight.

She pushed harder—and pain surged through her hand as invisible splinters dug more deeply into her flesh.

She wouldn't be able to discover more without using the key to open things up. If the Queen had laid a trap, she'd done an effective job.

Ivy hefted the Cross forward, nudging it against the death-magic that surrounded the hidden object, then twisted, letting the blunt end of the Cross loosen the knots that had kept the gypsy treasure from Nazi hands.

The flash of light seared her eyes even behind her closed eyelids.

"What the hell was that?"

"You finally saw something, did you, Zack? Welcome to the second sight."

With the outer layer unbolted, Ivy had no trouble reaching in and removing the clay vessel.

Her skin shriveled against it, as if it contained a powerful desiccant that soaked the life from her fingers.

It wasn't evil, exactly, but it didn't generate the life-affirming sensation she got from both Cross and Veil, either. And old? Eve might have poured Adam a drink from this small pitcher.

"Give it to me." The Queen's gnarled hands clawed toward the precious chalice.

"This held the blood from human sacrifice," Ivy said.

"Look more closely. That was long ago."

Which was true. The faith of the gypsies, or at least these gypsies, had changed. They still sacrificed, but for hundreds of years, flowers and fruits had, more often than not, provided the bodies offered to the deities. Rarely, a chicken or even a lamb might be offered. As Zack explained later, even the ancient Hebrew faith had gone through a similar transition.

Ivy felt a powerful urge to keep the chalice, to hoard its power to herself. Could the world really trust gypsies with this kind of object? Couldn't it be better used by those who saw one sacrifice forever eliminating the need for more?

Her fingers tightened on the clay pot and it seemed to cling to her more closely, whispering its promises of power. With this and the Cross, the Foundation would be no match for her. She could become the Foundation, transforming it from its present goals of war and destruction to those of peace and understanding.

That promise made her suddenly aware of the very personal danger the chalice represented. Ivy thrust it into the old woman's hands. She had been given a quest and two holy relics had fallen to her. Stealing others would pervert her quest, would turn her into what she had sworn to fight. "Guard it carefully and be careful not to listen to its whispers too much. It is a dangerous thing."

"They're almost here. You must leave now."

Chapter 19

They were less than a mile from the gypsy camp when Armageddon seemed to erupt behind them. The moonless sky lit up with parachute flares, heavy turbine helicopters thrummed their ground-rattling roars, and bullhorns shouted out messages in English, Turkish, Arabic, and Greek. Apparently the Foundation hadn't managed any gypsy interpreters because the one language that seemed completely missing was that of the people being surrounded.

"Will they be all right?" The Queen and most of the gypsies had stayed behind. The shotgun gypsy, the Queen's granddaughter, and one other gypsy, a man with a peg leg and a leering squint, had guided them out on foot.

Shotgun shrugged. "Gajikané always cause trouble."

That didn't comfort Ivy much. By gypsy standards, she was a gajikané herself. That seemed to be the gypsy equivalent of a gentile, someone outside the tribe.

"Including us, I guess."

Shotgun's grin exposed a gold tooth. "But you are our friend. You bring back the tribe's symbol of our days in India. You, we help."

She couldn't help wondering how many times he had said those words even as he gulled unsuspecting gajikané with one scam after another.

Shotgun urged them onward, until they came to a small farming village.

"Wait here," he insisted.

He hotwired a farm truck and bundled Ivy and Zack, along with the Queen's granddaughter into the freight compartment and set off.

211

"You're not going to make any friends around here if you just steal their trucks," Zack observed.

The girl laughed. "We no make friends anywhere. There are the Roma and there are the, how you say, suckers?"

"Sounds like something an American would say," Zack warned.

She scowled at him. "That is different. Americans are, what is the word, obnoxious? The Roma are beset. Every man's hand is set against ours. Is that not what it says in your Bible?"

Ivy couldn't remember that quote, but she also couldn't remember the Bible saying anything about gypsies.

The girl, though, wasn't waiting for an answer. She reached out and grabbed Zack's hand. "Let me see your fate, friend of vampire."

Ivy pushed down an irrational surge of jealousy when the girl caressed Zack's hand. She didn't own Zack and even if she had, the gypsy was barely a teen. Hardly someone Zack would be interested in.

"You will go through great adventures," she murmured although it was so dark, Ivy doubted she actually saw the lines on Zack's hands. "I see water and a strange circle of power."

"Aren't you supposed to tell me I'll marry happily and have three and a half children?"

"The second sight is also useful to see what people want to hear. For the suckers, even if I see their lifeline plunge into death, I promise them long years with grandchildren because then they give me money. You would not believe such nonsense. For you, I share the truth."

"No wife? No children?"

The gypsy girl shrugged. "If you survive, perhaps. If you die, the power of the Cross will not bring you back—you are not like the other, the vampire. If you die, you remain dead. And you may die. Soon."

"Glad I asked about that," Zack said. He was trying to joke, but he sounded shaken.

"Ordinary people who stand too close to the power are often burned." The girl put a bit of power into her voice, hinting at horrible danger, suffering, death. Thanks to her developing second sight, Ivy could block the effects of that power. Zack, however was unprotected.

"Sounds like tough times ahead," Zack quipped. "And after we've been having such a pleasant vacation."

"Those who lie with vampires rarely live long enough to joke."

"That's enough," Ivy said. "Do you have any idea where we're going or are you just along to keep us from catching up on our sleep?"

"I was sent with you to sense danger. This is my special talent."

"And is there any?"

The girl shrugged. "All around, of course. When is it not?"

"Yeah, that's a useful talent," Ivy said. "I'm going to take a nap. Wake me when we get wherever we're going."

She laid down her head against the Cross and closed her eyes just as the truck creaked to a stop.

"Quickly," the girl hissed. "The Americans have just given up searching the camp and are spreading out across the countryside."

Ivy picked up the shorter Cross section and hopped down from the truck.

Zack followed her with the other section. "Are we across the border?"

The shotgun gypsy shrugged. "Nearby. There is a passage. We'll leave you here. You will be met at the other end."

"Good enough," Ivy said. "Where's the passage?"

Pegleg hadn't spoken the entire time and, from the way Shotgun talked to him now, Ivy guessed that was because he didn't speak any English. Finally, though, Pegleg grunted, then gestured at them.

"You follow him. He leads you. Not to tell anyone, however. The passage is gypsy secret."

Pegleg grunted again, then gestured toward the nearby hills.

Five minutes of walking through an abandoned apricot orchard got Ivy a couple of clunks in the head from running the Cross into trees, and a windfallen apricot.

Pegleg finally gestured to the heavy iron grating over a corrugated drain that stuck out of the mountain.

"This is it?"

Pegleg shrugged.

"How do we get in?" Zack asked. The iron bars looked rusty but plenty solid enough to keep them out.

Pegleg looked disgusted, but he reached his hand through a couple of bars and tripped a latch, swinging the steel grate outward.

"Are you coming with us?"

Pegleg might not speak English, but he was doing a pretty good job understanding Ivy's questions. He gestured at them to enter the two-foot-high opening. Clearly he wasn't going anywhere.

"Looks like we either have to trust him or not," Zack said. "You did the Queen a favor. So, I figure we should trust them to pay us back."

"The Queen said it," Ivy answered. "If they wanted us dead, they wouldn't be doing anything this complicated." She crawled into the opening wondering whether this part of Thrace was big on snakes and scorpions.

Pegleg grunted again, shoved something at Zack, then slammed the grating behind them. They were alone again.

Dragging the Cross across the bumpy corrugated iron pipe felt blasphemous, but Ivy didn't have any choice. They couldn't stand upright and certainly couldn't just carry their burdens.

Dawn had provided a gray lighting outside as they'd scrambled through the apricot orchard, but Zack's bulk behind her cut off almost all of the light. What little got through diminished quickly as she crawled more deeply into the tunnel.

Then, abruptly, light dazzled, almost blinding her.

"Our one-legged friend gave me a flashlight," Zack admitted.

* * * *

The pipe dumped them out in a stone cave that felt ancient and holy to Ivy.

The blue tinge to the magic could have indicated Mary worship, but she felt certain whatever had been worshiped here had been ancient before Mary had been born.

Zack flashed his lantern around, stopping at the hammer and sickle hewn into the rock in one spot, at the lettering in another spot that didn't look like either the Greek, Latin, Arabic, or Cyrillic alphabets.

"What's that?"

Zack wrinkled his forehead. "I don't recognize it. Maybe it's Linear B."

"Linear what?"

"It's the old Greek alphabet that was lost in the wars during the Mycenaean dark ages before Homer. The Greeks didn't rediscover writing for hundreds of years and then they had to adapt a whole new alphabet."

Ivy shuddered, reminded again of the vision she'd seen in Mosul. She tried to imagine how a war could be that destructive. It wasn't hard to imagine cities being destroyed. Iraq was full of destroyed cities—some ruined thousands of years ago, others flattened by the American invasion. Even technologies could be lost as had Greek Fire, which had once defended Constantinople against the Arabs. But a loss of knowledge so complete that even the alphabet hadn't survived seemed a huge leap beyond even the massive destruction she'd witnessed.

"Another archeological dream," Zack whispered. "I don't think anyone knows that Linear B penetrated so far into Thrace." He sighed, clearly wishing he could stay and explore. "Still, we'd better go. I don't know how long these batteries are going to last."

"Good." Ivy led the way forward hoping that the cavern wouldn't have multiple branches. Without a guide, it would be easy to become lost in a maze. "Say, you don't think those ancient Greeks were Communists, do you?"

"You mean the hammer and sickle? More likely this was a hiding place and smuggling center during the Greek civil war," Zack said. "Or maybe part of the resistance during World War II."

The passage showed occasional signs of more recent use. Perhaps the gypsies, or maybe smugglers, had kept alive memory of an ancient cave system that had once been used to celebrate dark mysteries dedicated to a goddess whose name Ivy couldn't even guess.

The flashlight batteries gave out just as they saw the green light of day to the west.

They emerged from a tree-shrouded grotto, splashing their way through a narrow stream the last hundred feet, and finally squeezing themselves through a muddy opening small enough that Zack had to contort his shoulders to get through.

Ivy looked back at the hill behind them and spotted the high fence that separated Turkey from Greece.

Despite Pegleg's promise, no one was at hand to greet them.

"Looks like we're one step closer to Venice," she said. "Now what?"

"More walking," Zack said. "The Americans don't have as many bases in Greece as they do in Turkey, but I'm willing to bet that one more border isn't going to stop the Foundation from following us."

* * * *

Greece involved a lot more walking. Eventually, though, they made contact with some of the Constantinople Patriarch's allies in Greece and were bundled onto one of the many Greek shipping lines—on a ship heading for Venice.

"It's not exactly a pleasure cruise." Ivy filled Zack's bowl with a Greek lamb stew, then dished out another bowl to the Greek sailor behind him.

"Tell me about it." Zack looked as exhausted as she felt. Because he couldn't speak Greek and had no special on-board skills, he'd been given the most skutwork jobs on the ship.

The ship's whistle sounded before they could gripe any more and the dining room where Ivy had been put to work as assistant cook and food-slopper emptied out.

"Quickly, move." The cook grabbed her by the arm and dragged her toward his room.

She heard the telltale rumble of helicopter turbines just in time to keep from decking the aging sailor. Although they were hundreds of miles from where they'd finally broken contact with the Foundation, the Agents hadn't given up. It didn't help that they could have drawn a line from Mosul in Iraq through Turkey and Greece to get an idea of where she and Zack were heading.

The freighter's engine shifted tone as the captain hove to under threat of attack.

"No woman on ship," the cook insisted as he shoved her into his room. "Change."

That she could understand. Not that the baggy pants or blue workshirt she wore were especially feminine.

She packed a couple of towels into her shirt, hoping to make her breasts look like fat rather than female, and grabbed the cook's straight razor.

This wouldn't hurt at all.

It only took her about thirty seconds to shave off all of her hair, blacken her eyebrows, yank out her earrings, and head out to the deck.

The cook handed her a greasy sailor's cap which she stuck on top of her shaved head.

A U.S. Navy frigate rocketed through the gray waters of the Adriatic toward them while an ugly black helicopter circled overhead.

As she watched, a rope ladder dropped down from the gunship and two sailors scrabbled down.

The Captain met them at the base of the ladder, screaming at them that he was a registered merchant, that they were conducting an act of piracy and war, that he would notify his government representative, and that the sailor's mother had engaged in sex with a horse's hindquarters.

The sailor listened to the captain for a couple of moments, then shoved him aside.

An angry murmur ran through the watching Greek sailors and several stepped forward carrying improvised weapons, but the roar of Gatling gun bullets convinced them to pull back.

The helicopter crew had fired into the sea, but the warning was clear —they could turn the freighter into so much scrap metal in a few seconds of sustained firing.

"What cargo are you carrying?" the sailor demanded.

The captain brushed himself off. "Olive oil, incense, artwork. Some containers delivered by customers. Those are sealed by Customs. I don't have the keys."

"Yeah, right. Of course you don't. Well, we can get through seals. Show us where they are."

The captain protested for a moment, but everyone could see his heart wasn't in it. He didn't want to let the Americans into his cargo, but he wanted to get shot up even less.

"Tell the rest of your sailors to stay on deck. Anyone else going below will be killed."

The captain shouted something in Greek and, from the angry murmur from the sailors, Ivy thought he had added his opinions of the Americans, but he must also have conveyed his message because no one moved as the captain led the sailors below.

"The men from the chopper are dressed as Navy petty officers, but they stink of Foundation to me." Zack hadn't moved noticeably, but he'd closed the distance so they could talk. "And jeez, what the heck happened to your head?"

"No women on the ship. I didn't have time for a careful styling."

"It's, uh, unfortunate."

"Too bad. Here I was such a fashionplate before."

"Whatever. So, what are we going to do if they find the Cross?"

They'd hidden it as best they could, but the Foundation had proven able to track them down. These Agents, though, didn't seem especially alert. They were going through the motions of inspecting every ship in the area.

The captain popped up and shouted something else and the cook gestured to Zack and Ivy. "You four, go with the Captain." He signaled to a couple of others so it wasn't just the two of them. Ivy wondered if the Captain had decided that giving them up would be the safest strategy. Considering how the Foundation Agents treated their witnesses, Ivy didn't he'd be right. Still, it was way too late to warn him.

The Captain put them to work unbolting the cargo holds and bringing up samples of the cargo from below.

"No guns," he insisted as if he really believed that the Agents were U.S. military and that they were looking for terrorists. "No explosion. We carry same cargo we have carry for twenty years."

"I'm picking up something." The Agents appeared to have tuned out the captain. "Over to the left."

If Ivy needed convincing that these weren't real sailors, his use of the word 'left' rather than 'port' would have done it.

Rather than the crucifix Smith and some of the other agents had carried, this pair had a small electronic device the size of a palmtop computer, but with a cute little dish antenna on top. More evidence they were putting every agent into the field that they could.

"Seems to be close."

"Nothing below, in the hold?"

"I'm picking up a vague signal down there, too. Nothing big, though."

"All right. Let's focus on the big one." He turned to the captain. "Whatchew hiding behind this door?"

Rather than wait for an answer, he kicked his booted foot through the closed door.

The ship's chapel was fancier than Ivy would have imagined before she'd seen it. The Greek shipping crew was all Orthodox and, as far as Ivy could tell, relatively devout for a bunch of sailors. Still, she'd been blown away when she'd first seen the gold leaf, the dozens of paintings, and the continually burning and frequently refreshed candles. A huge crucifix with a lifesized but strangely flat-looking statue of Jesus hanging from it dominated the chapel.

"It's a goddamn church," the Agent said.

The senior agent pushed in and looked around. "The so-called Orthodox religion is as badly in error as the Papist faith. Both stray from the true word."

"Maybe so, but the detector is going crazy," the Agent said. "This place is full of faith."

"Let me see that." The senior agent grabbed the palmtop detector and pointed it around the room.

Sure enough, the device's proximity locator screamed but its direction sensing seemed completely out of whack. Even without understanding how the palm-sized device worked, Ivy could see that its signals were spiking aimlessly.

She took a couple of steps and the system squawked. Good. The power emissions from both Cross and Veil were stronger than it was built to deal with. Having them both in close proximity confused it and made it hard to get a fix on either source. Of course the ambient power associated with the chapel just added to its confusion.

"Just how old is this church?" the junior Agent demanded.

The captain shrugged. "We move our chapel from old ship to new ship when the old ship retires. This maybe come from a hundred years ago first, when Greece begins to build major shipping. Some changes, some things remain the same."

The junior agent scratched his head. "Could it be just another church? We've gotten funky signals before."

"Only one way to find out. Tear the place apart and see what we find," the Senior Agent demanded.

Ivy froze, but forced herself to relax. Even if they subdued the boarding party, they could do nothing in the face of the helicopter's

Gatling guns.

The Captain clutched the Senior Agent's arm. "No. This is our special place. It belonged to my father, to his father before him."

"Don't touch me." The Agent yanked his arm free, then shoved the Captain against the wall hard enough to, crack the wood paneling.

Real tears ran down the Captain's cheeks as the senior Agent radioed the frigate to send over a group of sailors with crowbars. The sailors cheerfully demolished the chapel, yanked sandlewood paneling from the walls, cut icons out of their frames, and spilled the liturgical wine and wafers on the floor.

A couple of sailors kept submachineguns trained on the Captain, who continued to shout curses at them, wave his fists, and threaten to rush them each time they attacked another panel, another old painting.

"Even the infidel Turks do not do such damage when they inspect us. Why do you do this?"

Evidently the senior agent had heard enough. He grabbed the Captain and twisted his lapels so tightly the Captain's swarthy face turned blue. "The end-times are here, Captain. The Gog-Magog war is already under way. You'd better start getting yourself right with the Lord. These icons aren't going to help you."

He dumped the Captain on the floor, then turned to supervise the damage.

"We haven't seen anything," the junior Agent reported. "I think we're wasting our time. Again."

"Maybe," the senior Agent admitted. "Still, there is a certain satisfaction from destroying these symbols of the Antichrist."

He looked around. "Tear up the floors."

The Captain hadn't learned his lesson from the choking he'd gotten. "No! These are priceless mosaics, ancient floorboards. Surely—"

"Surely nothing," the Agent said. "Down to the steel bulkheads."

For thirty minutes, six sailors and two agents used crowbars, electric screwdrivers, and a small jackhammer to tear out the floors and walls of the chapel, leaving the entire cabin a steel box with a large pile of litter in the middle.

They finally stopped when the senior Agent got a call on his cell.

"We've got another ship to inspect. Let's go," he reported.

"But the damage to my ship," the Captain protested. "It will cost many thousands of Euros to repair."

"The love of money is the root of all evil," the Agent responded. "Think of this as a small sacrifice toward your, admittedly unlikely, salvation. You Orthodox still believe in indulgences, don't you?"

By the time they went back on deck, the helicopter had vanished, possibly to refuel, and the Agents joined the sailors in the open boat for the ride back to the frigate.

"The Lord has given us idiots for enemies," the Captain said when the sailors motored away. "Unfortunately, their idiocy has not prevented them from doing great damage."

"Sorry about the mess we got you into," Zack said.

The Captain waved a hand. "I will not blame you for what your countrymen have done. Come, we still have many kilometers to cover before we reach Venice. I would rather not experience this kind of interruption again."

The freighter's engines rumbled as the Captain engaged propellers deep beneath the surface of the ocean and the ship picked up speed.

If the U.S. Navy and the Foundation were stopping all shipping like this everywhere in the eastern Mediterranean, the State Department would be getting complaints from every one of their allies and the Defense Department would be running through its budget even quicker than usual. All of which had to mean something.

The senior Agent had said something about the 'end times.' This was another area of Christian belief that the Catholic Church didn't emphasize but that Zack explained many Protestant faiths worried about a lot. But could the Agent have been speaking literally when he'd said that the 'end times' were actually here, rather than fast approaching? Perhaps that would explain why he didn't seem worried about offending foreigners or how much money his casual vandalism was going to end up costing his government.

Ivy wasn't sure.

"So, where was the Cross?" Zack demanded.

"You didn't see it? It was hanging right there in the open."

"You mean the Crucifix?"

She nodded. "They expected to see a Cross in a Church, so we gave it to them. It became invisible. Even its power, they could justify to themselves as the result of decades of sailors praying."

She looked into the shattered chapel. The entire chamber was filled with wreckage with only the Cross itself, along with the temporarily attached statue of Jesus, hanging over the shattered alter, unaffected by the carnage.

Chapter 20

Venice was magical.

Since their ship was going to be in the harbor for several days, they left the Cross in the ruined chapel on the freighter and set off to explore the ancient city—and to see if they could figure out what they were supposed to be doing here.

Ivy described the many colors of power to Zack, but to him, the city was a mosaic of more subtle shades—the dark gray of the water in the canals, the dull brown of motorboats and the inky black of the gondolas clogging up the canals like cars on a freeway, the paler gray of stone buildings, the dusty brick of tiled roofs, and the gleaming whiteness of ancient churches.

"Venice isn't actually as old as Istanbul or some of the other places we've visited," Ivy reported from a guidebook. "It was founded in 421 A.D. by Romans fleeing the destruction of that empire."

"I'd think being on a city of islands would make it easier to defend," Zack admitted.

"They hammered millions of wooden piers into the marshland to create many of the islands." She was still reading.

"Which means all these heavy stone buildings are being supported by wood that's been rotting for fifteen hundred years. Suddenly I'm not feeling so secure."

"Yeah, the whole place is settling." Ivy looked up from her book and grinned. "Another thousand years and we'll be in real trouble."

He was still having trouble getting used to the bald and fat Greek Sailor version of Ivy although it had certainly fooled the Foundation Agents when they'd invaded the freighter.

Troubled or not, she still looked good to him.

She looked good to the pigeons in Saint Mark's Square, as well. By the thousands and tens of thousands, they abandoned the tourists who were feeding them bits of stale bread and corn and flocked around Ivy. Dozens landed on her head, their little claws grasping for purchase on her newly shiny dome. Others settled on her shoulders, while thousands more scrambled around her feet, somehow managing to keep out of the way as she stepped forward toward the massive cathedral.

"If the city wasn't built until the fifth century, it wouldn't have the same sort of artifacts we found in Mosul or Istanbul, would it?" he asked.

Ivy shrugged, temporarily sending up a cloud of pigeons. "According to the guide book, the Venetians were prime thieves and pirates—a kleptocracy. They looted most of the great treasures of Constantinople, except the Veil. They stole the relics of Saint Mark from the Coptic Christians in Egypt, and collected treasures from the entire world for a thousand years. The major symbols of the city, the four horses over the Doge's palace and the Cathedral of Saint Mark both celebrate theft."

"So, basically, we have no idea what we're looking for and whatever it is, it was brought here as loot from some foreign conquest?"

Ivy waved her hand and the swarm of pigeons dispersed, several of them looking backward at her as they flew to see if she might relent. "I don't know, Zack. The priestess said to come to Venice and we did. I don't have a clue what comes next, except we've only got 48 hours to figure it out. Because that's how long before the freighter moves out and I don't think this is the kind of place we want to be lugging our Cross sections around in. It would be hard to be inconspicuous when we're surrounded by a hundred thousand Italians and another hundred thousand tourists from all over the world."

A small sign outside the massive Cathedral of Saint Mark indicated that Mass would begin in a few minutes. If there was ever a time when divine inspiration would come in handy, Zack figured this was it.

"What do you say we go to Church, then have a glass of wine on the plaza here and talk about next steps?"

Ivy brushed her fingers against her ugly blue coveralls, directly over where they'd sewn the Veil of Mary into a hidden compartment. "Why not?"

Mass was celebrated by an angelic-sounding choir, a massive pipe organ that looked to be at least a couple of hundred years old, and a bishop wearing the pointed hat and carrying the crooked miter of his rank.

The professions of faith, the liturgical Italian, and the massive solidity of the Church provided him a moral uplift, but Zack didn't get any brilliant ideas on what to do next. Inspiration wasn't that easy.

The Captain had grudgingly paid them for their work on the freighter, grumbling the whole while about the costs of the damage done by the Foundation Agents and the navy wrecking crew, but Zack wasn't surprised to see the ridiculous prices for food or a glass of wine at the restaurants on the plaza. They were tourist traps. Still, whatever else they might be, he and Ivy were tourists there in the ancient city.

He ordered a carafe of the house wine and a couple of glasses and then sent the waiter away.

"So, what next?"

Ivy took a sip of her wine. "Let's review what we know." She ticked off the points on her fingers. "First, the Foundation is a nominally Christian organization, but it appears to have no respect for Orthodox or Catholic denominations."

"That isn't unusual with the extreme Protestant factions," Zack reminded her. "Some of them think that the Catholic Church really is the Whore of Babylon from the Bible."

She looked blank. "If you say so. Second, there are at least hints that the Foundation, whatever it is, is trying to create some sort of new Crusade or war between the Christian world and the Moslem world."

"Which seems at odds with its lack of respect for the Catholics and Orthodox who would be on the front lines for that war," Zack said.

"Unless they think getting the two groups to kill each other off would be a good thing."

Now that was a depressing thought. "It seems more likely to me that the organization has fanatical members but that the leadership has more ecumenical notions of Christianity. They may think the Catholics and Orthodox are misguided, but that they're on the right side of the war."

"Maybe." They both knew he was just speculating.

"Third, the agent and the Queen talked about the Gog/Magog war. I have absolutely no idea what that is except they think we're in it."

Zack strained his memory. "It's from Ezekiel, I think. Part of some really cryptic prophesies that everyone thinks refers to themselves. Israel will be under attack."

"The last agent said that war had been going on for a while."

"Well, Israel has been under attack."

She shrugged. "Fourth, we know that the Cross is involved and is considered the key. Which I first thought meant it was critically important, but now believe is meant literally. The Cross is intended to open something."

He refilled their wineglasses and took a sip. Although he'd ordered the cheapest Italian wine the café offered, it still tasted pretty good to him. "And the Cross can unleash power that has been locked up for centuries."

"Yeah. That's about all we know. Unless you can think of something else, those four points are everything we've learned about the people who have been trying to kill us for weeks."

He considered, then shook his head. "We know one more thing."

"What's that?"

"There's someone working against them. Someone sent you a message to go to Byzantium to get the Veil. Someone told us to come here to Venice."

"Oh, great. Our one great helper is a priestess who's been dead for thousands of years and whose religion died out hundreds of years before Jesus."

Somehow that twinged wrong to him. "Really? Are you absolutely sure?"

* * * *

Ivy hadn't noticed she'd been drinking her wine but when Zack refilled her glass for the second time, she decided she had better slow down. The last thing they needed was to be arrested for public intoxication.

But Zack was right. Or rather, he was wrong about the Priestess being alive thousands of years later or Ishtar worship continuing after all that time, but he was right that they needed to find some opposition to the Foundation. Staying one jump ahead of the Foundation was a game they couldn't win. Sooner or later, an Agent would get lucky. They needed a more permanent solution. For that, they needed real allies.

She had no idea where to start looking, but if the priestess's message meant anything, at least they were in the right city.

"We'll start early tomorrow," Zack suggested. "Maybe you can use your second sight to pick up on something. In the meantime, we might as well head back to the freighter. At least we can sleep there for free."

"We don't have time." At least they'd had a chance to catch up on their sleep while they'd been sailing from Greece to Venice. Because Ivy didn't plan on resting until she'd either found someone who could help her or at least found a safe place to hide the Cross.

"If you've got a better idea, I'm wide open."

If she had any better ideas, she wouldn't be sitting her in the middle of a piazza drinking cheap red wine and surrounded by an admiring flock of pigeons.

Still, they had to do something.

"The Patriarch was helpful. And remember that the Agents seemed to hate the Orthodox Church. Maybe we could make contact with the local Greek Orthodox congregation and see if they could point us in the right direction."

Zack was unimpressed. "Even if there is an Orthodox Church, why would we be sent here to find it? I mean, we spent days in Greece. They have thousands of Orthodox priests there."

"Because it's something to do, Zack. It's got to be better than just sitting here waiting for the Foundation Agents to figure out how we got past them."

Zack considered, then nodded. "Why not? Let's get started."

Since they were wearing Greek sailor clothing, no one seemed surprised that they were looking for the Orthodox Church. After a couple of misdirections, they finally found the beautiful domed church standing near one of the many canals that cut through the island city.

The striking Church's red glow of faith was so similar to that of Saint Marks where they'd recently celebrated Mass that Ivy wondered how the different churches had managed to keep themselves at war with one another for so many centuries before Pope John had finally started the movement to bring people of faith together.

The priest who met them was as complete an opposite to Father Galen as Ivy could have imagined. He was over six feet tall, but he couldn't have weighed much more than she did. His skin clung to his skull like a mummy and he peered at them through a pair of bifocals that looked like they were about to collapse into a pile of rust.

"Ti?"

Okay, their Greek sailor uniforms were convincing. Unfortunately, she had no idea what he was saying. "Do you speak English, Father?"

"You're a woman." He started to make the sign of the Cross, then restrained himself. "Yes, I speak English."

"Father, we need help."

"Are you Orthodox? There are many Churches in Venice. Perhaps you should seek council from your own priest, or a pastor of your faith."

"That's the problem, Father. We don't know who to trust."

He squinted at her, took off his glasses and polished them, then looked at her again.

"If your problems are not spiritual, the police may be more helpful to you than a priest." His expression suggested that contacting a mental health professional might be an even better solution but that he was afraid of making the suggestion in case they turned violent.

"Father, have you ever heard of an extreme Christian organization called The Foundation?"

"Extreme Christian?" He gave them a benevolent smile. "I like to think that we are all extreme Christians."

"Enough that you'd kill to gain control of the True Cross?" Zack put in.

The priest laughed, then stopped abruptly when he saw they weren't joking. He looked at the doorway at the back of the church and lowered his voice. "Why don't you come into my office and tell me what this is about?"

The priest's office was a part of the late medieval Church. Unlike the rest of the church, though, it had been updated with comfortable leather chairs, air conditioning, and recessed lighting.

Everywhere around the room, Ivy saw images of saints and of Jesus. Oddly, though, she saw none of Mary or any other female.

He poured tea for them and Ivy accepted a cup. "Right. I assume you are using the example of the Cross as some sort of hyperbole."

"Not at all, Father," she said. In a few sentences, she summarized their discovering the Cross, the Foundation's chase, and the Patriarch's assistance.

"But how did you come to Venice?"

"We took the train," Zack interrupted.

Ivy hadn't been brought up to lie to priests, but when she looked at Zack, he frowned back at her. Okay. He didn't have the second sight, but he had an instinct for people she could only admire.

"And where is the Cross now?"

"We hid it in Saint Marks." Zack continued his lie. "It seemed safer there, surrounded by all of the other relics. And who would notice two more beams among the scaffolding where they're cleaning and preserving."

"Very wise," the priest said. "I have not heard of this Foundation. Until now, my vocation has dealt more with counseling local Greeks and performing marriages for those who think Venice would make a wonderful honeymoon than in battling American hate groups. Still, I can go on-line and see what I can discover. There are chat groups and bulletin boards where cults and heresies are discussed. My fellow priests have taken to the virtual world in a big way. As you suggest, I can get guidance from the Patriarch in Constantinople."

"We'd appreciate it if you could do that," Ivy said. She felt like an idiot for not thinking of it herself. There were Internet cafes all over Turkey where she could have done research.

"Perhaps you'd like to look around the Church while I, as you say, surf." He seemed proud of himself for using that outdated verb.

"Fine." She set down her untouched tea and stepped out of the priest's office.

"What was that lying about?" she whispered to Zack.

"Remember how Galen wanted the Cross and Veil for himself? I figured we'd be smart not to throw too much temptation in the way of this priest."

Ivy nodded, although she didn't think it was quite fair to assume all priests would be tempted. She busied herself walking around the church. It was, according to her guidebook about five hundred years old, with a tall dome and a heavy sense of religious awe and the bright red of power that should have felt peaceful and reassuring, but that somehow seemed almost oppressive.

After ten minutes, she couldn't stand it any more. "I'm going to see how our priest is doing."

"You know it can take time to do online research."

"I'm still going."

She opened the office door and the priest grinned at her. "I've been able to locate some information on the Foundation."

"Great. What have you learned?"

"They aren't just Protestant extremists after all. The Foundation includes Catholic, Orthodox, even Coptic leaders as well as a broad spectrum of the Protestant wing.

"They are men who are concerned about the loss of Christian faith to the secular and New Age movements as well as the Moslems and eastern occult movements."

"Interesting. Your Patriarch didn't seem to know about them."

"The Patriarch in Constantinople is a strange man. He is, perhaps, more liberal than many in our church. Unlike the Catholics, we do not recognize the authority of a single supreme leader for the entire Orthodox communion, despite occasional pretenses from Constantinople."

Zack must have been feeling some of the same warning signs Ivy was because he physically interposed himself between her and the priest. "And so who opposes the Foundation?"

The priest shrugged. "Moslems, worshipers of the occult, the Liberal Protestant faiths, heretical Catholics and Orthodox. The usual suspects, as you Americans say, Captain Hererra."

* * * *

He moved without conscious thought.

227

The instant the priest said his name, Zack threw Ivy over his shoulder and headed for the door.

"You won't get far," the priest shouted behind him. "We know where the Cross is now."

Once outside the Church's elegant courtyard, Zack set Ivy down. "We've got to get back to the freighter and hide the Cross."

"But we told them it's hidden in Saint Mark's."

"Which they'll believe for how long? We came in dressed as Greek sailors. You don't think they put two and two together and start looking in Greek ships?"

"You're right. And I have to admit that going to the Orthodox Church turned out to be a bad idea. Sorry."

"And I'm sorry I treated you like a sack of potatoes when we needed to get out of there. But at least we learned something."

"Do you think he was telling the truth?"

"Why would he lie? He thinks he's on the side of angels here, defending his church against evil influences of modern times. And I don't believe he thought we'd get away. At least now we have an idea of where to look for organized opposition to The Foundation."

"Yeah. Our big allies are liberal kooks. It's real reassuring we'll have them to count on when we go up against knife-fighters and gunmen. Maybe we we're in the wrong place. Maybe we were supposed to go to Venice, California rather than Venice, Italy. If we'd gone there, we could be hanging out with New Agers and surfers."

Ivy had been a tower of strength for weeks. Now it was up to him to suck it up while she suffered her doubts.

"I don't believe you misinterpreted what the Priestess told you. Now, let's get the Cross and find a place to go to ground. Then we can figure out what to do next."

Since those were so obviously the next steps, Ivy couldn't argue.

Unfortunately, following through on the steps was not so easy.

They crossed the first bridge with no problems. By the time they reached the second, Italian police had set up checkpoints and were demanding identification from everyone crossing over. Since Venice consists of dozens of tiny islands connected by bridges, the Foundation could cordon the city, sending Agents through each section while controlling all movement between them. With the Italian police as witting or unwitting accomplices to the Foundation, he and Ivy were trapped like rats.

"The Priest will have described us," Ivy said. "Time for me to be a chick again." She yanked the wadded fabric from around her waist, borrowed Zack's cap, and tied the ends of the baggy shirt over her navel.

The transformation was almost shocking. Those few changes altered her appearance from that of a pudgy male to a sexy female.

They'd retreated into one of the narrow alleys that actually seemed to be the main streets of this section of Venice.

"Don't you think we're past disguises by now?" Zack said. "The priest will have told them that you're a woman and he knew my name. You won't fool anyone by changing back to your normal appearance."

"It's worked so far. Besides, at least I'm me and not an ugly fat man," she said. "Now, how are we going to get out of here?"

They were trapped on a tiny island connected to the other parts of the city by four bridges. Foundation Agents and Italian policemen guarded each bridge. Across one of the bridges, on the island with the Orthodox Church, police were already checking in every shop and street corner systematically narrowing down their possible hiding places. The search would slow as it moved in concentric rings away from the last contact point, but it wouldn't take long before they moved to the neighboring islands. When that happened, if they were still there, they'd be caught.

Zack looked down at the narrow canals. "We could swim across that."

"That would be a bit obvious, wouldn't it? Besides, we'd just be on another little island."

A policeman carried his submachine gun on the ready as he patrolled the far side of the canal and Zack and Ivy retreated into a tourist shop to escape his prying eyes.

"We can't wait here like frogs hypnotized by a cobra," Zack protested. "We've got to move."

Ivy started giggling. "I've got an idea."

He followed her gaze. "Oh, no. Not going to happen."

* * * *

Zack looked quite charming in his striped shirt and white gondolier hat. Its wide brim hid his dark eyes and the broad red ribbon around the crown gave him a rakish appeal.

"I'm not going to sing," he promised.

"Don't be a sissy. Didn't your mother play operas when you were growing up? I'll bet you have a pretty voice."

She'd found a wig pair of skinny pants and a halter top for herself. A big floppy hat and a cheap camera completed the outfit. She thought she looked like a tourist from somewhere in Northern Europe. Germany, maybe, or Scandinavia. Definitely nothing like an American. And the

Foundation and cops would be looking for an American couple or a pair of Greek sailors, not for a single European woman who insisted on being rowed around the city by a handsome Italian gondolier.

At least she hoped so.

Obtaining a gondola was a lot trickier. Stealing one was the obvious solution but it didn't take a genius to guess that the owner would report the theft to the authorities, which would blow their disguise. And purchasing one was way beyond their resources. One question established that a gondola cost as much as an SUV, although Ivy did have to admit it would probably get better mileage.

They pooled what was left of their cash, threw in the fake ID's Cejno had provided them, and finally convinced a lazy gondolier that he would be happier renting them the boat and getting drunk than waiting for a fare. Ivy credited their persuasiveness to the power of the Veil, although Zack insisted it had more to do with her feminine charms. They even convinced the slacking gondolier to throw in a phone call—and warned the freighter Captain to offload the Cross onto one of the ship's launches, setting up a rendezvous for that evening.

"Home, Iago," she ordered as they stepped into the narrow vessel.

"We're going to look pretty silly when I tip this thing over and we all get wet," Zack said.

"You're right. So don't do that. We've got about four hours to kill so let's just get to the Grand Canal and blend in with the other gondolas."

The broad-striped shirt clung to Zack's muscles as he stood in the stern of the gondola and navigated his way through crowds of outboards, the other tourist-bearing gondolas, and the larger boats that brought groceries, supplies, and everything else into the city of canals and islands.

A police outboard roared by them, its engines leaving a wake behind that rocked their gondola and nearly made a prophet out of Zack.

"Hey, you're supposed to know what you're doing."

"Yeah? Well, you're supposed to be paying me. So maybe neither of us should complain."

The disguise must have been convincing, though, because no one gave them a second look as Zack slowly rowed through the dozens of canals of Venice.

Ivy snapped pictures of the major Venice landmarks—the palazzos, the 'Bridge of Sighs' which connected the Doge's palace to his prisons, a view of the Cathedral from the canals, and the famous bell tower, while Zack gradually became more comfortable with the single oar used to propel the long slender boat through the filthy waters of the canals.

The police were out in force and several helicopters circled the city, foretelling an even more active U.S. military presence. Ivy could almost feel their eyes glaze over when they saw the single European woman, alone on the gondola. To them, the olive-skinned gondolier was an object, not even noticeable.

As dusk began to fall, the other gondoliers steered their boats toward the docks, leaving only a few of the most romantic to tour by darkness.

Ivy lit the lantern at the bow of their gondola. It was time to connect with the men from their ship.

Which was easier said than done.

They'd arranged to meet at the dock near the train station, a central point connecting Venice to the Italian mainland. But the Captain had sent out the sailors as soon as Ivy had called, wanting the Cross off his ship before the Foundation Agents renewed their search—and tore apart more of his precious cargo.

Apparently the launch's crew had decided they'd be conspicuous just waiting at the pier and had gone into a local bar for drinks.

The freighter's launch was indistinguishable from dozens of other small boats tied up at the station's pier. Searching all of them would invite certain attention from the local cops.

"I can check out the local bars," Zack offered. "The sailors will probably be in one of the closer ones."

"You can't leave me on the gondola alone, Zack. And it would look suspicious if the two of us went barhopping dressed like this. Besides, we don't need the sailors. All we need is the launch."

"Surely they wouldn't have left the Cross unprotected."

"You think they took two big hunks of timber bar-hopping? That wouldn't look suspicious?"

He shut up and she closed her eyes for focus.

Just about all of the boats tied to the pier had some sort of religious glow. Italy remained a Catholic nation and Christian medallions, tiny statues, and other testaments of faith were scattered around most of the boats and nearby homes.

But the glorious shine from the Cross stood out like a searchlight next to a thousand flickering candles. She pointed toward the identifying glow. "It's there."

The Captain must have been having some guilt feelings. In addition to sending the Cross, he'd even thrown in a waterproof bag filled with a food and a couple of hundred Euros. It wasn't much, but it was more than he'd had to do.

They transferred the Cross to the bottom of their gondola and ate some of the bread and olives the Captain had left for them, Zack wolfishly gulping his meal down.

"All that rowing take something out of you?" she asked.

He nodded. "I can see why the gondoliers charge so much. You owe me for this."

Zack finished off his loaf of bread, then rowed away from the train station pier. "Okay, so what now?"

The Foundation and Italian Police were still everywhere around the city bringing Venice's normally wild nightlife to a low ebb. Zack and Ivy considered checking into one of the many two-star hotels carved into the ancient palaces of Venice, but finally decided to stay with the gondola, tying the boat to a pier and pulling a tarp over the cockpit.

"Just us, the Cross, and the Veil," Zack murmured as he shifted his weight looking for comfort. "Pretty romantic."

Ivy suppressed her sigh. Just a little bit of romance wouldn't have been completely out of place, would it?

Chapter 21

Dense fog shrouded the ancient city. Zack and Ivy ate the last of the bread, cheese, and olives the Captain had sent them, then set off.

In most cities, a boat would be a horribly impractical way to travel. In Venice, though, just about every building is accessible by water. Hundreds of docks, piers, and water gates had let medieval Venetians step from gondola to the palaces of their friends or rivals. Many of those gates remained open and available.

The challenge was to discover which of those gates was right, and which represented another trap. Ivy had guessed wrong when she'd decided on the Orthodox Church the previous afternoon—almost fatally wrong. Luck, rather than any particular skill or virtue, had kept them alive, if on the run. If she guessed wrong again, Ivy didn't think they'd survive the experience.

Zack seemed endlessly patient as she had him row through the smaller canals, the literal backwaters of the city. At this time of the morning, most of the traffic was motorized—small boats delivering merchandise and hauling away trash, but the fog protected them from prying eyes on the shores.

Their gondola raised a few eyes—tourists normally didn't wake up that early—but no whistles blew. After spending all night searching, maybe the cops were tired, too.

"Can't you use your second sight?" Zack suggested.

"And look for what? A mystical glowing banner that says 'enemies of The Foundation welcomed here?'"

"Hey, don't bite my head off. I'm on your side, remember."

"Sorry." Things would have been easier if she could just look for the red glow of the monotheistic religions. But she'd already learned that even within any one splinter of the red world, there were huge differences of opinion. The Orthodox Patriarch in Constantinople had feared and opposed the Foundation and his support had eased their way through Greece. The local Orthodox Priest in Venice had been a member or sympathizer. Yet their colors had been the same. The rare spots of other colors might be hotbeds of anti-Foundation activity, but they could also be remnants of the pre-Roman population of the swamps that had become the city of Venice or a local palm-reading establishment.

Ivy kept her eyes closed, letting her untrained but increasingly powerful senses reach out around her. Ultimately, though, she guided Zack through canals and open waterways by instinct and hunch rather than reason.

"Straight ahead," she said.

The teak and mahogany gondola gave a loud complaint as Zack ran it up onto the stone pier of a neighborhood church.

"Sorry, bad advice," she said.

"Thick as the fog is, it's amazing we haven't run into more things." He shoved the gondola away from the building.

A sense of wrongness hit her as they distanced themselves from the pier. "Wait, Zack. There's something about this place."

"Something good, or something bad?"

"I'm not sure."

Physically, the church was indistinguishable from the hundreds of others scattered around Venice. For generations, each neighborhood had built and maintained their own church, supported a priest or two to tend to their souls' needs, and gathered what small treasures of faith—relics, paintings, statues—that had been collected by the parishioners and bequeathed to their local Church in their old age or death.

The ever-present red glow of monotheism, though, was overlaid with the powerful blue that Ivy associated with the adoration of Mary.

"Remember how that Agent Jones worried about a 'fetish of Mary?'"

"You think Marianism may be some sort of key to opposition?" Zack had followed her logic, but doubt was heavy in his voice.

"We've noticed before that Mary, Queen of Heaven has distinct similarities with the ancient Goddess. Maybe those Catholics who have been drawn to Mary are following in that ancient tradition. Maybe they are part of what the Foundation is working against. The Greek priest did say the Foundation battled heretical Catholics, didn't he?"

"You're making some big logic jumps, Ivy."

She knew that. Things hadn't worked out very well the last time they'd taken chances, but that didn't mean they could afford to play it safe. For them, there were no safe choices.

"I'm going in. Want to come with me, or stay here and guard the Cross?"

"Nobody's going to steal a couple of old timbers. We're a team. We stick together."

Someone might just steal an unguarded gondola—taking the timbers along. Still, the risk of dragging the Cross with them into a public church seemed greater.

A youthful priest seemed to have just ended mass as they arrived.

A few elderly women in traditional black dresses gathered around the priest, pressing food on him and seeking his advice on the infirmities of old age. A couple of children, too young for school and left with grandmothers, orbited beyond. The church was otherwise deserted.

The parish church lacked some of the extreme decoration of Saint Mark's or the Orthodox Church they'd visited the previous day but the more simple paintings and statues nevertheless shone with the authentic passion of the artists and radiated a quiet holiness that, to Ivy's sensitized other-sight, bathed the church in a light that echoed and complemented the vivid stained glass images.

A childhood memory of churchgoing returned to her and she crossed herself as she entered the church, then sat in a pew to wait. Her second sight didn't give her any indication of special focal points within the church beyond the usual Stations of the Cross and the carved wooden altar. It didn't seem likely that they'd find any long-forgotten relics in the old, but far from ancient structure. Still, there was a rightness to the church that her instincts told her to trust.

One of the parishioners turned and scowled at her and Ivy realized she was a mess. She'd lost her wig and hadn't combed the four-day fuzz of hair that poked straight up from her head She hadn't brushed her teeth in over twenty-four hours. Her sleeveless top, tied at the waist to expose more abdomen than was appropriate for a church. And an obvious tourist who snuck her gondolier into a church could only be viewed with suspicion.

The priest was younger than most of the priests she knew back home, handsome, and completely Italian. No wonder there were so many older women hanging out at his church. With his thick black hair, soulful brown eyes, and muscular arms, if he hadn't received a calling, he might have made it big in the movie business.

He patted a little girl on the head, exchanged a few words with one of the older parishioners who lapped up his words as if she had been starving for attention, and then he headed toward Ivy and Zack.

Ivy's grammar school Latin was little help when he opened up on Zack, obviously blasting him for something.

Zack nodded, grinned at the priest, then turned to Ivy. "He says gondoliers should know better than to try to pick up on rich tourists and trick them into marriage," Zack said. "I can't speak the language but it's close enough to Spanish that I can make out most of the words."

The priest frowned. "You are the Americans?"

Uh-oh. Her muscles tensed, then cramped as she went into panic mode. He knew about them. They'd walked into a trap.

* * * *

"There are those in the priesthood who forget the Lord's first message," the priest told them. "I hope I am not one of them. I am not your judge. Tell me why you've come."

The priest's name was Father Paulo. After a brief explanation, he let them bring in the Cross and hide it in a storage room along with various broken pews and water-damaged artworks.

That taken care of, the priest sent a former altar boy to return the gondola, made them each a cup of truly excellent espresso coffee, and ushered them into the parish house where he with an ancient priest who looked up from his computer when they came in, then ignored them.

Father Paulo waited until they'd had a chance to sip on their coffee and munch a couple of cookies, then shook his head slowly. "I will not judge you, but I need to know that you are not a danger to yourself or those around you. Why should I believe you are not complete kooks?"

"We might be," Zack answered. "But people have been trying to kill us for weeks now. They've spent countless dollars, redirected entire carrier groups, and threatened the sovereignty of at least one allied nation, and conducted high-seas piracy. I'd say those are things worth worrying about."

"If your story is true," Paulo agreed. "Can you even prove that these particular pieces of wood really are the True Cross?"

"It brought Ivy back from the dead," Zack insisted.

Paulo waved away that objection. "Perhaps. Or perhaps your entire story is a concocted fiction."

The ancient priest interrupted with a burst of Italian much too fast for Ivy to catch.

"Oh." Paulo took a sip of his coffee. "Father Francis tells me that there has been chatter on the loops he follows. There are also somewhat veiled orders from the Vatican that we provide what support we can to the efforts of this Foundation. That much of your story, at least, is confirmed."

Zack appeared to relax but Ivy had spent too much time with him to be fooled. He was coiled, ready to erupt from his chair, to continue their flight—although Ivy had no idea where they would go next.

"Do you plan to follow those instructions?" Ivy tried to keep her voice soft, unthreatening.

"A Priest promises obedience to any lawful orders from his superiors and the Pope," Paulo admitted. "Still, online hints can hardly be called proper orders. Father Francis and I are left with a certain amount of discretion in deciding the proper response."

Ivy nodded, then considered next steps. "I didn't pick your church at random. There's something here that speaks not just of God, but of the Queen of Heaven."

Paulo laughed. "Naturally. We are the Church of Mary of the Sailors. As Catholics, you know that Mary is venerated above all other saints. Neither she, nor any saint is worshipped, of course, because worship is due only to the Lord."

His answer reflected official Catholic doctrine, but Ivy didn't think it was the entire truth.

"Yesterday, we had the misfortune to meet with an Orthodox Priest who told us that the Foundation was dedicated to scourging both pagans and heretics. He specifically mentioned Marian heretics."

Paulo's grin was unconvincing. "Every Christian abhors the heresies that lead men from Grace."

"Except that not all Christians agree on what constitutes a heresy, or on what leads men, or women, from Grace."

Father Francis interrupted with another burst of Italian.

"He thinks we're here to entrap them," Zack translated, his Spanish letting him get the old priest's meaning.

Ivy laughed. It was hard to imagine two more unlikely inquisitors than herself and Zack. "I suspect the Vatican has more serious problems than worrying about whether a couple of its parish priests are paying a bit too much devotion to the Mother of God."

Father Paulo shrugged. "With all due respect to the Holy See, what the Vatican chooses to worry about does not always match what is most important to the faith."

They didn't have time for this kind of fencing. "We're asking you to trust us, the way we're trusting you. We showed you the Cross. You can't believe that we would cart the True Cross around the world just to entrap you."

"If it is the True Cross."

"What we haven't showed you is this." Ivy reached into her bag.

Father Francis shouted something and picked up his computer keyboard, holding it as if it could somehow defend him from attack.

Ivy withdrew the veil, then unfolded it for the two priests.

"Clearly you think this object is important," Father Paulo's hands twitched with a transparent desire to touch the holy object.

"The Veil of Mary was the most holy relic in medieval Constantinople," Zack said. "It protected that city for hundreds of years against Russian, Slavic, Arab, and Turkish invaders."

"That could not be the Mary's Veil," Father Paulo protested.

"Couldn't it?" Ivy said. "The Patriarch of Constantinople disagrees with you."

"But look at it." Father Paulo's fingers, only millimeters from the fabric, traced the silver stars embroidered into the dark blue of the silk. "These eight-pointed stars are the symbols of the Goddess Ishtar. No proper Jewish woman would ever wear such a garment."

Which prompted a quick Italian conversation between Paulo and Francis.

"He says it could have been," Paulo admitted. "The Hebrews battled the other Semitic religions for a thousand years after the exodus from Egypt. For hundreds of years, the chosen people worshiped God but read the commandment to have "no gods before me" only to mean that the God of Abraham was to be first among many rather than the only God. And of course, women were not really part of the Hebrew congregation. It is certain that some of them worshipped a goddess cult. But that would have been centuries before Mary."

"And those Ancient Semitic religions?"

"Many had the worship of the Goddess at their center," Paulo admitted. "Ishtar was the name the Sumerians gave this great mother-goddess. They called her the Queen of Heaven and her color was blue."

Paulo's hand traced the shape of the veil, his fingers only millimeters from the ancient silk. "What you have here is a holy object. But it is the veil of a priestess of Ishtar. If Mary wore it, that would mean that the worship of Ishtar continued in Judea after the northern tribes were lost, even after the Babylonian Captivity.

"This would revolutionize the Church." Paulo's eyes lit as he considered the consequences. "Jesus is not merely the Hebrew Messiah and Holy Son of God. He is also the true Son of the Great Goddess. The holy trinity is not Father, Son, and some amorphous Holy Ghost, but Father, Mother, and Child. It is possible. Nazareth is far from Jerusalem. Far enough, perhaps, that the older religions might have lived on. Especially because the contemporary Hebrew religion was so male-centered. Remember the secret language of women in China? Perhaps Hebrew women maintained their secret religion through Biblical times."

* * * *

Ivy and Father Paulo waded into esoteric considerations of how Christian faith could be re-interpreted with the understanding that Mary was a Priestess in her own right. A Priestess or even, as Father Paulo suggested in an excited moment, an Avatar of the Great Goddess herself.

Zack listened for a few minutes, uncomfortable with this divergence from his beliefs. Finally he cleared his throat. "This is interesting, Father. But right now, we need to figure out how to stay alive, and how to keep the Cross out of the hands of the Foundation."

Father Paulo nodded. "The two go together, Zack. But your point is well taken. We must learn more about our enemy."

Zack wasn't sure how the Foundation had become their enemy, but he wasn't going to argue. It was about time he and Ivy had some allies. Unfortunately, their flight had been hard on allies.

"We know what the Foundation wants. They want a war between Christianity and Islam. A new crusade."

"Why would they need the Cross for that?"

"After Iraq, it's pretty clear that the U.S. needs help from other countries if it's going to continue its warfare," Zack said. "The Cross will whip up fervor. Remember, it was used in the medieval crusades."

"So, did finding the Cross whip up your fervor and make you want to attack Moslems?" Father Paulo demanded. "Instead, you found many Moslems, even their religious leaders, to be among your helpers."

"The Foundation literature called the Cross the 'key,'" Ivy said. "I think they want it for its power to open hidden powers."

"Possible." Father Paulo stood abruptly, then paced the room like a caged tiger. "I'm a priest, not an exorcist, not someone who has studied the occult."

"What's the Gog-Magog war?" Ivy asked.

"Is that part of their plan?"

"Several of the Foundation Agents mentioned it."

Father Paulo nodded slowly. "You know, all of a sudden, this has a horrible, sick logic."

"What?"

Instead of answering, Father Paulo turned to Father Francis and demanded that he search the Christian boards on the Internet for something tying together the Foundation and the radical believers in the millennium. Although the accent was dramatically different, twenty-four hours in Italy was honing Zack's ear to the point where he could hear the

Latin connection between the poverty-trained Texican-Spanish that had been spoken in his home when he'd been a child and the educated Italian spoken by the priests.

"I take it you have some ideas," he said.

Father Paulo's hand shook as he raised it to his forehead and wiped away a few small beads of sweat. "Perhaps."

"What does it mean to be a radical believer in the millennium?"

"Possibly nothing," Father Paulo admitted. "But the reference to a Gog-Magog War comes from the Prophet Ezekiel. Israel is threatened with horrible enemies from around the world. There are those, especially among the Pentecostal movement, who claim that these prophesies have not yet been fulfilled, but are a part of the same end-times as described in the Book of Revelations. Revelations is a part of the inspired words given to man by God himself. But it is also a particularly difficult work filled with strange and cryptic allusions. Revelations is where our concept of the end times is most clearly found."

"So, that Foundation agent was claiming that the Iraq war is the beginning of the end of the world?" It seemed like a strange belief to Zack, but he couldn't see how it was especially harmful, unless believers started neglecting their everyday activities in vain attempts to get ready for an end that Jesus had said no one could predict.

"There are those who do more than believe," Father Paulo corrected. "In every generation for hundreds of years, there have been those who predicted the end of the world. But recently, there have been those who not only predict the end, but who are attempting to fulfill prophesy and bring about the end times, to hurry the Lord along in his job."

"And you think—"

Father Paulo cut Ivy's question off. "I don't think anything, yet. But I do believe it is worth looking into the possibility that the Foundation is attempting to complete prophesy and bring about the tribulation and end-times."

"Would that be so bad? Haven't we all prayed for Christ's Kingdom on Earth?"

For the first time, Father Francis addressed them in English. Perfectly unaccented English. "Attempting to force the hand of God is the ultimate in blasphemy."

* * * *

Ivy wished she'd paid more attention in her catechism classes because listening to Fathers Francis and Paulo was like drinking from a fire hose. The more obscure Hebrew prophets and the Book of Revelations forecast certain specific events that would occur before the triumphant second coming of Jesus. Catholic and Orthodox doctrine had evolved to the point where the eminent return of Jesus was prayed for but not urgently anticipated. The Lord would return in his own time, when his return could do the most good for the world, for the souls of men, and for God's greater purposes. In the meantime, the Church would spread the word of forgiveness and salvation, as well as help the sick and weak.

Not all Christians, Father Francis repeated, were so patient. Many urgently anticipated the second coming, seeking connections between the events of their age and those predicted in Revelations. In its two thousand year history, the Catholic Church had seen many such moments of fervor—moments that led only to despondency and a turning away from the faith when Jesus did not return according to the artificial schedules of misguided prophets. Eventually the Church's leaders had decided to focus their attention on what they could control rather than on the eventual return.

But deliberately trying to bring about the end days was new. According to Father Francis, it was something that only the arrogant Americans would even contemplate.

Zack bristled a bit at what could be seen as a slam on Americans, but Ivy figured Father Francis was right. Her nation's great strength was also its weakness. It saw itself as unique in the world and wanted to act on that uniqueness. Sometimes that led to wonderful results. Sometimes it didn't.

"So, what does Mary have to do with all of this?"

Father Paulo shook his head. "Some Protestants seem to think that venerating the Mother of God takes away from the holiness of the Lord."

"Maybe they're right," Zack said. "Did you listen to yourself a few minutes ago when you were coming up with a new Trinity based on father, mother, and child? There is no Goddess in the Bible."

Father Paulo smiled. "Is that what you learned in your Catechism? Because it's quite wrong. Throughout much of the Book of Genesis, the Hebrew descriptions of God often take the female form. Although we Catholics prefer to think of God, the Father, it is certainly not anti-scriptural to speak of God, the Mother, as well."

That simple statement felt, to Ivy, like a punch in the gut. Her priests had never told her that. They'd gone on about how Jesus had accepted only male disciples, proving, to their satisfaction at least that women were second-class members of the human race. Her own disillusioning from religion had started with that discovery. Certainly that way of believing was not unique to the Catholic faith. Many officers and NCOs in her

National Guard unit had loved to quote from the Bible about how men needed to order women around because of Eve's sin and because only Adam had been created in the image of God.

While Ivy had known that the Priestess in her Iraq vision had worshipped a mother-goddess, that Priestess had been dead for thousands of years. Conceiving her own God, the God she'd believed in from her earliest memories as being a Goddess as well as a bearded male patriarch, changed everything.

"Father Paulo is correct about the literal translation of the ancient Hebrew," Father Francis interjected. "But that does not make it established doctrine. Because of the mystery of the Holy Spirit, the Church long-ago considered the possibility that the third person of the Almighty might have a female form—considered and rejected it."

"At the risk of repeating myself, do we really have time for this?" Zack interrupted. "We have people after us—people who don't hesitate to kill. I know that being in a Church provides the Cross a bit of protective cover from psychic detection, but we've got to figure out a more permanent way to hide. Deciding the true nature of the Trinity is a bit like debating the number of angels who can dance on a pin, don't you think? Not helpful."

"You might be right, Zack." Ivy was still trying to deal with the consequences of this revelation, with how her own faith was being transformed by new information. "But we've reached the end of the line. The Priestess told us to go to Byzantium and then to Venice. She didn't say anything about moving on after that. Besides, I'm tired of running. We've got the information now. I think it's time to stop hiding and start doing something."

Zack shook his head. "Hiding is exactly what we need to do. The Foundation needs the Cross. It's their key. Without the Cross, they have no ability to start their countdown to the apocalypse. If we can just keep it out of their hands, they're defanged. If we try to take the fight to them, they'll beat us and capture the Cross. Staying alive and keeping the Cross from them is our most effective tactic."

"I'm not saying you're wrong, Zack." Although she wasn't sure he was right, either. "But how would you propose permanently hiding the Cross? After they captured it in the Crusades, the Moslems hid it in one of the greatest mosques in Iraq, hundreds of miles from the nearest Christian country, and in the midst of what became a nation that was a great enemy of the U.S.

"Despite that, the Foundation still managed to find it and take it. Hiding it in Italy, a country shot-through with Americans and our spies, a country that was a part of the coalition in our invasion of Iraq, and a country where the Church has issued an order for all of its priests to cooperate with the Foundation, hardly sounds like an improvement."

"Wait a minute." Zack held up a hand as if he thought it could stop information from seeping through. "Surely you're not saying that the U.S. invaded Iraq just so the Foundation could gain control of the Cross."

"I'm not saying that--the Foundation said it. Vice President Cheney always claimed that there really were weapons of mass destruction in Iraq, despite all of the evidence that Clinton's bombing raids had destroyed everything Saddam had tried to retain. What if the weapon of mass destruction wasn't some nuclear or biological device, but something even more powerful, more primal, more ancient? What if it were the Cross, itself? Isn't that what the Foundation has been telling us?"

Zack sputtered, but no words came out.

"If you're prepared to believe that The Foundation is trying to bring about the end of the world and, as Father Francis said, 'force the hand of God,'" she continued, "how hard is it to believe that they'd trick our nation into invading a country that happened to be in possession of the one thing they need to make their dreams come true?"

Chapter 22

Governments lie. Zack hadn't been especially surprised when the original justification for invading Iraq had proven to be based on manufactured data, wishful thinking, and suppressing anything that didn't agree with what the generals and politicians had wanted to hear.

But he had believed that the American invasion, and the sacrifice of American and allied soldiers, had been undertaken on the nation's interests—however misguided the war planners might have been. That his native country might have been led into war by fanatics to access a tool they could use to create future wars sickened him.

"There's got to be a way we can hide the Cross so completely they'll never be able to find it." Or was that sensible? Maybe Ivy had a point about hiding being a doomed strategy.

Father Francis shook his head. "It could remain hidden as long as it was only because so many people believed that Saladin had destroyed it after capturing it from the crusaders. Now that its existence is known to so many, both within this Foundation and outside of it, it can never be truly hidden again.

"Already rumors of the Cross are circulating on the bulletin boards read by the religious and by conspiracy theorists. It can only get worse from here. How long before the sailors on your ship talk? What about the imams who helped you in Turkey? What about the priests in the Patriarch's circle? Men like to talk, like to share their secrets."

Unfortunately, all of that made sense. "Maybe we should go public with it. It was one thing for the U.S. to bomb a Mosque or raid an unknown little church. But imagine if we gave the Cross to your church, Father Paulo. It would instantly become a huge pilgrimage center. The

Foundation wouldn't dare pull anything then. Sometimes the light of knowledge becomes our best protection."

Zack didn't need to be a mind-reader like the gypsies in Turkey to see the temptation that offer posed to Father Paulo. Paulo might be happy with his congregation of aging women and his deteriorating church, but what priest wouldn't want to find himself at the center of devotion? What priest wouldn't want his church to be the repository of the holiest object in the Christian faith?

"Lead me not into temptation," the priest quoted.

Ivy shook her head. "Wouldn't work. How long do you think it would take before the Foundation snuck in a substitute and stole the real thing?"

This was getting a bit annoying. "I suggested hiding it and you say that won't work. So I suggested putting it in plain sight where it could be guarded and you say that won't work. Haven't you just backed yourself into a corner? Maybe there is nothing we can do and we should just give up."

"Hey, Captain. You're the planner. What does West Point have to say about this?"

"I came up through the ranks. I'm not a West Pointer." Still, Ivy had a point. Until his career had turned on him, he'd been a lifer. He'd attended officer training school. He knew how to fight. And giving up was no more a part of his makeup than it was of Ivy's.

One thing he'd learned from military training is the importance of seizing the offensive. They'd tried to turn the tables on the Foundation, seize control of the situation, but only in small ways. Basically, they'd spent weeks on the defensive, running away. They'd succeeded, which meant they'd managed to stay alive. But the Foundation only had to get lucky once. He and Ivy needed to get lucky every day, every hour, just to stay one step ahead of their doom. Neither hiding the Cross, nor simply handing it over to the Church would let them escape their fate.

"If this were a military campaign, we'd plan to seize the strategic offensive," Zack finally answered Ivy's question. "But I have no idea how to do that. We've followed your Priestess's orders, visited Byzantium and Venice. We've learned a lot about what we're facing, but we're no better equipped to confront aircraft carriers, drone missile launchers, and the world's strongest military force than we were when we started this adventure."

Ivy smiled at him. "Do you remember the name of that famous church in Constantinople?"

"Hagia Sophia?"

"Know what it means?"

"Saint Sophia, right? Whoever she was."

Ivy shook her head. "It means Holy Wisdom. Which might also be the third person in the trinity. We've gained wisdom in our flight and we've made a network of friends and allies. Now we've got to figure out a way to transform our knowledge into power."

Sure. That sounded logical and it sounded easy. But it was easier to believe that knowledge was power when you weren't facing helicopter gunships, armed only with the certainty of your convictions.

"The Foundation has effective control over the U.S. military, so we've got to think like guerillas, attacking where they aren't, seeking the soft spots in their defenses. Obviously, the two of us aren't going to attack them militarily."

"Two?" Father Paulo said. "But there are already the four of us. And you told us of so many others who have helped you."

Ivy frowned. "Keep thinking, Zack, but I don't think we're quite on the right track. We came to Venice for a reason. Why here? Sure, it was great to meet with Father Paulo and Father Francis, but we could have met with priests in Turkey or Greece. We need to know why the Priestess sent us here."

"Maybe she likes the canals."

"Yeah. And maybe she thought it would be handy if we crossed half the world just to hand the Cross over to her enemies. But I don't think either of those is true. She sent us to Byzantium to pick up the Veil. So, why did she send us to Venice?"

* * * *

The three men were getting a bit sulky and Ivy couldn't blame them. She'd asked for their plans and then, when they'd come up with any, she'd shot them down. Still, she couldn't help thinking that they were missing something fundamental.

From the guidebook she'd studied while she and Zack had explored the canals of this ancient city, she knew Venice had been a mostly uninhabited swamp until around the fall of the Western Roman Empire. A number of Romans had founded the city then to escape from the German tribes who overran Italy during that period. So, there couldn't be anything truly ancient here. Nothing dating back before the Christian era.

On the flipside, though, although the old city of Byzantium had dated back to the pre-Christian era, the Veil hadn't been hidden there until the 1400s when the Turks finally overran that last citadel of the two-thousand-year-old Roman Empire. Something old could have been brought to Venice in the fifteen hundred years since its founding.

"We were sent to Byzantium to pick up the Veil, so maybe we're here to pick up something else. Think about what could be hidden here. What is Venice famous for?"

"They've got the relics of Saint Mark," Zack said.

"Anything else?" Ivy didn't think an ancient skeleton, even that of one of the Apostles, would provide the kind of power they needed to confront the Foundation.

"Who knows what loot is hidden around the city?" Father Paulo suggested. "We were a merchant nation, but also a nation of pirates and thieves. But for all that is known, Venetian merchants may have looted the Holy Grail, the Ark of the Covenant, Kali's strangling cord, and the Ka'bah stone, in addition to the known treasures."

"Which of those would help?"

Father Paulo shrugged. "I'm not saying any of them are here, just that Venice is a hodgepodge of ancient stuff gathered over the centuries by Venetian noblemen intent on proving that they were among the wealthiest and most artistically inclined of their world. It wasn't for nothing that the Renaissance started here in Venice, you know."

"I thought it started because of all the Greeks fleeing the conquest of Constantinople and bringing their scientific and artistic skills with them," Zack offered.

Father Francis shook his head. "A very narrow-minded reading of history."

"Okay, is there any particular place where the loot would be?" Ivy asked. "I read something about the Cairo Museum having millions of uncataloged treasures. Does Venice have anything like that?"

"Not museums," Father Paulo said. "Just the city itself. And the mainland too, of course."

"But I thought—"

"When the city grew rich, noble Venetians competed by building palaces on the mainland."

"So, we've not only got to search the islands of Venice, we've got to search everywhere around it, too? All while the Foundation and Italian Police are everywhere in the city looking for us?"

"When you put it like that, it sounds like an impossible mission," Father Paulo agreed.

"Can you think of a positive way to put it?"

"Perhaps it would be wise to consider prayer," the priest said. "I have often found that, when I face impossible obstacles, the Lord shows me a way around them, through them, or simply moves them away."

"I've got nothing against prayer, Father," Zack said. "But I'm thinking we're as outgunned in the prayer department as we are in more obvious weapons. I don't know how many members the Foundation has, but it's a sure bet they have more than four. And all of the ones we've met so far seem to be big on prayer. When they aren't trying to kill us, anyway."

"Prayer isn't an additive thing," Father Paulo said. "The Lord does not set up scales comparing the numbers of prayers for one thing or another. If he did, we Christians would imitate the Tibetans with their prayer wheels to mechanize our offerings of thanks and requests for aid."

The obviousness of Father Paulo's suggestion almost took Ivy's breath away.

"You're right," she said. "We've done what the Priestess told us to do. So, now we need to reconnect with her. Prayer is the traditional way of connecting to gods and the dead."

"I wasn't suggesting turning to paganism," Father Paulo protested.

Ivy had tried not to confront that little problem in her own belief structure. If she was a Catholic and a Christian, how could she also be doing the bidding of a priestess of Ishtar? How like a priest to make her confront what she'd been trying to avoid.

Still, was there really a contradiction?

"Remember what you said. Based on the symbols on the Veil, we know that Mary may well have been a priestess of Ishtar or possibly even an avatar of Ishtar. And visions of Mary, messages from Mary are fully consistent with the teachings of the Catholic Church." She doubted that they would be consistent with the teachings of whatever strange breed of Christianity the Foundation pursued, but that wasn't her problem.

"We didn't conclude that Mary was a priestess," Father Francis protested. "We were speaking hypothetically. We don't know that Mary ever owned this Veil. The church recognizes that not every purported relic is authentic."

"Hypothetical or not, you convinced me. It's at least possible that my priestess is consistent with the Catholic faith. You said we need supernatural help and I'm going to ask for it. Last time we needed supernatural help, we got it from the priestess. Now, that person might be Mary. She might be just about anyone else, for that matter, but she's given us the only guidance we've had so far. I'm going to ask for her help again."

"How are you going to contact her?" Zack wanted to know. "She hasn't been in touch for weeks now, since that first night when we just happened to stumble into a cave that had once been a temple to Ishtar."

"We didn't just stumble," Ivy said. She hoped she sounded more confident than she really felt. "My second sight showed me the way, just as it has shown me the way here in Venice."

"But where should we go?"

She was glad that Zack had said 'we.' "We're already there. The Church of Mary of the Sailors is shot-through with the blue power of the Goddess. If she won't talk to me here, where would she?"

* * * *

Two days later, Ivy was beginning to wish she'd never asked that question.

Praying for a vision from the Goddess or her priestess had seemed like an obvious answer. They'd followed the priestess's orders, traveling through Turkey, Greece, and Italy and retrieving the Cross and Veil. Now they were ready for the next set of instructions. The only problem was, nothing was happening.

Ivy had lit candles, crossed herself with holy water, and gotten down on her knees and prayed for guidance from Mary, the Goddess, the Priestess, and from every saint and angel she could think of—male or female.

Praying hadn't hurt her any. From when she'd been a small child, prayer had always made her feel better, as if she'd been cleaned from the inside as well as on the outside. Two solid days praying made her feel cleaner than she'd ever felt before. But a good shiny feeling wasn't doing the job. The Foundation was still out there.

Father Paulo reported rumors from parishioners about Italian police officers accompanied by unidentified but definitely non-Italian men in civilian clothing who broke into homes and ransacked them, leaving the residents with wreckage to clean up. In a few cases, owners who had protested too much had vanished with the police. Few of those had returned and none of those who were missing could be found when their families hired attorneys to track them down. The Italian judiciary simply shrugged.

Overhead, American helicopters and fighter jets circled the city, creating a continual blanket of noise and of the crackling red-colored power that was seeking them out.

Venice had seemed like a refuge when they'd crossed Asia and Europe to reach it. Now, it felt like a trap. If she and Zack fled the city, with the Cross or without it, Ivy knew they would be detected, captured, and killed. If they stayed, eventually the Foundation would hunt them down, dig them out, and finish them that way.

It would take a miracle for them to survive the next week, and miracles were suddenly in short supply.

Ivy looked up from her prayer as a clutch of elderly Italian women shuffled into the church.

Several of them nodded to her. The priests had rounded her up a baggy dress that hung down to mid-calf and an oldfashioned wig. The combination made her look dumpy unattractive, and unthreatening. She'd spent enough time in the church over the past couple of days that she'd become a familiar figure. The women probably thought she'd been dumped at the altar by her handsome gondolier. All of which made her a lot more sympathetic than when they'd thought her a man-hungry tourist.

One of the women shoved a shopping bag at her, a couple of oranges and a small loaf of Italian bread poking through the mesh net of the sack.

"Grazie," she responded. She hadn't eaten in better than twenty-four hours and was feeling a bit weak, but completely uninspired.

"*Siete benvenuti,*" the woman responded before taking her place on a pew.

A pair of altar boys led Father Paulo up the center aisle of the Church, one carrying a crucifix and the other swinging an incense burner around so wildly that it smacked into Ivy's knee.

"Ouch."

Father Paulo gave her a frown.

Well, he was right. Better for her to suffer a few bruises than to let everyone know she was American. Venice might be a big city, but its rumor mill was equal to that of the smallest small-town in America. And rumors could go two ways. She had to believe that the Foundation was tapped into it at least as well as were Fathers Paulo and Francis.

The altar boy gave her an apologetic smile, waved another cloud of incense at her, then headed toward the altar at the front of the church.

She inhaled deeply.

Church incense had always reminded her of funerals and long, boring sermons. Although Catholic churches always smelled of it, and now that she consciously thought of it, Orthodox churches had too, her brain tuned it out.

But when the altar boy had waved the burner under her nose, she'd caught a hint of memory.

When they'd stumbled onto the cave, there she'd smelled fire and smoke. Zack had argued that they'd been drugged, that her visions had been hallucinogenic rather than real. He'd come to believe this wasn't the case, that her second sight was as real as anything else on Earth, but that didn't mean that the smoke had been meaningless.

For the first time in days, Ivy had an idea of what to do next.

She sat through Father Paulo's service, listening to the rich baritone of his voice as he chanted the holy creeds of the Church.

Father Paulo didn't look like a man conflicted with doubts about his Church's teachings. And, Ivy realized, he probably wasn't. He wasn't a simple man. He'd graduated from college in Milan and spent several years in Africa working with AIDS patients before returning to his beloved Venice. By examining him through her second sight, Ivy saw that his faith was pure. He believed in a merciful God who would forgive anyone who asked for forgiveness in his Son's name, who tried to do what was right, and who truly repented his errors when he fell short of his ideals. Not for Father Paulo was any notion of a cold and calculating God ever-watching for that momentary misstep that would lead straight to hell.

Father Paulo was certain that God would forgive him if helping Ivy was a mistake, but his God would have a harder time forgiving the priest if he refused to help any who fled to his church as sanctuary.

She almost dozed off during his sermon, not what any priest would like to see, but she understood so little Italian that she could only wallow in the rich tones of his voice and the shining color of his faith.

After the sermon, as always, the women from his flock gathered around him bringing him small gifts of homemade food and seeking his attention, his blessing. Which he gave without stint.

"Anything?" he asked when the last of them had left and he'd sent the altar boys off to school.

"No."

The priest's shoulders drooped a bit. "I'm sorry, Ivy. Perhaps you were wrong. There may have been something else you were supposed to accomplish instead of just waiting for the messenger to return."

"Maybe. But the incense gave me an idea. When I saw the Priestess the first time, herbs were burning nearby. I think they may have been a part of opening the pathway."

Father Paulo frowned. "I cannot allow illegal drugs in my church. You do understand that, don't you?"

Ivy bristled. They were facing a group of angry men who were trying to bring about the end of the world in what Father Francis had called the 'ultimate blasphemy' but Father Paulo was worried about petty legalities.

Going non-linear wouldn't help, though.

"First things first, Father. I don't know that she was burning controlled substances. There's got to be someplace in Venice where I can look for herbs and spices. I've got to try to find something that matches

251

what Zack and I experienced outside of Nineveh."

* * * *

Ivy was used to the farmers' markets of Pittsburgh and expected something similar in Venice. Instead, Venice's open-air market spread across the city's narrow alleys and spilled onto barges and flat-bottomed outboards in the canals.

Thousands of people shouted at each other, bargained over prices, insulted merchandise, or sipped on espresso shots while watching the next generation try their skills. Here and there, pretty girls and college-aged boys on motor scooters zipped through the crowds, always at the point of hitting someone, but always managing to swerve out of the way at the last minute.

Other than the scooters and the occasional sound of an outboard motor, the market seemed little changed from what it would have been in late-medieval days when Venetian ships ruled the Mediterranean, and when Marco Polo returned to the city with his fabulous tales of Kublai Khan and the glories of China.

Ivy tried to use her second sight to identify the herbs she'd smelled outside of Mosul. As at the pier on the Grand Canal, though, the multitude of religious objects overwhelmed her senses.

"Does anything look familiar?" Zack asked. He was wearing one of Father Paulo's black suits with the Roman collar while Ivy had been made up to look like an aging woman doing her shopping.

"Nothing," she admitted. "My senses are suffering from overload."

He sniffed the air then pointed down an alley. "I think the spices are this way."

She followed behind him, doing her best to ignore the submachinegun-toting policemen scattered through the market.

Sure enough, Zack's nose led them around a corner to a section of the market that she hadn't even guessed at.

Venice's herb and spice market featured people from around the world, most dressed in traditional garb. Nutmeg, clove, garlic, cinnamon, cocoa, and the complex odors of pepper all clamored for her attention.

From behind tie-died curtains, accompanied by the soft gurgle of water pipes, wafted the sweet scent of hashish, painfully familiar to Ivy after the time she'd spent with Cejno.

From below the decks of small boats, she picked up even more unsavory exchanges—cocaine, opium, heroin.

Second only to Constantinople during the middle ages as the hotbed of illicit behavior and decadent wealth, Venice didn't seem to have slowed down a bit.

Zack chuckled. "That smells way too familiar."

Ivy followed his lead, away from the drug-infested corner of the market where they'd emerged, toward the sunlight and open stalls.

In the midst of the familiar, they found hundreds of herbs, fresh, dried, and powdered, that Ivy had never heard of—many with odors that made her wonder what had driven anyone to taste them in the first place.

Trusting her nose rather than her overwhelmed second sight, she made her way to a small stall marked with Arabic lettering.

She didn't recognize the herbs and couldn't pronounce the names of the spices when the Middle-Eastern-looking attendant, an attractive woman who was dressed in a pair of pants that could have been painted on her body and a top that plunged between more than ample breasts, repeated them. But Ivy recognized the scents. They'd found what they were looking for—and they didn't even look to be illegal.

"I'll bet she doesn't dress like that when she goes back to the old country," Zack whispered.

"Keep your eyes to yourself, Father," she reminded him.

"Hey. Even a priest can look."

She wasn't sure that was good theology but couldn't afford to attract attention by having an argument with him. Not with the Italian police swarming the city.

Instead, she paid the ridiculous price the woman demanded for small plastic bags of the herbs Zack's nose confirmed as being correct, using money Father Paulo had forced on her.

Sun streamed down on the city as they headed back toward their base in the Church of Mary of the Sailors. Despite the omnipresent police, the city had taken a festive atmosphere. A young couple skipped past them wearing a pair of feathered masks of the type that spoke of the Venetian carnival.

Ivy wasn't fooled. Venice might be a vacation paradise, but danger lay close beneath the surface.

After a brief negotiation, Zack took the point with Ivy trailing about ten meters behind.

Zack seemed to have picked up a sense Venice, because he led them on a route Ivy had never seen before, circling back through the city rather than taking them straight for the church.

"You notice something?" she whispered when they momentarily got closer."

"Nothing I can put a finger on. But something feels wrong." He considered, then turned down a narrow street, a street that looked exactly like every other to Ivy.

Twenty feet down, a group of tourists stepped into the gap between she and Zack.

The tour guide, a tiny Japanese woman, gesturing to stone carvings high on an old building that seemed to Ivy indistinguishable from thousands of others scattered throughout the city.

One of the tourists snapped a picture at just the wrong moment, the flash only a few feet from her eyes, and she hesitated, abruptly blind.

Without her second sight, she would have been caught completely unaware.

Her physical blindness, though, opened her senses to the colors around her. The Japanese were almost colorless, dull beige glows. Behind her, though, a vivid maroon moved with implacable certainty.

She spun around, her hands up in a guard.

He didn't bother ordering her to surrender. Instead, he thrust his long knife at her.

Her second sight had let her to recognize the threat, but it didn't provide the detail she needed to defend herself.

The Foundation Agent, his blood-red glow reflecting the harsh certainty of the Foundation's faith, thrust straight for her heart, avoiding her warding arms.

The knife slammed into her sending a wave of pain through her body and she collapsed to the ground.

Chapter 23

The agent had used the distraction brilliantly, attacking when Zack and Ivy were separated, unable to provide adequate backup.

But a sound had alerted Zack and he turned in time to see the agent thrust his knife into Ivy's heart, then, as she started to fall, pull her too him as if she was a drunk he was helping home.

Zack bulled through the Japanese tourists wishing he'd brought a weapon even though that would have been horribly incongruous to his disguise as a priest.

Since Zack was unarmed, it would have been nice if the Agent had at least been distracted, but one of the tourists shouted something and Ivy's assailant looked up in time to see Zack bearing down on him.

The agent dumped Ivy's body and took an awkward-looking swing toward Zack.

Fortunately, Zack had seen the knife and knew the agent had palmed it. Like most knifemen, he planned for the knife to be a surprise.

Zack wasn't taken unaware, but that didn't give him much of an advantage. The very awkwardness of the agent's attack made it that much harder to block.

Adjusting his tactics to the situation, Zack blended with the attack rather than blocking. He shifted his center and let the knife come toward where he had been. As the blade sliced a layer from his priest outfit, he added his weight to the agent's momentum.

It wasn't much, but it was enough to put the agent ever so slightly off balance.

Zack flicked a kick into the agent's kneecap just as he used his hips to roll the muscular American's hand over, then down.

The man crashed to the ground, his face suddenly bloody as it brushed against his own knife as he fell.

Zack didn't think he'd managed a fatal blow, so he kicked the agent hard in the head to slow him down further, then picked up Ivy's limp form and fled.

The two-note sound of European police sirens, a sound Zack still identified with the Gestapo from the World War II movies he'd grown up watching on television, told him that the police were not far behind.

He wasn't going to be able to make it back to the Church of Mary of the Sailors.

But Venice was filled with churches and he wasn't in a position to be fussy. He doubled back, took a couple of random turns, then ducked into the Church of Santa Lucia.

He considered the confession booths along the walls of the church but rejected them. They were far too obvious as hiding places and wouldn't give him much room to help Ivy, assuming that she wasn't past all help. The Cross had saved her before, but they hadn't carried the Cross with them and he couldn't get her back to it now.

Ignoring its morbid connotations, he ducked down into the crypt.

Although much of Venice is built on piers, at least some of the city was constructed on the original islands off the Italian mainland. This church seemed located on one such spot because the crypt was dug a good twenty feet into the ground.

Stone tombs identified long-gone benefactors of the church. Intricate Byzantine-style mosaics covered the walls, reflecting the long history that Venice and Constantinople had shared as allies, competitors, and enemies. An iron door barred the crypt from the church's treasury.

He set Ivy's figure on a monument that looked like a coffin rising from the floor, took a deep breath, then grasped the stone doorway to one of the older-looking family tombs.

The door resisted, but finally yielded, opening with a groan. Fortunately, nobody had been buried there in a hundred years or more so he didn't have to deal with the odor of death and disintegration.

He picked up Ivy, carried her in, then set her on a stone table whose use he couldn't guess at and about which he didn't want to speculate.

Operating as much by feel as by the dim light seeping through from the Church above, Zack found a half-burned candle, lit it, the slowly closed the tomb door behind him. The Foundation might still be able to find them, but he wasn't making it any easier on them than he had to.

He tried to ignore the solid thunk as the tomb's stone door slipped into place. He'd have time to worry about that later. Right now, he was a lot more worried about Ivy.

He turned his attention to his friend.

She hadn't stirred, hadn't even breathed from what he could tell, and he'd seen that knife bury itself deep in her chest.

His own heart felt as if it had received that thrust. They'd shared so much, risked so much together, that Zack couldn't imagine going on without her. He couldn't remember when he'd fallen for her—that first night outside of Mosul, when they'd escaped together from the Turkish army, certainly before they'd shared that sensual experience in Aphrodite's temple. He'd always assumed that they would succeed together, or fail together, never dreamed she could leave him alone.

Swallowing hard, forcing his limbs to move, he bent to check her.

He didn't have much hope.

He wouldn't give up on that small chance that something had gone right.

Using the dim candlelight, he unbuttoned Ivy's ugly black dress.

When he took them away from the buttons, his hands dripped with crimson blood, made even more macabre in the candle's yellow light.

He pulled the dress back from her shoulders and ribs.

The Veil of the Virgin Mary formed a second layer of garments. He'd forgotten that Ivy never let it go beyond her touch.

He pealed that away.

A huge bruise marred the soft tissue between her ribs—right where the Agent had stabbed toward her heart. But beneath the veil, the wound seemed to be an abrasion rather than a deep puncture. Despite the man's power and training, the knife hadn't penetrated. How was that possible? And where had all the blood come from.

Ivy's chest moved, her small breasts rising as she inhaled.

"What happened?" Ivy's voice was a faint croak.

"You're alive."

"Good. If I hurt this much after being dead, that would mean I'm not in heaven. And you know the alternative."

"That's impossible."

She started to sigh, then stopped with a gasp. "Damn, it's hard to breath. And trust me, I've done a lot of bad things. No way is heaven a sure thing."

He shook his head. "That's not what I meant." Although if there were a heaven, as he certainly believed, its gates would swing wide open when Ivy arrived. The imans in Turkey weren't the only ones who recognized Ivy as a saint. "How did you manage to stay alive, and where did all that blood come from? I saw that Agent stab you."

Ivy shrugged, then barely converted a scream into a soft moan. "Think he broke some ribs. Hurts like the devil."

257

A knife might break ribs as it cut through them into her heart. But somehow, that hadn't happened.

He prodded at the bruise trying to ascertain the amount of damage and Ivy winced.

"I don't think they're clean breaks. I think they're shattered."

Unfortunately, there wasn't anything Zack could do for ribs, broken, bruised, or shattered. He buttoned back Ivy's dress. "I've got us hidden in a crypt. The cops and Foundation types are out there looking."

"It was the Veil," Ivy said.

No big surprise that she was hallucinating after the trauma she'd just faced. And Zack thought she might have hit her head when she fell.

"Sure. The Veil. Whatever you say."

"I'm not crazy. I think the Veil saved me."

He realized he hadn't put the square of silk back where he'd found it and so he looked at it more closely.

Ivy had folded the veil into a packet about six inches on a side. Despite the number of folds, the resulting square was still insubstantially thin, and deformed by the shape of a knife point.

"This is absolutely incredible, but it looks like you're right. Somehow the silk fibers kept the knife from going through. I knew Kevlar can do that, but I wouldn't think silk, especially two thousand year-old silk, would stand up to that kind of attack."

"The ancient Japanese used to make armor from silk. Besides, this isn't ordinary silk," she reminded him. "And if Father Paulo was right, it's a lot older than two thousand years. The priestesses of Ishtar would have handed it down over generations."

But he'd seen the blood. "It's another miracle."

"Miracle or not, it happened and I'm still alive. So, what do we do next?"

* * * *

Zack's crypt wasn't much for comfort, but Ivy couldn't have imagined a more secure hiding place. The church above them and the religious artifacts within the crypt itself would obscure any magical glow coming from Zack and herself, or from the Veil. The stone walls cut off any thermal impression and muffled any sounds they made.

She tried not to think about the pain ripping through her chest, or how much it hurt to breathe, and concentrated on relaxing, on letting her body begin the healing process.

After a few minutes, she asked for the Veil back from Zack and draped it over herself. It might be sacrilegious to use the relic like that, but she needed its power to help her. She couldn't spend months disabled and out of the fight. The Agent's sudden attack had proved that they were going to keep searching until they got what they were looking for.

Zack's candle slowly shrank into a puddle of molten wax, then winked out and they were plunged into absolute darkness.

Physical darkness, that is. Ivy's second senses picked up the emanations from everywhere around them. Mostly red, of course, from the great paternalistic and monotheistic tradition. But quite a few blue, and some of the other colors of the esoteric rainbow. As some Protestants complained, multiple traditions coexisted under the broad umbrella of the Catholic Church.

"This crypt may have been a horrible idea," Zack admitted. "I don't like enclosed places, I don't like the dark, and I'm not absolutely sure I'll be able to shift the stone door from inside of this place."

She reached for his hand and brought it to her cheek. "It's all right, Zack. I'm sure you'll get us out of here when the time is right. In the meantime, you've found us one of the safest spots in Venice."

"How safe do you figure that is?" His hand trembled against her like a baby bird cupped in her hands, needing the warmth of touch but afraid of being crushed.

"Not very safe." They're not going to give up. If I were them, I'd bring in every agent plus the FBI, the Navy, and every Italian policeman they can. Based on what Father Francis told us, I'll bet they have priests and Opus Dei scouring the city as well. Even if the Pope isn't completely in bed with the Foundation, he'll want the Cross for himself."

"You know, I'm not exactly comfortable with the thought of the Pope in bed with anyone."

"Sorry. Bad metaphor." Although the crypt's stone walls muffled sound, they kept their voices down, barely murmuring.

They stopped even that when they heard hard-heeled footsteps outside.

Ivy tried to project a vision of nothingness. It wasn't easy and she wasn't sure she'd accomplished anything. Still, it made sense that if the power could be used to heal and to hide or recover hidden objects, it could also be used for other purposes.

The sounds stopped abruptly and Ivy froze. They'd come a long way since Iraq, but in some ways nothing had changed at all. Once again, as in Mosul, they were huddled in a stone room waiting to be discovered and killed by gunmen. Although the insurgents had been tracking them in Iraq, and the Foundation was here, the difference didn't extend their life expectancy any.

Maybe trying to use the power had been an error. Perhaps it had sent the very signal she was trying to obscure.

But the echoing footsteps finally resumed, stumped their way down the stone walkway.

Rusty iron screeched against itself and then, abruptly, the sense of horrible presence faded.

"I think—"

She pressed her hand against Zack's mouth. It was too soon to assume safety.

He nodded, silently.

Ivy tracked time by counting her heartbeats. They seemed to come incredibly slowly. A hundred beats felt like an hour. Another hundred seemed like a year. Finally the footsteps returned, moving more quickly now as the agents completed whatever they'd been doing on the other side of the iron door and headed away from the church.

"I guess we can talk now," she said when the sounds had been gone for several minutes.

"We can talk, but what are we going to do? When we come out, they'll catch us. They'll be on every street corner now, not just on the bridges. There's no way we can make it back to Father Paulo and Father Francis. And we can't stay here. The only thing we have to eat is those herbs we bought in the market."

The herbs weren't for eating, though.

"We'll just have to do it here."

Zack's hand jerked against her face leaving her with a sense of coldness, aloneness even beyond that of the crypt itself.

"If we burn those things here, we'll suffocate. It's already getting hard to breathe."

"You're letting your claustrophobia get to you. It isn't that bad. Yet."

But it would get bad. The stone door was close enough to airtight to make no difference. She could only guess how much oxygen her body was consuming as it transformed energy from the veil into healing power.

"I could open the vault a crack."

"Might as well. If we wait too long, we'll be too weak to do it."

While Zack fussed with the door, Ivy opened the packets of herbs they'd bought, ran her finger through the course-ground powders, tried to visualize any essence of the Priestess, to call her into existence through sheer force of will.

The only response she got was a feeling of echoing emptiness, as if she were knocking at a door to a deserted mansion. Which couldn't be right. She'd seen the priestess only weeks before.

"Uh-oh."

"I don't like it when you say that."

"I don't like it either." Zack's voice was calm now, but Ivy knew him well enough to recognize that tone. He'd clamped down. There was bad news.

"Tell me."

"I can't budge the door. We're sealed in."

* * * *

Moments before, the air had seemed fine to Ivy. All of a sudden, breathing took an effort.

Zack sat down beside her and seized her hand. "I'm pissed about dying. And I'm sorry that I put us into a trap that I couldn't get out of, but I'm even more angry that this means the Foundation wins. They'll track the Cross down to Father Paulo's church in no time. They won't even have to bother fighting us. Thanks to me, we've taken care of that ourselves."

She squeezed his hand back. "We're not dead yet."

"Nope. We get to wait and wonder whether bad air or thirst will kill us first. I'll bet nobody has been buried in this particular tomb for better than a hundred years. I don't see the gravediggers opening it any time soon. Certainly not in time to help us."

Ivy hadn't known how much she'd counted on Zack's confidence, his willingness to keep going when things looked hopeless. She needed that confidence now, but realized it would have to come from herself.

"Calm down and breath slowly," she said. "We're not beat yet."

His pulse beat through his hands under the pressure of her fingers and she willed him to calm. They needed to think, plan. Sure they'd made mistakes, but after all they'd been through, could a blocked stone door really be the end?

"I'm healing. Wait an hour and we'll push together," she whispered.

She sensed his headshake. "The door is sealed. It doesn't move at all."

"Give me an hour. The air should last."

It would last or it wouldn't. The Veil had caught the knife, kept it from penetrating her heart, but the soft fabric had done little to stop the force behind the Agent's blow. Her shattered ribs meant she couldn't move, lacked any strength. They'd also been the source of the blood Zack had found. She must have exhaled pounds of the stuff as it flowed into her lungs. Her body was pulling itself together now, far faster than would have been possible without the protective healing from the Veil, but she knew she still couldn't stand.

"I'll give you the rest of my life."

He might have meant that as bitter humor but Ivy had to swallow hard to eliminate the choked up feeling in her throat.

"I'm not big on mushy stuff, Zack. But the past weeks with you have been special. You're a good friend."

She stopped abruptly. The bad air must have gotten to her. Ivy didn't talk to men that way--ever. She maintained her cool--always.

Zack squeezed her hand again. "Okay, now I'm motivated. We've got to get out of here for sure."

"Give me my hour, Zack. I'll think of something."

But Zack was the first one to think of something. After about ten minutes of sitting in the darkness, he stirred. "I'm going to move you to the floor, Ivy. If there's any inflow of fresh air, it'll be from there. Besides, hot air rises."

Carbon dioxide had three atoms rather than the two in pure oxygen. That meant it should be heavier, right, so maybe they should go up. Still, Zack might be right. She could hope that the ancient Venetians who'd built this tomb weren't scientific enough to build perfectly hermetically sealed doorways, or that the city's settling had opened cracks. A little seepage might be coming in through the cracks.

She tried to suppress her gasp of pain when he lifted her, but knew her efforts had come up short.

"Sorry."

"Don't worry about it. I'm getting better."

"Nobody can heal that quickly." He sat beside her, arranging her head over his thigh.

With the stone floor cold and hard against her back, she welcomed the warmth from his body.

"It's the Veil, Zack."

"That's imposs—uh, erase that. I'm going to eliminate the world 'impossible' from my vocabulary."

"Good thinking. Because we need a plan. And any plan we come up with will have a lot of impossibles in it."

He managed a choking laugh despite himself. "Okay, you've convinced me. Pretend I never got discouraged. Let's make a list of tactical assets. Once we've got that, we can determine a plan."

Ivy almost sighed in relief. Zack was back. "There's the Cross."

"Not exactly reachable right now, but clearly that's the big gun in our arsenal. And then there's the Veil. It's obviously important or the Priestess wouldn't have sent you to Byzantium to find it."

"It saved me."

"Okay. But you wouldn't have needed saving if they hadn't gotten us into this mess."

"That was the Foundation. The Priestess is helping, and the Veil was part of that help."

* * * *

Ivy's heart pounded loudly in her ears. Each breath seemed a bit more labored than the last. Talking had become too much of an effort. The hour she'd demanded for healing was clearly too much.

She brushed her fingers against the plastic bags filled with herbs for what seemed like the millionth time. Don't leave me now. She sent the words out to the universe in an unspoken but heartfelt plea.

The only answer she got was a quick memory of her days in Mosul, angry Arabs looking at both Americans and Kurds as hated enemies. Arab women scurrying through the destruction of war, frequently draping a bit of cloth over their mouths and noses.

Her mind, stupefied by the lack of oxygen, took a moment to grasp the power of the idea.

"Thank you, Priestess," she croaked.

"Save breath," Zack said. "Don't talk."

"Breathe through the Veil," she answered, taking her own advice.

"It isn't dust. Nothing to filter out. Just not enough oxygen."

"Humor me." She knew there was no scientific reason for this to work, but the Veil was a source of steady protection. It had saved her from the knife-thrust. Already, her mind felt more active as the veil somehow purified the air she breathed and oxygen flooded through her system.

Zack said nothing for a minute, but he shifted his weight and she felt the drag as he brought a corner of the veil to his mouth.

"This is amazing," he admitted after a minute or so of silent recovery.

"Yeah. But we're still trapped." Still, she couldn't help sharing his mood. They could breathe. They weren't going to die of suffocation. She believed that the Priestess had sent that quick mental picture. Surely she wouldn't have done it solely to prolong the agony of their death.

"I'm going to burn some of the herbs," she said. "The Priestess needs help to get in here."

"She got into that cave."

"That cave belongs to the Goddess. This crypt belongs to the dead."

There was a Goddess of the underworld, of death, she vaguely remembered. But life and regeneration seemed much more closely aligned to the female principle. Of course, they were also in a Church, which probably made things doubly difficult.

"You're the boss when it comes to miracles and magic."

She shook out a pinch from each of the five bags they'd bought, mixing them with a couple of shredded Euro notes to serve as kindling.

Finally she borrowed a match and stroked the phosphorous tip against the chemical sandpaper of the matchbook.

In the crypt's dead air, the match barely ignited.

She pressed the tiny blue dot of flame into the center of the small pyramid of shredded banknotes and watched as the slivers of paper smoldered.

"Not enough oxygen," Zack said.

"Not much. Maybe enough."

Ivy's eyes were so accustomed to the darkness that the smoldering paper, half burning, half simply oxidizing, shed enough light for her to see the thin line of smoke.

She dropped the veil for a moment, brought her face directly over that trickle of smoke, and inhaled.

The harsh herbs tore at her lungs, adding a jolt of pain to the steady throb from her still-healing ribs.

She held the smoke in, imitating the drug-smoking soldiers she'd worked with back in Iraq, trying to grasp every molecule of sustenance from the draught.

In her own cave, the Priestess had been a figure of compassion, but also of power. Here, she was practically a doll. A tiny, but perfectly proportioned, female standing on the tomb floor in front of her.

Over her shoulders and neck, the Priestess wore a veil that was a mirror image of the one Ivy had draped across her lap. White where Mary's veil was blue. Blue where Mary's veil was silver and white. But the eight-pointed stars of Ishtar were the same.

"You've almost reached the end," the Priestess said. "Wait for my day and give them my message. Then do what you must."

"What about the Foundation and the end-times?" Ivy asked.

"Humans must learn that the greatest evil is done by those who are most certain that they are following the word of their deity. That is why there must always be the Goddess, to balance justice with mercy, to moderate where extremes lead to destruction."

"But how do we get out of here?"

"Wait for my day."

* * * *

Ivy plunged forward.

Zack barely caught her in time to keep her head from crashing into the pile of ashes.

He'd seen her drop the veil, assumed she knew what she was doing. Obviously she hadn't. Between the herb-laden fumes, lack of oxygen, and babbling to someone who wasn't there, she'd fainted.

Worse, he hadn't seen a hint of the Priestess Ivy talked about so often.

It might be a kindness to let her go peacefully. Dying of thirst would be a hundred times worse than simply fading into nothingness. But he resisted the brief temptation. Ivy was as much a fighter as he was. She'd want to fight on, no matter how hopeless the battle.

He brought the Veil to her face, letting her breathe through the thin fabric.

Her breathing seemed impossibly shallow, but her pulse was slow and steady.

All he could do now was wait and see what happened next.

For the next ten minutes or so, what happened was nothing.

Then Ivy started coughing.

The attack was so violent he had to pin her down to keep the Veil pressed over her nose and mouth. Finally, he covered her body with his own and wrapped the Veil over her whole head. It wasn't pretty, but it worked.

Ivy's coughing stopped as abruptly as it had started. "You're squeezing pretty tight."

"Sorry. You were spasming. Anyway, too bad your idea didn't work out."

"What are you talking about?"

"No Priestess. I guess you were right about the tomb and all."

"She was here, Zack. I saw her."

"Then you were hallucinating."

She paused a moment. "I won't deny your reality. But she was here. And she told me that we'd nearly reached the end."

"No kidding? Glad we didn't have to figure that out on our own."

"She might have meant that we were just going to die here, but I don't think so. Because she said we had more to do. We're supposed to wait for her day and then spread her message."

"She tell you what message to give? Or who to give it to?"

"Something about remembering the female principle. Justice tempered with mercy. Retribution with forgiveness. That sort of thing."

"That'll set those Foundation types straight, all right."

"Sarcasm isn't helpful."

Zack felt like a heel. It didn't matter whether Ivy had actually seen a priestess, he still shouldn't be negative. If Ivy hadn't seen her, her hallucination wasn't hurting anyone and it made her feel better. If he was the one who was blind to the altered reality, and given what he'd experienced over the past few weeks, he couldn't rule that out, filling Ivy with doubt was the worst thing he could do.

"Sorry," he said. "Did she give any hints on how to escape this tomb?"

Ivy shook her head. "She said we had to wait for her day. Do you have any idea what day that would be?"

Zack strained his brain. He was Catholic and had never spent much time listening to the New-Agers. Still, everyone knows that certain days were especially important to the Goddess. The winter and summer solstices. The vernal and autumnal equinoxes. The full and new moons. The first of May. Many of these had been adopted or co-opted into the Christian faith. Christmas at the winter solstice. Easter at the vernal equinox. All Saints Day near the autumnal equinox. And May Day for Mary and the Rosy Cross.

Unfortunately, none of those days was anywhere close. Waiting four weeks for the fall equinox couldn't be the right answer.

"No clue," he admitted.

"Maybe Sunday," she said. "What's today?"

Being on the run made it easy to lose track of the calendar. He had to rack his brain a bit more than he would have wanted. "Tuesday, I think."

"Think we can make it until Sunday?"

"With no water? Maybe." But he doubted it.

But something about Sunday didn't feel right. "Sunday is not just the day of the Sun. It's also the day of the Son, S-O-N. The Church adopted it as the Sabbath in honor of Easter and Christ's resurrection," he said.

"Which means the Goddess's day might be something else?"

"Right. And Saturday was the original Jewish Sabbath. But that would be the day of the Father."

She shivered. "By that logic, Monday should be the day of the Goddess. Monday means Moon-day. And the Moon represents the Goddess, doesn't she?"

He didn't think they could survive until Monday. He also suspected they didn't have that long before the Foundation was back, equipped with more advanced search technology.

"That's good thinking. Sunday for the Son. Monday for the Moon. Today's Tuesday. Who the heck is Tue?"

"No clue."

He thought. "Mars?"

"Why?"

"Because in Spanish, Tuesday is Martes. And Martes is for Mars."

"Okay, so today is definitely not the day. I don't see the Goddess being identified with the Roman god of war."

"And Thursday is definitely Thor's day in English, Jueves in Spanish. Thor and Jupiter are the thunder god. No goddesses there."

"Wednesday?"

"Woden's day in English, Miércoles, or Mercury in Spanish. Another God."

"It's got to be Friday. Who's Fri?"

"Fria, goddess of the home. In Spanish, Viernes, Venus's day. And Venus was the Goddess of Love. The message the Priestess had shared with Ivy was that of love, not that of the powerful moon. "It's got to be Friday."

He sensed Ivy's smile through the darkness. "Venus's day. I like that."

Chapter 24

Ivy's throat felt like the deserts of Iraq. They'd been locked in the tomb for what seemed like forever, but the backlit glow of Zack's watch told them it had only been three days. Which meant it was finally Friday.

Overhead, the sound of a pipe organ shook the entire church and joyful voices proclaimed a new day and eternal faith in the Creator and Redeemer.

"Now," she croaked.

"We're still locked in."

"The tomb can no longer hold us," she said. "I have the power of the Goddess on her day."

She wasn't surprised when the stone door to the tomb fell away at her lightest touch.

The smoldering pile of herbs burst into flame as oxygen reached it. A huge cloud of smoke followed her out of the tomb, then up from the crypt.

She wrapped the Veil around her and climbed the stairs into the middle of the packed church.

"Che cosa?" the priest blurted.

"Enough," she said. "I'm sick of your petty squabbles in the name of God. Are you so blind you cannot see that your hatred and disputes hurt you far more than those you hate? Are you deaf to the cries of your brothers? Are your hearts so hardened that you joy from the suffering of others?

"What is the meaning of this?" A bald priest, smelling of bacon and coffee, stepped down from the pulpit to stop her progress. "Who are you to profane the sanctity of the Church of Santa Lucia?

"The message is not for you alone," Ivy explained. "The Goddess sends it to all the people. Not just Catholics, but Orthodox and Protestant and Nestorian as well. Not just Christian but Islam and Buddhists and Hindu too. Try to understand rather than condemn."

Her throat remained dry, but waters surrounded her in this city of multiple islands and she drew on those waters for comfort and strength.

"This is a House of God," the priest insisted. "We want none of your pagan kind here."

She looked into his soul, saw his memories and smiled.

"You are not the first to deny the message, and you will not be the last. Listen, for the message will not be denied. You had a calling once, Father. Remember why you chose the priesthood. It wasn't really because Isabelle chose another man, was it? It was because you saw the precious face of the Mother of God. Have you strayed so far from her that you cannot listen when she begs for your help?"

The priest drew himself up, a crazed look on his face. For a moment, Ivy thought he was going to physically attack her. Then he prostrated himself at her feet. "She is a true vision of the Virgin. The Church of Santa Lucia is blessed."

* * * *

Zack tried to keep a watch on the congregation as they reacted to Ivy's presence. He, himself, might as well have been invisible for all of the attention he got. Which was fine. Exactly how he would have wanted it, in fact. It was obvious to him that Ivy had thrown caution to the winds. If this was the mission the priestess had sent her on, he wasn't at all sure that Ivy's priestess cared about her long-term survival.

Despite his intentions, though, Zack found himself drawn to watch Ivy, to listen to her talk.

It took him a moment to realize what was wrong with the whole scene. Ivy didn't speak Italian. So, how was she able to communicate to the people? Surely not all of them spoke English.

"Una visione del virgin," the Priest cried as he threw himself on the floor.

Zack smiled ruefully. He didn't think Ivy was a virgin, although he couldn't have proved it. But the Priest was speaking in Italian. And Ivy wasn't speaking in English or Italian. Instead, she spoke a language he'd never heard before, yet one he seemed to understand intuitively.

She'd once babbled something about the language of the priestess being the true language from before the Tower of Babble. Could she be using that to cut through barriers between people?

No one left as Ivy lectured them on what was at the center of their shared Christian faith—and at the center of the faith of Moslems, Hindu, and others of the great religions as well. Trusting in God to judge, rather than leaping to condemnation. Avoiding violence, rather than creating new enemies to fight. It was pretty standard stuff, but from her, in the magical language of the ancients, it sounded different. It sounded True, and it sounded as if saying it made it inexorably true. It was a call to change, a cry for action.

According to a mythology class he'd taken while working on his degree, the supposed True language is different from any other language because words spoken in it are self-fulfilling. Ivy wasn't just repeating church doctrine, she was creating it and making it true with each word she spoke.

No one had left the church since he and Ivy had appeared from the crypt, but more and more people were arriving, already breathless with excitement about the mystery unfolding in their midst.

He briefly wondered whether Ivy had sent psychic reverberations throughout the city, but then saw the cell phones. Even in a world where the True Cross had been recovered, it made sense to look for technology before magic.

"There are those who are attempting to misuse the Word," Ivy insisted. "They call themselves The Foundation, because they hope to be the cornerstone of the new Temple, of the reign of God. But they are mistaken. A temple built on that cornerstone would crumble into dust."

"We'll fight them, kill them," the priest moaned near Ivy's feet. His body writhed in ecstasy from whatever vision he saw.

"Yes," Zack breathed to himself. The Foundation agents would be helpless if swarmed by the true believers of Venice. If these ordinary people got word out to their friends, it could make the parade in Constantinople look tiny by comparison. After all, Turkey was a Moslem nation. Italy wasn't just Christian, it had been the center of the Catholic faith for fifteen hundred years. Against the massed might of eighty million Italian Catholics, with as many more from nearby France, Spain, Southern Germany, Austria, and Poland, the Foundation would be a speck of driftwood washed away by a tsunami.

Ivy smiled, then shook her head. "I did not come to bring more violence, but to make peace."

Zack was a soldier. And there's nothing a soldier likes more than peace. But peace with the Foundation wasn't going to be a happening thing. Not until a lot of Foundation Agents were dead, anyhow. He could only hope that Ivy would realize that before it was too late.

As if his fears created their own reality, the main doors to the church burst open and four grim-faced Americans strode in, accompanied by perhaps a dozen Uzi-equipped Italian policemen.

"This woman is a known terrorist threat," the lead agent announced in English, then in Italian little better than what Zack could have mustered. "Please stand clear, people. No one needs to get hurt."

Ivy's laughter was the sharp tinkle of breaking glass. "Those who seek God using the tools of the deceiver will deceive and mislead themselves," Ivy said. "Do you truly believe that the Kingdom of God can be built on your lies?"

"Get her."

Zack moved to intercept the killers. Ivy was a fighter, but he feared she wouldn't fight now. He wasn't going to let them create a new martyr here in Venice. Not while he could still move.

Ivy laughed again, then swirled Mary's Veil like a matador waving his cape before a bull.

The small plastic bags of herbs they'd left smoldering in the crypt should have burned out long before. Impossibly, though, they hadn't. A rich cloud of smoke swirled around the Agents and they stumbled into one another, blinded by the acrid fumes.

"Shoot her down," the lead Agent commanded.

Seconds later, a flurry of shots rang out. Unaimed bullets sprayed from the cloud of smoke, ricocheting from stone walls.

Ivy shook the veil like a maid shaking out a dustcloth and a score of bullets tumbled from the sheer silk fabric to the floor.

One of the altar boys stumbled forward, blood turning his white robes bright red, his screams filling the church.

"Antonio, some day you will be a Cardinal. But that time is not yet. Better to keep the white of innocence for a while," Ivy said. She placed the veil over the wound, then drew it back.

The boy fingered the hole in his robe, then pulled the robe off, exposing his pale and unbroken skin. "It doesn't hurt."

"The Queen of Heaven accepts only sacrifices that are freely given, only that whose ripeness is full."

The smoke had cleared and the Agents still had their guns out, but they were clearly having second thoughts about another round of firing.

"Didn't you hear what she said?" the lead Agent demanded of the priest. "She's not a Christian. She's a New-Age follower of some made-up Goddess. Queen of Heaven, indeed."

"While you may scorn Mary, Mother of God, we do not." The priest squared his shoulders and looked straight at those guns. "The Virgin has come to us with a message of mercy and goodness, and you welcome her with violence and gunshot. You are not welcome in this house of the

Lord. Leave."

"These guns are all the welcome we need," the Agent blustered.

"You will put your weapons away." The Italian police lieutenant pushed his way between the Americans and Ivy. "We've seen a great miracle today. We won't let you continue."

"You're forgetting who's in charge here."

"Am I? We are in Italy, not America."

"I'll get you fired."

The cop laughed. "You threaten me? Even if your threat had any weight, I would still stop you. Now, lady, what are your intentions?"

* * * *

"What are your intentions?"

She'd preached the message of the Mother of God, Queen of Heaven, as the priestess had asked her to do. But the Foundation was still there. The locals were impressed with what they had seen, but Ivy knew it wouldn't be long before they started selling cheap china figurines of the messenger and forgot the message.

And the Foundation was still out there. They seemed immune to the message, separated from the truth by the twisted power of their sanctimonious beliefs. High on the Priestess's promise and on the vast power that she suddenly could access, Ivy had believed it would be possible to reach them. That she could remind even Foundation Agents of their shared faith, show them how their actions were taking them away from Grace, were based on a wholly misguided view of the divine. Horribly, the very certainty of their faith shielded them from the truth.

She could mobilize the entire city to come to her aid. Water is at the secret heart of the female principle. And Venice was the city of water, a city of the Goddess as were few others in the world. This, then, was the true reason they'd been sent to this city. In Venice as much anywhere in the world, she could draw on the power of the Goddess, use it to perform little miracles like the healing she'd done on the altar boy, or even greater miracles. But the human mind, especially a mind protected by the shields of fanaticism, remained beyond reach of her powers. She could destroy one easily enough, but she couldn't heal those who clung to their illness.

She tried to remember everything the priestess had told her, everything she'd learned in studying for her Confirmation. But no easy lessons jumped out at her. She'd have to figure what to do on her own.

She had access to all of the power in the world. She could destroy anything. She could kill or heal. She could declare herself the Goddess Incarnate, and rule Venice with a velvet fist. She could reach around the world and crush anyone who made war.

But she followed the logic of each of those choices. Each led to the same result—a world ever-more crippled by religious violence and religious hatred. And that world was the world of The Foundation.

She hadn't lied when she'd told the congregation that a City of God based on hatred and violence could never stand, but if she used the power of the Veil, the Cross, and the City, she could only become like them.

With the power in her, she could peer into the origins of the Foundation—to that group of frightened men who had gathered to celebrate their faith and work together to create a better world. They'd been then like she was now, seeking only good.

To succeed in the face of all the obstacles, they'd needed power. And seeking power, they'd discovered its allure, been perverted by it, until power became their unspoken goal.

Now, she had the power. But the only way she could see to use it would lead to that same result.

Realizing that, seeing those frightened men in her mind, brought the answer to her.

She headed toward the Church's open doors.

As she stepped past them, parishioners reached for her, their hands brushing against the Veil but unable to hold it.

"The Virgin," she heard whispered again and again. "We've seen the Virgin."

She smiled at them. She could joyfully do what needed to be done now.

"Come with me," she said. "Follow." The words rolled from her, spreading out like the ripples spreading from a stone thrown in a still pond, reverberating through the church and beyond where a still-growing crowd stood and waited. Some of them, she saw, had knelt in silent prayer. Others looked thoughtful, or angry, or filled with greed.

"Come," she repeated, knowing as she said it that her words made it an imperative, that they could no more resist the compulsion than they could talk a tornado into changing its path.

* * * *

The people parted around Ivy like water yielding to a ship. They clutched at, but their hands didn't stick. Yet, even as their hands slid from her, their lips turned upward into smiles, or opened into prayer.

Zack was blind to the colors of power that Ivy spoke of so often, but even he could sense the electrical nimbus that surrounded her.

She brushed near the Agents and for a moment, hunger lit the lead

Agent's face.

His thoughts were completely transparent, and they weren't about Ivy being a saint, either. He wanted to grab her, snap her neck, kill her once and for all, and then rape her body. With Ivy dead, the compulsion would end. Even if the Italian cops reacted instantly, killing the Agent, it would be too late to save Ivy. And the Agent would welcome martyrdom.

"Watch out," he called to Ivy. He pushed himself forward but the mob didn't respond to him as it did to Ivy. People shoved back, jealous of their closeness to their vision of the Virgin.

"Come, Zack," Ivy said, laughter in her voice. "You were with me from the beginning. Try to stay with me to the end."

"Watch the Agent."

His warning came too late. The Agent threw himself at Ivy, a knife clutched in one hand while the other reached for her neck.

Zack shoved forward, desperate to reach her in time, knowing he would be too late.

Ivy must have heard his warning, though, because she turned toward the Agent.

Rather than stepping into a defensive stance, she simply held the veil in front of her.

The Agent hit the thin layer of silk—and bounced off as if he'd rammed a brick wall.

"Do not harm him," Ivy said to a couple of Italian policemen who had drawn saps and were heading toward the Agent with serious faces.

"But make sure he can't get away," Zack added. Ivy might have converted to pacifism, but that didn't mean they couldn't take reasonable precautions. Not if he had anything to say about it.

Outside the church was a stone courtyard filled with a growing crowd.

An eerie hush descended as Ivy stepped into their midst.

"Follow me," Ivy repeated.

She walked through the crowd and stepped onto a gondola that couldn't have been waiting for her, but seemed to be.

"Need me to row?" Zack asked.

She smiled at him, then reached out and brushed a hand across his cheek.

"Call ahead to Father Paulo. We need the Cross to finish this. But this part, I have to do on my own. As we used to say when I was little, 'no boys allowed.'"

Okay, Ivy had a plan. Zack felt a little better with that realization.

He borrowed a cell from the bald priest at Santa Lucia and put through a call to the Church of Mary of the Sailors.

To his surprise, Father Francis answered. Zack told the older priest that Ivy was coming and to have the item ready. On an open channel, that was all he dared say. Even that was probably too much.

"The Saint is exultant in the power that flows through her, but not all those whom she faces will be powerless," Father Francis warned him.

Those weren't the most encouraging words for Zack to hear. He handed the cell back to the bald priest and took off to share the warning with Ivy.

She stood in the center of a Gondola as it moved down the canal. Although there appeared to be no oarsman, the gondola's single oar cut through the water, moving her at a steady pace that the joyful crowds could just follow.

Each time they passed a building, more people flooded into the streets and walkways along the canal, their voices a babble of Italian and other languages as they demanded to know what was going on, who that woman was, whether she was breaking city code by sailing a gondola without a gondolier, what holiday had been declared.

Zack spotted a bridge ahead and hurried toward it. He needed to get Father Francis's warning to Ivy and there was no way he could make himself overheard over the hubbub from the increasingly huge crowd.

By the time he got to the bridge, it was already filling but he was able to secure the last front row location.

A woman next to him tossed flower petals onto the canal's brown waters. Past her, a barefooted Franciscan monk was down on his knees praying.

Children ran, laughing, over the crowded length of the bridge, then up the other side of the canal as Ivy's gondola approached.

* * * *

Things were going too easily.

While Ivy hadn't been able to penetrate the Agent's warped beliefs, protected as they were by his strong but perverted faith, he had been too weak even to touch the veil.

Which meant he was just a foot soldier in the Foundation's army. But surely they had more senior agents. Ivy wasn't naïve enough to believe the Goddess would assign her an easy job.

Still, she'd caught them off-guard, and the crowds of people and the energized Italian police could slow their reactions and jam their communications with so much chatter that they would find it difficult to react.

It seemed barely possible that she'd be able to pull this off, make it to the Church of Mary of the Sailors, to the Cross before the Foundation brought in their heavy guns.

The whine of a helicopter's turbine engine overhead put a lie to that speculation. The Foundation wasn't going to be fooled again.

The chopper's rotors stirred up murky canal waters and drove a few of the celebrating children, joyous in their escape from school, back under cover.

She couldn't see faces behind the black glass of the helicopter's canopy, but she felt the gunner's eyes on her, sighting on her through a missile rangefinder.

She called up a bit of power from the waters that surrounded her and sent it into the sighting mechanism.

The backwash almost stunned her. She hadn't meant to hurt the man but his eye had been pushed tightly into the sight. His pain rippled through her body. Her newly found resistance to violence and death suddenly made sense not just as a philosophical virtue but as hard-edged reality. She felt every bit of the pain she caused. Although she could draw power from all around her, she was still physically frail from injuries and days without food or much sleep. Fighting physical battles where she suffered when she won as much as she suffered when she lost couldn't be the right answer.

The helicopter banked away, then returned and dropped a rope ladder.

She gestured at it and the ladder fell from the chopper, its Kevlar strands sliced like so much cotton candy.

The wave of anger from above didn't scare her at all. Anger was more destructive for the man holding it than for the woman he assaulted with it.

Her trick with the ladder didn't phase the Foundation agents, though.

A man stepped into the chopper's open door and jumped down toward the water.

He hit the water as if it were solid ground, splaying his legs to take the brunt of the energy, then stood and walked across the canal toward her.

From the crowd, she heard an amazed gasp. If she'd wowed them with a gondola that steered without a gondolier, walking on water was a big step up.

Ivy's surprise though, was less from the manner of his approach than from his identity.

"Smith?"

"Guess it's time to finish what I started."

"We left you dead in Mosul."

His laugh was cutting, nasal, nasty.

"As I left you. But you don't have the Cross with you now. This time, when you die, you stay dead."

She didn't dare close her eyes, but she used her second sight to view the power surrounding him.

As with the other Foundation Agents, it pulsed a deep maroon red. In his case, though, the ugly mustard of yellow crept through, like hotter flames through a glowing bed of coal.

She recognized that horrid yellow from the temple to the bird-god. There, it had been associated with human sacrifice. Without access to the power of the Cross, had the Foundation crossed that line of evil?

"Your leaders must have really wanted you back if they resorted to human sacrifice."

"Liar. You don't know what you're talking about."

It didn't take second sight to hear the hint of doubt in his voice. So, they hadn't told him what they'd done, but he suspected, or feared.

That didn't surprise her. Need to know was not limited to government spy organizations.

"Can't you see that your precious Foundation is destroying what it is trying to build? Remember the message of Jesus. He forgave those who offended him. He preached peace even in the face of the warmongers."

"Don't pervert the words of the Lord." He strode across the water, closing the distance to her gondola. "It is not I who has forgotten the message of the Prince of Peace. You've succumbed to Lilith. Your New-Age interpretations of the Holy Word have no power over me and every word you speak is condemned by the true Church. Even your precious and misguided Catholicism spurns them."

Hatred and rage contorted his features.

Smith drew a knife from his jacket and, despite herself, Ivy's body trembled. That was the same knife he'd used to slit her throat. The laws of magic applied. It had killed her once, it could kill her again. Unwashed, still carrying her life-blood, it held a magical power over her that no ordinary weapon could claim. Against it, the Veil would be useless fabric.

"Killing me will accomplish nothing," she said. "The powers of the Goddess are not so easily defeated."

"Your so-called Goddess, like all of Satan's demons, has no strength before the Lord. And spare me your misguided reinterpretation of the Trinity. True Christians have rejected that blasphemy from the earliest times."

Although she'd kept the gondola in motion, heading down the river and away from him, Smith was faster, closing the distance.

He reached her boat just as they crossed beneath a bridge.

A blue-tinged figure dropped from the bridge and grappled with Smith.

She had just a moment to recognize her rescuer. It was Zack, of course. He really hadn't gotten it. Like Peter in the Garden, when the soldiers had come to arrest Jesus, Zack thought he could use violence to solve the problems that violence creates.

She just hoped he could survive his error.

All of Smith's attention had been on Ivy and Zack landed feet-first on the Agent's head. Which would have incapacitated any human. But Smith wasn't quite human anymore. Like herself, the man had been transformed by death and resurrection.

Zack's face contorted with pain when his feet smashed into the Agent's head and the Agent simply shrugged, turning his knife casually to slice at Zack as he went by.

Unlike Smith, the water didn't support Zack. Where he splashed, blood turned the water red.

Anger swept over Ivy. Zack was her friend, had sacrificed everything he had built to help her survive. And Smith had swatted him away as casually as he might squash an ant.

With the powers available to her on the water, she could call up a whirlpool to swamp Smith, or hit him with a wave of fire hot enough to melt through even the powerful wards of faith that surrounded him.

She barely fought down the temptation. Smith was trying to make her lose her temper. If she reacted in anger, the Foundation would win, and humanity would lose.

Instead, she changed the texture of the water beneath Smith, making it more slippery, more open, less willing to bear weight.

He'd been expecting something overt and strong, not something sneaky and subtle.

Smith's splash followed Zack's by less than a second.

She reached tentacles of power into the water and yanked Zack out, placing him on the ground near a group of Italian policemen. A flicker of life remained within him. Maybe their first aid could be enough to save him. Unfortunately, she didn't have time to wait and see. She'd never know.

She fought back the urge to cry, putting the energy into the gondola's oar, increasing her speed as she moved through the city toward the Church of Mary of the Sailors.

A few blocks from that church, the crowd must have sensed where she was going because they got louder and thicker. The entire city seemed intent on gathering in one very small area.

Overhead, the Foundation helicopter had been joined by U.S. Navy fighters but then Ivy noticed that the Navy fighters weren't alone. Italian Air Force fighters scrambled. It looked as if they were trying to keep the Navy away from the crowds.

She guessed that made sense. The Foundation had shown it didn't mind civilian casualties, especially if they were Catholic or any other religion that didn't meet the Foundation's exacting standards. But the Italian government wouldn't be so sanguine about the slaughter of their civilians. They would also have been getting word from the local police. And Ivy doubted that the U.S. Government had bothered to ask for official permission for these overflights.

She spared just a bit of power to raise the spirits of the Italian pilots overhead. They were facing the world's most powerful military without clear orders from their government. She didn't want them to fight, but she appreciated them being there, providing just that little extra reason to discourage the Foundation from doing anything truly stupid.

The church of Mary of the Fishermen loomed closer, the stone walls of its sea-gate shiny with slime from the canal.

For the first time since they'd been trapped in the crypt, she let out a small sigh of relief. She was going to make it.

She only blinked for a moment, but when she looked, a hand emerged from the filthy canal and seized the stern of her gondola.

She let out a choked squawk and commanded the wood of the gondola to liquefy, to deny Smith any grip.

Like so much else that was primitive, wood was sacred to the Goddess. It should have obeyed her command. But it didn't react. Smith's physical touch overrode her commands and dissipated her energy like a monolith dissipated waves washing against it.

The Agent hauled himself out of the water with one hand, his other still gripping the knife.

"You didn't think you'd get rid of me that easily, did you?"

Chapter 25

Ivy shook her head. She'd hoped Smith might be held by the superslippery water. After all, water was the native element of the Goddess. Just as Air was the element of the Son, and Fire the element of the Father.

She'd hoped, but at some level, she hadn't really believed it could be that easy. If a stitching of submachinegun bullets through his gut hadn't stopped Smith, a dumping into the canals of Venice, no matter how dirty or magically enhanced, wouldn't either.

"I slowed you down. That was enough."

His laughter was too high-pitched for a man his size. "Enough? Enough to let you bring me to the Cross, that's all. I suppose I should thank you, although I would have been a lot more grateful if you'd just died in Mosul where you were supposed to."

Church bells rang, echoing first from the Church of Mary of the Sailors and then from nearby churches until the entire city echoed.

Smith hissed. "Another of your tricks?"

Ivy shrugged. "None of my doing. Why? Does their faith frighten you?"

"It frightens me that so many are damned because of the errors of your so-called Catholic so-called religion. It frightens me that its sins have prevented the return of Christ for centuries. Their puny powers frighten me not at all."

But Ivy wasn't fooled. Smith was frightened. The church bells didn't create power, but their vibrations awakened power from within the waters surrounding and underlying the city and from the ancient stone buildings of Venice.

Venice had survived its share of fanatics. Smith would find plenty of that power available to him. But most of the city's fifteen hundred years had been lived under the guidance of a more practical faith. Venice had been a city of merchants for far longer than it had been a city of conquerors. As the gateway between East and West, it had enjoyed a mix of Orthodox and Catholic heritages and a tolerance for those of the Moslem faith. And in those Catholic and Orthodox practices, even if denied in official doctrine, adoration of the Queen of Heaven remained powerful. The church bells changed the balance of power between herself and Smith, helping him less than they helped her.

Unfortunately, the future wouldn't be decided by a climactic mage-battle, like in the movies. Being filled with the Goddess meant that Ivy was incapable of attacking. She knew from her military training that defending alone is ultimately doomed.

From the waters and the earth below, though, healing and protective powers welled up, comforting her, promising her that they were available to her if she could figure how to use them.

In the clouds over the city, a sense of impending power hung like an electrical charge before a lightning storm. Unlike the gentle and healing power of the Goddess, this power was harsh, hot, and hasty. It was not evil, but its raw strength was still something Smith could draw on in support of his narrow-minded definition of virtue.

The doorway to the Church of Mary of the Sailors flew open and Father Paulo, Father Francis, and more than a dozen other priests carried the two sections of the Cross into the courtyard.

Silence began at the Cross, then spread in concentric circles until only the distant sound of fighter jets overhead remained.

The Cross had always been an object of power. But now Ivy realized how undeveloped her second sight had been before the days and nights she'd spent in the tomb. Where she had seen it as gleaming with a red light, now it shined as bright as the sun.

As she watched, the Priests assembled the two pieces, bringing them together not as two pieces of lumber, but as a traditionally shaped Cross.

The Cross's power blazed even more brightly, so much so that Smith flinched. But then he stood strong, soaking in power like a sponge.

The Cross was whole.

It seemed to Ivy that the world stood still for an eternal moment.

Smith's eyes were drawn to that blazing symbol of power and his knuckles whitened on the knife.

"Finally," he breathed. "It will be mine."

The church bells resumed chiming, a glorious celebration of the recovery of the very symbol of the Christian faith. The bell's sonic vibrations mingled with the psychic emanations from the Cross. Ivy felt a snap as the universe changed.

All through the world, long-buried objects shifted in their places. Artifacts, weapons, forgotten temples, secret lore responded to the key, readied themselves to be called up, sent into battle. They waited only for the power of the Cross to call them out, arm them for the last days, the ultimate battle as described in the Bible—and in the dark legends of the Germanic gods.

"Under this banner, we shall conquer," Smith gloated. "We shall redeem the Holy Land at last. We shall prepare the physical throne of the risen Christ on the Holy Mount. With the Cross to lead us, we can cast all who oppose us into death and damnation. And I shall stand at the Lord's right hand."

"Not yet," Ivy said. "God's timing is his own, not to be rushed by fanatics."

"Must you continue to deny us? Your power would be welcomed by The Foundation, Sergeant."

She was sure. They'd drain her, then kill her. The angry men who had created The Foundation half a century earlier would never accept women in any role other than that as subservient creatures. For all their loud repugnance to the ancient rites of temple prostitution, those men thought of women as vessels for sex, to be used and forgotten.

Not that Ivy would join them even if they could accept her as an equal. Their faith was real, but it was horribly perverted from what the Goddess demanded of her people.

"The Goddess demands balance," she answered calmly. "Your Foundation strives to overturn that balance."

Smith snickered. "Balance is overthrown. The Cross is found, is unleashed on the world. Keep it if you're strong enough. It will not matter. The days of Prophesy are at hand and cannot be averted even by your false Goddess's evil power."

He was deluding himself about the nature of the Goddess's power, but his words rang true. With the Cross unveiled in an anxious and war-torn world, The Foundation would accomplish its goals of hurrying the final cataclysm.

Smith's mouth was open and his eyes slightly out of focus. Like her, he could see more than the mundane. Perhaps, Ivy thought, it was one effect of coming back from death.

He stepped toward the Cross, shoving aside the pilgrims who reached to touch it, to affirm their faith with the very real and wholly tangible power of the Cross.

She moved to block him. If he took the Cross, he'd be too powerful for her to face.

If he'd been able to keep the corners of his lips still, he would have had her, but that hint of a smirk gave her warning. He still had the knife.

She shifted her weight, twisted her hips, and let the knife pass by her, then draped the veil over his wrist.

His look of surprise changed into one of horror and he jerked back, screaming.

Where the veil touched it, his hand shriveled to bloodstained bones and dried tendons.

He pulled back, barely holding onto the knife, then transferring it to his left hand.

"Bitch."

Interesting. Hurting the soldiers in the helicopter had nearly crippled her. Damaging Smith hadn't hurt her at all.

She'd thought the vampires the gypsies had feared were mythical. Apparently not. Smith hadn't been brought back to life in the same way she had. Then again, he hadn't had access to the True Cross. Rather than being resurrected, he'd been reanimated, sucking up lives of the sacrifice, or sacrifices, that had been made on his behalf. If she hadn't spent time with the gypsies, she wouldn't have known that, wouldn't have guessed the meaning of what had just happened. The path the Goddess had set them seemed ever-more connected.

Mary's veil undid the magic that had brought him back. The concerns of the Father and Son were for eternity. The concerns of the Mother, the Great Goddess and Queen of Heaven, were for the living. Smith was not one of those.

He snarled. "What did you do?"

"You're still trying to deny it, aren't you? They lied to you if they said they resurrected you. Only the Cross can do that. And they didn't have the Cross."

"You're lying. Lazarus was resurrected through faith alone. And even if you're not lying, I have the Cross now. It will save me." He angled around her.

"Don't let him have it, but don't touch him," she shouted to the priests holding the Cross.

The vague orders were a mistake. Their previously coordinated efforts in bringing out the Cross scrambled, each priest pulling in a different direction.

She stepped to block Smith, but he gestured with the knife and spoke two words in the true language. The first, 'time,' she heard clearly. The second came too fast for her to hear.

The world speeded up around her. She seemed to be moving through an ocean of tar, the very air resisting her movement while Smith moved unhindered.

"Time," a voice whispered in her ear. A female voice, speaking the true language. "His God is identified as Chronos, the lord of time."

She didn't stop to thank the priestess, or Goddess for the information. There'd be time enough for that if she survived the next few minutes.

She pulled the Veil back, slowly wrapping it around her shoulders, over her head like a hood.

The instant it covered her, she was free of Smith's curse. Free, but desperately late.

Smith's eyes gleamed as he reached his shattered, dead, hand to the Cross, touched it, and then grasped the ancient symbol of power, trying to pull it away from the priests.

Ten priests held onto the Cross, unwilling to let it be taken from them. Decades of prayer strengthened them. These were not ordinary men filled with doubt, but priests filled with the certainty of their faith, strengthened by the presence of the power and solid reality of the Cross itself.

Smith's eyes widened at the strength with which they resisted. His muscles strained as he attempted to rip it from their grasp.

Strained and failed.

Ivy closed the distance. She only needed a few seconds.

She was only a meter away when one of the priests stumbled and brushed against Smith.

Like time-lapse footage, the priest withered on himself, aging, turning gray, then collapsing into powdery bones.

To Ivy's second sight, it looked as if the power of Smith's energy field had been hit with a surge of pure oxygen. As the priest fell, Smith soaked up his faith, gathered the power to himself.

Smith clenched the fist of his shriveled hand and the priests stood back as it healed, adding flesh and muscle while they watched.

The remaining nine priests could have held on, continued to resist, but the shock of what they'd seen was too much. First one, then another loosened their grip on the Cross.

Smith took advantage of their weakness, jerking it free of the others until only ancient Father Francis retained his grasp at the head of the Cross.

The Agent lifted the massive weight of the heavy wood object over his head and shook it, but the Priest hung on grimly.

Ivy reached into the waters beneath her to send a line of power to the stubborn Priest. It was little enough, but it was all she could do as she prepared to confront the undead man.

The gypsies had told her about vampires, but had they prepared her? She wished she'd paid more attention. Certainly the myth that they couldn't stand the sight of a crucifix was mistaken. Smith wasn't bothered by the True Cross at all.

She knew they hated garlic but didn't think that would help, either, not even in Italy.

But the thought of garlic reminded her of the burning herbs of the Goddess.

Flames had almost consumed the last of the herbs but back in the tomb, a few smoldered on.

Using the power of the Earth, Ivy reached across the kilometers and pulled those burning herbs to her.

The smoke hit Smith like a fist, dropping him to one knee.

He released his grip on the Cross, stood, and turned to face her, glowing with the power he'd seized from the Cross and from the priest he'd desiccated.

"You might have lived if you'd run."

"If you give up on your insane dreams, you can live forever," Ivy answered. "Even now, the Queen of Heaven can wash the sin from your soul."

"The Queen of Heaven is a cursed demon," Smith screamed. He summoned his powers, then slashed at her, his long knife flaming with fire and hatred.

* * * *

It had taken Zack too long to persuade the policemen that he was fine, that the blood was worse than it looked, that Ivy had pretty much heal him and if they'd just bandage up his arm where he'd scraped it trying to get up, he could get on with his day.

Only the word that the True Cross had been unveiled persuaded them that they had more important things to do. They might be cops, but they were Christians, too.

He hurried after them, arriving in time to see Smith seize the Cross and destroy one of the Priests who had guarded it.

With that brutal murder, the crowd eased back a bit. Nobody was in quite as much of a hurry to get close to the Agent, no matter how strong the allure of the Cross. No one Except Zack.

Zack pushed his way forward.

"The Queen of Heaven is a cursed demon," Smith shouted.

Impossibly, it seemed as if the heavy incense from the Priestess's herbs had followed them, surrounding the Agent.

The smoke took the shape of dozens of beautiful women clutching at Smith's arms, brushing their hair across his eyes, whispering secrets in his ear.

The Agent dropped the Cross and turned on Ivy.

He missed with his first slash, but flipped his wrist and swung it back, moving twice as fast as anything Zack had ever seen.

Ivy saw it coming and moved.

For a moment, Zack thought she'd slipped it entirely. Then blood blackened the royal blue of the Veil she wore as a shawl.

She pressed a hand over her rib where the knife had struck. The Veil wasn't protecting her.

Smith knew he'd won and pressed the attack.

Ivy backed away from him, ducked under one slash, then jumped over another.

Almost. The knife caught her heel, dumping her on the ground.

It wasn't the opportunity he'd been waiting for, but Zack could wait no longer.

He leapt at the Agent, throwing punches as quickly as he could.

He landed one solid shot to Smith's gut and another to his chin—and felt the bones in his hands shatter as if he'd tried to punch out a rock.

Smith gestured with the knife and Zack was thrown backward.

If the pilgrims hadn't caught at him, slowed him down, he would have been crushed when he hit the church's stone wall. As it was, he still had the wind knocked out of him.

He could barely stand, but he forced himself forward. Smith might be unstoppable, but Zack wasn't going to give him a free ride.

Zack had bought Ivy time to run, but she hadn't taken it.

"Give up, Smith," she said. "You cannot win."

"I have won." He waved a lance of flame at her.

Ivy countered with a wave of water, drowning the flame in a roar of steam. But the flame had been a feint. Smith followed it, shrugged off the steam, and struck again.

Ivy batted the knife away, but Smith twisted the blade as she blocked, slicing deeply into her palm.

"Good-bye, Sergeant."

"Good-bye, Smith." Ivy gave up trying to hold her side and blood spurted from what could only be a cut artery, spraying over the Cross, the Veil, and the courtyard.

She ignored the blood and her injured hand, pulled the veil off her shoulders and unfolded it again and again until it became flimsy, gauzy, almost nothing.

Smith edged back for a moment, uncertain about Ivy's plan, then moved forward for his kill.

As he struck, Ivy threw the veil into the air.

Smith's stab ripped through the veil and into Ivy's forehead.

She collapsed, the Veil slowly settling over both her and the Cross.

Smith laughed, then reached for his prize.

His hand went through the Cross.

The sound of church bells went from glorious celebration to clamoring lament as Ivy, the Cross, and the Veil shimmered, then melted into nothingness.

Smith turned on the crowd, his knife ready. "Who stole it?"

"Neither the Veil nor the Cross were meant for this age," Father Francis explained. "Saint Ivy has returned them to safety."

"Her? She's no saint. And the Foundation would have kept them safe."

Father Francis laughed. "The Cross and Veil were always safe. Their existence is tied up in the very persistence of the universe. Our own brief lives are far less secure, but our souls are protected."

Smith slashed his bloody knife through the fading clouds of smoke and the gradually diminishing sparkle that marked the spot where Ivy had vanished.

"It isn't possible."

"On the contrary, Saint Ivy did the only thing she could do," Father Francis said. His voice was soft, but it expanded through the crowd. "She sacrificed herself to lock the key inside itself, beyond the reach of anyone who will attempt to use God's awesome power to compel the Lord."

"Your petty blasphemies offend me." Smith waved the knife at Father Francis and sent the aging priest stumbling backward, then launched a lance of fire into the survivors from the group of priests who'd carried the Cross out from the church.

"If I burn down your city, I suspect I'll find the Cross at the bottom of the embers, with the Sergeant's bones turned to ashes around it."

He launched a firebolt into a garbage boat that had docked nearby, its attendants more interested in miracles than in the city's cleanup. In seconds, unquenchable fire hit the boat's gasoline tank and it exploded, sending fiery streams floating across the canal.

"We've got to stop him." With Ivy's death, Zack wanted to give up. But he couldn't just let the Agent destroy a city that was home to so many tens of thousands. A fear that Smith might be right and that his destruction would release the Cross to the Foundation only made Zack more certain.

"Wait." Father Paulo clutched at Zack's sleeve. "I've got an idea."

The Priest darted into the Church of Saint Mary of the Sailors.

Zack followed, just in time to avoid another of Smith's fireballs.

"Try to throw this on him." The priest handed him a pitcher filled with a colorless liquid.

Zack sniffed the pitcher. Water? "Ivy already tried that. He isn't the Wicked Witch of the West. I hardly think he's going to melt."

"It's the best chance we have. Hurry."

For a second, Zack was an altar boy again, following his priest's commands.

He took the crystal pitcher and hurried out of the church.

Smith was still tossing the occasional fireball, but he was also on his radio, screaming at the Navy fighters to start missile launches against anything that moved in the city. Pretty clearly the Navy pilots were arguing, but Zack suspected they would be ordered to obey Smith's commands.

Unless Zack stopped him.

"Smith."

The Agent whirled around. "You're still not dead, Captain?"

"Not yet. Which makes one of us." He tossed the water over the Agent, then, realizing that the crystal decanter would make a far better weapon than simple water, threw it at Smith's head.

Smith knocked the pitcher back at Zack with his knife and glared at him contemptuously.

The liquid settled into Smith's skin and began ripping through it, exposing bone, rotting flesh, a grinning skull mask.

Zack hadn't seen Father Paulo come out from the church, but the Priest threw another pitcher of the horrible killing liquid over the Agent's body.

It gradually crumpled to the ground, skeletal ribs holding a heart that continued to throb despite the fact that no blood reached it.

Zack backed away from the skeletal remains. "What the heck was in that pitcher? Hydrochloric acid?"

"No, my son. Something far more powerful."

Zack's brain was too tired for riddles. "What's that?"

"Pure water, Holy Water, blessed by the Lord and Lady."

* * * *

With no Agent commanding them to send their missiles into the civilian population of an allied nation, the Navy fighters didn't stick around long, heading back to their aircraft carriers and the chance to prepare to face real enemies.

Zack helped the Priests and police with the firefighting and cleanup, then collapsed.

He'd lost a lot of blood in his brief encounter with Smith.

Fathers Paulo and Francis visited him in the hospital a few days later. They'd signed him in as a local gondolier, avoiding any indication of his nationality or his current AWOL status from the U.S. Army.

"We were wondering if you had plans?" Father Paulo admitted after exchanging a few pleasantries about his health and healing.

"No." Losing Ivy had ripped a hole out of his life and Zack didn't think he could ever heal it.

"In this increasingly secular world, too few men turn to God," Father Francis said, speaking softly as if someone might overhear and accuse him of treason to the church. "Yet, consider this. You've spent time with a Saint, carried the Cross that our Lord carried, touched and been protected by the Veil of the Mother of God. What man, more than you, could be said to have received a calling? The church would be honored to have you consider the seminary, accept your calling into the service of the Lord."

When he'd been an altar boy, Zack had briefly considered the priesthood. But he'd discovered girls and then the army. Those had driven any inclination from him.

Now, it was a possibility again. The Catholic Church, unlike the Orthodox, required that its priests be celibate and unmarried, but that would hardly be a problem for Zack. He had found his woman and now she was lost. He wouldn't be interested in another. And he did have a message. He'd listened when Ivy had told him about her priestess, he'd heard her create new truths of peace in the Church of Saint Lucia. It was a message the Church, and the world, needed to hear.

"I'll think about it," he said.

Father Francis beamed at him, patting him on the shoulder. "You will make an excellent priest. People would come from miles around to hear your account of the flight of the Cross across Europe and Asia. And what better advocate could Ivy have for her canonization?"

"Canonization?"

"Surely she deserves that. She died for the faith, protecting the Holy Cross from abomination. The Veil of the Mother of God came to her after being lost for hundreds of years. She received several visions from Saint Mary and became a vision of the Queen herself, an avatar. It will take time, but I feel certain that the Church will eventually recognize her as one of its martyrs."

"And there's wonderful news," Father Paulo interjected. "We're reconsecrating the Church and consecrating Ivy's relic next week. You'll have to be there."

Dread fell over Zack. Had Ivy's sacrifice been wasted? Had they recovered the Cross despite everything. "Her relic?"

"Smith's knife which marked her with Christ's stigmata. Wounds in her hands, feet, and side."

"You're making Smith's knife into a holy object?" The thought sickened him.

Father Francis touched him lightly on the forehead. "Don't be concerned, Brother Zack. The Faithful recognize the implements of martyrdom to remind them of the sacrifice. Think of the Cross itself. Forget the superstitious belief that it came from a seed from the Garden of Eden. What is a Cross other than the device the Romans used to torture and kill our King? Yet it became the perpetual symbol of our faith."

"I'll be there," Zack promised.

Chapter 26

Church bells rang through the city.

The waters beneath the city of water responded to the bells, small waves in the nearly glass-smooth waters rippling in cadence with the sounds.

Over time as they sailed down the Grand Canal from the causeway to the Church of Mary of the Fishermen, Zack's heart began to resonate to that same powerful beat.

Fathers Francis and Paulo had been joined by two Bishops and a Cardinal, but the local priests were the stars of the show, holding the still-bloody knife high in the air as their gondola sliced through the city's ever-present water.

Zack, along with the surviving priests from the group that had carried the Cross, followed in a second Gondola. The priests from the Church of Santa Lucia, where he and Ivy had hidden, followed behind, their censers billowing blue smoke that mimicked the smells Ivy had produced with the herbs she'd bought rather than the Church's familiar bitter myrrh. Behind them came other religious and civic leaders.

Crowds lined the walkways along the canal and the bridges over it.

Portraits of the Virgin Mary and of Ivy, many of them ethereal creations representing nothing close to the very human woman Zack had known, hung in banners over the river.

Zack had to pinch himself a few times when he thought he saw familiar faces. Surely the Patriarch of Constantinople couldn't have come to Venice. And that first imam from the village in Turkey? Gypsies could travel anywhere, but the Greek sailors would have left long before.

The whole city of Venice seemed intent on squeezing into the Church of St. Mary of the Sailors. A couple of burly priests opened a passage for the dignitaries from the first three boats leaving the others to fend for themselves, and the Cardinal blessed the assembly and conducted a Mass.

As they blessed the knife, adding it to the Church's treasury of real and suspected holy relics, Father Francis slipped next to Zack.

"Have you reconsidered our suggestion? Today, many men receive their calling later in life, perhaps after losing a loved one. You would not be alone."

Zack shook his head slowly. He'd always be alone. Only one person had shared that horrible, yet wonderful journey across Asia and Europe. No one could replace her in his mind and heart. And believing that he could be her advocate in the Church was self-delusional.

"I'm not ready for that," Zack said.

Father Francis shook his head slowly. "Don't retreat from human contact, my brother. You've done much to be proud of, but we humans are not designed to be solitary. If you don't find companionship in the church, find it somewhere. Otherwise, what you have seen and survived will make your crazy."

It sounded like good advice and Zack thanked the aging priest. Still, he wasn't sure how he could take it. He didn't want the company of others.

The next person who joined him was the imam. "The Saint has defeated the powers of Shaitan, for the time at least. Allah will not look unkindly upon you for all you have done."

"Don't Moslems think Christians are doomed to hell?"

The holy man shook his head. "Not at all. Our faith teaches that the compassion of Allah extends to the many. I pray that even the Agent, Smith, will be cleansed and receive Allah's grace."

Which was part of what Ivy had been trying to say. Moslems, even more than Catholics, resist the notion of the Goddess or Queen of Heaven. Yet Ivy's teachings of the Goddess and her final decision to accept the pain of the knife rather than fight back were more in keeping with those of the imam than they were those of the Church itself.

"We recognized her as a Saint long before her fellow Christians did," the imam concluded.

"For all the good it did her."

"Bitterness is not the tree she would wish to grow from the seed she planted," the imam admonished him.

The Mass wound down and the citizens and tourists of Venice returned to their everyday lives leaving Zack and a few of the ubiquitous black-clad women alone in the church.

"You are hungry, perhaps," one of the women said. She shoved a bag holding bread, cheese, and apples at him.

Zack nodded. He hadn't been able to eat for days since they'd faced the Agent. Suddenly he felt famished.

"Thank you."

"It is what I did for her."

He'd forgotten, but the women of the church had helped Ivy during the time she'd spent in what had seemed unanswered prayer.

"I thank you for your kindness to her as well."

"We would have done it even if she hadn't been a saint. Being a woman is not so easy."

Being a man wasn't any great shakes either, Zack thought. But Ivy had had it tougher than he had. "I don't imagine so."

"That one never speaks." The woman gestured at another woman who was kneeling in front of one of the small chapels off to the side of the main church.

The statue of Mary, rising from the sea, caught Zack by surprise. It was definitely Mary, but the sensuality of the carving hinted at a different Mary than the Church had taught him. This was both Mary and Aphrodite.

He swallowed hard. Things were going to remind him of Ivy for the rest of his life. He couldn't get all choked up every time he saw a statue.

Still, he stepped over, plunked a two-Euro coin in the slot, and lit one of the white candles.

"I hope you're in a better place, Ivy," he whispered as he placed the candle in the holder beside the dozens of others burning down to nothingness.

"Ivy?" The female voice was hoarse, as if it hadn't been used in a thousand years. "Who is Ivy?"

* * * *

She was one with eternity.

The Goddess floated on a sea of celestial harmony. No boundary existed between herself and that outside herself. She simply was.

"Do you wish to remain?"

She started. If there was nothing outside of herself, who could ask her a question? Then she smiled. She could ask it of herself, of course. Did she wish to remain here?

Why not? She wasn't in a place, she was everywhere. Ordinary restrictions of space and time were meaningless. She couldn't remember it, but a part of her knew she hadn't always been the way. Once, she'd been more limited. Time had been a linear thing that could only be experienced and never repeated. Space had been solid thing. Then, she'd been limited to a single point in space and time.

Why would she want to return to that?

"I hope you're in a better place, Ivy."

She considered the words. Why would she say them to herself? The word hope meant nothing in the universe she occupied. Whatever she wished was. Hope implied limitations, that something desired could fail to be attained.

And Ivy? The word resonated with her; it should have meaning, but it didn't.

She shared the pain. The voice was suffering.

She'd forgotten suffering. Now that she was reminded of it, though, she knew she wouldn't forget it again.

She peered into the pain and saw something called loneliness. Another almost incomprehensible meaning. How could one be alone when one was whole and filled the universe?

"Ivy is the person who all this procession and celebration was about. Didn't you know?"

More confusion. This voice couldn't be hers. Why would she think such disconnected thoughts?

But the pain and loneliness brought back memories and shook at the foundation of her oneness with the universe. Because memories implied time, and time implied limitation.

She hadn't always been the Goddess. Once she'd been Ivy. Or a part of her had been Ivy. Or maybe even she had been a part of Ivy. Confusion too was new.

"You can go back if you wish."

Now she recognized that voice—it was her own voice, the voice of the Goddess speaking absolute truth.

"You have done much, headed off one hideous attack, but there is more to do."

"Aren't there others?" She remembered pain too well. Horrible pain shooting through her body. The Agent's knife had not just cut her physically, it had assaulted her soul.

"There are others. You may rest. Do you wish to stay?"

Another foolish question. How could she not want to stay here? She was complete here. There, in the shadow world, she'd be incomplete, would forget.

"I need to go back." Her answer startled both her limited self-aware self and her greater self that was the Goddess.

"If you go back, you'll go without the gifts."

"I must go. I'm needed."

The part of her that was the Goddess nodded, slowly, eternally. "So be it. Our doors will open when you seek us again."

A thousand pale lights flashed in her eyes and she staggered.

Strong hands caught her.

"Are you all right?"

It was the voice that had called her back.

She looked on his face. He was a man. Strange. She'd forgotten men.

"I don't know."

His eyes narrowed as he studied her. "This isn't possible."

"I have more to accomplish."

"God, don't you remember me?"

She laughed. "Goddess, not God."

"Ivy, I'm Zack." He pulled something from her eyes and everything became sharper.

"You healed my sight."

"I pulled back the veil you were wearing."

"Ah." She reached a finger and brushed it against the scratchy skin of his face. "There is always something hidden behind the veil."

"I can't believe you're back. I saw you dead. I watched you seal the Cross with the veil and your own blood."

Despite herself, despite the font of wellness and healing she'd just left, she winced at the sudden memory of pain.

"Yes. I sealed the Cross. Its time is not yet, man."

"Zack. Call me Zack." A tear trickled from one of his eyes, rolled down his cheek to touch her finger.

She brought that drop of water to her mouth and tasted it. Salt, water, and life were its flavors.

"Are you real, Ivy? Or are you just a vision? Or am I dying, too."

"Oh, Zack-man. Of course I'm real. And I've come back because there is more to be done."

"I hope you're saying something like, the two of us joining up, getting a cottage in the forest somewhere and living our lives together."

Ivy laughed again. Joy wasn't the same in this limited plane as it was in the expansive universe she'd recently left. "No, Zack. Nothing so easy. Those who seek to alter the flow will strike again. I must continue to stand against them. But you've done your part. No reason you can't go back. You'll find that your old life is available to you again. The Goddess would not offer less than that."

He shook his head. "I can't go back to what I was, Ivy. I'm with you until you tell me you can't use me."

It was an awesome responsibility. But as the memories returned, Ivy realized it wasn't her responsibility alone. She and Zack had shared. They were partners.

"I can't see the way I used to, Zack. When I returned to your world, I closed my third eye and can't open it. I can't see into your heart any more. It scares me."

"If you want to know what my heart has to say, how about this? We're in a church. We know the priests. Why not get married. I don't know how long the two of us will be around, given the way trouble has of finding us out. But I'd rather spend what time is given to us as your husband and lover."

Ivy felt the corners of her mouth turn upwards. A smile. "The Goddess cannot be limited."

"Which means?" He didn't look happy.

"I don't know where my future will take me, only that I have more to accomplish." Memories were coming back now, as the overpowering presence of the Goddess, in all of her glory, faded from her, leaving her diminished, but still transformed from what she had been.

"You've done enough. Surely we deserve a break."

She laughed. "I said the same thing. But I still have things to offer to the world."

"What about me?"

"You do, too, Zack. If you want a family, a wife and children, you can have those."

He got a stubborn look in his eyes. "I want to be with you."

"But I can't offer you those things, Zack. Not now. Maybe never."

"All right."

"All right, you'll take the family?"

"No, Ivy. All right, I'll take you, no matter what conditions that come attached."

"The Foundation is still out there, Zack. Smith won't be coming back, but others will be looking for tools to rush the end times. If you stay with me, you're dooming yourself to more of what we've faced."

Zack caught her hand and held it. "If I can be Sancho Panza to your Don Quixote, that's good enough for me. And if the promises of the Temple of Aphrodite can come true, I'm even more happy with that."

"All right." AS she said those words, a wave of joy washed over her. Yes, the Goddess demanded, but she rewarded as well. Ivy couldn't give Zack the life he'd dreamed of. There would be no growing old together, surrounded by loving children and grandchildren. Against the power that remained to the Foundation, against the powers that had been unlocked during those moments when the Cross had come together, they could only battle without hope of complete victory.

Still, having Zack at her side made her think that they could win some battles. Perhaps, in time, they could even explore the promise that Aphrodite had made.

"We must leave then," she continued. "And I'm counting on you to come up with a plan, Captain."

He laughed. "As long as we're a team, Sergeant."

She wrapped her veil more tightly around her, then stopped and looked at it. The stars glittered even in the Church's darkness. So, maybe they weren't so completely ill-equipped for the future after all.

CPSIA information can be obtained at www.ICGtesting.com
Printed in the USA
LVOW04s0135050815

448804LV00034B/1555/P